AFTER

Melvin Jules Bukiet

ST. MARTIN'S PRESS ✿ NEW YORK

AFTER

Production Editor: David Stanford Burr

Design: Nancy Resnick

Library of Congress Cataloging-in-Publication Data

Bukiet, Melvin Jules.
    After / Melvin Jules Bukiet.—1st ed.
        p.   cm.
    ISBN 0-312-14536-5
    I. Title.
    PS3552.U398A69   1996
    813'.54—dc20   96-8502
                                       CIP

First Edition: September 1996

10 9 8 7 6 5 4 3 2 1

To: my father, Joe, and my uncles, Al and Jack, and Sarah, and David and Selma, and Katzi, and Ben, and Yitzhak and Shoshana, and Kuba and Sesha, and all of the other survivors.

Contents

Grateful thanks to those whose work I have used in this book:

Thomas Pynchon for the *Anubis* and Rocketmann and the harmonica from *Gravity's Rainbow*

Hal Prince, Joe Masteroff, John Kander and Fred Ebb for the Emcee from *Cabaret*

Arthur A. Cohen for "The Legend of the Last Jew on Earth" from *In the Days of Simon Stern*

Bernard Bukiet for being United States Table Tennis Champion, 1957, 1963, 1966 (no relation)

BOOK I

FREEDOM

CHAPTER 1

The April sun leached through gaps in the wall. Since the inmates' daily routine commenced before dawn and concluded after dusk, they had never seen sun in the barracks. It illuminated the splintery wooden floorboards rubbed smooth as butter with the footfalls of the dead.

Isaac Kaufman was the first to break the silence. "They're gone."

"Hush."

"It's a trick."

"I'm telling you, they're gone." He stood up and went to the door.

"Don't!"

He stepped out. The guard towers were untenanted, but he couldn't tell if electricity still surged through the barbed wires. Isaac had always been more terrified by the men in the towers than those on the ground. Though the latter were more likely to kill him, it was the sense of being watched that was most disturbing to the shy boy who had gone straight from the Rabbi Yochanan Ben Zakhai Yeshiva to the lager with his graduating class. Now, for the first time, the only remaining graduate of his school was able to examine at leisure the construction of the tower that contained him.

Five-meter sections of wood were set into concrete footings and braced by cross beams that kept the tall verticals from shearing in a wind. A miniature cabin sat on top with a pitched roof to protect its occupant from the elements. A ladder led to the cabin.

The other prisoners huddled in a mass by the entry to the barrack watching Isaac wander across the yard, past the stack of the last week's bodies, toward the kitchen. A hose cock was dripping and Isaac knelt to sip.

One by one, the others inched tentatively forward.

Still fearful, Isaac's friend, Schimmel, remained in the doorway and called out, "They're having a picnic, the Führer's birthday, they'll come back and kill you."

It wasn't the Führer's birthday—just the opposite. Berlin lay in ruins and two hours later an American tank rode into Aspenfeld, a tiny subcamp of Buchenwald, in Weimar, home of Goethe and the Republic, beneath the forged metal sign that read, ARBEIT MACHT FREI or "Work Makes One Free."

Isaac had never seen such a vehicle, an armored, ungainly monstrosity that crashed through the wire and stopped, snub-nosed cannon to the door of the administration house, its treads crushing the nasturtiums that had been painstakingly planted by the kommandant's daughter. For a prisoner, it would have been death to touch a petal.

Off in the distance, a column of tanks approached, and one of them flew a banner that shocked the pale umber landscape, vivid red, white, and blue, stripes and stars. Three years locked away from any shade but German black, even the densest of prisoners knew what these colors meant. They had heard rumors, and for the last week they had heard the rumblings of battle. It was the Americans and they had won. The War was over.

All the barracks doors opened like a bank of synchronized cuckoo clocks and the prisoners stumbled into the open, an army of ghosts and skeletons clad in gray-striped uniforms who tripped, fell to their knees, stood, and surrounded the liberator.

Isaac plucked a nasturtium and put the stem into his mouth.

The top of the tank opened up like a lid, and a boy no older than themselves poked his head up. "Hey, youse. Is this the way to the Grand Concourse?"

Isaac smiled, revealing a row of uneven teeth, broken the previous winter. Groggy and unkempt, he had been one of the hundred-odd survivors who stepped into the frigid world the morning after the thermometer sank so low that doors froze to their hinges and stones shriveled into pebbles. There was no snow and no wind, but the air might as well have been a glacier. On milder days, the masters in their leather tea jackets had compelled the prisoners to do calisthenics, but that day they did not leave their heated quarters for fear the arms of their twisted crosses would snap. Instead, a Ukranian Kapo was allowed to exercise his own brutal ingenuity over the diminished ranks so thoroughly rigid that they walked like stick figures, unable to bend a joint. That morning, Isaac thought he was lucky because the round-faced Kapo singled him out for a cup of hot coffee. He was naturally suspicious of the sly, obsequious smile as the man proferred him the steaming concoction, but he was starved—not for nourishment, but warmth. His hands wrapped about the circumference of the tin cup, drawing every degree of heat from its surface, for he was sure the man would kick it from his grasp. He could see the color returning to his fingertips. He raised it to his lips.

"Uh-uh," warned the Kapo.

Isaac paused, tempted to gulp it down despite the lethal punishment that would undoubtedly follow disobedience.

"One sip only," the guard said, "as big as you wish, but one sip."

If those were the ground rules, Isaac would make the most of them. He took the cup to his mouth and drank. But he had never experienced a cold that penetrated so deeply it congealed the marrow in his bones. He did not know what would occur when the hot liquid came into contact with the brittle surface of his teeth. He did not know that Eskimos returning from the Arctic hunt first ate cold strips of fish to ease the change in temperature. The second the steaming liquid hit his mouth, it cracked all his teeth, and when the Kapo said, "Smile," he did, and tiny bits of enamel snowed onto the ground.

Isaac's exposed nerves gradually healed over a season of pain, aided by the lager's doctor who dabbed arsenic onto the openings to kill any nerves. Eventually, the skin grew over the openings and he learned to speak again, pushing his voice farther back in his throat to avoid the gumming he associated with age, and death.

Then came the miraculous day when the Germans fled the camp without bothering to obey their last order to incinerate the Jews in their wooden barracks. Isaac woke to a silence as pervasive as the previous winter's cold, wondering why there was no roll call as the sun climbed higher. One by one the rest of the section woke to the weird hush. These men who whispered to each other under clear threat of instant execution were as quiet as the camp that surrounded them, more fearful of the silence than they were of the usual clatter of dogs, guns, and shrieking SS.

The boy soldier in the tank flinched at the sight of Isaac's teeth and said, "I guess I made a wrong turn."

Swarms of military personnel descended upon the camp. Following in the wake of the tanks came the rest of the U.S. Army, a vast apparatus nearly as impressive in its own way as the German killing machine. There were convoys bearing clothes and food, and mobile shops disgorging soldier-carpenters who set to hammering up temporary headquarters while soldier-electricians strung wires to communicate with other units while soldier-cooks put together a galley and soldier-tailors stitched uniforms rent by bullets while soldier-doctors repaired the bodies pierced by those same bullets as the army established a base and prepared to move on. Aspenfeld was only one stop on the Americans' sweep across the Continent.

The soldiers were standing in the funny little turrets like birds peeking out from iron nests, distributing candy bars to the prisoners as if they had arrived solely for this purpose, Hershey's advance men.

The prisoners accepted the offerings with glazed disbelief, and stuffed them immediately into their mouths. They stood agape, chins dripping with dark brown goo like dirty little boys.

"There's more, hey. Want some?"

"Yah!"

"Yah," they echoed.

"Something else?"

"Yah!"

And the soldiers poured forth Lucky Strike cigarettes and K rations, in a vain attempt to alleviate the hunger that had no end. The soldiers knew that this was a prison, but the frenzy for a tin of chipped beef shocked them.

"More chocolate," they called to the sergeant from the Quartermaster's Corps as they were accustomed to shouting for more ammo.

So the inmates were not as pretty as the grateful French girls of

6

Lyons; nonetheless a giddy carnival air prevailed as the liberators enjoyed their role. Eventually, though, the smiles left their faces as the true nature of this particular institution dawned upon them. The reek of human decay was too pervasive to be hidden by the temporary aroma of melting cocoa, and the field of nasturtiums was insufficient to ornament the perimeter of the suffocation pit. Inured to death on the battlefield, they were staggered by death in the lager. At Normandy, death existed as a function of War: Aspenfeld existed as a function of death. Aspenfeld, like the hundred other camps situated from Poland to France, was one star in a cannibal galaxy, one duchy in the kingdom of death.

The captain of the regiment was so stunned, his eyes clouded by ashes and despair, that later that first afternoon, at the tail end of the military parade, when the entourage of General "Hammerin' Hank, Scourge of the Hun" Smith entered underneath the gate, the motto of which had already been changed with a hand-lettered plywood sign strung ungrammatically over its first word, to read, TANKS MAKES ONE FREE, he forgot to salute.

The heavyset general, chest bedecked with medals, dismounted from the jeep, and stared straight in the captain's face, waiting.

The captain looked right through him.

An expression of anger at the indignity struck Hammerin' Hank. Then he saw what his men had been staring at for hours and the general sank to his knees.

One by one the rest of the soldiers kneeled before the dead Jews stacked head to toe like cordwood.

Isaac and Schimmel and a group from C Block looked at the amazing scene. The saviours from beyond the sea were not unexpected after the rumors that had been circulating since the invasion at Normandy nearly a year before, but their sheer size and vigor was astonishing. The Germans who had run away seemed runty all of a sudden, pallid and cowardly, downright un-Aryan. Here was the true master race—half a decade too late. And they were down on bent knee, war-hardened eyes flinching from the sight that met the student from Proszowice and the tailor from Boiberik every waking day.

Journalists who traveled with the battallion angled to take pictures of the general on his knees.

"Parson," he called, "A speech."

A Negro chaplain stepped forward, saluted, and began an impromptu service. "Hear O Israel," he cried. "That's how the Hebrew prayer begins. And this is the fate of the chosen people. This . . . this . . . this abomination, this holocaust . . ." With the correct word upon his lips, the parson hit his stride and began thumping on the post beside the gallows.

"Who's that?" Schimmel whispered.

"Like a Rabbi." Isaac replied. "From Africa."

Schimmel had never seen a black man before, and he asked, "Are they all like that?"

"No, can't you see the others?"

"Was he in a fire?"

"No, idiot," Isaac scoffed, "you were."

The chaplain could see the flames in their eyes. "A great and terrible crime occurred here," he said.

But these words—they were translated and they were true—did nothing to soothe the pain they implied.

"It's a sad day when man stoops to the level of beasts," he said. "But it is also a glad day when man can rescue his fellows from that condition. Today we celebrate and we mourn. Let us pray."

"For what?" Isaac commented.

The general invited the neighbors from the adjacent villages in through the gates to meet the inmates, a starving, shaven-headed Sanhedrin, who watched the innocent burghers of Weimar shake their heads and claim, "We never knew what happened here."

"Lies," Schimmel cried, shaking with fury.

"Of course they're lying," Isaac replied, "But we lied to them, too. It's even."

"Tell them," Hammerin' Hank spoke through his translator, "that if it was up to me, I'd lock them all up. Tell them to get out of my sight. No, take that back. Tell them to go home and come back with a broom or a shovel, with rags and sponges and soap, pronto."

"What for, Sir?"

"To clean."

"Clean?"

"Yeah, clean. I want this place as spotless as their sainted grandma's kitchen. It's a Goddamn pigpen."

The order was duly translated and duly obeyed. If Hank had expected shirking, he was wrong. An hour later, the entire village was back with wash buckets stuffed full of every utensil in Weimar's domestic armory.

Clean, the Germans did, with a native talent and enthusiasm that were miraculous to behold. The matrons took brooms to the feces that covered the latrine floor while the men carried stacks of debris to a pile in the corner. They scrubbed the floors and scoured the walls. Even the village children in their pale brown shorts lifted bits and pieces of dead Jews while the living Jews squatted and sucked on chocolate bars. Then, when the Germans were done for the day and vowed to return to finish the task, they lined up as dominoes to beg for food in return for their labor.

The citizens were hungry. Naturally obliging, they were even more eager to help if they might be rewarded with a portion of Allied largesse. During the last months of the War all domestic shipments of nonessential, which meant nonexplosive, materials had ceased so they looked enviously at the prisoners with tins o f tuna fish stacked in front of them as army bulldozers pushed the reeking pile of flesh into a pit and soldiers wearing gas masks sprinkled lime powder before the bulldozer covered the bodies with dirt.

Then it was onward for the general, who assigned his Fourth Division to remain to administer the dismantling of this one messy blot on the face of the earth.

The battle-weary soldiers who were left behind were happy to be benched for the duration of the War. Clearly, it was already won, but every one of the last few steps to the finish line was still potentially lethal. Somebody would die on every mile to Berlin.

Despite the enormity of the terror it evoked, Aspenfeld was a resort to the soldiers. It reminded Private Second Class Herman Weinglass of the bungalow colony in the Catskills his parents had taken him to before the war. There was no pond here for late afternoon dips and no veranda on which to sip iced tea, but the bunks were made of the same slatted wood as those in which the prosperous Brooklynites summered and the conversation he overheard was spoken in the same Yiddish vernacular that his elders had used when arguing business or politics. Herman and the other soldiers shut their eyes to try to eradicate the vision of death that surrounded them while the Jews just naturally assumed that life went on.

Overnight, a small bourse developed in the corner where they had assembled for work detail. Commerce, the same kind that existed underground in the camp, was conducted in public now, but instead of trading labor for crusts of mealy turnip bread, the stakes were raised, and the former prisoners swapped cigarettes for chocolates and exchanged information concerning the services suddenly available to them. Every hour, Aspenfeld was more like Warsaw. Every hour, it was harder to believe that the War was over. Every hour, it was harder to believe that the War had ever occurred.

But no one asked Isaac to smile, so he didn't, so he didn't feel happy until he saw a woman journalist dancing around the gallows. It was Elizabeth Smith Moss, First Lady of the Front Lines, dressed in army fatigues tucked into stylish boots she had picked up while accompanying the Allied forces into Florence a few months earlier. She was fiddling with the three cameras slung about her neck on worn leather straps and considering which perspective would make for a good shot. The gallows was a crude structure composed of three pieces of wood, two vertical, one horizontal, and a hook approximately seven feet off the surface of the earth.

"Interesting, yah."

"Could you stand there?"

"Why?"

"So I can take a picture."

There was something about the pose that made Isaac break into a grin. As soon as she saw his winning expression, the journalist took a calf-leather billfold out of her pocket and handed him a dollar. Such a mouth was a real asset.

Isaac smiled again and other photographers fell over themselves as if it was Eisenhower himself pointing toward the gallows.

The situation grew even funnier when Elizabeth Smith Moss inquired, "What did you do here?"

The answer was obvious. "We died."

"Bad times?"

The sentiment was translated into German.

Isaac smiled, "Yaah."

A soldier turned to the photographer, "They're crazy, aren't they?"

"Wouldn't you be?"

Isaac whispered to Schimmel while the cameras were clicking, "Once, before, I was in the Cracow Zoo. The monkeys they learned what the people liked, whatever it was, begging, swinging from the bars, so they would do that to earn a peanut. Not so different, hey."

Neither was it so different from the posing they had done over the past one thousand days; it was just a different pose. If the image of strength kept them from selection before, now weakness impelled generosity.

Of course, the best images were those of the Musselmen, the living dead who still scuffed along on feet that never seemed to leave the ground, the hours left to them evident in the snail's track they left behind them. The army doctors found these Musselmen the most intriguing patients, as well as the most frustrating, for there was nothing discernibly wrong with them, or no moreso than the rest of the Aspenfeld population, yet their sentence, self-inflicted, was more absolute than the one the Reich had imposed upon them—no mere army penicillin could grant them reprieve. It was not the German's truncheon, boot, and chamber that killed them, but the knowledge of those atrocities they could not bear, and that knowledge did not diminish once the boot itself disappeared. All the doctors could do was to try to make them comfortable in a special infirmary established in the mess hall with genuine fiber-stuffed mattresses—with pillows.

When these accommodations came to the rest of the camp's attention, a plague of imitation Musslemen slouched into the infirmary, heads hung down in burlesque of their soon-to-be-dead peers. It was easy to fool the Lucky Boys, since the only proof of their imminent demise lay in whether they dropped under the Americans as they would have under the Germans or the Rabbis of Jerusalem. Change happened for everyone but the Musselmen; they were beyond the moods of release, and no matter the fluids the Yankee doctors poured in their mouths, it sluiced out their asses with the rank taint of mental dysentery.

Their impersonators yawned and fluffed up their pillows.

A day after the War, it seemed unreal. Isaac was nineteen, and all he had known since his Bar Mitzvah in 1939 was war. It was ludicrous that an empire had collapsed merely because its gate had been opened. Already the barbed wire fence that had seemed as enduring as the pyramids turned to rust. Isaac wondered what would have happened if he had strode straight through the gate two years before, if the earth would have opened and swallowed the Germans then, as it appeared to do once the Americans came knocking. He felt as if gravity or magnetism had ceased to operate. All his ideas about life were no longer valid.

"Now you are free," the Negro chaplain said during Sunday services he conducted on the plaza where the daily selections had been made.

"So, what is freedom?" Isaac replied, formulating against his will a hazy memory of childhood romps in the woods outside of Proszowice.

Just then a slat of wood detached from the tower, and drifted down like an autumn leaf, exposing the place where a vanished master's feet previously hid, shining. One commodity the Germans never lacked was boot polish. Until the day they left, they had sat in a grim circle every morning after breakfast sausages, buffing their heels with chamois cloths for sheer pleasure. They stocked so much polish at Aspenfeld that they had once forced a prisoner to smear his face with it and perform a minstrel show. Then they hung him. It reminded Isaac of the American chaplain.

Sergeant Campion did his best to accommodate his services to the Hebrews, but Isaac refused to join in prayer. Neither did he feel any inclination to play, but now that he could acknowledge his desires, he became aware of a tremendous impulse to climb.

"Hey, hey, dreamer."

Isaac woke from his reverie to discover his right foot planted firmly on the first rung of the ladder that led to the guard tower platform.

"Where you going?"

"Up," he replied.

"Up?"

"Up!" Foot after foot he rose until Schimmel's knobby head was directly beneath him. The climber was about to enter the doghouse under the little roof pitched to protect its former occupant from the harsh rays of the Thuringian sun.

"Isaac, I don't know if you should be there."

"Why not, is it Hitler's birthday?" He stepped in, and waved his big toe through the hole in the platform.

Sure enough, an American lieutenant marched over and said, "He shouldn't be there."

"I know," Schimmel said.

"Tell him to come down."

"Come down."

"No."

"He says 'No.' "

"He has to."

Another soldier wandered by. It was Private Weinglass, in the wrong place at the wrong time. "Go and get that guy down," the lieutenant ordered.

"How?"

"I don't know."

Weinglass tilted his head back to peer up at Isaac basking there as if on a widow's walk in Cape Cod. "Maybe I should just shoot him, Sir."

Elizabeth Smith Moss, renowned among the press corps for her uncanny ability to appear at the scene of any dramatic moment, stood at the ready, lens uncapped, exposure set.

"Yah!" Isaac called to her.

"Yah," she called back.

The lieutenant shrugged and hastened to the canteen. The Jews were all crazy, those from here and those from home. He didn't care anyway. So Isaac remained in his perch.

"Lessons," he called to Schimmel from the guard tower as he surveyed the blurry fields that led to the demure hamlet whose good citizens serviced the camp that had taken in a tiny portion of the Jews of Eastern Europe and, in their spare time, were known for the intricate carving of chess figures and cuckoo clocks. Isaac Kaufman would not pray; he could not play, but climbing provided him with a divine satisfaction he had not felt since the day he was orphaned. That was freedom, too.

The Americans treated the prisoners like pets; they cleaned them with a solution of peroxide and DDT to kill the lice that infected them, and then they groomed them. As hair began to grow on the shaved heads, they distributed bright blue plastic combs that the more fashion-conscious tucked behind their ears. Of course, a few hothouse specimens able to tolerate beating but not bathing caught a chill and, of course, they died.

Those who lived were offered a choice of clothes unpacked from the storehouses of Canada. This was a cordoned off area of the camp so named because of the immense natural resources it contained: teeth and hair and gold not yet shipped off to the repository at Lieb-knecht and a mountain of suitcases stuffed with the lace of Vienna and the wool of Lodz. There were Bibles and dolls and small toys for children and photograph albums of those who did not know that they were going to meet their ancestors sooner than they expected.

All of this except the gold was distributed to the prisoners by Private Second Class Weinglass. He was the perfect choice for the job, because he had the manner they understood.

"I used ta woik at a habadashery on Flatbush Avenue," he said. "Stetsons, fedoras, Panamas, derbies for evenings at the thee-a-ter, boaters for afternoons in Prospect Park, you name it," he listed his erstwhile inventory while dispensing from the heap. "Even the Rabbis came in for their headgear. Lot of yarmulkes here, lot of yarmulkes. Nobody could size a head like me. Now I'd say you was a 7¼. We specialized in Dodger baseball caps. But I know fabric, too. I'm no stranger to a tux. Here's a fine example of a Dutch weave, you see the extra stitching around the collar, that's for durability. Jacket like this will last as long as you do." He blushed.

The Americans were embarrased in front of the skeletons who lined up to accept their offerings.

"Here, take it, you get a second pair of pants, free."

The prisoners' waists were so thin that the pants circled them like the ring around Saturn.

One man suddenly dashed to another and tore a brown hound-stooth garment from his hands.

The first one grabbed it back.

"It's mine."

"They just gave it to me."

"What's the fuss?"

"He took that coat from me."

"It's mine."

"Hey, hey, a little civilization, please."

Without understanding the precise words of their benefactors, the Jews grasped their meaning. "Here?" one replied.

"But they gave it to him."

"It wasn't theirs to give. It's mine."

"Yours?"

"From Before."

It took a moment to comprehend that there was a before, but the coincidence was astonishing. "There are a million coats like this."

A crowd began to gather. "What's happening?" they asked.

"Berger's gone nuts."

"Crazy Hungarian."

"There may be ten million, but that's mine. It was my father's, and now it's mine."

"He thinks he's back in Budapest."

"Don't be ridiculous, how can you tell?"

"Give me a razor." This request from a man who was shaving himself with a piece of broken glass a week ago was remarkable enough. More remarkably, the MP gave him a blade from his own kit, as if responding to an order from the general, although he remained watchful. He didn't want the Jew to use it to stab his opponent.

Instead, the man called Berger sliced the lapel as if for mourning—a Jewish custom—while Weinglass, who knew fabric, shrieked, "Hey, watcha doon?"

Before anyone could take away the rent garment, the Hungarian plunged his fingers into the gap behind the lining and came out with a tiny velvet sack that had been sewn in behind the buttonhole. He swiftly turned the sack upside down and three diamonds spilled onto the dusty ground. "These are mine," he said, "You can have the coat."

Thus the camp acquired its first rich man, and Isaac studied the lesson well. Berger was immediately granted anything he wanted on the bourse based on his word, which was backed up by the collateral he never touched.

"What do you think of that?" Schimmel asked, while parading in his own new attire.

"Credit," Isaac replied, as if witnessing a miracle. He was one of the few ex-prisoners still wearing a striped prison outfit, because he had been too busy coming to terms with the new customs to bother with exchanging his old garment.

"But . . ."

"Money," Isaac explained, "exists in a social context. It's the agreement between the members of a community that they will allow abstract pieces of gold or paper to represent labor. If one requires food to exist, a piece of this representation will stand one better than a tomato, because a tomato will rot while a diamond retains its value."

"But why?"

"Because enough people are still willing to believe in money, and everyone believes in food—except the Musselmen."

"How do you get money?"

"By providing something tangible that people desire."

"But Berger provides nothing."

"Au contraire, my dear Schimmel Shlemiel. He provides the sense of something, the idea of wealth. Of course, someday, he may have to relinquish one of his bright stones to prove his contention. Then, someone else will possess that value."

Fingering the bill he had been given by the lady photographer, Isaac resolved to be further compensated. There was nothing he wished to purchase at the bourse, but money was freedom and the first thing he did to obtain some was to accept a new jacket, the pockets of which were empty, though beautifully stitched. Like everyone else in the camp, he examined the hems, collar, lapels, and lining thoroughly just in case it hid diamonds. No such luck.

Liberation was easy to take for granted. Where the acquisition of food and the avoidance of death from Tuesday to Wednesday had been the sole aims of lager society, it shifted instantly to wholesale extraction of goods and services from the pity-struck Americans. So what if the Yanks had opened the gates to Aspenfeld. It was obvious that the Jews were no more people in their eyes than they were to the Germans. The substantial difference was that they were objects of sympathy rather than malice. But this could change as quickly as the sign over the gates, which had been altered one more time from TANKS MAKES ONE FREE to $ MAKES ONE FREE.

Isaac had not edited the sign; nevertheless he appreciated it. Cynicism was a new and strangely satisfying emotion; it assumed a distrust of benevolence, yet it also assumed a benevolence to distrust. Isaac enjoyed his doubts, never more so than when he allowed Elizabeth Smith Moss to take his picture beside the sign. In keeping with its aphorism, she offered him another dollar. This time, however, he refused her donation.

"But why?" she asked through the translator who was also being paid. A dollar was a dollar.

Isaac smiled, gratis, and replied, "I prefer credit."

"Fine," she said with the obliviousness of a patrician signing a blank check, "I owe you." This was truer than her subject could know, for Isaac's photograph had already been reproduced on half the front pages in America and she was hoping for a Pulitzer.

Nor was Miss Moss alone. The camp became a focal point for all refugees in the vicinity, and where the refugees went, the refugee industry sprang up. British and French politicians appeared, while a second wave of journalists, enticed by the imagery of catastrophe, poached on Elizabeth Smith Moss's territory. There were representatives from the Red Cross and the United Nations wearing starched white uniforms. Even the Vatican sent a cadre of prelates on a fact-finding mission.

New people kept arriving at Aspenfeld, for the excellent rail connections had not been bombed in the Allied attack on the military targets of the Rhineland. Any Frenchman in Vienna wanting to travel east or any stray Czech hastening southwestward home from Antwerp had to make do with tracks that often terminated abruptly at a blown out bridge or collapsed tunnel. Before they could make other arrangements they were compelled to bunk temporarily in the lager barracks, which rented out for dollars like frontier hotels.

The Westerners seemed to experience a vicarious pleasure in simulating the rigors the Jews had undergone. An American senator stood in the suffocation pit for hours, reveling in the frisson of horror, and his only comment was a hearty, "Tain't as bad as a Democratic filibuster."

Of course, these tourists needed a memento to take home as proof of their stay in the world's capital of atrocity—words would not do justice—so a market in striped uniforms and yellow stars was immediately established on the bourse next to the booth that already sold Iron Crosses for deutschemarks and Swiss kroner. Much to haberdasher Weinglass's consternation, the prison tailors traded their fine Dutch weaves to the good volk of Weimar for bolts of yellow cloth in order to mass-produce yellow stars to meet the demand.

Between trade and manufacturing and travel, Aspenfeld took on the airs of a small city. It had a government in the form of the Military Police and a church in the body of Chaplain Duane Campion and it had a fourth estate to rival London's. It even had a social aristocracy in the Jews; they were the *Mayflower* to the arriviste, and much sought as dinner partners by the visiting intelligentsia. As in any boomtown, however, the manners at Aspenfeld were subject to a swift degeneration from discipline to anarchy. One day, Berger's diamonds were stolen.

The theft occurred during a movie, *Oliver and Hardy at the Biergarten,* watched by troops and inmates together on ranks of long benches set up in the mess tent with a projector borrowed from Weimar's own cinema. Berger strode in, blocking the beam of light from the projector in the rear and creating a giant shadow on the screen, to assume his rightful place in the front row, but in the midst of the hilarity generated by Laurel's fumbling with a tray of tankards during the third reel, Berger cried out, "My jewels."

The lights were switched on and the MPs investigated as best they could, and went so far as to detain the man who sat beside Berger, Shmuel Karten, a Bundist, who distributed copies of *What Is to Be Done* on the sly. But the rabble-rouser, claiming that such an outrage would never have occurred if the Russians had liberated the camp, was released when no proof that he had picked Berger's pocket was forthcoming.

Berger, meanwhile, wandered around like a Musselman, lamenting his lost fortune more bitterly than his lost family.

The prisoners made the same comment they had when Berger first became rich: "Crazy Hungarian."

Aspenfeld's own Rothschild's instantaneous, inglorious transition from wealth to indigence was a lesson, too, and one that made Isaac

18

feel pleased that he had incurred a debt from Elizabeth Smith Moss rather than a dollar.

If money was freedom, credit was freedom from money. Isaac began to bank favors and broker deals in return for promises and influence. *De Tellegraph* from Amsterdam wanted an interview with a Dutch Jew—Isaac could arrange that in return for yellow cloth. Then he could trade the cloth for a Prussian cavalry saber, and the saber to the base telephone operator for a transatlantic connection, and the connection to a sad sack who yearned to talk to home for a three-day pass for yet another American soldier whose assistance in who knows what endeavor might come in handy. It was Isaac's doing that led to the establishment of a bank with Berger the bankrupt as its president. It was his doing that enabled a constant supply of movies from abroad. Thus within six working days of the moment he had woken to sunshine in the barracks now occupied by a Hollywood newsreel crew Isaac Kaufman had situated himself as someone in the know if one needed food, papers, or a bed in the infirmary. And on the seventh day, he kept working.

Along with crime came charity in the shape of a squadron of gray-suited representatives of the Jewish Diaspora headed by a tall, elegant man named Alan Foyle (né Fogelstein) who stepped through the camp gates as if he was boarding the *Titanic* and dispensed newly minted business cards that identified him as Deputy Director, Refugee Affairs, Joint Distribution Committee. Commonly known as the Joint, Mr. Foyle's organization was a unificatory body created by the American Jewish community to supercede its own sectarian impulses. Nobody knew precisely who had authorized their mandate to serve their wounded co-religionists, but Mr. Foyle was given a complete tour of the facilities by Major Hiram Hamilton, a tedious young West Pointer whom General Smith had left in command of Aspenfeld, now known as Sector 14, Field HQ.

Hamilton had already escorted the American senator and the Vatican reps so he knew which aspects of camp life were most interesting to visitors, and delivered his spiel as effectively as a tour guide at Madame Tussaud's. "On your left, the spot where Himmler gave a speech during his one visit to the camp in March of 1943. Since then, this avenue was known as Himmlerstrasse. And this," he pointed to the gravel path that lead from the train station to the barracks, mixing history and geography, "is the "Highway to Heaven."

All of this was quite charming to Mr. Foyle, but his eyes lit up when he saw a sturdy Quonset hut used for the camp laundry. "I suppose this is no longer in operation," Foyle said.

"Affirmative."

"So I suppose we could use it for an office?"

Instructed to offer every assistance to anyone inclined to take the Jews off the army's hands, Major Hamilton promptly agreed.

"And I suppose you could see to it that we have tables, chairs, and proper office equipment?"

Imitating the manner he had learned at the seat of Hammerin' Hank, Major Hamilton groused, "What do you think this is, Chase Manhattan?"

"Affirmative," Mr. Foyle drawled.

And in less time than it took to spin dry, the Quonset hut was filled with all the amenities of a Larchmont youth center, from water coolers to a sentimental lithograph of a rabbi blowing a shofar.

As the first step beyond seeing to their own bureaucratic necessities, Mr. Foyle gently explained to the chaplain that services ought to be held on Saturday rather than Sunday, "at least for your Jewish constituents."

Isaac said, "I'm glad we have a religious authority here."

In short order, Foyle's office unearthed a mimeograph machine that cranked out a newsletter composed of schedules for inoculations, death notices, free advertisements concerning lost relatives, and articles culled from the *Herald Tribune*. It even reproduced Elizabeth Smith Moss's famous photograph of Isaac at the gallows.

"What do you think?" Schimmel said excitedly, "You're famous."

"I'd rather be free," Isaac replied as he took the paper into the latrine.

Thus the newsletter acquired a nickname, "The Daily Shitrag," and the initial volume that flew off the presses could hardly meet the demand—much to the gratification of its editors until they realized that it was being used merely to clog the facilities.

Major Hamilton complained to Mr. Foyle, who wrote a front-page editorial espousing the use of American toilet paper. Civilization was a learning process and Mr. Foyle, much chagrined by his people's

20

lack of proper deportment, apologized to Major Hamilton, "They're not ready for Boston, yet."

Representatives from the Bund, the Socialist Zionists, Agudas Yisroel, and the Musicians Union busily joined the fray, contending for lost souls like there was no yesterday. Much to Mr. Foyle's displeasure, they, too, were placed in the laundry that became a convention hall of competing agendas. Nonetheless, the Joint was clearly first among equals. Only they had the power to do more than issue statements and manifestos. They had money and they had passports.

"Come with me," Schimmel said to Isaac. "I'm going to be processed."

"It sounds like being turned into soap."

"What a disgusting idea."

"That's what they tell me was done elsewhere."

"Another lager?"

"Yes, I've heard rumors of lampshades, too."

"How?"

"Skin. Finely ornamented with elegant tattoos."

"Isaac!"

"Hey, I don't make this stuff up. It's just what I hear through the grapevine. Could it be true? Who knows?" He shrugged.

"Well . . . come with me then—for the lesson."

Approached this way, the young fixer could hardly refuse to accompany Schimmel to the table set up beside the huge tubs in which the prisoners had been compelled to wash their warder's socks. Three American volunteers flanked by three newly recruited translators made notations in tall blue ledgers while several hundred emaciated men snaked around the building waiting patiently for their turn.

Isaac marched Schimmel to the front of the line and interrupted a small-boned American girl in the center of the registration table in the midst of her first, exciting interview in the Land of the Dead. "Is this dance taken?"

"Please return to your place in line, Sir."

"This is my place in line."

The girl's chocolate eyes stared out from under a curtain of straight brown hair while Isaac asked the man who was hunched earnestly over the table, number 14-46-02, one question and dashed off a promissory note good for a bicycle in response to the man's answer.

The recipient of this scrip obligingly tipped his fedora and walked away.

"Very cute," the young woman said, accordingly translated by a Romanian professor of economics who had also translated for the Germans. "And what do you have for me?"

Despite Isaac's intuitive understanding of her tone, the professor's flat translation failed to communicate sarcasm. Responding therefore to the literal question, he answered, "Perfume."

"What about a dress?"

"That, too, can be arranged . . . yellow, the color of sunshine."

"And what if I still refuse to process you?"

"I do not wish to be . . . processed. That is for my friend."

"And what if we refuse to process him?"

"Then you will break his heart and waste my perfume."

"Is there a problem, Miranda?"

Mr. Foyle had stepped out from behind his own desk to investigate the delay. According to his schedule, she ought to be able to process two hundred prisoners a day, but at this rate she wouldn't be able to get through a dozen.

Isaac answered, "Miranda has no problems. She is most obliging."

The girl recalled the training that should have prepared her for the fact that manners were different in the lager than they were on Beekman Place. She sniffed with untranslated disdain and turned to Schimmel. "Name. Age. Country of Origin."

Schimmel answered the questions while Isaac filed his nails. Isaac had better things to do. There was a fur coat to be located for a blacksmith. "I'll see you later. Adieu."

The Romanian interpreted, "Good-bye."

The young woman ignored him, but Schimmel ran after his friend as soon as he had given her the names of his mother, "Sarah," father, "Mordecai," and other family members, "Dora, Chaya, Leah," and the last place they had been seen, "Smoke."

"Is that the name of a camp?"

"It is the name of all camps."

"I don't understand."

"Neither did we."

"Please ask him to elaborate, to explain further."

"Smoke. Chimneys. You know, crematoria."

"Oh." The girl named Miranda's naturally pale complexion turned even paler. "I didn't know. I'm sorry."

"She's sorry," said the translator.

"Don't worry. You're new at this."

He received an application for a visa.

Issac was examining his manicure, the palm of his hand resting against a tank's enormous tread when Schimmel caught up to him, brimming with excitement. "Isaac you should go back. They are taking names to make aliyah, to go to Palestine."

"The last time names were taken, it was to come here. My name is my own now. They can have my number."

"Isaac, they're Jews."

"You think there's no such thing as Jewish vultures?"

"They are helping. And this girl, she is very sympathetic."

"Maybe yes and maybe they are just helping themselves."

"For what purpose?"

"I cannot say."

"But at the least, they can make it easier here. Everyone who registers gets a package. Money, they give us expense money. Look," he riffled five dollars and a package of food chits.

"And what happens to that? You pee it away on cigarettes. Money is a boomerang. Where do the cigarettes come from, the Americans? It always returns to the place it came from."

"Please, Isaac, give them a chance."

"I don't know. I just want time to consider my options."

"Why?"

Isaac looked at him, and spontaneously leaned forward. "Can you keep a secret?"

"Yes."

He explained that he was preparing to leave.

"Leave?"

"And why not, is Aspenfeld such a paradise?"

"Where are you going to go?"

"I don't know."

"Home?"

"Nah. What's going to be there?"

"You could always say Kaddish."

"Yah, I can always say Kaddish—so I don't need to go to a graveyard. These feet will never enter Poland." He glanced down at the snazzy alligator shoes he had recently procured from Weinglass, but had already committed to trade for a package of wax candles, which he had already decided he was going to trade for more yellow cloth for the girl who processed Schimmel. A debt was a debt.

"Where then?"

"Maybe New York."

Schmimmel pursed his lips and nodded with respect. This he understood, but other camps had been liberated before Aspenfeld and the girl had told him that there was already a two-year waiting list for emigration to the States. "Good luck."

Suddenly Isaac was afraid. In a moment of weakness he had revealed his plans. Who knew, perhaps Schimmel was correct and there was nothing to fear, but distrust had kept Isaac Kaufman alive for six years, and he would continue to doubt until it was proven that faith worked better. He resolved to leave immediately. The gates were open, but no one had yet dared to step beyond their boundary. The inmates were too happy in their fairyland of pillows and chocolate. Isaac had had enough chocolate; he was ready for real freedom.

Resolved, Isaac packed his suit and the notebook in which he kept a record of his financial transactions. Before departing, however, he climbed to his perch atop the guard tower overseeing C Block for one last view. By now it was a familiar climb, like that to the roof of the Rabbi Yochanan Ben Zakhai Yeshiva where the boys had helped feed the janitor's pigeons until they were eaten during the early months of the War. He stood watching the human traffic of Jews entering the laundry, soldiers on parade, a hundred different people on a hundred errands, and wondered if the ebb and flow from this bird's-eye perspective looked anything like it had when the only occupants of the camp were the predators and their prey.

There was a commotion from D Block. A German was found; he had slept late with the prisoners that lucky day when the sun shone into the barracks and had been hiding in a loft over the garage ever since then. Finally the odors of his defecation lead to his detection. The man was still in uniform and his boots were clean.

For the American soldier who found the German soldier, it was a

24

shock. Private Monroe had gone through an entire campaign shooting into dark woods and never coming face to face with the enemy.

"What sort of disgusting . . ." he began, assigned to investigate the odor by his lieutenant when he recognized the black uniform and reached for his weapon.

The German was as quick as Wyatt Earp. He extracted his own gun from a leather shoulder holster and there was a moment when Private Monroe winced, expecting a bullet between the teeth. The moment passed, Private Monroe opened one eye and saw the handle of the German revolver being offered to him, in surrender. "That's better," he said, "you're coming with me."

Intending to bring his captive to his superior officer, like a proud cat presenting its owner with a half-dead mouse, maybe get himself a medal or a weekend pass, Private Monroe proudly marched the German out of the garage. But the sight of the German created a stir before they got ten feet beyond the glistening Mercedes-Benz grilles. Everyone on the line in front of the laundry turned. There was pushing and shoving. Heads along the Highway to Heaven bobbed up and down to get a view.

"Shame!" a voice cried.

"Killer!"

Isaac recognized the German, Sturmmann Hans Lichter. He was a quiet fellow who had hardly ever killed any of the prisoners. He had even been known to give leftover bread from his sandwich to a hungry child, smiling with a bemused expression like a pensioner feeding pigeons in the park. Perhaps it was only the path that emphasized the man's stature. The German was paraded directly past the gallows by the still nervous American soldier at a gunpoint stance that may have furthered the illusion of danger.

"Killer," someone else in the crowd repeated.

"Kill him," came the imperfect echo.

"Kill the Nazi beast!" went up the cry.

From above, it looked like a nautical scene to Isaac, as if the soldier was a tugboat, his prisoner the figurehead on the prow, splitting the waves of Jews, who spread behind. But the American soldier was an uncertain navigator and slowed his pace and the waves of skeletons pressed in, and some of them began to slap at the German with their sticklike arms.

One blow must have landed because a blotch of red appeared on his upper lip.

The boat began to founder in the choppy sea.

Elizabeth Smith Moss raised a camera to her eyes.

"Kill the Nazi beast!"

"Vengeance," Isaac thought from his peaceful aerie—did he really want vengeance? He was King of Aspenfeld now, but he was no longer happy, and his teeth had begun to ache again.

Despite his evident thriving within the changed lager, the circumstances of Isaac's success were disconcerting. There were too many lessons to be learned: about America, about credit, about living without fear, and about freedom, which was also fearsome. The difference between the Before and the After was that learning before had to be instantaneous, because a student received no second chance. The postliberation lager was less demanding, but Isaac had no patience. Despite his failure to test the effect of a cup of hot coffee once upon a time, he still swallowed his drink in single gulps. He was ready to leave and going to leave. He started down the ladder.

Major Hamilton heard the ruckus and came striding out of his tent. "What's going on here?" He fired a pistol into the air, and the crowd hushed. "What's going on here?" he said quietly.

The private tried to explain how he found the hiding German, but the shrill outcries of the Jews gave their own testimony.

One of the last Musselmen looked on impassively.

A voice from the crowd called out to him, "Maxie! Look Maxie, we caught one."

The American officer was trying to decide whether to defend his prisoner for due process, but he had overseen the burial of too many bodies and his revulsion was as clear as his desire to please. He turned to Mr. Foyle, who had followed the crowd out of the laundry, and asked this only authority from the West, "What do you think?

The question was so far removed from the bureaucrat's domain that he blanched and looked in turn to the silent Musselman, Maxie. "What do you think?"

Maxie peered at the German soldier with his sunken eyes and said nothing. That was his judgment.

"Take him," Major Hamilton said.

Take him, they did, pushing, shoving in the direction of the gallows. Sturmmann Lichter went silently as Maxie's eyes met his one-time master's in a moment of mutual understanding.

From nowhere, a rope appeared, thin and rough. It was strung around the German's neck, three times—not precisely a noose, but sufficient to the task—and knotted.

"A chair."

"We need a chair!"

The item was requisitioned from the office of the Joint; it was the heavy metal swivel chair the slim girl with the straight hair occupied. She looked out the window.

The German was enthroned on the chair and it reminded Isaac of the party he had attended when one of his teachers back at the yeshiva was wed to the daughter of another Hasidic Rabbi, and the community celebrated. A crowd of men surrounded the groom, placed him on a chair, lifted the four legs, and danced him awkwardly across the floor to the music of two fiddles and a clarinet.

The gallows at Aspenfeld was not a mechanical contraption. There was no trap to give way and let swing. There was only a bar and a rusty metal hook. The swivel chair was the platform. The rope was looped around the hook by a man who climbed atop the horizontal cross beam, and the prisoner was pushed off the chair. For a fragment of a second, he hovered, before gravity took hold.

"Heil . . ." he shrieked as his weight pulled him down, his hand jerked up in final salute.

CHAPTER 2

Imagine a map of Europe with cities obliterated, boundaries irrelevant, mountains flattened, and rivers run dry. Imagine only the camps delineated, blue for labor, yellow for concentration, red for extermination, jewels in the helmet of the Thousand Year Reich. In the spring of 1945, however, the jewels were plucked out like eyes by crows from dead Jews, as the gates were opened to the final dissolution of the bastions amid the flux. Two hundred miles east of Aspenfeld, also two hundred south, at a hundred camps and sub-camps, the same kinds of liberation, pandemonium, and recrimination were occurring more or less simultaneously. The triumphant armies of the United States, Britain, France, the U.S.S.R. and individual battallions representing dozens of other nations from the Philippines to Palestine marched in, allowing fifty thousand-odd refugees to stream out.

It was Passover in Dachau, the holiday celebrating the Jews' Exodus from Egypt. The actual calendar date of the festival had come several weeks prior to liberation, but some of the inmates decided to organize a belated seder, and, in the name of restitution, the British occupying force airlifted in the necessary ritual foods.

There was matzoh and horse raddish and parsley, the first green vegetable the inmates had seen in years, hard-boiled eggs and salt in which to dredge them, and apples and nuts requested by the Jews to mash together for charoses, which represented the mortar their ancestors used to cement the pyramids on the Nile. There was also a single lamb's shank bone attained from a kosher butcher in Belgravia to be singed beside the pyre of bones already present on the grounds of the lager. Better yet, there were lingonberries and cream. Manna excepted, Moses never tasted such a treat, but the British commander took the opportunity to add these items to his requisition list, aiming to serve his own private table as well as the mess built for the remnants of Zion.

"Jews," they scoffed in Whitehall.

But they had seen Elizabeth Smith Moss's photos reproduced in their magazines and Churchill knew the benefits to be reaped by one single image of a seder under the auspices of the Union Jack that had so abjectly surrendered Czechoslovakia years earlier. It had taken Dunkirk to negate John Bull's reputation for physical cowardice. Perhaps a seder could do as well in the ethical domain. London duly sent a carton of green lingonberries along with the more Yiddische items on the list.

So what if they had to go to New Zealand for the berries. The pilots dispatched on this mission to the southern hemisphere knew it was vital. "Probably microfilm inside the crate of Maori Brand," one speculated to his copilot as they touched down at Gatwick.

So determined were the Whitehall authorities to make the first postliberation seder an occasion to remember that they recruited a British rabbi to travel with the food, as if clerics were stacked in aisle three of the military warehouse next to matzoh. He wore an ill-fitting combat uniform and shrugged at the lingonberries he escorted, but accepted his mandate with grace.

Two days later, newly commissioned with the rank of Captain in the Queen's Guards, Chaplain Simon Levi set foot in the lager. He took the obligatory tour of Hell, evinced the same repulsion as his less spiritual predecessors, and immediately sought refuge in one of the hundred Haggadahs provided by an American coffee manufacturer trying to cosset the Jewish market.

Rabbi Levi was eager to commence the service he had been sent to conduct in the large tent decorated with grapevines strung along barbed wire for the purpose. It was dusk and the place was jammed with Jews, English soldiers, and reporters from the *Times,* the *Sun,* the *Mail,* and half a dozen other papers that had received press releases along with the government's invitation to a junket. Levi, whose Highgate congregation had hosted Disraeli less than seventy-five years earlier, scanned the ranks of his fascinating co-religionists, who were as foreign to him as Zulus, and recited the Hebrew kiddush with a British accent, "Blessed art Thou, Eternal our God, Ruler of the universe, Creator of the fruit of the vine. Blessed art Thou, Eternal our God, Ruler of the universe, Who chose us from all peoples and exalted us among all nations."

Before this line was out of his mouth, came the first rumblings of discontent, as a young French Jew whispered, "Look at us—exalted."

"Sssh," a Hasid whispered back. He showed off a newly recaptured fur shtreimel and examined the wisps of hair that would grow into payes beneath the brim. For those who measured time in messianic terms, the duration of their stay in the lagers was but a blink, and their footsteps temporarily detoured were back on track to Panacea.

Between the stare of the British rabbi and the glare of the Gerer Hasid, the young Frenchman hushed, but there were others under the enormous tent who did not share the messianic attitude. These secular Jews disdained gabardine in favor of linen trousers that hung in unintended pleats on their emaciated frames like the first oversize pair of long pants presented to them on their Bar Mitzvahs—"don't worry—you'll grow into it." Rather than being religious, they were curious or, more pertinently, ravenous, heeding the call of their faith in return for a mortal reward of broiled chicken and carrots glazed with brown sugar sauce, cut in coins and heaped like a pirate's ransom on a genuine plate. They hadn't seen a plate in many Passovers.

The rabbi continued, "With love You gave us the festivals for happiness, holidays and seasons for rejoicing; as this day of the Feast of Matzoh, the season of our freedom . . ."

The French Jew's expression twisted with anger on his narrow face made narrower by starvation, his enormous, black eyes made larger by the shrinkage of flesh nearly to bone. "Now?"

"Sssh," came the second angry whisper from the minyan of would-be graybeards in front. The faithful had found each other swiftly after liberation.

Marcus Morgenstern heard the comment, smiled grimly, heard the rejoinder, smiled again, and waited. He couldn't see very well for his Coke-bottle glasses were fitted to Special Projects' specifications, but he knew a storm when he smelled one coming.

"Yves is getting warmed up," Reznikoff said.

"I know," Kline said.

Marcus was sitting off to the side with Reznikoff and Kline, the men he had worked with on "Special Projects."

The rabbi paused to peruse the assembly, which lifted the first of four glasses of sacramental wine. Unlike the heavy sweet Malaga they were used to Before, their glasses were filled with a strange bubbly concoction that was white instead of red. Their waiters were English privates, who might as well have been impressed into serving royalty at Bath, and the wine was a '28 Rhine vintage decanted from bottles in the camp kommandant's cellar, since Major Castleton preferred it to the red.

The service lead on to the Four Questions, traditionally asked by the youngest at the festive table. There were no children in Dachau, but one twelve-year-old worked in the brothel for the SS, some of whom preferred boys. Morgenstern listened with keen anticipation, knowing that the response of Billy—as his jackbooted lovers called him—might not be precisely what the rabbi expected.

"Why is this night different from all other nights?" young Billy recited, and before an elder could respond, he answered the question himself, "Because we do not spread our cheeks."

"Alors, Velvel," shouted the Frenchman.

"Hmm." The rabbi began to sense that this was no ordinary seder. Nonetheless he proceeded with the ritual discussion. "No, yingeleh, it is because on all other nights we eat leavened bread, but this is the bread of affliction," he said as held up the matzoh from London.

The Hasidim duly savored the crackers' gritty texture while Yves innocently asked an unscripted second question, "Tell me, Reb, what other nights have we eaten challah?"

Despite the undercurrent of discontent, the seder ran through the traditional recitation of the Passover story. It told of the ancient Jews' enslavement in Egypt and Moses' divinely ordained liberation of his people after ten plagues were called down upon Pharaoh. It told of how the Jews' final escape was executed in such a hurry that bread for the journey had to be removed from the ovens before it had a chance to rise, which is why matzoh became a ritual food. It also told of the esoteric commentary on these events repeated through the ages, such as Rabbi Yose the Galilean's higher math: "How can one show that following the ten plagues in Egypt itself the Egyptians were smitten with fifty plagues at the Red Sea. Of one of the plagues in Egypt it is said, 'The soothsayers said to Pharaoh, the plague is the finger of God,' while at the Red Sea it is said, 'And Israel saw the strong hand which the Eternal had shown against Egypt. . . . ' If one finger of God in Egypt caused ten plagues, we may assume from this that the whole hand of God at the Red Sea would cause fifty plagues."

And, they moved on to the listing, with a drop of wine spilled to represent each biblical plague. The Hasidim carefully dipped their little fingers into their mugs and dabbed them on the paper table-cloths provided for the occasion, blots spreading and overlapping.

"Blood.

Frogs.

Vermin.

Beasts.

Murrain.

Boils.

Hail.

Locusts.

Darkness.

Slaying of the First-Born."

The Hasidim wiped their fingers on the tablecloth so they would not inadvertently bring a finger to their lips and imbibe the symbolic plagues, but there was something about the notion of plagues them-selves that seemed to inspire the rest of the crowd

Yves sucked meditatively on his little finger and said, "I can think of a few more."

"More plagues!" another cried, and the rest took up the chant. "More plagues. More plagues," and they began banging tin cups on the tables to the rhythm of the demand. "More plagues! More plagues!"

The rabbi raised his eyes to meet Major Castleton's. It was worse than Czechoslovakia and the journalists were snapping pictures of the rude frenzy.

It took another, less refined rabbi, Hirsh Baer, wise in the ways of the lager, to understand that the analogies to recent history were too clear to be avoided. Baer had been deported from Bialystok early in the war and conducted illicit Yom Kippur services in the camp. He understood that only by acknowledging them could one calm the crowd. "Fine," he said, as he joined Simon Levi at the head of the table, placing a yarmulke on his shaved head, feeling the strange texture on his scalp for the first time since Before.

"Fine," he repeated. "Let us list the modern plagues." He agreed to recite the history of the last month as if it had occurred four thousand years earlier.

"Auschwitz."

"Here. Here."

"L'chayim."

The British rabbi translated for the major, "That means: To Life."

"Treblinka."

"La Mort." It was the weasely French Jew who spoke with true Gallic savoir faire, and raised his battered tin cup of white wine.

Marcus Morgenstern said to Reznikoff, "Yves is just warming up."

"I know," Kline nodded.

Tasting freedom, they hoisted a glass to the next plague, "Majdanek."

"La Merde."

The rabbi turned to the major, who spoke first, "I know."

One by one they named the rest of the plagues and after each one, they raised their glasses in bitter jubilee.

"Chelmno.

Sobibor.

Belzec.

Mauthausen.

Buchenwald.

Dachau."

And with each plague they sipped at the wine, until they arrived at the last, all-encompassing scourge, "Europe!"

There was a universal pause as they contemplated the Continent of the Diaspora, the Europe of the Magna Carta and the Rights of Man, the Europe of the Inquisition and the Crusades, the Europe of Copernicus, Goethe, and Goebbels. Then the French Jew, Yves, said, "What is this piss we're drinking? Why, on all other Passovers do we drink red wine and on this night white?"

"Why?"

"I'll tell you why. Because they did not let us mix in the blood of Christian children."

"Hallelujah."

"Go on," Major Castleton said warily, watching the creatures, and preparing for the next explosion. Marcus sipped along with them, humored and removed.

Fortunately, they had now arrived at the point in the seder when the ritual foods were to be eaten and the meal served. The rabbi gave silent thanks that his ordeal was nearly over, and distributed fragments from the matzoh.

Still, it was not enough. "Matzoh, who wants that?"

Those who had tasted their first real bread of the decade in the last month were in no mood to make sacrifices. They refused the matzoh and called for, "Rye, pumpernickel, whole wheat, just give it to me and see what happens."

"But it's Passover . . . here."

"I don't care if it's Passover everywhere," Yves replied. "Any bread is good bread as far as I'm concerned. Raisin bread. Corn bread. Onion bread with caraway seeds. Tortillas. Chapatis. Baguettes."

"It is the bread of affliction."

"No bread can ever symbolize affliction again."

"More wine."

"More plagues!"

Suddenly there was an impromptu debate leading to the Hasids' Talmudic resolution that although the substance of the ceremony was to be kept intact, its form could change, and because it was not really the calendar date of the holiday they could eat bread to represent matzoh if they wished.

This was not satisfactory. The unrepentant contingent's representative declared, "I'll eat it whether you want me to or not."

"So eat."

Trying to salvage a remnant of decisiveness, he said, "I'll eat it whether I want to or not."

"So eat the bread of affliction."

"You are the bread of affliction."

"Ten seconds after the War, and they think they're in cheder again," Marcus Morgenstern commented with the same brand of cynicism that Isaac Kaufman had found two hundred miles away.

Just before the opposing parties arrived at blows, the meal itself arrived, and this more than matzoh created an island of silence punctuated by chewing sounds. Rabbis and atheists alike tore into the food as fast as the English privates could deliver it.

Only the Musselmen didn't eat. It might have been their last supper, but they were as ready for eternity as Jesus at the Upper Room. Every day was a fast day in the sacred universe.

Ignoring their ascetic peers' air of passive contemplation, the rest of the crowd cracked the fowl limbs from their joints and devoured the flesh with undisguised relish. A barnyard of chickens was swallowed, yet insufficient to sate their appetite. They swabbed up mashed potatoes and digested forests of the broccoli the British chefs deemed fit to accompany the main dish.

Still, it was not enough. They reached toward the Musselmen's plates with fingers thin as chicken feet before the English waiters could retrieve the untouched portions. "You don't mind, do you," they said as they grabbed.

Still they wanted more. "Pork, please," the young Frenchman requested.

"There is no pork."

"What is there?"

"Well, mately, we've got Yorkshire pudding back at the canteen."

"What is that?"

"Sort of eggy, like big cakes cooked in milk and roast beef drippings."

"Treyf," the Hasidim cried with great satisfaction at the first time they could afford to refuse food in years.

"Bring it in," Yves said . . . "along with more wine, s'il vous plaît."

The Brits had sent a batch of individually wrapped puddings with their kosher catering so that their own men would feel appreciated, but in the name of international good will and publicity, the whole platoon of yellowish cubes were broken out, and promptly ripped to pieces, fat dripping from the former inmates' fatless knuckles, but it was still not enough. The more the men ate, the more they craved, until the kitchens were depleted, the cooks exhausted.

The photographers clicked their shutters with the same abandon as their subjects ate. The major had to provide something else to stop the seder's total degeneration, but there was only one last carton of edibles he could volunteer in the name of His Majesty. "All that's left are berries and cream."

"We'll take it," Yves replied, "Right, Rabbi?"

"Right." Even the Hasidim agreed, planning to eat only the berries and leave the unkosher cream to the apostates with shaved heads.

Major Castleton looked on with pain as his private cache was opened, and the Jews plowed into the berries first and followed them with a tub of clotted cream.

"We win the war and they eat cream," he said.

"Pah, strange stuff," the ungrateful Jews said as they gulped down New Zealand's best lingonberries by the precious bowlful, celebrating their own freedom despite the major's affliction.

Then they moved on to what ought to have been the second glass of wine according to the order of the service, but was really the fifth or sixth or seventh after the drinking to the plagues and additional guzzling during the meal.

Morgenstern sat at the corner with Reznikoff and Kline. They were the only ones who had not participated fully in the orgy, because they had been well fed by the masters who respected Special Projects' work. They did, however, drink.

"Freedom," the ex-inmates shouted, downing another glass of wine before the designated moment in the service.

The flow of liquor continued through the ostensible third glass and the fourth. That was the end of ritual consumption, but they drank a fifth that was actually a tenth. Bottles tumbled to the floor and rolled underneath the table. Jews rolled underneath the table, too, giggling with the luxury of frivolity.

"Is this Passover or Purim?" the outraged rabbi referred to the holiday in which oblivion was commanded to the extent that when reading the *Megillah,* the story of an earlier generation's salvation, one ought not to be able to tell the difference between Mordecai, the hero, and Haman, the villain. "It's a shandeh,"—a Yiddish shame—the rabbi declared.

"It's a party," they replied and began singing the boisterous songs they had heard the masters singing when lubricated by the liters of schnapps sent to sustain them in Dachau's noble endeavor. Instead of "Dayenu" and the other traditional melodies, the ex-inmates' voices rang into:

> *Bei mir bist du schoen*
> *Please let me explain.*

"Explain!"

"Tell us, Rabbi."

And he tried, retreating from Hebrew to the Aramaic ditty that had concluded innumerable seders, "One little goat, one little goat, My father bought for two zuzim. One little goat, one little goat. Then came a cat and ate the goat, My father bought for two zuzim. One little goat, one little goat. Then came a dog and bit the cat . . . Then came a stick and beat the dog, That bit the cat . . ." And on through the fire that burned the stick, the water that quenched the fire, the ox that drank the water, the butcher that slaughtered the ox, the angel of death that killed the butcher, to the final verse, "Then came the Holy One, blessed be He, And slew the angel of death, That killed the butcher, That slaughtered the ox, That drank the water, That quenched the fire, That burned the stick, That beat the dog, That bit the cat, That ate the goat, My father bought for two zuzim. One little goat, one little goat."

But the sounds of the foreign song washed over him and obliterated his voice: "Bei mir bist du schoen means that you're grand."

"A sheyne meydele!"

> *I could say Bella Bella . . .*
> "Even say Wunderbar," sang the Frenchman.
> *Bei mir bist du schoen.*
> *How grand you are!*

One little goat!
Let's eat the goat.
Scapegoat soufflé.
Warsaw pudding, cooked in roast Jew's dripping!

The voices, a mixture of Talmudic disputation and raucous hilarity, mingled under the canvas tent. Shy, shabby, sly, and disputatious, the Jews reverted immediately to the variety they had known before the War. United for the duration in a place that did not distinguish between orthodoxy and aspostasy, holy or profane, the remains of the Jewish communal body broke into a million fragments as the monolith of Europe crumbled.

It was the wine that made Morgenstern giddy, then queasy, and sent him reeling outside, first to vomit the precious Yorkshire nutrients onto the dusty earth. It was drizzling at Dachau, a foggy mist that made him believe it must be spirits hooting and hollering to beat the band back under the tent.

Merrymakers dozed off; the rabbi droned on. Squashed lingonberries stained the floor. Outside, Marcus felt like Moses, safe on the eastward shore of the Red Sea, his enemies drowned betide. Ahead lay the waste of Sinai, but there was the Hebrews' vision in the desert to guide him, a pillar of smoke by day and a pillar of flame by night.

He thought he heard someone, and replied, "Allo. Who is there?" but nobody answered.

Morgenstern could see no farther than his knuckles, let alone the image of God—not here, not now. His genetic nearsightedness had been deliberately magnified by those who compelled him to wear too strong a pair of spectacles to accomplish the fine work they required. The glasses had originally belonged to a half-blind upholsterer in Tarnów whose speciality was tapestry: "A forest, Mrs. Cohane, I'll make you for curtains. You'll think you're in the Congo."

Naked, six months later, approaching a ditch she helped dig amid birch trees, Mrs. Cohane said to her tradesman, "Is this the forest you intended, Mr. Green?" before his glasses were collected along with her earrings and teeth, wiped clean and shipped back to the Fatherland. The glasses were intended for distribution to the Aryan populace, all except the extraordinarily thick pair from Tarnów that was requisitioned by Special Projects. These lenses fit the man of embroidery, whose own vision required such drastic correction, but their new tenant, Morgenstern of only modest myopia, was not able to see more than half a meter from his eyeballs once he put them on. That had been three years ago.

Reznikoff was lucky. He had perfect vision; he was a jeweler who had never required a loupe, not even Before, when he and his brother-in-law rented a booth off the Vistula Arcade, and he took easily to the task imposed on the Special Projects group.

Like Morgenstern, Kline, a typographer, had his sight distorted by new glasses, but unlike Morgenstern he did not care. When Marcus nudged him and asked, "What's going on?" he answered back, "What's to see?"

"Whatever there is."

"Why bother?"

They were in the midst of this discussion when the wine started churning in Morgenstern's belly and sent him pitching through the flap, heaving putrid, macaroni-shaped nodules of Yorkshire pudding and digestive fluid into the shallow trough that ran through the camp, toward Canada, the warehouse that Marcus drunkenly realized must contain other glasses.

In Dachau Canada was a converted airplane hangar, a vast, low-ceilinged structure built in the early years of aviation, used once by Lindbergh on a trip that may have contributed to his admiration of the Reich. It was unlocked, because there was nothing worth stealing amid the stacked and massed property of the Jews. All the gold and currency had long since been sieved out of the mountain of suitcases that nearly reached the ceiling.

Marcus maneuvered between piles of sweaters, photographs, boots, and books, all neatly categorized. Hebrew Bibles were kept aside as rarities from an extinct religion, artifacts esoteric as cuneiform tablets, salvaged for the ethnographic museums of the future. He passed shoes and more suitcases until he came to a chicken-wire bin stuffed with spectacles. The tangle of wire and glass and Bakelite frames glittered in the moonlight that glowed through a row of transoms under the hangar's pitched roof. There must have been thousands of glasses and the only way to find out which one matched his pre-War prescription was by trial and error. Marcus sat down cross-legged, and, like a seamstress commencing to unravel a skein, he extracted a pair of horn-rims from the edge of the thicket and tried them on. They turned the far corner of the warehouse into a brilliant telescopic picture, of as many eyes as there were stars in the sky, that turned out to belong to a cairn of toy dolls. Unfortunately, the view left the viewer's own hand fuzzy. How many fingers were there?

It reminded him of a legendary guard who cut off prisoners' thumbs and wore them inside a cartridge belt.

Morgenstern set the horn-rims aside and tried on a succession of other glasses, without regard for style. He tried whatever his fingers were able to tease out through the mesh, this one with pink rhinestones, that with sleek metallic shades for bathing at Nordensk, and a dozen narrow steel rims shaped like teardrops, octagons, and circles until he finally found a pair of cracked tortoiseshell frames that put the world in focus. Delighted, he stood up to explore this new universe, but, remembering the old universe, he first slipped his old glasses back through the chicken-wire for the ghost of the upholsterer of Tarnów or some future unfortunate who needed just that same dead man's defect cured—either that or someone else who required them for fine work or crewel.

Instead of leaving by the front door, the newly observant Morgenstern noticed a back exit. What clarity, what perception! Seeing was thrilling. The gray rectangle stood out in the tenebrous dusk. It was the door to the masters' quarters. The warehouse was attached to the administration building by a kind of tunnel, so when that door was open, as all doors were open now, now that the war was over, and he could see, he entered. Nobody stopped him.

The long galvanized corridor was still lined with a row of drooping flags jutting out from tarnished bronze holders set at eye level for a stretch of ten meters. Bulletin boards were interspersed between the banners and various notices were tacked onto the cork: health warnings, inspirational phrases, cartoons from the military newspaper, and train schedules printed on cheap gray newsprint, curled at the edges, describing shipments of Jews yet to arrive.

At the end of the hall was Kommandant Luster's private domain. That was where the pretty secretary who used to stroll onto the killing grounds and point to a prisoner for her man to lash to death had sat. At least they assumed this woman they christened "The Princess of Pain" was pretty. Neither Morgenstern nor Kline could see beyond their drafting tables, while all that Reznikoff really saw of her from Special Projects window was a flash of black hair crossing the frame. Such a black, though! He described it to his hyper-nearsighted coworkers as patent leather.

There were a dozen other stations where underlings tended the mundane details of camp administration, one for vehicles, one for supplies, one for Jews, and there at the end of the room was the brown leather chair rubbed smooth where Luster sat and supervised all of them and, once a month, reported to Berlin. There were three telephones on the corner of his desk, one presumably for internal use, one for external calls, and the third a hot line to the Valkyries of the Niebelung for all Marcus Morgenstern knew. A cap bearing the branched cross hung from a peg on the wall.

Head coverings had a different significance for a people trained to humility before their Lord. It was ironic that there was a hat without a head in a world of heads without hats.

Marcus idly took the cap off its peg and set it on his own brow at a slant. He could see his reflection in the window, beyond which a last few Jews wearing skullcaps still rang out the songs of their ancestors. The carousers of "Bei Mir Bist Du Schoen" had succumbed to exhaustion and inebriation while Hasidic chants still permeated the night, since the rabbis were more accustomed to hard drink than their emancipated cousins. Morgenstern tried the chair, found it comfortable, and reached toward the desk. Like the warehouse, it was unlocked. There was nothing to hide.

All that was left in Kommandant Luster's desk was the stationery of Moloch, thumbtacks that held up train schedules, rubber bands that bunched together hundreds of passports stamped J, paper clips, and a green-covered ledger and a photograph album.

The ledger was a record of shipments out from Dachau, a series of numbers, "12, 8, 17 . . . ," representing kilos of teeth sent to have their gold fillings extracted and smelted before a trip to the Lieb-knechtwerke, a minor camp that acted as the repository of the Reich's human excavations.

As for the album, there was Luster's own baby Otto in knee breeches on skates, baby Otto atop a stepstool in a low-beamed kitchen, baby Otto making a funny face while being snuggled by smiling grandparents in a mountain setting, and every picture was attached by four black corners as if in mourning. Indeed baby Otto might be buried under the ruins of Ulm by now, along with his whole collection of Hitler Youth outfits and paraphenalia.

There were also pictures of Jews in the album—marching, praying, dying and dead, limbs tangled as the frames of their glasses. These were clearly taken by a different camera and a different sensibility. The finger that pressed this shutter was both closer to its subject and more composed than the shaky, sentimental hand that recorded baby Otto's first steps to mail to his father on the domestic front.

Morgenstern well remembered Anton Koff, a German soldier who was a photography buff, a pale sickly boy who reminded Marcus of the ephebes of Poznán, always with a Leica 202 that must have cost a summer's salary around his thin neck, who created an ongoing record of the Jewish experience in the lager from arrival to airborn departure. Koff was always present at a new train's arrival and a new group's selection, his face hidden by the black metal camera box. He was a fixture, yet who could have guessed that the images he created would be chosen with such an eye to beauty.

Morgenstern was mesmerized by these photographs, especially one cleverly double-exposed shot with a pale impressionistic scrim across the bottom that was actually a line of dishevelled figures viewed at a distance while the closeup of a candle flame superimposed at the left was vivid enough to singe one's fingers.

Marcus wondered how the pictures got into Luster's desk, whether they were presented, confiscated, or commissioned. He wondered if the soldier with the camera was given a medal or hung as a traitor.

He was still sitting in Luster's chair, death's-head cap sitting at a jaunty skew, when two British privates and a captain broke in and aimed guns at his chest.

"Nice and easy, bub," the captain said, then turned and congratulated the private who had spotted the figure in what ought to have been a vacant office. "Good eyes."

"Vos iz dos?" Morgenstern rocked back and forth.

"I don't know how we missed you, Heinz, but you'll have plenty of time to swing." He jerked his neck sideways and grinned.

The British soldiers were, in fact, surprised to find yet another

German because the camp personnel at Dachau had not been as fortunate as their peers at places like Aspenfeld; they had not received any advance warning of the Allied approach and were not able to flee or hide. They just woke one morning to find the camp surrounded, and for no more than a minute was there the question of a final battle, before they wisely chose to surrender. This avoided the kind of spontaneous retribution that occurred to Sturmmann Lichter at Aspenfeld and a few stray dozens of murderers across the Continent. The British simply lined up the camp personnel, all except the Princess of Pain, who said she was visiting her cousin and hitched a ride out of town with a French journalist before anyone could stop her, and marched them to their own POW camp. It was not as fancy as Dachau, lacking banquet halls and sports facilities and murder compartments, but it had all that was necessary to keep the local high command alive until their trials.

Nonetheless one German officer apparently remained, and on this, the night of His Majesty's seder, the British soldiers were not going to let the Kraut escape. Three carbines aimed directly at the man in the armchair, who lifted his hands from the photo album he had been perusing.

"Crimes against humanity" was the term already bandied forth, and Morgenstern, who had studied English as part of Special Projects' mandate, caught the gist, and turned it back on his accusers.

"Humanity, you say. Please to allow me to ask what crimes were committed against you? If you want to be, how do you say, accurate, let us say crimes against Jews. But the logic would then suggest that Jews are human. But your own immigration policy differs, eh?"

"There's a difference between not lettin' 'em in and wipin' 'em out, matey."

"Not from my perspective."

"And what is your perspective?"

"I am a Jew."

"Is that how you got so chubby while your cousins weigh about six stone?"

"Aha!" It was Morgenstern's Special Projects' good health as much as his cap that misidentified him as a German. "Healthy or not, nevertheless, I am a Jew." He rolled up his sleeve to offer proof in the shape of the blue number tattooed midway between his elbow and wrist, 189941. "Then again, I am an expert with the pen and ink. So you can't really know if this is authentic."

"Sir?" the private turned to the captain with sudden doubt.

Morgenstern's insistence was half-convincing, but he spoke with such a heavy Yiddish accent, naturally mistaken for German, that the soldiers were still suspicious.

"Sure talks like a Jew."

"So what is he doing here?"

It was time to end the misunderstanding, so Marcus explained, "I was looking for a new pair of glasses. I came in here from the warehouse."

"The door is locked."

"It wasn't when I came in."

"It is now."

"Perhaps I locked it by mistake. Perhaps someone else locked it— the angel of death, say, or the holy ghost. In any case, a closed door does not change my race . . . Look, this is ridiculous. Just bring in any one of the men from the seder and they'll tell you who I am. Bring in Reznikoff. Bring in Kline."

Uncertain, the captain nodded to one of his men, who saluted, left, and returned a couple of awkward mintues later with a Jew— neither of the gentlemen Morgenstern requested. Who could tell the skeletons apart? Why bother? The soldier brought, instead, the only one left sober after the debacle of a seder, the British rabbi, Simon Levi. There was a hushed conference among the victors, while Morgenstern, the vanquished, looked cooly at them. This was interesting. He had never been interrogated by the Germans, who had respected his skills and left him alone.

The rabbi circled around the prisoner, like a peasant examining a horse, Morgenstern thought. Eventually, he had no choice but to address the suspicious merchandise, "Hello."

"Hello."

"My name is Rabbi Simon Levi."

"I know."

"How?"

"I saw your seder."

The rabbi nodded, but could not bring himself to query Morgenstern about the seder or indeed anything that occurred on this side of the barbed wire. Instead, he asked, "What did you do before the war?"

How this might resolve their dilemma, the rabbi could not have said, but it seemed like a logical question. Morgenstern replied, "I was a dentist . . . but I've become an artist, after a fashion."

"Hmm." The rabbi decided to pry further into the prisoner's self-declared aesthetic knowledge, to trip him up. "Interesting art is being uncovered." He was referring to the butterflies and menorahs drawn by the handful of children incarcerated during the War. He had an envelope of their pictures entrusted to him by the new camp authorities tucked into his waistcoat pocket. He opened it and showed the images to Morgenstern. "It was the last thing they did. Remarkable, no?"

"I'm sorry if these children were murdered, but that does not transform their scribblings into art."

"What is art, then?"

"You want to see?"

"Yes."

"Here." And Morgenstern pointed to the photos he had found in the Kommandant's desk, "Here's your twentieth-century genius. Someday they'll be in a museum, but you can see them now. Bow to the work of Herr Artmeister Koff."

Simon Levi tried to look, but he couldn't. His own stomach churned. Only two categories of humanity were able to face this art without flinching.

It was Koff who had inadvertently saved Marcus when Kommandant Luster was seeking men for the Special Projects group. The photographer was kneeling, shooting into the sun while the prisoners were being interviewed. Why Marcus cared whether the pictures came out, he could not have said, unless it was to preserve his last moments on earth, but he addressed the German, a lethal error in lager etiquette. "Your photos will be ruined."

Koff, the genius, ignored him.

"I'm telling you, they will all be overexposed." The dentist of Poznań knew this from X rays of teeth.

"It depends on the f-stop."

Koff knew precisely what he was doing, and Morgenstern's layman's advice was less than useless, but the kommandant overheard their dialogue. "You are an artist?" he asked Marcus with a faint undertone of respect. These people were known for their Kultur.

In that moment, Morgenstern made the leap that saved his life. "Yes," he said with, he hoped, suitable conviction.

"A modern artist?"

This was a trick question, but Marcus was aware of German criticism. They disdained the radical imagination of people like Picasso. Give them an apple-cheeked Rhine maiden instead. "Unfortunately not," he bluffed. "I am more of a traditionalist, a realist."

"Why unfortunately?"

"Because, modern artists are very successful. They make a great deal of money."

"Here, you will make a great deal of money."

That was what the Kommandant said and he meant it literally. Marcus was recruited on the spot to join Reznikoff and Kline in Special Projects' Operation George Washington, an attempt to forge American currency to destablize the United States economy. As it turned out, his fine hand-eye coordination served him well, as did Reznikoff's jewelry skills and Kline's typesetting. Though forced to wear overstrong spectacles to focus solely on their labor, the three men were granted privileges that none of the other prisoners shared, like food.

Then, in '44, as it appeared that Germany was going to lose the war, the three men were set to working extra hours into the night producing documents for German escape, although the masters never had the opportunity to use them. Somewhere, there was a box filled with half a dozen imaginary people with birth certificates, passports, driver's licenses, library cards, all the papers that proved they were as real as the Jews who went up in smoke.

Marcus remembered those imaginary people well, better than the real people who had once been his parents and friends. There was Rolf Costello, of Trieste, a commercial traveler whose description bore an uncanny resemblance to Kommandant Luster, and Irina Fet, a Russian émigré with patent leather black hair. He had particularly enjoyed concocting Irina's heritage, including an embossed letter from St. Petersburg testifying to her loyalty to the deposed Tzar.

He told the British rabbi. "I was a forger for the Germans."

There was another whispered conference between the rabbi and the soldiers. Eventually, the captain spoke to Morgenstern, "Can you prove this?"

Marcus pushed a sheet of paper from a stack in Luster's upper left drawer—it was a requisition form for shoe polish—across the table, and said, "Sign your name."

"What?"

"Your name, please, and rank if you wish. You have serial numbers, too, I believe, just like us."

The captain scribbled with a hasty flourish as if there was something distasteful about the exercise.

Morgenstern concentrated on the page, noting the particular crossing of the *T*, the slant to the left. Then he took the captain's pen, set the nib facing inward at forty-five degrees, and followed the lines of the signature without looking at what he was writing, tracing it in his mind. Keeping one's eyes to the original rather than the reproduction was the secret. Time enough to admire one's handiwork later. Then he did it again, and again, above and below the original. Then he handed the paper filled with signatures to the captain, and said, "If you can tell me which one is yours, I will tie the noose around my neck myself."

The captain started to play the game with the man's life at stake, carefully comparing the row of signatures up and down the page, trying to remember where on the page he had signed. After a moment in which his men watched him as intently as he examined the page, he threw the paper down and said, "Bloody Hell here, only a Jew would risk it."

Morgenstern nodded with acknowledgment of his skill, but he smiled because he could tell that they didn't care and that even as they stalked off they rather wished that he was a German instead of a Jew.

He sailed the Nazi cap across the room back onto the peg. A week later, he would leave the camp, but in the meanwhile he reopened the book of photographs.

CHAPTER 3

The morning Mauthausen was evacuated, Fishl was given a DDT shower to exterminate his lice.

"A shower in the shower room," Alter Kaufman said. "How novel."

Novel or not, the water washed off a peel of grit and left the disinfected young man's skin itchless and as shockingly smooth as a newborn's. Thus, despite the clatter of machinery. Fishl went to sleep. He slept, but he dreamed that he was moving, and it wasn't until the truck bumped over a pair of unevenly graded train tracks that he gazed blearily out the window and discovered the countryside flying past.

Fishl was perpetually late. Eighteen years earlier, he was a ten-month baby. Five years ago, he had been late to leave Ostrowiec and it saved his life. "Quick, quick, Reb Fishl," cried Zalman, the oat-monger's son, "the Germans are in the marketplace, and anyone who isn't there in ten minutes will be shot. Hurry."

Fishl looked up from the tractate he was studying and asked, "How long does it take to get to the marketplace?"

"Fifteen minutes," the boy said.

"So if they're going to shoot me anyway, why should I make it easy?"

The messenger left, returned to the marketplace late, and was duly killed—along with everyone who had arrived at the prescribed hour.

Fishl licked his finger and turned the last page of the Talmud's discussion of whether music was a language.

Sadly, his lethargic nature did not always serve him so well; he was also late to escape Ostrowiec. That was another chapter, one that took half a decade to arrive at its own unusual conclusion when the Russian Army blasted the gate off its hinges at Steyr and raised the red flag.

Waiting in line for his DDT shower, Fishl had stared at the Steyr section of Mauthausen with a purity of wonderment unmatched since the day he arrived. The camp was being disassembled by a flock of enormous cranes that lifted entire barracks off their foundations and set them as gently as uncooked eggs upon a convoy of flatbed trucks bound for Baku, where Stalin's peacetime army planned to house a population of "volunteer workers" to restore the USSR's devastated oil fields. All of the DPs were offered jobs.

"Work in the east, rings a bell," Alter Kaufman, Isaac's older brother, said.

"Communists are not Fascists."

"Only the moustaches are different."

Fishl, threading between the conversations, wanted to go, but overslept instead.

The barracks were hurtling along so close to the speckled oaks that longer branches kissed the windows in arboreal farewell, and jolting roughly from side to side. In order to move forward, Fishl had to grip one bunk post after another until he reached the front door that opened onto a cab in which a Russian soldier was driving. There was a stiff-brimmed cap with a red star on the seat, and the driver was singing. Through his windshield, Fishl could see another truck with another barracks and as many ahead as stretched to the horizon. It was Steyr on wheels. He wondered if they also packed up the crematoria.

Fishl didn't say anything, but the driver must have felt a shadow or sensed a presence, because he adjusted the rearview mirror and their eyes met, the driver no less startled by his passenger than the passenger had been by his unexpected journey. The truck swerved violently and pulled to the narrow shoulder. Barrack after barrack roared past their unscheduled rest stop.

The driver waited until the last truck's license was too small to read, then said one word, "Raus."

That, Fishl understood. He stepped through the door and climbed over the hook that attached the flatbed to the driver's cab.

"What are you doing?"

Fishl shrugged.

"Where are you going?"

"Where should I go?" he replied.

"Baku." The driver spoke a pigeon German. "People to Baku on different route. No people here. Houses."

Fishl could see. It reminded him of a tractate that posited a farmer's apples falling in a neighbor's yard. But what if someone picked up your home and took that away, the opposite of Before—when they left the homes and took away the people.

"Town." The man gestured in the direction they had come from. "Go to town," he said, pointing backward before he left his stowaway in a cloud of diesel fumes.

Inside, Steyr had been a controlled institution; outside was subject to random force, to choice, to intuition, to town. Why not? The Russian's oracular advice seemed natural. Fishl walked, feet scuffing the dirt road crossed by train tracks, pausing to watch a single jet screaming across the sky.

The nearest municipality was a dark-windowed main street like a cow's spine with a few side streets branching off like ribs. At one central intersection there was a tiny public square, like the cavity where the beast's heart might have pumped, with a waterless fountain beside a gray stone church where stray dogs foraged for scraps.

A signpost at the square bore arrows in two directions:

BRATISLAVA 80K →

← BRNO 55K

"Now let's see," the traveler thought back to his geography lessons. He sat on the edge of the fountain while the dogs sniffed his cuffs, and tried to create a map of Europe from the two facts he had been given. Bratislava was in the north of Hungary, Brno toward Prague. Assuming that the distances were correct and that the sign had not revolved on its pivot, he was somewhere in Czechoslovakia, south of

Poland, east of Germany. Mauthausen was in Austria, so the barracks must have been traveling all afternoon before he woke.

Drawn to the sound of water behind the church, Fishl found a narrow river spanned by a delicately arched bridge bearing a plaque that informed him that King Stanislaus had dedicated the bridge in 1542. Although the inadvertent tourist had not studied much secular history recently, everyone knew of Stanislaus's valiant defence against Charles I of Sweden, the horses slaughtered and piled as ramparts. It was definitely Czechoslovakia, and probably Hodonín, and it was drizzling. For a few minutes Fishl stood while the rain slid over the nubby, lice-free surface of his head and under the collar of his jacket before he realized that he could take shelter beneath the bridge. He lay down to rest, although he felt as if he was still traveling, by barge perhaps, floating down this tributary to the Danube and on to the Black Sea.

A coin dropped onto the ground beside him. The sound roused him. It was a long time since a gold piece had weighed in any of his pockets, not that many had found their way from Zurich to Warsaw to Kielce to Ostrowiec Before. A man was standing between Fishl and a streetlight that glowed in the mist.

The man was wearing a vest with a button hanging loose, swinging like a watch fob, and looked like he could put the money to better use than the object of his misplaced generosity. Fishl picked up the coin and returned it to his would-be benefactor.

"Juden?"

Why deny it? The worst that could happen would be that time would run backward, the truck with the Red Army driver return, pick him up, redeposit the barracks, and life under the Reich resume. "Da?"

"Juden . . . there."

"Where?" To a selection?

Despite or because of the man's insistence, Fishl felt a personal inclination to go the other way, north out of town in obedience to an inner compass that pointed beyond the Carpathians, through the flat farm country of Galicia, past Cracow, not quite all the way to Warsaw—to Kielce and the shtetl of Ostrowiec, that insignificant speck where he had missed one train to death and caught another that apparently led, after a detour, to life.

The man in the vest, however, seemed determined to guide him elsewhere. He spoke an urgent, gutteral Czech dialect Fishl clearly could not understand and then, in frustration, he extracted a pencil from his pocket, like a dagger from a sheath, and began to draw on the pavement, starting with a sketch of the bridge they stood beneath, shading it with the side of the lead, quickly notching a lacy fretwork, and then extending beyond artistry to a more abstract diagram of streets. Two corners in, he held up two fingers; then his hand swam to signify a right turn. "Juden . . . there."

Why not? Fishl started over the bridge and turned around. The man shook his head and put his palms together. Fishl walked until he found the destination. He knew it when he saw it. The citizen had pointed the Jewish stranger to the synagogue of Hodonín. It was a curious three-story building showing Dutch influence in the gabling, not much newer than the bridge, and wedged between twin apartment houses where a variety of flowers on the tenants' windowsills glistened with moisture. A stained glass window over the synagogue door was black, but approaching it from the side Fishl could discern two intersecting lead pane triangles that formed a Star of David. The door was open.

The synagogue had been neither burned nor desecrated, just abandoned after its congregants marched off to eternity. The same books they had left stood on the same shelves, accumulating dust. Fishl lifted one—what a familiar weight—and riffled the pages and seemed to hear a sweet, faraway chanting emanating from between the covers. It was Ma'ariv, the evening service, of love for and gratitude to God, and Fishl, who retained every line of liturgy, history, and commentary he had ever heard, recognized not only the words, but the melody of Before.

Tears came to Fishl's eyes; the book flipped open to the correct page; the words came tumbling out. Prayer had not changed nor had a dim body of men he now perceived mumbling in the depths of the cavern, bodies swaying with the ancient rhythmns of the faith. Fishl was drawn forward through some atavistic yearning.

His eyes met those of the other worshippers. Their heads nodded, as they continued, and he joined them. Only after the last "Amen" did they turn to him and say, "Sholem aleichem." Welcome.

Fishl gave the traditional response, "Aleichem sholem," and looked at the group forming a semicircle around him. They all had hair.

The man on the left, a slim elderly gentleman wearing a pince-nez, said, "Please, allow me to make introductions. I am Dr. Albert Kepler, retired, just returned from a prolonged stay in Shanghai. There," he gestured to the two men beside him wearing rugged peasant clothing, "are Reuven Kaplan and Lester Wolfe, partisans. They spent the last two years in the woods. We are what is left of the local congregation, Ohavi Zedek. David," he named the last man on the far end of the arc, "is our shammes."

David the caretaker was a squat, ungainly man, not a student but a keeper of texts, who described himself bitterly, "A shammes for an empty shul."

"At least you have books," Fishl replied soothingly.

"But no Torahs." David pulled aside the velvet curtain that adorned the empty ark. "They took the Torahs. Why?"

"I don't know."

"Maybe they wanted to read them," one of the partisans laughed.

"Never mind," the doctor said, and turned to Fishl, "What do you need?"

Needing itself was an odd concept—like money, or choice. He understood the language, but required an interpreter. Did one "need" to live?

"A shtickle herring?" The shammes offered the guest first helpings from a single plate of sliced fish and crusty black bread.

Yes, he needed food, of some sort, no more than a stray dog, water, retrieved in cupped hands from a river under a medieval bridge. "Thank you." He ate. The salty taste of the herring was as evocative as Proust's madeleine.

"Where are you from?"

"Ostrowiec."

"A shtetl?"

It wasn't even that. "A shtetelkh." The town returned more vividly to him with each chew. "Near Kielce."

"Poland?"

"Yes."

"Of course. And then?"

"Mauthausen."

The doctor nodded his head and asked a question. "Did you know Koplowitz?"

Fishl ransacked his brain, but he came up empty. Certainly Alter Kaufman, the lagermacher who had befriended him, would have known. "No."

"How about Schine, from Warsaw? Big family. Four brothers. I think two of them went to Mauthausen."

Fishl shook his head.

"Everyone knew the Schines. If you were in Mauthausen, you must have known them."

A curious expression crossed the face of the shammes. It was doubt, not at Fishl's history, but his character. The stranger's cheekbones vouched for his authenticity, but still, who could fail to know Schine? That was like living in Washington and not knowing Roosevelt. Worse than not knowing was not reciprocating with his own, "Do you know . . . ?"

Fishl had more than someone to ask about; he had too many, and the herring bones brought them all back. He had the Rabbi of Ostrowiec, a big sweaty man who looked like a butcher, and, of course, Lebedkin, the butcher. Most butchers were brawny, red-faced giants, right arms thick from wielding a cleaver, but Lebedkin was a small gentle man, rich with any butcher's eye to a slim cut, but idiosyncratic, a vegetarian who seemed to regret his occupation rather than relish it. There was also Emanuel, the beggar, to whom the butcher gave the shavings he kept from the matrons even as he urged them to stop eating flesh. There were the short-changed matrons themselves, all fullfilling their roles in the life of the community. There was even an enlightened teacher who produced small dramas in the library, paraphrasing Shakespeare for the local audience, "Ostrowiec is a stage, and the men and women merely players." Fishl had a family there, a mother, a father, brothers, sisters, cousins—half the town was related—and a wife.

If they had their roles, his was yeshiva bokher bookworm at sea on a raft of commentary. He had not expected to be saddled with the additional rights and responsibilities of the men called "husbands."

The betrothal was a great ceremony, for Rivka's grandfather was a renowned rabbi and his followers descended on Ostrowiec in a swarm of gabardine. They drank and pounded the tables of their beleaguered hosts for seven days of celebration, made passionate by the concurrent announcement of the first edicts levied against them: No Jews were allowed to employ gentile servants. No Jews were allowed to sue gentiles. No Jewish doctors were allowed to examine gentile patients. Afterward, alone together for the first time, recumbent on the nuptial bed in the attic of his parents' house, Fishl had looked on his bride, and seen, not as he was afraid, a great beauty, but a frightened breastless girl with a ring of curly chestnut hair.

She saw that he already had a high forehead and that the fringe of hair he bore was but a temporary ornament. But the lumpy scalp, so filled with millenia of biblical lore that the new husband could not be bothered with the hour of day nor grasp his marital responsibilities, was exposed sooner than either could imagine, as was his wife's. The hairs due to fall upon down-filled pillows would be shaved, and used to stuff the mattresses of Frankfurt and Hamburg and Cologne and Düsseldorf and Munich and Ulm and Mainz.

When the Germans marched in, the first thing they did was to separate the men and women. While the others cried for what they lost, Fishl felt the intellectual's abstract pain at his ignorance of what there was to be lost.

He couldn't bring himself to ask, "Did anyone meet a girl named Rivka from near Kielce?" because he felt that he had hardly met her, and would recognize only her hair. It brought up the sages' question of lost objects; there are those with individuality and there are those that are featureless. The example used was that if a cow is lost on the road to the market it may be claimed by its owner, because no two cows are exactly alike, but once the cow has been sold at the market and the proceeds lost on the return from the market it is considerably more difficult to identify.

Fishl's father and two brothers were shot in the marketplace.

The men in the synagogue of Hodonín were staring at him.

"And you?" Fishl stammered. He was not generally inquisitive, but unless he asked them something about themselves, he would never be able to stop talking about himself.

The men looked around, as if afraid to be overheard. It took the shammes to break the silence by leaning forward to explain. "I was hidden."

"Hidden? By who?"

"People who live here."

He explained that there was a secret tunnel under the Stanislaus bridge that linked the synagogue basement with the church crypt, where the priest allowed the living to cohabit with the dead, and fed the former from the leftovers of his own meager meals.

This kind of behavior astonished Fishl. He didn't particularly regret that he had not been hidden, nor did he dare to wonder which of his family might have been hidden; it was sufficient that the shammes of Hodonín had been hidden to go one step toward endowing a world he could abide. It also made his need to leave town, travel north, more immediate. It gave him a goal.

As if reading their guest's mind, the doctor unfolded a map of eastern Europe. Together, they examined the web of lines that confirmed Fishl's geographic intuition. He was three hundred and seventy-five kilometers from Kielce, not so far. At thirty kilometers a day, he could traverse the sector and find his old home in two weeks, but he also had four years to traverse, backward, and that was a distance.

"Nonsense," the men in the synagogue said, and they led Fishl back over the bridge, flanked by the partisans like a prisoner, and beyond the stone church to a single-roomed train station attached to a large glass shed. There was something strange about the preserved town that had sheltered a single Jew that was as perfect as a child's model city made of balsa. Perhaps the presence of the shammes buried undead in the church crypt protected it from the fury of heaven.

Fishl thought of Abraham the patriarch's argument with God when the Lord announced his plans to destroy Sodom. "If there be but a hundred righteous people, would he act thus?"

"No," the Lord said, "For a hundred righteous people, I would save the city."

"And if there were fifty righteous people? Twenty? Ten?" Abraham continued to negotiate.

For ten righteous people, the Lord would withhold his anger.

Sodom was obliterated from the face of the earth, but Hodonín remained.

The 5:14 train was not on time. Nor did anyone at the information kiosk seem to know when it was arriving or where it was, as frantic calls went out over the wires in search of the locomotive last seen somewhere between Trieste and Riga.

"It's missing," the man in the kiosk said with a shrug of solicitous regret.

"Missing? How can a train be missing?" one of the partisans demanded.

"I'm afraid that I can't answer that, Sir."

Europe was a continent of trains. It relied on trains to cross borders and link cities. Frequently, the only language neighbors had in common was written in eight-gauge steel. Maybe the web of tracks could still lead to the ten lost tribes of Galicia, Silesia, and the General Government region of Poland. Maybe they had spent the last four years shuttling back and forth from Lisbon to the Volga, nibbling smoked salmon and sipping currant jelly tea from tall glasses in the dining cars of a mobile, metal-clad caravan, only to disembark now that the whistle blew and the War was over—except those Fishl had personally seen made dead.

Dr. Kepler inserted his long fingers into a narrow vest pocket in order to extract a billfold containing a mix of krona and one hundred-zloty notes, which he used to purchase a ticket, which he gave to Fishl along with the change. "Good luck," he said.

The embarrassed young man tried to return the money, but Kepler squeezed his hand shut. "No, no, I insist," he said. "Here's the train."

"On time, after all."

"No," the man in the information booth said. "That's not the five-fourteen. It's the seven-twelve."

"Early or late?"

"Maybe it passed the five-fourteen."

"On one track?"

However it managed to avoid detection, the snub-nosed locomotive came heaving to a rest within the confines of Hodonín's tiny station. Steam floated up from between the train's wheels and clouds formed under the peaked glass roof. It was damp enough to rain inside, but that made no difference. Other trains were cancelled, detoured, or derailed; the 7:12 was running.

Fishl had only been in one train during the War, but it was very different, and he knew that railroads had already assumed a vital metaphoric position in the iconography of Hell. Their tracks were the strands along which the pearls of fire were strung. Nonetheless, this train had comfortable seats, windows that opened, and thick rubber luggage racks for those passengers who traveled with goods. Only one thing was missing. Torn blue ticket stubs littered the floor, but there were no passengers. Fishl walked the empty aisle between the empty seats, setting a hundred dainty white antimacassars fluttering as he passed. He was certain he was in the wrong place, but was unable to disappoint the committee he had left on the platform so pleased with the service they thought they had done him. He was nervous until a lady clutching a wicker basket that stank of some curdled organic material bustled in and sat down in front of him. As if it had been waiting for her, the train lurched forward.

Fishl looked at his benefactors from the train window and waved.

The shammes waved back and said to his friend, "Musselman?"

"No, not exactly. Could have been, but took a different turn."

"He didn't have someone to ask for?"

The doctor shrugged.

Hodonín was gone in seconds, church steeple no more than a mirage in the benign Czech mist. The only proof that he had really been there was the cash in Fishl's pocket, the herring in his belly, and a kind of satisfaction he felt at the thought of the shammes sharing a crypt with the Christian saints. The train flew past a dozen smaller towns, traveling faster than a Russian truck, blurring farm country into forest. Every once in a while Fishl peeked at the woman who kept the malodorous basket on her lap, despite the empty seats beside her. The basket itself seemed to wobble, even when the ride was smooth.

Fishl watched the woman. He had nothing else to do, neither books to read nor reason to delve into the books in his head. She was a squat, fiftyish farmer's wife, her clothes as woebegone as her baggage except for a thin gold necklace that peeked out from under two woolen scarves and a dingy yellow kerchief.

The scenery had gone dark, and a row of dim bulbs kept the car in perpetual twilight. Eventually Fishl nodded off. He didn't know how much time passed or how far they had advanced, but when he awoke it was dawn. If they had stopped during the night it made no difference, because nobody had entered, and the lady with the basket remained.

As if she had been waiting for the new day, the woman reached into her basket, presumably for breakfast. Suddenly, there was a wild, explosive panic, and a fluttering wing swept out. "Aye!" she screamed and inadvertently let go of the precious basket she had held steadily since she had entered the railroad car. It tumbled to the aisle, lid popped wide. In a flash, a duck leapt out, feathers gray with slime. The bird tried to waddle down the aisle, or better yet to fly, toward Fishl, but its legs were bound with a knot of rough twine, and it fell sideways onto its beak and honked with strident complaint.

The lady was on top of the escaped creature immediately. She scooped him off the floor and clamped the duck to her chest. Only its head was able to pivot round, and its eyes met Fishl's over the lacy trim of the antimaccassar that had been stained by the back of its mistress' kerchief. Before the duck was able to make another sound, the woman grasped the creature's neck and deftly twisted it as if she was rinsing a towel. The duck's eyes bulged, and the squawk ceased mid-plea.

The woman began to pluck the feathers. At first she placed them in a neat pile on the empty seat beside her, but a stray breeze that gusted from between cars blew them into a flurry, which alit gradually among the torn blue tickets.

The draft was a precursor of the conductor, stamping his feet as if he had come in from a storm. He cast a disgusted look at the woman and quickly strode past Fishl.

"Excuse me, I have a ticket."

"Good, when we get to Vienna you can go to the theater."

"Vienna?" Fishl was alarmed that he was traveling in the wrong direction.

"Vienna. Warsaw. What's the difference?"

"Does this train stop at Kielce?"

"Why not?"

The conductor sat down at the rear of the compartment and unfolded a Bulgarian newspaper. The system was in total disarray. Some trains got lost while others would not start. Sometimes there were trains without fuel, and sometimes there was fuel without a train. Some trains had engineers without conductors, others had conductors without engineers. Some had no passengers. In the meanwhile, any trip might be one's last, and the conductor hardly gave a damn. The only forces to be relied upon were inertia and momentum, the tendencies of a body at rest to remain at rest, and of a body in motion to keep moving.

"Excuse me," Fishl interrupted the conductor again, "but what are the rules for this train?" He didn't know precisely what he had in mind, but he didn't want to get in trouble for refusing to pay when it was the conductor who refused to accept his payment.

"Only one rule," the conductor replied. "No chicken plucking."

"It's a duck."

"Then she's OK."

"That's it?"

"It. No rules. No schedules. No laws."

"No Jews." It was a daring statement that Fishl let slip, a sign of freedom. What did he mean? Did Jews and laws go together, or was it just one more lack in the modern world?

The conductor smiled. If, during the War, one wondered, "Will he turn me in?" one received an answer. There was a clarity to experience. Now, every question was hypothetical, like, "Would he have turned me in?" and one could never be certain. If, during the War, one inhabited a world of actual murder, the end of the War ushered in an era of murderous contemplation. If thoughts could kill . . .

Fishl remembered the only real advice Alter Kaufman ever gave him. When Fishl told Kaufman that he needed time to consider whether to join a particular work detail Alter said firmly, "Stop thinking—keep moving."

Alter was neither the strongest nor the smartest man in Steyr, but he was the most optimistic. Despite his cynicism about the nature of the world outside the barracks, Alter was the only one in the barrack with an absolute faith that the world outside still existed. "Wait till you meet my little brother," he once said.

"I don't understand."

"Eventually you will arrive in a place where you will hear of a man named Isaac Kaufman. Go to him. Knock on his door like this." He rapped on Fishl's head, once, a pause, twice, a pause, once again.

"How can you tell he's alive?"

"Isaac lives. No question about it."

Fishl was the opposite. He knew his loved ones were dead and couldn't believe he wasn't. That was why he and Alter got along. Both were naturally contrary; Alter thought his brother was alive despite the evidence, whereas Fishl thought himself dead despite the evidence. It was only since he met the shammes of Hodonín that he felt hope.

Whether it was God's will, the military government of Czechoslovakia, or some international railway authority that was so marvelously efficient, the train did not run out of fuel or off the tracks before it stopped at Kielce, sixty kilometers from Ostrowiec, a distance imponderable Before, insignificant now. The doors opened with a hydraulic whoosh, and a blizzard of feathers cycloned out onto the gravelly bed. The woman slaughterer gave her sole companion a vicious glance as he departed onto the tall, black metal folding stairs, half-expecting the response that had met him the last time he left a train. Instead of guns and dogs, only a solitary man smoking a pipe atop the driver's seat of a horse-drawn cart was there to meet the 7:12. The back of his cart was filled with a load of dead rabbits incompletely covered with rough burlap sacking to discourage a swarm of flies that buzzed about in an angry cloud, but he was lingering near the train station hoping for an additional paying passenger.

Fishl recognized the distinctive Gothic architecture of the station because his parents had once taken him to a fair at Kielce, but he could have sworn that the station had been surrounded by a warren of ancient alleyways. Then he realized that although the building itself was intact down to the etched glass symbols on the lavatory doors—a top hat for gentlemen, a bonnet for ladies—the city itself was reduced to a field of shattered timber broken by solitary chimneys that jutted up from the wreckage.

Unlike Hodonín or Mauthausen, Kielce had been bombed, and there was no way of telling whether they had been German or American bombs. Bombs bear no signatures. The craters were signs of a modernity that both nations shared, because no weapon could have done that Before. Nothing could have devastated the landscape like this short of an act of God. "Where to?" the man on the cart said as he released a puff of caraway-scented smoke.

"Ostrowiec."

"Fifty zlotys . . . but for you forty . . . All right, tough guy, all right. Twenty-five."

By the time Fishl dug into his pocket to see what the community of Hodonín had given to him, the price was ten. "Here," he said. He gave the man a hundred. The man offered no change.

"Jew," the man declared, gazing at the train that was already receding into the distance. "Hop in."

As soon as Fishl climbed up onto the splintery wooden plank, the peasant lowered his whip flat across his pony's back, where a line described years of lashing. The heavy wooden spokes were set to turning along the rutted drive. The rabbits in the back jostled about as if animated, and a long, furry ear bumped out from under the bloody canvas.

Sholem Aleichem knew that every city was different in its own way, but all shtetls were alike. Kielce was not Babel's Odessa, Cahan's New York or Kafka's Prague, but Ostrowiec was awfully like Proszowice or Anatevka. There was a loose scattering of thatched huts amid the fields, except for the village square where five or six buildings were clustered together about a cobbled courtyard. It was the same as Before except for a charred hole in the roof of the tavern where lightning struck during a summer storm back in '43. If indeed it was not God who had demolished Kielce, this ragged hole was clearly His handiwork.

No one else would bother to bomb such a pathetic hodepodge as Ostrowiec. Besides, who could tell the difference? Nobody would waste bombs on a marketplace filled with moldy turnips, sour sweet potatoes, carrots and kohlrabies stacked in enormous pyramids not quite so large as those of chestnut hair or gold-dotted teeth.

The driver dropped his passenger off and set to bartering his rabbits for vegetables.

Fishl wasn't positive, but he thought he recognized some of the faces at the market. Lined and a little thinner than Before, they were still familiar. The man who spat over a hastily erected corral was

Veselka, the horse trader. The man who lay dozing on a bench in front of the tavern was Renko, Bailiff of the Regional Court. Hanka Smokolniki, holding forth a bunch of garlic, wore the same sweater she always had, with the same unraveling green thread at her wrist. Michael Plesak, the blacksmith, wore the same gunmetal blue trousers and leather apron. Styles never changed in the shtetl.

Fishl headed immediately to the synagogue. He needed no directions, no map drawn on the side of a Czech bridge. Blindfolded, he could find any shul in any shtetl. He just couldn't find anything else.

The building that had once been the home of Ostrowiec's tattered faith was still there, but since the roundup of Ostrowiec's Jewish citizens, it had been transformed into a variety store that sold sundries arranged in piles set upon the cardboard cartons in which they had been shipped: spinning tops, mirrors, thimbles, sponges, and, especially, tubes. There were miles of hollow cardboard cylinders. Some were pencils, others tree trunks. Laid end to end, there were enough to reach Mauthausen. What the people needed with them, they themselves could not imagine, but each was stamped with the talismanic name of an American manufacturer and that was sufficient to sell them as tokens of the new world. Everyone in town bought an American tube, and Ostrowiec was proud to possess its first rich man, Klepish, the tube magnate.

Although the bookshelves remained, they were empty. Most shocking was the glaring nave that had once been shielded from human sight by navy blue velvet curtains with embroidered silver thread. The curtains were long since transformed into some local matron's finest gown, and the three Torahs they had protected, one of them donated by Fishl's father-in-law at his daughter's betrothal, were gone, too, stolen, scattered, burnt.

Maybe they wouldn't have recognized Fishl on the street, but slack-jawed in the doorway to the emporium that had once been the Ostrowiec shul, without a tube, he couldn't be anyone else. "A zhid," a little boy born since the intruder left pointed.

"Yes," Klepish said, standing arms akimbo beside the cash register that stood on the bema from which Fishl had been made a Bar Mitzvah.

"Didn't you used to sweep out the cheder?" Fishl asked.

"No," Klepish lied. He had always been a tube magnate, and the synagogue had always been a tube store, and nothing had ever been different from what it was now.

"Fishl," Mama Kottler declared.

Her wicked, toothless grin was exactly as it had been Before. She tugged her shawl close to her neck. There was a goiter beneath, pulsing like an egg about to hatch.

Everyone called her mama, because rumor had it that every man was her "dada."

"It's a ghost," shrieked Mama Kottler's mother, a wrinkled, shrunken, half-ghost herself, Madame Katski.

"Shut up!" Mama Kottler swatted the fearful maternal hands clutching at her scarf.

"Ay, ay." The old lady continued to moan and point in terror, but other braver souls gathered.

"He came back to find his treasure." Anna Plesak said. She was married to the blacksmith. Her eyes gleamed with visions of buried candelabras.

"Is that true?" Mama Kottler asked. "Are you looking for your treasure, Reb?"

That was true. He was looking for his treasure. He asked what he did not have the strength to ask the Jews in Hodonín. "Is Rivka here?"

"Rivka?"

"Born Weiser. Become Fishl. Rivka Fishl."

"I don't know," Mama Kottler replied. She turned to the women buying tubes, "Is there a Zhid Rivka here?"

They laughed, mouths full of rotten teeth.

She peeked under the bench, "Rivka!"

There was no answer.

Anna Plesak still believed Fishl was looking for silver. "When you find your treasure, you should give some to us, Reb. We fought the enemy, you know. We showed them."

Mama Kottler hoisted herself on tiptoes to peer toward the loft where the Jewish women of Ostrowiec sat during services, "Rivvvv-ka," she called.

Fishl turned and started down the rutted street, but he had acquired an escort of teenage boys, not so much younger than himself, "Rivka!" they called to the dogs. "Rivka," they looked under the porches. "Rivka?" they asked the squat Polish girls, who giggled. "Rivka!" they shrieked and laughed.

The train of youngsters that followed Fishl imitated his distinctive slump-shouldered gait. As he looked, they looked, peering into kitchens and swiping leaves off trees as they passed, but they understood that they were looking only for the sake of looking, while Fishl the idiot still thought he had a chance to find what he could barely remember. What he would do with her if he found her, he could not imagine.

Rivka was neither in the square nor in the shul. They approached the stuccoed hovel that had been home to the entire Fishl clan. He peered up toward the drafty attic window, and though he knew that her bridal quilt was torn, its feathers flying, he still called out, "Rivka!"

"Rivka," his chorus echoed.

"She's not here," a strange man filling the doorway said, standing firm with a shovel to protect his house from the intruder who might have wished to reclaim it.

They could have the house and the damn candelabra, too, which really had been buried three paces due north from the base of the tree in the yard. There was only one other place she could be. Without thinking, Fishl lead the group there.

It was outside Ostrowiec, a patch of country land surrounded by a low brick wall breached by a single arched gate with a Star of David embedded in the center of an ornamental iron grid. Untended, the iron had rusted, and inside the Jewish cemetery the ranks of eternal tablets had been toppled and torn from the earth to be used in construction. There was a sidewalk in Munich paved with the names of Ostrowiec's dead. All that remained were the bones, since the excavators did not dig so deep, and hundreds of tiny stones strewn across the weedy acre. It was a Jewish custom for mourners to add to the monuments they visited. Every engraved granite rectangle had once born the modest weight of a handful of pebbles that had tumbled off when the tombs themselves had been stolen. Those miniature cairns were now the only monuments to the wordless dead.

"Where is the treasure?" the littlest boy asked.

Fishl turned to him, and said, "There is no treasure."

They could not bear the thought that no treasure was to be had, by him, them, or the masters. Was it all for nothing? The good children of Jewless Ostrowiec had no recourse but to open their hearts to the treasure within, to search their souls and discover the purity of the hatred they bore like a vein of gold in the fertile Polish earth.

Whether it was Fishl's Jewishness or the stubborn fact that Ostrowiec was still Ostrowiec without its Jews, they could not bear it. Who was first to raise a tube in threat? Who was first to level it in attack? They seemed to act as one. The first hundred blows were a children's game, and the players were gleeful at the hollow, clopping noises that Fishl was too ignorant to pretend to fall beneath. Had he collapsed, they might have considered this a victory and left him, but he stood, and the flimsy cardboard tubes bent, and their delight turned to dismay. They needed something more substantial, less American, with which to berate the homecoming hero. And all they had were the stones that lay in tiny piles that had slid off the flat surfaces of the tilted graves.

A quartz oval flew, and although Fishl saw it coming, he could neither turn from it nor pull back his neck in time to let it skim the first bristlings of beard. The ragged edge tore a line in his cheek. Another bruised his shoulder. Another stung his shin.

Fishl faced the ragged urchin army. They reminded him of the Polish militia that rose against the Panzer Blitzkrieg. Moblized the day the War began on 1 September, 1939, the last brave garrison surrendered less than five weeks later, October 5. But it was different here. Here, they might win. Unfortunately, there was no barrier to keep their target within range of their weaponry, nor any mechanical brain to guide their ammunition on its way. And Fishl was no longer at Steyr, circumvented by electrified wire. He was no longer in modernity. He was in Ostrowiec, which he was too slow to escape once before.

Before he knew it, Fishl was taking long, loping strides, and then a graceful arc over the low brick wall. The children ran after him, but they couldn't maintain the Yiddish pace, swift as language, fleeting as thought, strong as sorrow. Fishl was a ghost running, without a family or a wife or a God to slow him down.

The stones clattered onto the path behind him. They beat a musical tattoo that finally died as he entered the forest. Was music a language?

Odd, for the first time since he was placed in the lager, he felt fear. Now, the War was over.

CHAPTER 4

Awesome in death, puny in triumph, the Jewish population shrank from masses to handfuls, yet was more evident than Before. If they had been vast and invisible, traveling in sealed cars, at night, under guard, now they were a public presence.

They were everywhere. A shaved head and exposed ribs were a passport universally recognized in the new, borderless Continent. A striped suit helped, but was not mandatory. Restless, deprived, and diminished, at least some of the hollow-cheeked horde wore the mothballed garments of their ancestors. Everyone knew that Jews were good with a needle and thread.

Even in the midst of cities with blocks flattened, bridges twisted, stanchions toppled, beside smashed power stations and exploded armories, the ravages the refugees bore within themselves stood out. It was a rot of the soul that emanated from them that only commenced after the decay of the body. Each carried the scent of his ancestors as he moved beyond the barbed wire into every crevice and knothole from Luxembourg to Lvov. It was the aroma of smoked fish and smoked meat.

Mr. Alan Foyle of the Joint Distribution Committee was not looking so well either. His cheeks had turned jowly from the lardy army mess, a far cry from the sole Véronique at La Bibliothèque, and his nose was pinched to avoid the stench of his surroundings, which was hardly Murray Hill. As for his elegant clothes: the army laundry could not press a suit as nicely as Monsieur Philip of Escapade French Dry Cleaners on East Thirty-fifth Street, New York City.

Promotion or not, field command was inferior to life at the Joint's walnut-panelled office tucked into a brownstone on a sweet begingkoed side street. Each day, he was set upon from both sides, by the misery and lunacy of his charges, and by the calls of his American constituents, their compassion inflamed by reams of publicity.

It was a sign of New York's faith in him that Alan Foyle was given the most newsworthy assignment that had ever come to the Joint. With the surrender of the last German soldier, hundreds of battlefront reporters started dredging for stories behind the lines. Every day there were more photos and articles. The world audience could not get enough. Concentration camps went above the fold. Every day there were additional claims on Foyle's time.

Partisan Review was dedicating a special issue to "The Tragedy of Europe" and sent a commission full of shaggy intellectuals to convene and analyze. The first thing they did after insuring the local supply of Sauvignon Blanc,'43, was to establish a glossary in which Yiddish and German words were finally acknowledged to have entered the international lingua franca, the mamelosh'n of Heine contributing terms like "lager" and "musselman" to the contemporary polyglot. In any language, phrases like "cattle car" and words like "camp" acquired new meaning. "Gas" became a verb.

Mr. Foyle was the first to hear the current vernacular because of his proximity to the primary sources. Yet, when his superiors asked him to introduce a special visitor from New York to a voice from the lager, he needed his assistant's help to find the perfect spokesman. "I've heard that there is one prisoner," he said.

"Ex-prisoner," Miranda corrected him.

"Whatever."

There were many terms for the residents of Aspenfeld and Bergen-Belsen and Dachau and Flossenbürg and Ravensbrück and Balanowka and Dakovo and Danica and Zemun and Jadavno and Klooga and Sobihor and Sachsenhausen and Stutthof and Ebensee and Auschwitz and a few more. Words and phrases were minted as rapidly as deutsche marks as journalists contended to define the moment. "Displaced Persons" was the most accurate, "DPs" its catchy short form, although "survivors" was gaining popularity. Others used "remnants," which had a nice connotation of the shmatte business, and Isaac himself rather liked "remainders" because it echoed remains.

"Who is known to act as a liaison," she admitted.

"So get him."

"Get *him*?"

"Get him!"

Finding Isaac was easy. If he wasn't contemplating the horizon from his perch atop the guard tower, he was bound to be trading favors, fabric, or currency at the position he had staked out in the center of the bourse. Mr. Foyle's emissary found him in the latter spot, sitting with a half dozen American soldiers in a circle around an ammunition crate, with a pile of dollars and coins and a few chits of paper mounded in the center. Isaac was learning to play cards.

"Psst, is a full house better than a flush?" Isaac whispered a little too loudly to his companion, Schimmel.

The disgusted Americans overheard and threw down their hands.

Isaac raked in the biggest pot of the day, and lay down a pair of fours.

"That's not a full house," said an American who had folded three Queens.

"So maybe next time maybe I'll have one." Isaac began to stack his winnings.

"Mr. Kaufman?" she said.

Isaac turned to Schimmel. "Poker is a skill that will come in handy. The Americans think they are going home, but their manners and their games are going to be with us for a while. Learn." He said the last word in a heavily accented English.

"Learn?" the American loser snorted. "Teach me. I'm tapped."

"Number five-four-six-seven-eight?"

Isaac turned and grinned at Miranda. He rolled up his sleeve to show the numbers she had called. Out of order, they formed a straight flush in aniline blue. She was the only one who knew numbers as well as names. Her days were spent tabulating columns of figures from the ledgers of Gehenna and her memory was impressive. She'd be a remarkable poker player. "Very good," Isaac said. "If you worked for the Germans, we wouldn't've had a chance."

Her hurt, appalled expression gave way to the stifled, girlish gasp of a bobby-soxer yearning for Bing.

The poker players glared at Isaac, but Miranda would not give her tormentor the satisfaction of allowing them to comfort her. She blinked back her tears and said, "Mr. Foyle would like to see you."

Isaac replied, "You're not wearing your yellow dress."

"I thought we had gotten beyond uniforms."

"Are you kidding? This is a world of uniforms, mädchen. Look," he gestured to the American soldiers who stayed in the game, fanning newly dealt hands in front of them. "And me, if you think this suit is not just as much of a uniform as camp stripes you're wrong. The only reason I changed is because I needed the pockets." He tucked his profits beside his breast. "Sure you wear a uniform, a pretty American dress. All I'm asking to see is the yellow uniform I gave you. Best tailor in Weimar made that. Put it on and then we'll talk. Now ante up, boys, Papa needs a new pair of shoes." He was also learning a new language.

Miranda sulked back to her quarters in the former camp visiting house. There were only a few women in Aspenfeld, and they were treated well. Her room was dominated by a heavy French armoire that was taken from a Provençal village early in the War, when the Wehrmacht was rolling so smoothly that its captains had time to spare for antiquing. She opened the wide-planked cherry doors to stand in stockings before her few stained gray skirts, treated as shabbily in the army laundry as her boss's Oxford cloth, and the one bright yellow dress, like a canary in a coal mine. Furiously, she threw the dress on, taking a small revenge by pulling the sash out from its loops and letting it fall to the floor of the cabinet, where it lay like a bright tropical snake among her shoes, before she returned to the card game. "Besser?"

Isaac smirked and said, "Much besser."

Their conversation took place in Yiddish. Miranda was the child of wealthy intellectuals. She attended progressive private schools and took folk dancing while her mother arranged charity dinners and her father's firm advised bankers who would not accept him in their club. Still, her parents were horrified when their only daughter dropped out of Pembroke and volunteered for a job at the Joint, and began to study Yiddish evenings at the Workman's Circle, where she was embarrassed by the limousine waiting for her at the curb. When she requested an assignment to Europe, they pulled strings to have it rejected. Miranda went on hunger strike.

Two days later, she received a message through her father's secretary. "Don't you think this is silly?"

"Sorry, I can't speak now, I'm feeling faint."

Two days later, she was at the airport, trying not to gloat.

There the senior partner embraced her, said, "Farewell, Quixote," and folded a single sheet of embossed stationary into his daughter's passport. It was the private telephone number of his college room-mate, the ambassador to Switzerland. "Just in case you need it."

She explained what Mr. Foyle wanted, but Isaac's reply was blunt. "Not interested."

"He needs someone to speak to Randolph Weiss, that's Rabbi Weiss, he's President of the Union of American Synagogues. They are the single major contributor to the Joint's operating fund."

"I don't care if he's King Solomon. Does he play cards?"

"Why don't you ask him yourself—unless you think you can't play that game?"

Isaac had a healthy respect for the position well taken. He nodded.

So, Randolph Weiss appeared. Despite his rabbinical title, he was unlike the other prelates and delegates who maundered on among the bones and shook their heads. Accompanied by an entourage of note-taking assistants, he was a well-groomed, businesslike presence, who might just as well have been the man from IG Farben come to make a deal for prisoner labor on behalf of the Bayerwerke at Lud-wigshafen.

Weiss had an agenda that made his visit pivotal to the Joint pro-gram in the states. He wanted to know assets and liabilities, not in terms of dollars, but the more abstract balance sheet of the organi-zation. What were they "giving" in human services, what were they "getting" in public relations. As the Joint had geared up for dealing with this particular, peculiar huddled mass whose needs were very different than the puschcart vendors of Eldridge Street, the question he had come to investigate was whether the organization would also have to host the refugees under its own roof sooner, or later.

According to Isaac's agreement with Miranda, he dutifully walked the premises with the visitor, who spoke an elegant Sephardic Hebrew, but not the gutter Yiddish of his guide. Isaac knew Hebrew, too, but nobody had asked and he did not volunteer. Instead, he explained to Miranda what she already knew about the camp's workings. Here was the parade ground. Here was the gallows. She in turn translated into English for Rabbi Weiss and his staff, and whenever Isaac's commentary was too harsh, she softened the edges.

It was for their own good. Hateful as they were. Miranda was determined to help. Her boss was a bureaucrat and her boss's bosses were politicians, but she was out to save the world. It was infuriating that Isaac, at least, showed no desire to be saved.

Prime examples in the new field of atrocity studies, the remainders' own empirical knowledge was inconsistent with that of the experts. Because they had survived, most assumed that others did. To think that they were the only ones was too great a burden, too random for chance to effect.

Yes, there were the mountains of hair and teeth and toy dolls, the impromptu graveyards, the daily deaths, but that their experience in one camp could be extrapolated to a universe of camps, killing nations of friends and cousins, was too intolerable a fact to grasp. It had to be fiction.

The War must have been a novel written by a Jew in a basement in Prague. Jewish writers were fabulists, fantasists, ravers, howlers, messianic dreamers, and modernists whose stock-in-trade was the fractured tense, the irrational development, and the absurd character. They were luftmenschen, would-be cruisers through the air whose feet were chained to the earth. Who else could imagine that theirs was not a sole idiosyncratic catastrophe, but the shape of Jewishness in their age?

When the Americans, lead by Mr. Foyle and Rabbi Weiss, listened to the narrative and arrived at the conclusion, they beat their breasts in token of grief and guilt and said, "We didn't know what was happening."

Isaac simply agreed, "Neither did we."

The group was baffled. Miranda explained to Isaac on their behalf, "They mean that they did not know until now." She was attempting to give the answer without implying the unpleasant question—why didn't they use their great American power when it might have made a difference? She did not ask why they waited to book tickets on the *S.S. France*—or, better yet, the *St. Louis*—until Elizabeth Smith Moss's photos started appearing in *Life* magazine.

Timing was irrelevant to Isaac. A day, a decade, an hour, history, what was the difference? Isaac was learning to live in a world of debits and credits, what he was owed and what price he had paid. "I still don't know," he insisted with a willfully obtuse naivete.

"But . . . but . . . the ovens."

They looked to the incinerators, still thick with the rendering of their tribe, and Isaac replied, in English, so that Miranda could not make the phrase any more palatable, "Bread today?"

Of course, the Americans did not understand. That's what made them lucky boys, whether they wore the dog tags of the army, the IDs of the press, or the clipboards of the charity corps. The difference between them and the locals was that they believed that, now, with the image-obliterating light of day shining in their blindfolded puppy blue eyes, they did know. Postrevelation, even the Yankees were not so brazen as to assume that the nickel tour was precisely equivalent to the experience, but, yes, yes, yes, they got the gist of it, whereas the dumb survivors seemed incapable of the same basic perception.

Not wisdom, not comfort, all the survivors wanted was to eat and to recover the ashes dispersed over the Continent. And so a search began for a familiar name or face, as they read the daily bulletins issued by the laundry hut press, and peered through the lineaments of bone structure into every shrunken skull to determine if it really was Uncle Moish from Lublin.

That was the way it was. An army of men wandered Europe and compared notes with everyone whose face bore the stamp of their common experience. When was the last time anyone had seen a father, a brother, anyone from the same village. Tracking down rumors, they created a timeline. The aunt on one's mother's side, last seen late in 1943, then someone who had crossed paths with a schoolmate in February 1944. Then, on line in Salzberg in 1945, there might be a familiar face, shrunk down to the bones but familiar nonetheless. It was the past and the future, history and emigration, how they got there and how they were aiming to get out, that were the mainstays of conversation, the purpose of communication.

"Anyone see anyone from Zweirzyniec?" Misha Tolkin asked, again and again until it slowly became apparent that what was left of Zweirzyniec was the shtetl in his mind, at which point he went mad, and Zweirzyniec was finally gone like so much smoke up a chimney.

There was a note on the wall that appeared from nowhere and said, "Chaim from Chelm. Your brother is in Mainz."

The note was dated a month earlier. Nevertheless, Chaim from Chelm rushed to see if it was still true, but once he arrived at the Joint office in Mainz he was greeted with a newer message, "Chaim from Chelm. Your brother is in Budapest."

From Budapest to Trieste to Düsseldorf. Chaim from Chelm traveled back and forth at the mockery of a cruel miscommunication. It was Chaim from Chelmno who had been summoned, and he was dead by the time the stranger from Chelm found him in a field hospital near Ansbach. The wandering Jew thus returned to the one home left to him on the third bunk in the fourth barracks in D Block at Aspenfeld.

Despite the odds, a few people did find each other as the smaller installations were shut down and inmates were assigned to larger encampments. They were shifted and rearranged like the racks of Panama hats in Sergeant Weinglass's store in Brooklyn when the new fall line arrived. They were bussed by cushioned army transport to the camps that acted as central organizational points, confined for ease of treatment and definition. The information they brought initiated a new round of "Who was last seen where?" queries. People from the same region began to congregate at the same sites, re-creating the geography of the pre-War era, Galizianer to the south side of the camp, Litvaks north. A brother and a sister discovered each other when they were sent for inoculation at the same station. Their joyous unification was duly reenacted for the cameras. Amid much hoopla, twin skeletons embraced, and one reporter whispered to another, "I can see the resemblance."

Only Elizabeth Smith Moss disdained the performance, preferring to catch a fortuitous moment on the wing or miss it altogether. Her photo of a desolate Chaim from Chelm ran side by side with the posed siblings. The caption read, NO FAMILY.

All relationships jumped several notches in the chain of consanguinity. Cousins were now brothers; neighbors became cousins. Strangers were neighbors, and enemies friends. Only gentiles never became Jews.

There were endless lists, cross-checked against the murderers' own documentation by the Joint's army of do-gooders. The numbers in their ledgers grew each day, as the volumes of documents replaced the people they had erased. New columns of the dead were toted up, mimeographed, and distributed to other district offices for further indexing. Until a name appeared on the verified roster of the deceased, there was hope. In the meanwhile, there was the hypnotic effect of the columns, some of which bore a hundred numbers in sequence, while others were more gaps than substance. It was like a list of Babylonian kings that was the sole hieroglyph for interpretation of a lost civilization.

In search of file cabinets to store the lists, Captain Hamilton set off one morning. This ought to have been a simple enough task, but the Russians had already established themselves in the Weimar City Hall, and would not allow the Americans so much as a paper clip without an official intraservice requisition. Undaunted, the captain and his men pressed southwest in a convoy, passing though town after town, asking by the side of the road "Files? Files?" to the baffled shrugs and knowing smirks of the natives.

It became a matter of military pride for Company C to return with files; as they drove farther from base, their determination increased. Hamilton, who had worked as an actuary before the War, craved all of the the stuff of office life, not merely file cabinets but rubber bands and manilla envelopes. He wanted pencil sharpeners and staplers, inkwells and gummed labels. He wanted rulers, in inches not centimeters, and carbon paper. He wanted an imitation leather swivel chair, but he had to settle for the two hundred men of Company C who hated his guts.

Eventually, the Gothic spires of Heidelberg loomed and the captain could scent victory, like a miner who suddenly tapped on the mother lode. A university had to have file cabinets. The quaint cobbled streets of this Princeton on the Rhine may have contributed to rocket research. but they were overlooked by the Allied bombers. The students hunched into their books might as well have been frozen in place seventy-five years earlier, cramming for Professor Hegel's final exam. Captain Hamilton entered the first building he saw and announced to the provost in charge that he was commandeering all files.

The provost peered at the invaders over steel-rimmed bifocals and asked, "In whose name?"

"What do you mean?"

"If you are acting contrary to the normal rules of society, and I assume that as a military man you are not a rogue creating your own rules, you must be acting in the name of some higher authority. Before I surrender any file cabinets, I must know who that authority is . . . Who?"

The excursus gave Hamilton pause. He turned to his lieutenant and whispered, "Whose name am I doing this in?"

"Pretend we're British and do it in the name of the queen."

"I can't."

"How about George Washington?"

"He's dead."

"So?"

"I don't think you can claim file cabinets in the name of a dead president. It's not done."

"OK, then Franklin Roosevelt."

"He's dead, too, and he was crippled."

"You mean you've got to have an athlete?"

"That's it."

"What's it?"

"Ted Williams."

"Oooh," the German said, "Der Splinter."

Hamilton nodded somberly and gave the order.

The privates unceremoniously dumped stacks of obscure philosophy manuscripts out of the cabinets in which they had been moldering for decades. Yellowed theories of being and analyses of ethics seemed to expand upon exposure to the air. Pages of footnotes spread across the floor and heaps of multisyllable words broke into hyphenated debris while the empty trucks were filled with the files to be refilled back in Aspenfeld with names, some of whom had once been students.

Gradually, Foyle and the Joint grasped the first tenuous grasp of the dimensions of the situation they faced. Fortunately, as the stack of documents grew, the numbers of survivors they represented lessened. The DP camps were hives of infection. No one had a chance to get sick during the heyday of the lager. Sickness was an indulgence punishable by death—of course, so was life. Now, to lie back and retch in the sun was as sultry a pleasure as tanning on the Riviera. Eventually, however, one had to bear the responsibility for one's condition. Eventually one had to get well or die. The last of the Musselmen closed their eyes. Even those who bore their predicament well succumbed to disease. Freedom did not cure typhus. Liberty was not penicillin.

The institution struggled to alleviate the more obvious physical complaints, but their attempts were still haphazard and their ability incomplete. Depending on which division had liberated them, some of the DPs were cleaned, clad, and fed while others still wore their stripes and starved.

They starved, but each had a Pendaflex file with his or her name and number neatly typed in the left hand margin, individually tabbed, thanks to Hamilton's daring stationery raid.

Isaac Kaufman theoretically required a notification of transfer to leave. He could have obtained the necesssary documents in return for toilet paper, but as far as he was concerned the documents were less valuable than toilet paper, so he packed a stout canvas duffel that he had received in exchange for three cans of corn.

"Watch out," Schimmel warned.

"What are they going to do, arrest me?"

Schimmel urged Issac to stay put. Compelled to give reason to his plea, he said, "New movies are coming . . . *The Three Stooges Burn the Reichstag.*

"I arranged those movies, idiot. You think I don't want, snap my fingers, they'll send them to Berlin, hang a screen on the Brandenburg Gate. I'll see movies in America whenever I wish."

"But here it's . . ."

"What?"

"Safer."

"Precisely," Issac said. He scoffed at those who chose safety, "What are you going to do, work with the sergeant from Brooklyn, America, be a tailor again? I'm no tailor."

Stuffing his pocket full of cash, he wedged chits good for money and service from DPs and MPs alike into his money belt, a lovely tooled leather that had belonged to one of Aspenfeld's officers that Isaac had acquired in return for the delivery of a cryptic one sentence telegraph to Brazil. It had been sent from Regensburg and said, "Waiting for ball bearings." That piqued Isaac's interest. There was someone in Regensburg who was thinking the same way he did. Those lesser favors that he couldn't fit, he passed on to Schimmel, for distribution as he wished. "Keep half of what you get. I'll collect the rest."

Isaac shouldered his bag and set off for the gate, with Schimmel and a half dozen of his employees in tow. Most of them believed that he couldn't leave; none of them believed that he would.

The American guard saw this group approaching and blocked the way, inwardly cursing the officer who had told him that this post was easy duty. He offered Isaac a chocolate bar, but Isaac did not pause to accept the gift because the gate that could be opened could also be shut. It was already September, and he had already wasted a summer in this backwater.

First, the soldier tried logic. "Do you know where you're going?"

"Do I care?"

Isaac leapt out of the path of an oncoming jeep like a matador avoiding a charging bull. He was was going south, certainly to Regensburg, possibly through to Switzerland, then maybe further to the Mediterranean, and a port to elsewhere, or New York. He could have bought a ride, but as he had walked in, he intended to walk out.

"Wait!" the soldier cried.

"Why?"

Stymied, the guard retreated to his booth to dial command from a field telephone, but the secretary refused to patch him through to any of the officers. Desperate for any imprimatur to avoid responsibility, he used the camp intercom to call a representative of the Joint from the laundry, and Miranda came running. The soldier informed her, "He wants to go."

She clearly did not expect this particular "he." Wearing the yellow dress with the sash that emphasized the fullness of her American figure, she blushed and fumbled in her pocketbook for a hairbrush.

Isaac sneered. The girl probably brushed her teeth, too. He wasn't asking for anything. He was leaving, and he laughed that she or the soldier thought either of them had a decision to make. "Have a chocolate," he said. "Stick around and eat all you want." He took another step.

"Halt."

Schimmel closed his eyes.

The only shot was that of Elizabeth Smith Moss, who caught Issac's back under the gate. She could almost read the caption, A FAREWELL TO ARMS.

As if he had eyes in the back of his head. Issac turned, and notched another imaginary obligation on an invisible chalkboard.

Elizabeth Smith Moss smiled, "Good luck."

He didn't need luck any more than he needed hair or teeth. He had credit.

Miranda grew teary and, for lack of any other ingrained response, the soldier saluted.

A kilometer from Weimar, Isaac met a young German boy who was trying to straighten the rim of a motorcycle broken down in a pine-shaded clearing beside a plane tree. The tree's bark was scarred by a lightning bolt-shaped gash, and the boy's exposed knees were bloody pads. Behind him was a picnic ground where the good volk of the Reich had once gathered to celebrate their native customs. Isaac could picture girls in embroidered skirts dancing about a campfire.

It was an SS cycle with the death's head emblem stenciled to the gas tank.

The boy was no more than sixteen, and although Isaac was no more than twenty, he felt oddly paternal. He remembered his own father painstakingly gluing together the uneven halves of a plate purchased from an itinerant beggar collecting money for a yeshiva in the Holy Land. The plate was an olive wood disc with a relief of the Western Wall that Isaac had inadvertently broken while roughhousing with his younger brother. It had been supported by two prongs that emerged from the stucco above the fireplace until Isaac rammed Levi's head into the plaster so hard that the prongs vibrated like tuning forks and the plate tipped infinitessimally forward. Isaac stood paralyzed for what seemed like forever until the plate hit the brick hearth and split in two. Both brothers had trembled for fear that their clumsiness could not be rectified.

"Can you help me?" the boy asked.

Isaac silently gripped the handlebars, cool silver metal on the left hand, a thick-ribbed rubber throttle on the right, but the position was awkward to maintain as the boy jerked ineffectively at the edge of the rim that held fast between the grooves of the front tire. Without thinking, Isaac lifted a foot over the black leather seat and clamped the tank between his skinny thighs while the boy continued to tug. Still the bent chrome rim did not budge.

"No good," the boy sighed.

"Let's change places," Isaac suggested.

"Gut."

"Yah, gut," Isaac replied as the boy followed his instructions. "Now hold tight," he said, inserting fingers under the jagged rim to pry it from the wheel.

"You are strong," the boy said.

"Strength of character." Isaac spun the wheel freely within its orbit.

"Danke schön," the German said, the first time Isaac had heard those words in three years. He watched the blur of the wheel slowing down until he could distinguish each spoke. Open palm, he slapped the boy's ear as hard as he could. He was strong.

The boy fell sideways to the ground with a look of smitten surprise, while Isaac started to walk the motorcycle off the gravel lot to the road. It was clear that having fixed it, he had decided to claim it. The word that was already being used was "reparations."

The boy began to cry. He sat crimson-eared, cross-legged, and sobbed. Resigned to accidental injury, willfull transgression was too much for him to bear. "The motorcycle is all I have. It is my father's."

"Amalek," Isaac said.

"Who?"

Amalek was the name of a tribe that fought with the early Jews for a piece of the promised land. They were so notably vicious in a vicious age that God told the victorious Jews to kill every one of the tribe, but the Jews took pity and allowed one infant boy to live—a mistake. That boy was the ancestor of every tormentor of the Jews through history. Isaac remembered the village teacher who taught the cheder boys the events of thousands of years ago as if they happened yesterday. He said, "This bike is Amalek's."

"No," the boy insisted, "it is my father's."

There was something slow about the boy. His eyes were dull, his speech thick. He had none of the guile that Isaac associated with the German character. Some of the guards were no geniuses, but they all had the cruel slyness of a disobedient child getting away with something.

"Did he work over there?" Isaac gestured in the direction he had come from, along an aisle of trees that lead directly to the camp.

The boy said, "Yes."

Isaac wondered which one of the Nazis was the boy's father. It was probably an officer if he had a child of this age—possibly the shy guard hung by the inmates.

Isaac knew that he should kill the boy. It would be easy. They were standing in a widened shoulder by the side of the road, next to a planked redwood table and a circle of stones that bore the familiar scent of smoke. He could lift a rock and crush the boy's head. Bury him in a pile of last autumns's leaves. He could strangle him with his hands. Leave him to rot. Perhaps he could use no weapon but his words. There was an officer in the camp who had once commanded a prisoner to die. The prisoner collapsed, dead at Amalek's boot. Was that master this child's father?

Isaac could smell meat from the garbage can and peddled the cycle over to inspect. He was no longer hungry, but the instinct to scavenge after years of starvation had not been eradicated by a single summer's K ration feast. There was a half-eaten piece of chicken, which he extracted from a wax paper wrapping and began to nibble, starting with the dried crisp of skin. Because of his bad teeth, he had trouble in gumming every last shred of meat until he was able to suck on the bones, while the boy watched.

Isaac finished and dropped the bones to the ground, the first litter despoiling the pristine picnic area. He was tempted to slap the boy again, but the fear in those blue eyes stopped him. Instead, he threw the candy bar the American soldier had given him to the ground, pressed on the pedal, and left.

There was once a photograph in the Warsaw *Tribuna-Ludo* of a boy flying. It was a special effect from the set of *The Dybbuk* that accompanied a review of the performance. Theater was not a part of the shtetl routine, but Isaac remembered that picture as he revved the throttle.

He had never ridden a motorcycle before and wobbled precariously, but as the velocity increased his balance improved, and he automatically knew to lean into the road on the curves. He liked the throb of the engine beneath him, and the gentle heat from the motor. He liked the roar that obliterated the sweet vernal forest sounds. More so than on the day of liberation, Isaac felt it was the first time he had ever known such freedom.

He recalled the era Before only vaguely. Was Proszowice really an island of home, family, and Shabbes afternoon cholent? Motoring through the woods, sun filtering between the branches, he could not imagine any other time or place. It was early autumn, and pale magenta flowers were visible through the underbrush.

Two years earlier, on the march to Aspenfeld, he stopped to eat some of these same flowers while a German guard watched him like a shepherd watching his flock. Ravenous, Isaac gnawed at the stems, grinding them, relishing the acidic juice that flowed down from the tip. Then came the winter when he lost his teeth. Even now, after the chicken, Isaac's mouth watered at the sight of the flowers and he had to tell himself that he had no need to stop for nourishment. At a crossroads, he slowed down and looked at the signposts for directions to the nearest large city.

Weimar itself was out of the question. Goethe's oak was too pastoral a symbol, the Republic too evident a failure. Leipzig was next closest, sixty kilometers east, but the odd message about ball bearings from Regensburg stuck in his mind, and he recalled other rumors that the Liebknecht camp outside that city was the central disposition point for the wealth of the Reich, the Canada of Canadas. In his weeks on the bourse, he had learned that proximity to value created value. For a second, he thought of Proszowice, his home, all thirty-six houses clustered together in brutal poverty and absolute faith.

He had no desire whatsoever to return to Proszowice, and intuitively knew that a city, any city, ought to be his destination. Aspenfeld had gone from shtetl mores to urban manners in a week, and he had felt more comfortable every day, but it was still an outpost. That was why he had left so soon. If he didn't he would have stayed, like the others, reduced to an infant sucking on the Joint tit. He thought of Miranda. He didn't understand why, but he knew that she was another reason to leave. But where to?

Regensburg lay in a valley at the periphery of the Tyrolean Alps, the focal point of all commerce between Munich and Vienna. Why not?

Still at the crossroads, he looped the motorcycle in an enormous wide arc until he was traveling back in the direction he had come from, and although he felt he had been traveling forever it was no more than minutes until he saw the German boy, still sitting like a Musselman next to the chicken bones in the dirt.

Disgusted—more with himself than anyone else—Isaac pulled into the clearing, and parked the motorcyle near the blubbering child. He told himself that his behavior was his own choice, a sign of strength rather than weakness. Then he kicked the motorcycle over with a clatter, half hoping it would redent the rim. As he had found it, so he would leave it. As he had marched into Aspenfeld, he would march onward, with no trace of his past, no shame, no chocolate, just a perfect emptiness, like that of a magic lamp he could use to create himself anew.

CHAPTER 5

Frayed flags hung from the few lampposts that still stood among the craters along the main street of Regensburg. There were no signs left to indicate the street's name, but its dimensions hinted at the grandeur that had preceded its devastation. In front of the Opera House three massive stone muses shouldered an enormous clear dome of sky that had once been a roof. Across the boulevard, a row of four-story offices that served as the regional National Socialist Party headquarters had been taken over by various Allied agencies, but one was already being evacuated because the building was no longer structurally sound. A steel girder jutted into space like a diving board. File cabinets to make Captain Hamilton drool lined the streets, extension cords snaked to generators parked on flatbed trucks, and chaplains of all denominations were set to praying for a dry season.

Municipal services had fallen off in town. The streets, bomb-pocked and broken, were filled with the detritus of War while the sidewalks that used to be scrubbed with Teutonic thoroughness were covered by scraps of résumés, diaries, magazines, and every possible form of paper except for cigarette butts, because everyone smoked them to the stub. Isaac noticed a particular gesture in the men of Regensburg, a kind of twitch of the thumb and forefinger as the last tobacco-tinted shred flared up, singing fingertips and obliterating fingerprints, a secondary benefit for any smoker with an unsavory past. Even marks floated in the desultory autumn breeze; they were worth less than the leaves of the linden trees that ceased growing as a monk's tonsure halfway up the Tyrolean Alps.

There was a German soldier with one leg begging from the passersby in front of the Opera. Next to him, another, more entrepeneurial, veteran was offering to swap one hundred-mark notes for ten-mark coins because the metal held more future than the paper, but the locals were already too wise for this maneuver, and there were no takers.

There was a soup line set up in the Regensburg Gymnasium by the occupying forces, but the patrons first had to pass a gauntlet of defeated grannies of the Thousand Year Reich. Bundled in multiple layers of Bavarian underwear, they sold eggs directly from the wheelbarrows they had pushed in from the country. Neither line, however, had chocolate.

Isaac heard someone say, "You want chocolate, go to Vienna."

"Or go to the Vivant!"

Everyone laughed because the Café Vivant was the most exclusive place in town. It was the only establishment that seemed to exist in the amber of the prior decade. Outside, its woven cane chairs spilled onto a small patio in calculated Continental disarray. Inside, who knew? Isaac watched as an elegant couple in clothes more appropriate for the opera entered.

"Make way!" a delivery man cried, bearing a brown carton from the seat of a truck as he stepped up to his ankle into a stream that appeared out of nowhere. Two children had dammed the flow from a broken hydrant with a bureau without any drawers. At the precise moment the delivery man was about to step down from his cab, the children lifted the dam to flood his feet, which, until their dousing, were unusually well shod in oxblood cordovan. He cursed and chased them away before shaking the water off his shoes and slipped through the café's service entrance.

Isaac stepped to the front door of the Vivant, but his entry was blocked by a tall blond man with a clipboard. "Your passport, Sir?"

Even as he was wondering why the young man was not in a Waffen SS uniform, Isaac felt unafraid as he replied, "I don't have a passport."

"Then I'm sorry, but I can't admit you, Sir."

Rather than reply, "What else can't you admit, asshole?" Isaac peeked inside at a roomful of locals, refugees, and American soldiers. "Do they have passports?"

"The best kind. Without one, I cannot seat you, Sir, that is unless you pay . . ." the man rubbed two fingers together, "in advance."

Isaac dug into his rucksack and brought out a chocolate bar.

"Look," the doorkeeper called into the club.

A man behind the zinc bar beside the doorway shouted back, "He thinks he's in kindergarten."

To the contrary, Isaac thought he had graduated, but his degrees meant nothing here. That was fine. He was a quick study. He took a band of notes from his bundle of currency. "Which do you prefer?"

"Anything but marks."

Isaac pushed several francs into his hand and moments later passed a few more across the counter, where the newly respectful bartender said, "Mais oui, monsieur."

"A seltzer."

Just as Isaac took a first sip, an entertainer stepped onto a semi-circular stage at the opposite end of the room. The man's face was entirely covered in white pancake makeup and his lips were carmine red. Some of the audience swiveled to watch him, but it was mostly foreigners who seemed eager for the show. Natives remained hunched over their tables, negotiating.

"General Eisenhower!" the entertainer snapped to salute and half the soldiers in the room jumped up while the other half dove under their tables.

"Regrettably cannot be with us today," the entertainer announced as he mimed a doleful countenance. "Eisenhower is visiting his ancestral home. The guy is Kraut. He's going to be president of the United States one day, but he's a Kraut from way back. So are we all, now. Ladies and gentlemen. Meine Damen und Herren! Will-kommen. Perhaps you saw my act Before. But you know, it was no act. Elsa! Stop that, you naughty thing."

He called to his assistant, a girl with a round face and Betty Boop curls, busy flirting with two soldiers stageside, who wagged her finger back at her boss.

"Hey, you know what this reminds me of—the old days, Before the War. Or was it after that other war? How can you tell? Ah well, as our Parisian friends say, vive la différence." Then he broke into a song,

Alsace Lorraine. You say LaRhine.
Lorraine. LaRhine.
LaRhine. Lorraine.
Let's call the whole thing off.

On cue, Elsa made her way back onto the stage and snuck behind the performer, from which position she reached a snaky, blue-nailed hand between his legs.

"Call it off, Elsa," he said. "Don't Jack it off. . . ." Her head appeared between his legs, and he removed her wig, revealing a suddenly toothy young boy. The performer screamed, "It's Jack, oy vay!"

"You prefer girls?"

The bartender rolled his eyes to the end of the bar, where two teenage girls in leather skirts lingered. Isaac had felt no sexual urgency for years and the girls' fluttering, kohl-colored lids shaped the first stirrings of libido. Here was an economy that could accomodate change if German whores more authentic than Elsa had already made the transition from heroines of the Fatherland to servants of the Conquerors. Something intriguing was going on on the premises.

He could smell it, not only sex, not only money, but business, trade, opportunity. It was survival at the Opera, but prosperity rampant at the Café Vivant. Isaac thought he was going to like it here.

Meanwhile the entertainer was doing impressions by changing hats, from Stalin in a stiff-brimmed olive military kepi, to Winston Churchill in a derby.

"Guy's pretty funny," the delivery man addressed Isaac.

"He seems to draw a crowd."

"Best act I've seen in years."

Isaac had not exactly frequented the café society of pre-War Warsaw.

Then the delivery man asked, "How'd you make it through?"

There was no need to wonder. He knew how Isaac had spent the last five years. An inocuous question deserved an inocuous answer, "A bis'l this. A bis'l that."

"Me, too."

"A landsman?" Isaac should have identified him by the fancy shoes, a Canadian import for sure. He thought he could tell a Jew at ten paces, but it would clearly take him a few hours to adjust to the rules of the new world. Perhaps the man had been a Kapo. Regensburg was the kind of town where the skills one may have learned elsewhere might serve one well.

"So what's your name, yungfleysh?"

"Isaac Kaufman."

"I knew a Kaufman once."

"I knew several," Isaac replied. He didn't want to get caught up in the game, but despite his contempt, even Isaac was susceptible to the fragile hopes that flooded him whenever he heard a strange voice. Asking a stranger if he knew one's mother was like trying to guess the serial numbers on a bill in the stranger's pocket. Nonetheless, one guessed; everyone did it, and every once in a while, successfully. It was that one in a milion chance that lead the other 999,999 suckers to believe that miracles were possible.

"Which?" the man asked.

"Any Kaufman. There were forty-three that I knew of: from Abraham to Zalman." Once upon a time there were photo albums full of Kaufmans, herds of Kaufmans, carefully posed and candid Kaufmans, Kaufmans on parlor chairs and garden swings, on football teams and school plays, dozens of Kaufmans, all descended from some first Kaufman who alit on Polish soil and disseminated his seeds.

"Yehudi?"

"I think there was a cousin Yehudi in Tishivits."

"Where was he last?"

"Plaszow, near Cracow, forty-three."

Tishivitz was gone, the synagogue in cinders, the usual Torah debris. That they had known for years. It was harder to understand that Plaszow was gone, too, those rolling Galitsianer hills where the overseer sat on a shady veranda from which he practiced marksmanship with human targets—like flat metal ducks paddling across a conveyor belt in a carnival booth.

Now there was no point of reference. There wasn't even a frame.

The delivery man just said, "There's an office of the Joint here if you want."

And that was the end of the discussion as far as Isaac was concerned. "There's an office of the Joint everywhere," he said. "There's also a pissoir on the corner, but I don't feel like peeing."

"You're right . . . where were they when we needed them?" the delivery man agreed to Isaac's unstated comment with a universal bitterness that may or may not have been feigned.

"I never needed them. My father did. My mother did. My sister did. My little brother did. I didn't. That's why they're all over the place now that nobody needs them."

"But they have information."

"Information," Isaac repeated.

"But information may be dangerous."

"Oh, good, then maybe I'll buy some . . . And you? What are you doing in Regensburg?"

"It's . . ." the delivery man looked around suspiciously.

But before he could finish the sentence, Isaac finished for him, "Business."

"How did you know, greenhorn?"

"It's obvious. What was in the carton?" The man hesitated, so Isaac said, "Oh, don't tell me any military secrets. How's life here?"

"It's not so bad. Once a week I make a drive to Zurich, pick up whiskey, bring it back."

"So it's whiskey in the carton." Liquor was illegal; social control was imperative.

"I didn't say that."

"And that's all you do for a week?"

"But if I get caught . . ."

"But you don't."

"Of course not."

"That's why it's easy."

"Nobody else is willing to work." He looked out the window at the same two children who had ruined his shoes. They were peering into the cab of his truck, until one grabbed a radio. "Thieves!"

"Aren't we all?" Isaac replied, but the delivery man was already out the door, chasing the kids and then on to another delivery or to pray, while Isaac remained at the bar, watching the entertainer prance among a chorus that had appeared from backstage during a show-stopping "Battle of the Bulges" routine. Listening in on other conversations, Isaac heard one that drew his neck forward like a chicken's to the blade.

Three men were huddled about a table, an elderly Jew in his thirties, wearing thick bifocals, and two razor-shaven Westerners. The latter were examining a passport.

The first returned the passport to the Jew and said, "Sheer artistry," but the second complained, "I don't understand what this has to do with ball bearings."

The Jew, probably a DP, explained, "There was artistry in death years ago. It must have been something to have a red-cowled priest lace one up with Jesuit knots that would have done a sailor proud, before being set afire in the midst of the Artiz River, the towers of Grenada silhouetted against the Spanish sky. There was a funeral worth sharing with the cheering Christian mass. A scene fit for El Greco."

"Very nice, Professor."

"Doctor," he modestly corrected them. "So name your poison." He signalled the waiter, any waiter, for another round.

In front of the quartet of high-kicking girls, the Emcee sang,

> *Frrrom the halls of Montezuma,*
> *to the shores of Normandy.*
> *Did I say that, oy vay!*
> *Ve shall fight our country's battles,*
> *on der land or under der sea.*

The doctor continued, "Then there were the Cossacks. Though the ungrateful residents of the Pale did not appreciate their beauty, imagine the drama of a herd of horsemen sweeping through the shtetl. Contemplate watching your little sisters swept underarm to create new generations of pig-faced little brothers." He leaned back and sighed with the appreciation of a rabbi listening to a theological point well made.

Parodying a clipped English accent, the Emcee sang phrases from half a dozen military songs,

Ve are marchink to Prrretoria.
Prrrretoria.
March, girls, or you will lose your slippers.

"There was, however, no elegance, if all too much intelligence, about the massacres of the last decade. It was an ungraceful era."

"But the . . . you know." He suddenly glanced around suspiciously.

The Emcee on the stage was saying, "It's familiar, my act, no? Or should I say nu? You recognize the tune. You've all seen my face. Where? On postage stamps, silly, jawohl." He took a toothbrush from his pocket and clamped it between his nose and his upper lip and started goose-stepping toward the wings.

"And I," Dr. Marcus Morgenstern leaned back, "am a fellow who appreciates beauty. So, if you wish something more beautiful than ball bearings, you can contact me." He lifted a finger to pick up the check for the entire table, grandly dropping a thousand-mark note on the round tray that hovered immediately, obediently, beside his elbow. It was the last local currency with any value. Isaac looked at the note and followed the waiter past the zinc bar.

Moments later, the man the doctor assumed was the waiter returned, but Morgenstern blinked under the bifocals and said, "Keep the change."

"Sir, may I speak to you?" the young man with the tray murmured obsequiously.

"Can't you see that I'm busy?" The lordly Morgenstern was irritated by the interruption.

"Excuse me, Sir, its quite important."

Morgenstern shrugged to his company, "There's no end to this. Probably wants me to get him in good with the management. I'll be back."

Together Morgenstern and the waiter stepped into an alcove between swags of heavy green drapery. "Now, now, what's on your mind, young fellow?"

"I'm sorry, Sir," he stammered, "but I can't take this money."

"And why not?"

"It's counterfeit, Sir."

"What? This is an outrage. Are you accusing me of counterfeiting? Do you know what the penalty for counterfeiting is?"

"Hanging, Sir."

"And for perjury, too? Perhaps you would like to repeat your allegations in a court of law where they must be substantiated?"

"Nonetheless, it's fake." The slim waiter held firm.

Both spoke a rough German to each other, but it was Morgenstern, rattled, whose language started to bear a Yiddish inflection, "Ah, well, that scoundrel in the taxi must have passed it on to me in change. Give it back and I'll replace it with something, shall we say, bona fides, as well as a little extra for your vigilance."

"No, Sir, the rules say one must turn all counterfeit currency in to the local police." He tucked the incriminating evidence into his vest pocket.

"So what, you wish to waste five hours in the station. A lot of gratitude they'll give you. They'll grill you, suspect you. Here, give me back the bill, for a sample, so I can spot other fakes." Morgenstern was sweating. Then he joked with the desperation of someone who is trying too hard to be funny, "It's cheaper to steal them."

"Even cheaper to make them," the waiter replied, his German now also tinged with a Yiddish that didn't seem quite so obsequious.

They looked at each other and the first hint of understanding passed. Morgenstern ventured a tentative smile and whispered, "But how could you tell?"

The young man answered, "By your manner. You produce lovely scrip, but your face gives it away."

"And you can do better?"

"I already did."

"I do not understand."

"There are many kinds of forgery. One is the falsification of currency or identification papers, the other of identity itself."

"So prove it. You're just a waiter here."

"No, as a matter of fact, he is." And Isaac pointed poker face to a older man limping across the room. Then the forger of identity started waltzing toward the café door.

Morgenstern looked back at the men he had been speaking to, but decided to catch up with Isaac. "Mayn Kuzin."

"Yes?"

"Oh, I didn't pay."

"Don't worry, I took care of it for you."

"Um, and my companions?"

"Of course."

"And a tip?"

"Genererous enough to be remembered. I may wish to return."

"So now we're really cousins."

"You have any others?"

"Not that I know of."

The Emcee giggled as he stuck his head out from the curtain for one last punchline, "So what say every twenty years we have a little excitement and then After, we have a lot of fun. See you at the next set."

The foreigners in the audience clapped and stamped their feet, while the locals barely glanced up from their discussions. They had seen the show Before.

Out on the street the sun was setting between twin hills to the west. "We need a place to stay," Isaac said.

Fortunately, there were empty apartments all over Europe. More people were killed than apartments were destroyed. Some didn't have water because the mains were still flooding, and others didn't have windows because they had been shattered by nearby explosions, but enough were available for those who needed them, walls, floors, stove, some ramshackle chairs, and a carved black walnut sideboard too heavy to remove.

"I have a flat on the Weinerstrasse in Liebknecht," Morgenstern said, "a quaint working-class neighborhood. Near the camp. The landlady is the widow of a former postal worker, happy to give a representative of the United Nations cheap rent." He showed off the false ID that got him into the Café Vivant as cash had been Isaac's passport. "I am sure that my assistant would also be welcome."

Isaac said, "That's very nice, but if the only ones you can fool are the grannies, it won't do you very much good."

"I was working on more substantial company when you interfered."

"They knew you were fake. You thought you were milking them, but they just wanted a free drink. Bubkes." Isaac shook his head and took the one thousand-mark note from his pocket, held it up to the last orange rays of the sun.

"Notice the watermarks," Morgenstern said proudly.

"Such small rewards for such beautiful work."

"And you, pip-squeak? So you want to conquer the world?"

"Everyone else does, the Germans, the Russians, the Americans, why not a few Jews?"

"Sounds like the *Protocols of the Elders of Zion.*"

"An exemplary text, something to aspire to, something to learn from."

"Sounds like Talmud."

"Revised."

"And you are the commentator, I suppose. You put a gloss on the text of the new world and interpret history for the people of the book."

"Call me Rashi."

Book II

OPPORTUNITY

CHAPTER 6

Crusoe washed up on shore, woke with sand-covered lips, salt-caked shirt and trousers, crazy, hungry, bruised by the waves, curled into a question mark beside a dead crab on the sandy crescent of the new world that was, above all other qualities, his, his absolutely, if temporarily, for as long as he could compel the scattered palms to relinquish the coconuts necessary to sate his hunger, slake his thirst, and give him strength to proclaim his kingship among the seaweed citizenry of his realm. Property laws aside, survival is nine-tenths of dominion.

Driftwood from the befoundered ship of state and a few goods of civilization rolled in with the tide: a nautical compass, a sheet of diamond-stitched rigging, a barrel of nutmeg, and one of gunpowder. Food and armaments had already attained prominence on the black market; all other commodities were either unavailable or irrelevant. Now that Isaac was out, in the zone, the payment required for these basics was not so simple as the favors he was able to dispense back in the lager. He didn't have clout and he didn't have friends. All he had now was his self-defined cousin, Morgenstern, who said, "What happened to your teeth?"

"They broke."

Isaac recognized Marcus's talent, but he didn't want any intimacies yet. They were walking along Weinerstrasse, the avenue that turned into a highway that connected Regensburg to Munich. Their route into the suburb of Liebknecht led past stolid apartment blocks and approached an enormous Gothic mansion and, farther, the gates through to a barreled arch of linden trees. Though he had never been here, Isaac knew the look: the ornamented facade with the ring of bright wire interrupted by a series of towers. Here the towers ended at the base of a small mountain.

The camp had originally been a mine, but when it was no longer productive its elegantly incongrous chalet-styled offices had been converted to a sanitorium and, indeed—once coiled steel took the place of hedges—its first occupants were its first prisoners. It was such an idyllic spot that later arrivals thought they might as well have gone crazy and been retired to a haven in the Bavarian forest. For those who had been transferred there from extermination camps in Poland, the Liebknechtwerke was like liberation; they didn't see what there was to complain about. Of course death, random and vicious, was a constant companion, but there was more food and a better quality of shelter in the wood-beamed medical buildings than the barracks they were used to; some of the rooms even had cuckoo clocks that chimed out the hours. The gas chamber was used as a punishment rather than as the sole purpose of the place.

Down below, inside the mountain, the entrance to which had been sealed shut in the closing days of the War, engineers labored on circuitry that would be used to direct the Liebknechtwerke's missiles northward while Wehrmacht cadets forced teams of Jewish slaves to help construct labyrinthine tunnels connecting up to the railroad tracks that would bring their brethren there to work and die.

Oddly, the bodies heaped about the perimeter far outnumbered the original residents of the camp. Marcus explained that new ones were shipped in daily from other lagers. It made sense for the Allies to consolidate the bodies they had to dispose of, and Liebknecht suited the troops for the same reason it suited Isaac and Marcus. Equidistant from the boundaries of Austria and Czechoslovakia and the south-German metropolis of Munich, Liebknecht was a centrally located dumping ground for this sector of the zone. Roosevelt, hence his employees, was a great one for wiping out lesser problems with enormous TVA-style programs. Huge lights illuminated mass graves.

"Home," Marcus said.

"The lager?"

"No, there." He gestured to the last in the line of apartments. "It has a view, though."

"Vunderbar."

The apartment may have been desirable during the operational days of the Liebknechtwerke, when a bird's-eye panorama of the comings and goings along the Weinerstrasse passage was an excellent thing to have whether one was angling for gleanings of the rubbish or a spy's kind of firsthand. Once the Allied bombers had penetrated the German veil of security, however, the good volk of Weinerstrasse evacuated with the swiftness of the rockets they helped to develop. It was empty now except for the landlady.

"Don't wake Frau Mannheim," Marcus whispered as he tiptoed in through the front door.

"Is that you, Herr Morgenstern?" a voice rang out.

"Yah, Frau Mannheim."

"And who is that with you?" She had read the footsteps.

"A friend."

The voice from behind the door cawed, "It's gut to have friends."

Marcus waited until they were upstairs in the small flat to explain, "Her husband worked for the post office. So did the other men in the building, but they're all gone now."

"Maybe that's lucky," Isaac pointed out, "there's no mail."

"Right." All such systems had gone to the dogs. Postboxes in town overflowed with uncollected and undelivered communication. They might as well have been trash cans. Ever since Frau Mannheim's late husband and his coworkers were drafted, the only safe route for a letter was via private delivery services.

Morgenstern set a pot of ersatz coffee to boil in a teardrop-shaped flask from the Scheissmund Laboratory for Genetic Blood Diseases and described his own journey. He had left Dachau after Passover with a pitchpipe of five varying thickness Rapidograph pens in his breast pocket, a bag full of inks along with his ancient dental instruments, and a suitcase of different bondage paper. Perforce a quick study, he traded his sweater, a nice gray Canadian, for 1,186 marks, one each of 1, 5, 10, 20, 50, 100 and 1,000 denomination bills, their imagery hastily changed by the caretaker government from the ubiquitous moustached profile to a collection of placid natural scenes—slopes not cliffs, ponds not cataracts—from the Black Forest, and set out to master them to earn his keep in the manner he had learned under Reznikoff's tutelage. Once he had created sufficient counterfeit capital, he would buy the identification, requisition, and transport forms of zone life, which he would reproduce and sell for authentic cash.

"And your teacher, Reznikoff?"

"Poor Adam," Marcus sighed. Reznikoff had written an admiralty pass for himself and was headed west, where he was intercepted and shot at the Spanish border by a renegade loyalist who didn't know the War was over. Marcus was more cautious. As a dentist and freelance forger, his skills were those of the workshop not the market, the wings rather than the proscenium. He left the camp, but could not yet bring himself to leave the zone. Instead, he found an island of comfort on the Weinerstrasse where the nearby lager was a familiar comfort as well as a financial boon.

When Isaac met him he was attempting the kind of impersonation that came naturally to the younger man. Dr. Morgenstern knew his own face betrayed his paperwork. Even the fumes of drinks in the Café Vivant made him tipsy.

Isaac asked, "Why did those men want ball bearings?"

Marcus shrugged, "Who knows? Someone in town put out the word, they go crazy. Probably has to do with weapons."

"Food, I understand," Isaac said. "But arms? What do they need them for?"

"To tell the truth, I can't say. Getting ready for the next war, I suppose. I only know the market; the second their bellies are full, it's guns, bullets, and tanks they want. Man, you get yourself a rocket, any rocket, V-2, say, you can write your own ticket, as the lucky boys say, 'legit.' Self-defense, maybe. Perhaps they're afraid."

"Of what?"

Marcus shrugged, "Vengeance." Then he poured two cups of fake coffee and sat at the scarred table.

Isaac sipped his own mug of the smoky chicory brew and said, "Wishful thinking."

Marcus went on. "Weapons and food. Food and weapons. Soldiers at camp distribute 'grub,' they call it, twice daily. We're supposed to eat it there, but no one watches or cares. So it moves out onto the black market. That's what the locals want, but they need paper to get it. Sometimes a permit, sometimes money. It's all paper to me."

"And you need someone to move the paper? That's what you thought those guys in the café could do?"

"So I made a mistake—with them."

Isaac had deposited his bag next to the door in case he wanted to leave in a hurry. Nonetheless, he was drawn into Marcus's world. He stood up and peered out the window. He had always liked heights. He was able to make out the shuttered windows of the empty mansion and several details of the camp at Leibknecht. Down the long arched passage of trees, past the faint scrim of the gate, in front of a bulbous Quonset hut, sat a four foot cube—like a massive die from outer space. "What's that?"

Marcus joined him at the window, impressed by Isaac's instinctual gravitation to the most fascinating object in the zone. "Good eyes, cousin."

"So, what is that?"

"Ah," Marcus said, "that's another story."

Eighteen tons of golden ingots created from fillings pried from the teeth of the Jews of eastern Europe lay behind the locked and guarded gates of the U.S. Army installation at Liebknecht.

"Think of the pain it represents," Dr. Morgenstern said as he flicked a dead moth from the sill with his fingernail, like a child playing marbles. Frequently, he had castigated himself for not becoming more aware of the dental horde that sat unguarded beneath an olive canvas tarpaulin until a British general too stupid to send it home to his wife and kids in Conventry ordered a more secure escort.

Clearly, the gold had been due to be extracted once again, probably under cover of dark, but whether the Camp kommandant missed his date with fortune because his horse lost a shoe, or the shoe a nail, or the soldier his life in the last Allied raid, it never happened.

Despite the missed opportunity, Dr. Morgenstern still perceived the value of the location that the locals had abdicated once they lost the War. Besides, he liked the view of the canvas, glittering with gold dust, slipped askew, and leeching wealth into the trenches of urine that overflowed into the gutters of the village. "Think of the pain," he repeated.

The doctor was not referring to the more recent pain the onetime owners of that gold had undergone, but the original dental work when the precious mineral was set into a million mouths to alleviate the toothaches of Cracow and to cleanse decay from the mouths of Warsaw and Budapest. All the baklava the Jews of Salonika ate and the tortes of Vienna had been replaced with dots of gold, which were subsequently hammered from their skulls, refined and sent to Liebknecht where they were intended to sodder the circuitry that would have obliterated the inedible puddings of London had they the chance.

The doctor's companion, however, was less abstract. "Screw the pain. Think of the money," he replied.

"And what would you do with that money, cousin?"

"To start with, food. Truffles from France and spices from the Indies. Herring and sable, slices as thick as a book."

"Very nice," the doctor muttered.

"Steaks from Argentina. Coconuts from the Congo. Pig meat."

The doctor squinted.

"Perhaps women," Isaac dreamed.

"Hah. That's all you need."

"Then maybe weapons."

"But to start with: food."

"You have?"

Marcus went into the kitchen and returned with something hidden behind his back. "Egg?"

Isaac looked at the perfect opalescent embryo that appeared in his host's fingers, like a rabbit from a magician's top hat. He hadn't seen one for years, and recalled gulping them raw in the roost in the barn back in Proszowice. Any egg that cracked during handling was tossed down any Kaufman gullet lest it go to waste. Sometimes, Isaac ate half a dozen raw eggs a day. Sometimes, when his touch had been too delicate, the boy would surreptitiously set an egg down on the hard edge of a plow.

Morgenstern handed it over like a jewel for Isaac's appraisal.

This egg was not cracked. The would-be purchaser turned it in the light, letting the moon's rays catch the veins. It might as well have been Fabergé, a perfect world cupped in the palm of his hand, and not a plow in sight. He returned the egg with care.

Morgenstern said, "Scrambled? Poached? Fried in butter?"

"And all you need is a cousin to move the merchandise?"

"Yes."

"Fried."

The War was over. There were girls to woo, kinder to grow. There would be jobs, too, as soon as the uncertainties of the minute passed. Yes, a certain satisfaction had been taken in military endeavors, but eventually the stench of dead Yids got to even the most battle-hardened of Nordic nostrils.

1945 moving into '46 was no time to dwell on the evils of the far distant past. The first half of the decade was gone in a blink. Better to blame a few big shots, bury the lads at Bitburg, and get on with it. The Germans were glad to surrender, lay down their arms, and embrace the peace—as long as they could repurchase their beloved Mausers a month later. There was contentment in the eyes of the soldiers tramping Reichward in a pair of good strong army boots. Two or three or six or twelve years after leaving the gymnasium, they were blissful with the defeat that meant one more taste of their mama's stollen. Even those veterans without legs sang the marching songs they had learned as recruits and temporarily forgot at Stalin-grad, joyous now as if they had won.

> *When Heine comes marching nach haus again.*
> *Jawohl. Jawohl.*
> *We'll give him a hearty velcome haus.*
> *Jawohl. Jawohl.*

Come the wreck of the decade's ideology, they were Crusoes of their own.

Trade in paper served Isaac and Marcus well for the first ninety days. Marcus sat at home, eyes shaded by a green-tinted clerk's visor, inks aligned, reaching for the proper width nib as he had for the proper drill in his previous existence while Isaac established a retail office by a mirror-topped table in the blue-lit comfort of the Vivant and made it known that he could, for a fee, acquire the paper that was being composed even as he sipped yellow Chartreuse on the rocks.

If the money itself was desired, he could obtain that, too, for barter. Certain things never changed.

The Allies initially attempted to reestablish older boundaries out of the Greater Reich, and boundaries meant passports, but the effort was doomed. Everytime they set a border, Churchill changed it, that giant baby playing with countries like blocks on the parlor rug.

"Wait, I've got an idea, let's call it Yugoslavia."

That meant new papers and new maps.

Isaac spent those evenings he was not working perusing a dozen plus maps he had tacked to the kitchen wall and considering the opportunities the broken lines represented. Every time he sold a border crossing card to a refugee who heard that his sister was alive in Ravensbrück or a gas ration chit to the delivery man from the Vivant, Isaac insisted on a map in addition to his fee. The surcharge could be topographic, geographic, or political; it made no difference; each bore a wisdom of its own. Thus he acquired street maps of Strasbourg and Lvov, a subway map of London, and, once, an antique celestial map stolen from a rare book library. It made no difference. He tacked them all to the walls, and then, starting with the map of the constellations, to the ceiling. Overlapping scales created a weird disequilibrium in the three-by-four square meter kitchen. A pale pink, bud green, and piss yellow 1890s Austro-Hungarian Empire met a newspaper schematic of Allied landing sites at Normandy at the corner over the stove. Every map contained some new piece of information, and all information was useful.

Papers functioned as maps of identity. The Allied forces had separate documentation for the army, navy, air force, and marines, OSS, IB-4 Brigade, and various special projects groups, while DPs, alien nationals, local residents, and discharged Luftwaffe copilots were issued their own text of the moment by the agencies whose purpose it was to monitor them.

The bureaucracy to check papers consequently grew to rival that of the horde whose papers were checked, but even the most bureaucratic of minds could see the irrelevancy of paper in a broken world. Sitting, pondering maps, Isaac worried that what had begun as a tiny stamp of certitude might become a frivolity when climbing over live sparking wires from downed electrical lines.

The ebb and flow of peoples was so tidal that there was no way to manage it effectively. One might as well try to place a lock on the Atlantic. Only the line farther east delineating the Russian sector was ineradicably drawn by Stalin's steel pen, since the fraternity of crimson and khaki had disintegrated as rapidly as that of red and brown shirts five years earlier. But nobody wanted to go eastward. Those on the other side of the Iron Curtain might have been interested in foreign travel, but theirs was as separate a sphere from Isaac and Marcus's chosen planet as Mercury is from earth; the temperature was intolerable, and anybody sane kept away.

It seemed that every day ever more extravagant IDs were circulating. Isaac swiveled toward the window to watch the latest manifestation of paper power at work. He used a pair of WWI Leica field binoculars—exchanged by a deputy mayor with pleurisy in return for a Pullman reservation to the Sad Baden Spa—to focus on a series of visitors to the Liebknechtwerke. They arrived in long black sedans and waved what appeared to be baby blue passes at the gate. The American guard saluted, and lifted the barrier that had been installed under the familiar slogan.

Isaac sneered, " 'Arbeit Macht Frei' ought to be changed to 'Papier Macht Frei.' "

"What?" Marcus muttered, distracted from his attempt to figure out an effective way to crimp the edges of an ID that Italian transient workers were issued in Bologna, which incidentally meant safe passage through Switzerland—and who was to say if the passer-through never passed out again.

"Nothing."

Isaac's attention returned to the scene at the gate where several men in knee-length laboratory coats gathered to greet their visitors. There was much handshaking. Due to the exegencies of post-War realpolitik, a new generation of Germans was already being defined in contrast to their elders. The most venerable of gray-haired scientists were given "Letters of Discretion," good anywhere from Berlin to Buenos Aires, that allowed them to recapture their youth by inverting the numerals of their age from say sixty-two to twenty-six and spit in the face of anyone who said "Boo!"—thus absolving themselves from the responsibilities of their cohort and granting them retroactive immunity from prosecution by the courts at Nuremberg, where a few famous names were already in prison.

Under the aegis of Operation Security Blanket, the scientific beneficiaries of this 80 percent rag content Fountain of Youth were taking their Allied peers on guided tours of the Liebknechtwerke. Isaac watched them stroll past the tarp-covered cube of gold, wielding tapes, gauges, and notebooks, trying to reconstruct their lost research for the benefit of the Free World.

Isaac said, "A new place is opening to compete with the Vivant. It's called the Green Hen."

"Where?"

"The street behind the Opera. It used to be the chicken warehouse. That's how it got its name."

"Uh-huh." Marcus nodded absently. He was examining an embossing stamp from the private library in the mansion across the street and trying to determine if the letterpress that read "Property of Count Geiger" could be reconfigured to simulate new French Sector rules in effect since Thursday.

"What's that?"

"I picked it up in town." Various properties from Der Geigerhaus glittered in the barrows of the peddlers along with shoes, used bandages, and individual cigarettes. "Why?"

"Never mind, Kuzin. Keep working," Isaac said. "I'm going into town myself. If I meet any enticing company, I will bring it home for dessert."

"Yes, yes." Marcus squeezed the stamp on the edge of a paper, then lifted the paper up toward the light, shaking his head with displeasure and complaining more to himself than Isaac, "I don't like the mesh. It won't take tiny striations of ink. It should resemble skin under a magnifying glass."

Issac had greater worries. In a world of Letters of Discretion, a mere worker's ID would be worth less than an hour of the worker's labor. He feared that ID's would eventually lose credibility, too—sixty-two to twenty-six, Hah! There was such a thing as reality. He lost patience with Marcus's perfectionist concern about paper that couldn't simulate skin and said, "So use the real item."

"What?"

"Skin."

Marcus lifted his head up and said, "Can you really get any?"

"I'll ask at the bar."

"What bar?"

"Never mind."

It was a pleasant stroll into town for Isaac, past the Geiger mansion from which the letterpress had been liberated, and a row of garages with triangular roofs with shuttered loft windows and the mass grave that grew regularly as new bodies were brought in from other lagers.

Plenty of skin there, but not fresh. It put Isaac in a mood to drink.

He had already become accustomed to the taste, texture, and effect of alcohol in a way that would always elude Marcus. The burning liquid numbed the perpetual ache in his gums and gave him the cozy warm feeling of Shabbes wine. Of course, the Kaufman homestead where all of his previous imbibing took place never had pink neon breasts with bright red nipples blinking over the door, but family was now as abstract a notion as paper. Taverns were real.

The Green Hen, two days old, was so popular that a crowd had gathered at a velvet rope that barred entry to all but the elite. It was amazing that Regensburg, hardly worth the bombs that had been expended on its devastation, was able to turn out a mass rally of clamoring citizens and wayfarers sufficient to jam the place on a random Tuesday in November. Word traveled fast in the zone. Isaac recognized a peddler from the market—maybe he had sold Marcus the Geiger letterpress—and an American sergeant from the lager as he flashed his own identification card over the heads of the crowd at the rope.

The doorman, a thuggish young Regensburger with a distinctly military crew cut, unlatched the hasp to grant the newcomer a coveted entry, but there was something about the fellow's half-second pause that Isaac hadn't seen in the first ninety days of wonder. The power of paper was weakening. "You wouldn't have a cigarette, would you?" the doorman asked with only a hint of a threat.

That a shred of paper with some rolled up leaves was worth more than some of Marcus's most labored documents ought not to have surprised Issac, but it did, and set him thinking . . . After all, he had the paper—the other half ought to be easy. "Here," he gave the doorman a precious smoke.

Inside, the Hen, as instant regulars already referred to the place, was cut to the same pattern as the Vivant, its competition. There were small, round tables, a long zinc bar, and a wobbly stage where three girls without underwear danced almost in synch. Behind the bar, a mirror reflected ranks of watery booze served to drunk and AWOL marines, burghers, and the random displaced person who had passed muster at the door. Nor was it only the natives who were in perpetual motion across the Continent; the charity corps moved, too, to experience the different camps in different cities. Like gourmets determined to dine in every three-star restaurant in Paris or pilgrims to genuflect at every station of the cross in Jerusalem, they would touch the earth in every lager in Sector C, they and the scholars and the diplomats angling for a better view of the girls' crotches.

Isaac squirmed through a cluster of decorated colonels hung over the bar and passed the card that had barely gotten him past the hoi polloi across the metal surface, wet with the wiping of the bartender, reflective as a lake at dawn.

The card lay like a raft alone on the lake.

Then Isaac recognized one of the bartenders from the Vivant, which meant that the Hen either had the same owner or was stealing personnel from its rival. "What's wrong?" he asked.

"Sorry, Isaac, that paper will last as long as this napkin," the bartender said, as he wiped down the zinc surface for the ninth time, then poured Isaac a schnapps on the house.

Isaac tipped him more than the cost of the drink.

"Thanks, cash does do nicely."

Isaac inwardly resolved to set Marcus back to currency. Later that night, when he saw an amateur swapping documents a third grader would be ashamed to have produced to a waiter for a Scotch on the rocks, not even a double, he knew for sure they needed a market that was not subject to the fashions of the minute.

He was thinking of cigarettes, and the tobacco that might be trucked in along with the illegal whiskey. "Who's behind this operation?" he asked the bartender.

"An American."

Isaac pursed his lips. On the other side of the room there were the contending players in the paper exchange, Herr Freidrich Wuppertal, the German journalists' union official in charge of the only operative local printing press, and Jerome Pinsker, a survivor who provided a slew of teenage messengers to deliver Wuppertal's second-rate documents. Everyone from the camps was a potential ally or a potential competitor or both. It was rather like the relationship between the Café Vivant and the Green Hen; each tried to steal the other's clientele, but each knew the other helped to create a district that was good for business. And if one did manage to slit the other's throat, and if it happened to result in suicide as well as homicide, well, "Vat vuz, vuz."

Isaac took his drink and sat down to engage in shoptalk among his peers. It was Lloyds of London in the coffeehouse circa 1760.

"New regs due out from Southern District HQ."

"There's always new regs."

"New legs," Pinsker said, commenting on the stage show.

"We could use some around here."

"New blood."

"Tastes the same as old blood."

"Waiter, tell the bartender to mix a little vodka into the vodka next round."

A river of imitation liquor flowed across the bar, while a trickle of the genuine stuff dribbled out to special customers underneath, but all the patrons felt drunk, if only on the atmosphere. One set followed another, a three-piece jazz combo alternating with the dancers. The Hen had not yet swayed the Emcee at the Vivant into bringing his retinue across town, but that was only a matter of time. The heavy at the door had to toss out a teenage pickpocket, while the saxophone player performed a solo, and the crowd applauded the bouncer more than the bopper. A few parcels were swapped at the bar, a few telephone numbers written on napkins.

Marcus entered after midnight when the company was on its sixth or seventh round. He, too, had passed the rigorous test at the door. "Good news," he said, signaling the waiter for a hot water with lemon. "I figured out how to crimp the edges, with a potato scaler."

"Good to have a use for that since we don't have any potatoes," Isaac replied.

Pinsker said, "I've heard they may be available in the East."

"Yeah, but who wants to go for them?"

"Maybe we can put together a train."

"We'd need a pass," Marcus said, already thinking.

"I'll have it delivered tomorrow," Pinsker laughed.

For Isaac the question was not one of production of paper or acquisition of potatoes, but supply and demand. Mulling over the bear market, claws outstretched, inches from his throat, or, worse, wallet, Isaac lamented the numbers. "Too bad we didn't start this earlier. There were alot more people Before."

Marcus sipped at his drink and showed a moment of uncharacteristic whimsy. "There still are. Only problem is they're dead." He too had passed the graveyard on the way into town. Around-the-clock shifts from the Army Engineer's Corps were bullozing lime back and forth over the latest pit dug to accommodate a shipment of Hungarians. He had stood there in the glare of the emergency lights, and now tried to describe the scene to the fellows at the table. "Each time the bulldozer went over them, a dozen arms popped up behind it, like they were trying to escape."

"Just another form of DP," Isaac said.

"What?"

"Not displaced persons—dead persons," Isaac explained, in English.

While the majority of refugees spoke the mamelosh'n of their childhood, the group of adults at the Hen was already getting the hang of the vernacular that had become the linguistic boundary between the old world and the new. They showed off their snazzy verbal passports by their ability to play games with letters. Crossword puzzles were the rage.

Marcus said, "Those DPs, can't stop 'em from doing anything."

"It's the ultimate immunity," Pinsker chimed in. "Better than Letters of Discretion."

"Get me a DPID, I'll conquer the world."

"I'll settle for Liebknecht."

"Remember Rabbi Yoel's advice to the Vilna Gaon: Never think small. If you think small and get what you want, you get bubkes. If you think big, you don't necessarily get what you want, but if you do, Wow!"

"Wasn't that Pascal?"

"No, Rothschild."

Isaac raised a glass. He was already dreaming of the square of gold in front of the Liebknechtwerke, but all he said was, "To thinking big!"

CHAPTER 7

There was a knock at the door.

Minutes earlier Isaac had begun rubbing the first of a row of dearly purchased American cigarettes between his thumb and forefinger while Marcus chopped a small pile of straw into powder. For a second, the two men looked at each other in alarm and then both moved swiftly. Isaac tossed the cigarettes he was working on into a gap in the bricks behind the stove and set a pot to boiling on top. The doctor swept the straw into the garbage.

The knock was followed by two short knocks.

Isaac went to the door while the doctor paused.

There was one more belated knock.

Isaac stared at the door as if the wooden panels had been transformed into some evil apparition before his eyes. The last time he had heard that knock was in the ghetto. But the knock wasn't that of SS hammering the door in, shouting, "Raus. Raus. Come and be killed or be killed." It was a code, yet despite the correct repetition of the pattern, the last long beat had followed too slowly after the short ones. It was an academic version of the knock rather than a communicative one. He placed one hand on the latch and said. "Who is it?"

"My name is Fishl. Alter sent me."

Isaac looked back at the doctor, who continued to wipe the kitchen surfaces.

Isaac opened the door.

The stranger was nearly six feet tall, but hunched with the weight of his enormous head from which an enormous nose protruded like a beak. He looked like a "Der Stürmer" cartoon come to life. Isaac looked at him and said, "Alter's dead."

"May I come in?"

"If you couldn't, I wouldn't open the door."

"Thank you."

"Tea?" Marcus offered.

"Alter told me you were hospitable." The man grasped at the glass with both of his large, bony hands and drank its contents at a gulp.

"Perhaps you would like some lemon and lingonberry jam?"

The doctor looked at the man and then at Isaac, who stalked from the kitchen to his perch by the living room window. "Food, perhaps?"

"Thank you."

There was a pot of mixed vegetables on the stove. The doctor spooned out a plateful over barley and continued to watch as the man ate the entire thing. "Thank you."

"More?"

"Thank you."

"Don't be so grateful."

"Thank you."

They could see his belly slowly distending like a blown-up balloon.

"Don't eat any more or you'll explode," the doctor said.

"Thank you."

"I just don't want to clean up after you burst."

"Th—"

"Enough," Isaac said. "Why did my dead brother send you here? Where are you from? What can you do?"

"You must be Isaac Kaufman."

"I must."

"I met your brother in Mauthausen." Fishl started to roll up his sleeve to prove it.

Marcus said, "I don't need to see your diploma," but Isaac was suspicious.

"No one lies, but it's better to be sure." He leaned forward to examine the tall man's tattoo to make sure it had the particular shade of aniline blue that was used at that camp. The number on the man's forearm was in the fifty thousand range, a low number that probably meant he had arrived in 1943.

"So you can lift stone," Isaac declared. Mauthausen was located in a quarry outside of Linz. Anyone who couldn't carry stone up the steep incline from the quarry floor was thrown off the precipice, and someone from the next crew would carry his broken bones up later that day.

"Yes," the man said. "I'm very good at lifting stone. I can also recite every verse in the Torah, the Mishnah, the Talmud, the Gemara, and most of the commentaries."

"Can you sell cigarettes?"

The man turned his mournful eyes to the two black marketeers. "If I could sell cigarettes, would I be so hungry?"

The doctor finally acknowledged the man's boundless appreciation, "You're welcome."

Isaac still wanted to know something. "And Alter, who is now dead, what did he tell you?"

"He's not . . ."

"Tell me what he said before he died."

Going slowly, Fishl answered, "He said that if I came to a place where there was a man named Isaac Kaufman, I was to knock in such a manner, and that I would be helped. He also said, and I don't know what he meant, that I would be of help."

"If you knock again, do it faster. Otherwise, it interrupts things." Isaac retrieved the cigarettes from behind the stove and handed one to the fellow and lit it with a spiral of newspaper he stuck under the boiling teapot.

The man inhaled with the same greediness with which he had eaten.

The doctor stared at his cousin. The cigarette was worth ten marks on the street.

Isaac shrugged.

❖   ❖   ❖

The doctor showed the newcomer how to stuff the cigarettes. Once the cylinder was empty they refilled it—nine-tenths straw, one-tenth tobacco. Like magic, from a cigarette a pack, from a pack a carton.

The man did what he was told without asking. His fingers were nimble. He repacked a dozen cigarettes in quick succession and then asked, "Pardon me, but is this illegal?"

"Of course."

"I just wanted to know."

Isaac said. "The important thing about your background, Rabbi, is that you can learn."

Learning held them in good stead, learning not what the Talmud's notion of moral behavior was when one found one's neighbor's goose on one's property, nor which fish of the sea were acceptable to eat under which circumstances, but learning how to squeeze an extra spoon of rancid treyf from the bottom of the rusty pot that served a barracks, learning which Ukranian convict one had best not be noticed by, because he would take a whip and lash you behind the knees until you could not walk, which meant you were dead—real-life learning.

There were the smart, who learned swiftly, and the tough, who could afford to learn slowly, and the lucky, who didn't have to learn at all. Of all the virtues, luck counted for the most. Intelligence failed; strength waned; only luck endured.

"Are you lucky?" Isaac asked Fishl after they had finished their work.

"Who is lucky? He who dies in bed."

"What if his bed is set on fire?"

"At least he has a bed."

"Well, I think you're pretty damn lucky you knocked on our door. And if you don't agree, you can leave right now. I don't want a Musselman on my team."

Fishl stood up, his head swaying atop his thin neck like a Japanese lantern. He was ready to depart, bearing no ill will. "Show me a lucky man in Europe," he said.

"And I'll show you his tomb," Isaac finished.

"That's because you're a lucky boy."

Isaac laughed at the stranger's spunk. The Americans were called Lucky Boys, because they gave out Lucky Strike cigarettes, but they didn't like the nickname. A look of fear and resentment flashed into their Yankee eyes as they dispensed goodies from Red Cross packages to the refugees. Even the German civilians, who were compelled to purchase diluted smokes secondhand from Isaac and his peers, called the soldiers Lucky Boys.

"I mean it. You have their cigarettes and then you increase them."

"Now you know the trick, too."

"But I am too stupid to take advantage of it."

There was something about the tall scholar calling himself stupid that struck the brash young entrepeneur silent. Isaac looked at him.

"I mean it," Fishl declared. "By the time I could organize such an enterprise, a ship of cigarettes will cross the ocean, flood the market, and there will be no need for my product. You on the other hand will be on that ship back to the States. Once you arrive in the city of New York, you will find your way. You will be Moishe Rockefeller by the time I stub out this butt." He ground the last quarter inch of his cigarette into the ashtray for emphasis, then peered at the ceramic. It was a souvenir of the mud baths at Wiesbaden left by the previous occupant of the flat who had spent a week soaking to heal her game knee early in the war, when the prosperous citizens beside the Liebknechtwerke had stipends to spread around the Fatherland. "On the other hand," Fishl said in the Talmudic tradition of examining the opposite side to any coin, "I was lucky to meet Alter."

"Who is dead."

"If you say so." Fishl was a rarity—generally, there was no leisure for thinkers in camp. There were just Jews who scrounged for crust and Musselmen who didn't. Fishl, meanwhile, used most of his time behind barbed wire to study Talmud with his neighbor.

"And how did you study—in the camp library, perhaps, finding Hillel next to Himmler?"

"It was a strange coincidence," Fishl explained patiently, failing to respond to his interrogator's mockery, "I was a student from Kielce, whereas my partner, one always studies with a partner, was a modern man from Italy, a chemist. His name was Pietro Salidano. Our trains arrived the same day, and our numbers were within twenty of each other, 49,753 and 49,735, eighteen away as a matter of fact. Are you aware of what eighteen means?"

"I may blaspheme, but I know my gematria," Isaac sneered.

According to this esoteric medieval doctrine, one could discover the secret mystical significance of language through numerology, and vice versa, since both words and numbers were designated by the same Hebrew alphabet. Chai or Life, for example, was composed of Het and Yud, which also denoted eighteen. Therefore eighteen meant life. That was a common cultural reference, but the extension of this theory was weird and suspect. It led one to discern meaning where none existed.

Each of the two new inmates of Mauthausen had already begun to dwell on why they were assigned their particular numbers, seeking more than the blunt truth of their position in the line to the brand, so when they discovered that their numbers consisted of the same digits and that they were separated by eighteen, they joined together to solve the enigma.

"Every day there was a countdown," Fishl told Isaac and Morgenstern, each of whom had forgotten the value of their cigarettes and lit one up while listening to the bizarre tale.

"49,750!"

"Here."

"49,751."

"Dead."

"49,752."

"Dead."

The Kapo answered for those who had lost the ability to answer for themselves in the twenty-four hours between one countdown and another. "Every day there were those numbers that did not respond. They were the lucky ones."

"49,759."

"Here."

"No."

"No?"

"Dead," the caller declared and took out his gun.

"Dead," the Kapo repeated after the shot.

"And on and on through my number and the rest, and then to work. Between shifts at the quarry, the chemist and I discussed the incident, how that number had died that day. Though he made his living as a scientist, Salidano was a spiritual man. He said that if only one had known who number 49,759 was, that knowledge might have kept him alive. In fact, if one could remember all of the stories of the community, one might keep that community alive. As reward for such a feat, one might attain heaven.

"My background was more scholarly. I said that back in cheder we had memorized pages under the same assumption, the reward of heaven.

"So we made a pact. I would try to recall as many pages of text as the number on my arm, while Salidano would compile the stories of our peers, as many as the number on his arm. Of course, the internal edifice I constructed within myself was created from the raw materials of memory, while his emerged from events. I looked back while he looked around, but we helped each other in our endeavors, and when I found a new inmate I would refer him to my friend to add a story to his compilation, and when he came across a rabbi who might have additional lore to add to my store, he passed that along. We were to compell the German figure to signify something. You understand?"

"So what happened to Salidano?"

"He would tell me of a girl who had been stolen from her mother and I would tell him of Solomon's decision about the stolen child. Every story referred to a passage of law, while every passage of law was illustrated by a story."

They bounced Talmud and the catechism of cataclysm against each other. It was a new scripture they assembled—The Book of Terror— and it was redacted not on paper but the knobs and curls of their brains. In essence, they were walking, breathing volumes, and could refer to each other's pages.

"Fifty thousand stories he had, each one beginning with the word "Jew."

"So what happened to him?" Morgenstern repeated the question sadly for he was sure that he knew the answer.

"What else? He died. I suppose we were separated by chai after all."

"Yes."

"All of his stories began the same, and all of them ended the same way, with Kaddish—'and then my mother died,' or 'and then my brother died.' " He looked at Isaac for a pregnant moment and went on. "The happier stories ended, 'and then the German soldier who had tormented her died.' Maybe you've got stories like that yourself."

Isaac and Morgenstern were silent.

"And then Salidano died. He turned into a Musselman when the Russian Army was twelve miles from the gates. I tried to encourage him, because we had heard rumors of liberation, but he was convinced that none of us would be allowed to walk out of the camp. Unable to summon the strength to eat, he succumbed to typhus and then he died, as mundane a death as you could want, coughing one night and not waking the following morning. Of course, his life was entirely insignificant, like all of ours, but what about his memory? Did all of those stories die with him?"

The logical extension of his thought was obvious. Fishl wondered if the Torah and its sages would die with him. There was Rabbi Akiva, flayed for a martyr, wandering skinless through the millenia, only to expire on the killing grounds of Mitteleuropa. There was the Sanhedrin tramping along dirt roads in Silesia, trying to save their energy to avoid the showers, and ultimately there were the forefathers of the Bible buried in the pits and burned upon the pyres of the faith.

"Yes," Dr. Morgenstern said, "The mind disappears, the body decays, and only the teeth remain."

"But I don't care about teeth. What I want to know is did the stories die with him?"

"Especially those teeth," Isaac said.

"Yes," Morgenstern agreed, "All that's left is the teeth."

Fishl did not understand their pointlessly literal reference. He could tell that his hosts were serious though, so he did not inquire further.

Morgenstern apparently changed the subject. "What do you think of, say, Baba Metzeva, the suggestion by Rabbi Oshaya that finding an object is as good as manufacturing it."

"Is it luck to find something that incurs an obligation? First one must determine what the obligation is, nu?"

"So what does it say if you find something that doesn't belong to anybody?"

Morgenstern was looking out the cracked windowpane toward the barbed wire fence and the tarpaulin.

As if reading their minds, Fishl scratched at his chin and said, "Don't forget the murderers."

Isaac grinned, "I never will." It was the first time he had smiled and Fishl stared at him in astonishment. Isaac's teeth were as jagged as the Alps.

Frau Mannheim, their landlady downstairs, shouted at a boy tossing a ball against her stoop. A clatter of American trucks rattled over the bomb-pocked road to the Liebknechtwerke. Still the three Jews sat, immersed in their own thoughts, as dusk set over the chimneys to the west. The water in the tea kettle boiled off and the kettle itself turned a bright red. Isaac noticed it first and watched, idly wondering when the spout would burst into flames. Moments later, a hole like one formed by a cigarette in tissue paper began spreading and fire itself started to crawl up the side of a glazed cabinet beside the stove. Fishl saw that and stood, but did not know what to do. He remained paralyzed until the doctor jumped to grab the blazing kettle with a towel and plunge it under the tap. The water turned to steam instantly in a violent hiss. The doctor slapped the towel at the side of the cabinet. The room stank of charred metal.

Fishl delicately opened the window to allow the smoke and vapor to escape.

Morgenstern snorted with disgust, and turned his back on his cousin to retrieve a thick brown bottle from the blackened cabinet beside the stove. He also brought out three dusty glasses, and poured amber liquid from the bottle into them, pushing one to Isaac, warning him, "Don't say a word," and another to Fishl.

"What's this?"

"Schnapps, Rabbi. If we can't drink tea, the liquid of gentlemen, we may as well have something less gentlemanly but a little more potent. Besides, company will be arriving soon. It might be best to be drunk."

What kind of company it would be best to be drunk to greet, Fishl did not know. He said, "But—"

"Just say 'L'chayim.'"

Fishl clinked his glass to the doctor's and downed what was clearly his first alcohol since before the war. He broke into a fit of coughing.

"Just think of it as Shabbes wine, Rabbi," Isaac laughed again as he sipped at his own drink.

"Now, now," Dr. Morgenstern said.

Whether he swallowed too quickly or whether Isaac couldn't really hold his liquor any better than Fishl, he, too, began choking, yet he still managed to imitate his cousin by wagging his finger and repeating, "Now, now."

Fishl was quiet, but after the bottle disappeared, and another besides, he could not restrain himself. "Where do you get this?"

"From the fount of all good things, the American PX. They cannot give us good memories, so they help us to forget bad ones."

"Inequity," Fishl intoned, made lugubrious by the drink. "Tell me about a God who gives the world to the German murderers and to us, who bow and pray, he gives worse than nothing, he gives . . ."

"Dreck and claptrap," Isaac declared. "He gives dreck and I've never heard such self-indulgent claptrap in all my life." He stood and slammed his empty glass down on the straw-covered table, "If this is what freedom brings, then put me back into the lager where I can understand what people are saying. At least you knew where you stood, and what you needed. The last thing I needed then and the last thing I need now is theology."

"Now, now, Isaac."

"Don't hush me, Marcus. I'm sick of this shit. I don't want to think about justice anymore. I've had it to here with theory. Give me schnapps."

"I am very happy to satisfy your primitive cravings, young man." Morgenstern cracked another bottle and poured generously.

The young man turned on his elder, who was no more than thirty himself, "And what do you want, Mein Herr Doktor Professor?"

"What?"

"Tell the yeshiva bokher what you want, Doctor."

Marcus Morgenstern wished to save enough money to go to Australia, "where you can travel for a thousand kilometers without seeing another face."

Isaac wiggled a finger by his ear to signify lunacy, but the scholar would not play this game. "And what do you want?" Fishl asked Isaac.

"Me?"

"Yes, you."

Isaac thought for a moment and then answered, "It's not what I'm interested in; It's when. I want nothing for tomorrow. I want anything you've got, however, today. Skoal!" He raised his thin cut crystal glass, drained it and threw it at the oven besides the broken kettle.

"And yourself, Rabbi?" Morgenstern asked the stranger.

"You really want to know?"

"Almost as much as I want to go to Australia."

"I want to stop remembering. I want an aide to recollection so I don't have to keep it inside me. I want a Torah."

Isaac was scornful. "One with a velvet cover and silver ornaments, two crowns and a shield hung over the top by a silver loop chain."

"Yes," Fishl sighed dreamily, "Mostly, I want to see the words of the Lord again once before I die."

"Torahs are rare nowadays," the doctor pointed out.

"Hey. If Fishl's any indication, maybe there's a market."

They may have been mocking him, but Fishl did not notice. "Nobody's yet reprinting," he said quite seriously.

"It's a business like any other business," Isaac replied. "And if there aren't enough like you around, we can sell them as souvenirs. I can see it now, an antiquity in the making. Get 'em before the Jews forget how to write 'em. Ever think of writing a Torah, kuzin?"

"Shut up and have a glass of tea."

"Sure," he said, and poured water into the top of the kettle which came sieving out the bottom.

Before they could finish laughing, there was another knock at the door. This time it was three swift beats, repeated and repeated again emphatically.

"That's not what I was told," Fishl said.

Isaac smiled. "I knew you were a quick study. That's why Alter sent you. Even though he's dead."

The knock was repeated, but Isaac took his time to explain to Fishl, "For every occasion there is a language."

A knock with syncopation was a Jewish knock. A number counted straight out was a German knock. Three knocks meant three girls. Isaac opened the door, "Wilkomen."

✢   ✢   ✢

One girl was dressed in a tight black leather outfit, one wore a loose peasant blouse, and the third sported an American flyer's jacket. They worked outcall from the back of The Green Hen, providing services for barter and sale.

"What do they want?" Fishl asked Morgenstern.

The girl in the leather overheard this and answered, "Love, darling."

Isaac said, "But they will settle for cigarettes. You can't inhale love. See."

"So what do you have for me, darling?"

"Sorry we can't make you tea."

"You can do better, perhaps, if you have some incentive." She pulled the leather strap off her shoulder, revealing the triangular edge of a black tattoo.

"Better close the door or you'll scare the children."

"Don't be silly, we *are* the children." The girl, lank hair a gauzy screen over her bekohled lids, couldn't have been more than twenty, but neither were her customers, except for Marcus. Neither were the American soldiers down the road. It seemed that nobody between Paris and Moscow was any other age; the old and the very young had disappeared. One category had faded into history, while the other failed to enter.

"Have some missile fuel," Dr. Morgenstern offered, bringing three additional glasses from the cupboard.

Several schnappses later, the liquid in yet another bottle depleted, Morgenstern was drunkenly elaborating upon the nature of the experiments at the Liebknechtwerke. "You see the Germans were best at close killing." He rubbed his spectacles on his vest and continued, "Like Auschwitz where they could get the raw material together with the end product, live bodies in from the left, dead bodies out to the right." His hand simulating a conveyor belt swept across the table, knocking two of the empty bottles to the floor.

Fishl leapt to pick them up.

Isaac was bored; he had heard this speech before. He turned to the girl with the black triangle extending up from the lacy edge of her brassiere. "Come now, fräulein, don't be shy. Show the yeshiva bokher the rest of the mascot."

The women tugged her undergarment to her hips and stood with a vast tattoo of a large black bird, wings spread across her exposed chest, eyes glowing red.

Fishl stared in astonishment.

Morgenstern paid the scene no attention. "But this was long-range killing they had in mind," he explained. "Here they had to transfer heavy machinery. Assembly was different from activity. Different materials were used. For instance, they required gold."

Fishl blurted out, "One question."

"Ah, yes, a voice from the back of the class. You, with the Torah? A question about the mechanism, perhaps?"

"Why three?" He was referring to the girls.

Isaac answered instead of the doctor. "You think I can't handle two of these fräuleins, I can, but what's mine is yours. We're partners—like you and Salidano, but it's not fifty thousand stories or fifty thousand pages we wish to accumulate, but fifty thousand dollars."

"Or fifty million," Morgenstern corrected Isaac without missing a beat.

"I'll drink to that," Isaac laughed.

"Big talker," the German girl said, "How about action?"

"You want action, I'll give you action . . . Or maybe I won't." Ignoring the bird-woman, Isaac lowered his pants and faced the second girl, the one in the peasant blouse. "Mitzie, it's your turn, you fortunate wench."

"We are so fortunate indeed to have met you, you big businessmen."

"Big Jewish businessmen and getting bigger all the time," Isaac laughed and gestured to the girl with the tattoo. "Try Arabella," he told Fishl.

The girl shrugged and the bird's wings appeared to flap.

"She knows how to handle sensitive men."

Arabella stuck out her tongue and licked her lips with scarcely disguised boredom.

"I like a girl with spirit."

"I like a man who likes a girl with spirit."

"I like spirits."

"Try," Dr. Morgenstern urged Fishl. "You are in good company, genius." Then he focused on the last girl. "You are new," he said. "Let's see your teeth."

The girl in the flyer jacket appeared confused. She was even younger than her friends. They had warned her about the crazy Jews, but she said that she preferred them to the young Americans who had bombed her city and given her a profession as well as a jacket.

"Now, now, I am serious. I cannot entertain any girl whose mouth has not been properly cared for. Open wide. Ah, yes," he peered intently. "Any gold?"

Finally, the girl understood. She entered into the manner of the discourse and replied, "The only gold I know is in your pocket."

"The only thing in his pocket is not gold," Isaac interrupted, abandoning Mitzie now to return to Arabella with the gigantic bird, who was lying on the sofa perusing a catalogue of army supplies.

"You don't know what you're missing, boychik. Arabella was once the mistress of Wachtel. He was the deputy of the werke. He was very generous to her."

"But not so generous as you boys."

"Tell us about your master," Morgenstern said.

"He was a good man," Arabella addressed Fishl as Isaac kicked his pants beside the sofa and lay down next to her.

Morgenstern meanwhile finished his examination of the new girl's teeth. "Healthy as a rat," he sighed, "healthiest creatures on earth. They only spread disease, they never suffer from it. They're lucky."

"You know what luck is?" she said. "Luck is a tank."

Mitzie in the embroidered blouse now sat beside Fishl and offered, "A song, Sir, do you think the occasion calls for a song?"

He recoiled.

"So, perform," Isaac said, and turned with a wink to Fishl, "They are such a musical people."

She looked down at him and sang in a sweet, rhythmic soprano,

> My love, he knows no anger.
> My love, he knows no fear.
> My love, he lies too still for me.
> On the field at Hanover.

Isaac shifted his weight and entered Arabella.

Flinging her hair left and right, the bird on her chest wildly trying to escape from the boundaries of flesh, she continued to tell about

Wachtel, "It was most ironic. He could not bear to be imprisoned, yet he had lived, ahh, in a prison the entire war. So he decided to take his Jews with him, ahhh. He invited them into his offices where a bomb was set to ticking."

"That's the good part," Morgenstern interposed, "Now tell him the sad part."

"Yes . . . He decided he made a mistake. He was too young. He had regrets. So he wished to leave, but the keys slipped to the floor and the prisoners snatched them up."

"Those dirty Jews," Isaac cried.

"Outside the chamber, his secretary could hear him shout, 'I promise you, we will all leave, together,' but none of them left. Together, the boom!"

Isaac grunted once, and removed himself from the girl. "You see, they tell stories, too, and they end with death."

"Except Alter's." There, he said it. Fishl's eyes bulged as if he was attempting to reverse them to look at himself.

Isaac stared at the interloper with unrepressed fury. He zipped his pants and closed the window. "Once upon a time . . ."

"Your brother is in Czechoslovakia."

This was truly unacceptable. "I have no brother." Isaac smiled. The line of shattered stubs in his mouth was a tool to strike pity and fear into anyone who beheld them.

Fishl winced and continued, "Be that as it may, I just left him eating potatoes in Theresienstadt"

"Liar, there are no potatoes in Theresienstadt."

"And there are no eggs in Liebknecht," Marcus muttered.

Isaac glared at his "cousin."

"Go," Marcus entered the talk. "Come back when you need your teeth done."

"What if I like them this way."

"Got tsu dank."

Isaac remembered the Chaim from Chelm who traveled halfway across the Continent and back in search of a brother who had died before he left. He started to tell the story, "Once upon a time . . ." but Marcus had heard it before.

Morgenstern interrupted, "That's not you. You're a lucky boy, Rashi. Go."

"I'll find a corpse."

"You are a corpse. You'll have something in common. Go."

"I'll come back."

"That's up to you."

"I'm not going anywhere."

But if there were potatoes anyplace, it was the Theresienstadt, the model camp that had been built by the Germans for display to the Red Cross when they were inclined to pretend—and if anyone had potatoes at Theresienstadt, it was Alter Kaufman.

CHAPTER 8

Mealy, moldy, pale, and flaky, there were nearly as many rotten potatoes among the picturesque turrets of the armory at Terezín as there were dead Jews.

Without Yankee bulldozers, the Russian soldiers kept shoveling them off dump trucks whose gears refused to engage. New soldiers were, however, cheaper than new gears. The Russian soldiers looked like potatoes themselves, their lumpy, starch white faces broad expanses broken by the pocks and scars of childhood disease. Isaac had seen his first contingent of the Red Army at the border. It was a crew of three, two sergeants playing pinochle and one private tending a vine of yellow flowers climbing up the post that held the crossbar between sectors. It was only a few hours from Regensburg, but the border to the Russian zone might just as well have been the passage to another universe.

Although the boundaries of the lagerworld had been clearly defined, the practical shadings of life on the other side were more delicate. Beyond the barbed wire still lay enemy territory. From the Liebknechtwerke to the village of Liebknecht to the city of Regensburg were but different hues of brown. The shift in enterprise from the slaughter of Jews to their succor was as easy as retooling a tank factory for the production of Volkswagen Beetles. Here, however, the jump from materialism to Marxism was of a different order.

It was an odd kind of border, like a kitchen where a schematic map of the Louvre was pasted up next to a guide to the synagogues of Salonika that overlapped the fjords of Norway, but it was odd in sense as well as space. All of the frenetic uproar of post-War Western commerce disappeared. It was so quiet that Isaac could hear birds, cardinals commissioned to perform as musical harbingers of the Pax Communista.

Before, brother Alter had flirted with socialism. A charter member of the Proszowice Junior Bund, he had read the pamphlets of Lenin and Chernyshevsky and discussed them in secret cadre meetings after hours in the shtetl icehouse. Clever lads, they mounted a guard, who greeted midnight arrivals with the coded query, "What Is to Be Done?"

Only initiates gave the correct password: "The Will of the People."

"Enter."

Inside, the organizers shivered against massive blocks sawed from the river the previous winter. The only light came from a pair of Shabbes candles "liberated" from the Kaufman family cupboard, but the reflections of the two slim flames made a hundred blocks glow as if there were candles embedded in the hearts of the large, icy cubes. Once everyone in the Proszowice cell arrived, the frozen adolescent revolutionaries plotted, and ultimately decided to march in public protest against the invasion of Spain.

Some march; it was half a dozen beardless boys less than a summer's remove from the Talmud Torah, forbidden copies of Herzen hidden under their shirts beside their tsitsits, but confident that their voices would shake the world. Hand-scrawled placards read, FASCISTS OUT OF MADRID and WE'RE WATCHING as they strode single file into the Tuesday marketplace in front of the shul.

Gil, the shammes, sweeping the threshold, rubbed his eyes and said, "Is this a parade?

The Rabbi, no less baffled, stroked his beard and wisely replied, "It can't be a parade. Where's the music?"

Mortcha Kaufman, yard goods salesman, Alter and Isaac's father, also the father of Sarah, Rebecca, Levi, and baby Israel, asked his eldest son, "What are you doing?"

"Bearing witness, Papa."

"Who's to see?"

"I want you to see," Alter told his father while the line moved forward among the booths selling turnips and sugar beets. "The Fascists are doing terrible things in Spain. We must help the people of Catalonia."

"Why?" Mortcha asked. "We were chased out of Spain four hundred years ago. I'm not ready to help."

Alter replied with the arrogance of youth, "Franco's not asking you," and rushed to catch up with his comrades, but instead ran into Vilnik, a Polish horse trader, who had come to the Jewish market with a nag that he knew would hardly fetch enough zlotys to justify his trip. Ill-tempered by nature, Vilnik had stopped at the tavern on the Cracow Road outside of Proszowice where he swallowed a tumbler of harsh, local vodka, which only fueled his disdain. He peered suspiciously at the sign he couldn't read, and smacked Alter with a blunt cudgel that caught the child under the left eye, raised him off the ground, and dropped him flat. Blood streamed from the thin tissue. Vilnik rode the unsold nag home, swaying and singing the Polish National Anthem at the top of his lungs.

The cut had to be stitched by the local barber, and for a month there was a blotch that changed color from purple to greenish to faint yellow, before it finally faded. Alter never saw quite right again. He squinted, and just shy of his seventeenth birthday, the vision in his left eye disappeared forever. All that remained were the barber's stitches like a single traintrack connecting his upper nose to his lid.

Then the War traveled east and Spain was forgotten in the twentieth-century totalitarian extravaganza, a roadshow complete with posters, banners, songs, salutes, and armies. Madrid was the introductory act; Berlin was the main event. The 1930s gave way to the 1940s, and the Iberian Generalissimo's dreams of domination were dwarfed by those of his master, the Austrian corporal.

Isaac, several years and four dead siblings younger than Alter, never understood his brother's politics. He was still studying the wisdom of the Babylonian Exile when the great march occurred. A decade later, here was the historical nexus Alter had sought, clarified by a red circle on a white pole guarded by the two sergeants from the Caucasus who put down their cards, entertained by a break in the endless stretch of hours.

"You sure this is going to work?" the driver Isaac had recruited from the Vivant whispered.

"Pish." Isaac waved a document with a signature that could have been that of Frederick the Great or Henry Ford for all the drones at the border knew. It could have been Trotsky announcing his return from Mexico or Lenin his resurrection, "Honey, I'm back!"

The guard pretended to examine the pass. At least he managed to hold it right side up, although he had the benefit of a fifty-fifty chance. There was no photograph of the bearer, but he glanced from the incomprehensible writing below the blurred insignia of Count Geiger's letterpress, to the passenger and narrowed his eyes.

"Is there a problem?"

"That is up to me to determine."

"Jawohl."

"What?"

"Nothing."

The two sergeants conferred, while the private searched the truck. Sure enough, he discovered a bottle of Scotch whiskey under the driver's seat. He handed it to the first sergeant, who grabbed the bottle and demanded, "And what is this?"

"Contraband," declared the second sergeant.

Isaac said, "It's a present."

"For who?"

"You."

The guard smiled and the barricade was raised. Marcus's papers still worked for the time being, along with a bottle.

Everything broke into components of value. Liquor, eggs, even vehicles were currency, and the driver knew the power he possessed by token of the ignition key that could lead to the border where Churchill's whims, Glasgow's brew, and Marcus Morgenstern's papers would hold sway. They passed a death's-head motorcycle puttering along on an afternoon's joy ride; Isaac laughed.

"You need a dentist, man," the driver said.

"I've got a dentist. I need a psychiatrist. That's why I'm going to Austria."

"They got the best damn head shrinkers in the world."

"Yes, I picked up this beautiful brushed felt fedora that's too small for me." He rubbed his scalp and said, "Lose another size and it'll fit perfectly."

"You're nuts."

"Hazelnuts or almonds?"

"Good Sacher tortes in Vienna, too."

"Still?"

"Take my word."

"You've got to know the source," the driver said.

Isaac corrected him, "You've got to have the capital. Then the source knows you."

Two hours later, parking in the tiny hamlet of Terezín, the driver said, "You want me to wait?"

"You want to get paid?"

"I'll wait."

Isaac left the driver and entered the armory complex that had served as a showplace for the Germans. It was a lager sure enough as Treblinka, but here the mass graves could accommodate their tenancy and there was only a modest pile of corpses as the old castle grounds were reduced to a vile, unclean necropolis. The first thing Isaac noticed, however, was that there was no ARBEIT MACHT FREI sign, either because it had never been erected in this particular camp or because the Soviets had removed it, a statement that everyone was free in the East. Indeed, Isaac was free to wander beneath the corbels and groins of the medieval courtyard.

Theresienstadt was clearly not as organized as Aspenfeld or Liebknecht. The Russians had entered later than the Americans in Germany. The cleanup here was still underway. Those Red Army soldiers who weren't on grave duty or potato brigade were lounging, smoking Stolichna Brand nonfilters, surprised that anyone was coming in instead of going out. One of them looked cursorily at Isaac's documents, jotted down a note to himself, and made an ironic welcoming sweep of his arm. Isaac was the king of paper.

In the distance, three men sat on upended ammunition crates. Grouped around a small campfire, fishing half-boiled potatoes out of a tin pot, they looked like Indians. A woman wearing a blue suit stood in front of them, holding a clipboard, the universal symbol of bureaucracy, perhaps counting how many potatoes they ate.

Isaac was sufficiently unusual a presence for the clipboard to interrupt her vigil and approach the stranger. "May I help you?" she addressed Isaac in Yiddish, the universal language.

Such politeness, such gentle, graceful assistance. Isaac wondered if she was the representative of some Russian version of the charity corps, a Natasha instead of a Miranda, working out of a cozy chapel nave with a mimeo machine and a calendar with a sentimental lithograph of the Wailing Wall. Isaac had to bite his tongue to keep from asking where the clipboard was in 1939. He thought fiercely of Fishl and Marcus, who had sent him on this wild-goose chase, put him in the same position as the many desperate men wheeling through Europe in fruitless search of lost time. "I am looking for Alter Kaufman."

"There are two thousand men here."

"Fine," Isaac said, ready to take the driver to Vienna for a Sacher torte and cappuccino.

"But you're lucky."

Isaac was startled.

"Alter happens to be one of our inmate trustees. I am coordinating local relief efforts with him."

"Yes, yes." Isaac was growing uncomfortably eager. The woman was speaking in the present tense.

"He's over there," the woman lifted the arm with the clipboard like a wing and waved toward the three men around the pot of boiled potatoes.

"There?"

"And you are . . . ?"

Isaac didn't answer. He moved slowly toward the simmering fire as if he was sleepwalking. Alter wasn't the man on the left with a giant nose and heavy lips that hung off his face like twin balloons. He could have been the man on the right, but Isaac wasn't sure. It wasn't easy to recognize a brother he hadn't seen since the woods outside of Proszowice, who had undoubtedly changed much in recent years. There was a third body, back to Isaac, arms shoveling chunks of potatoes from kettle to mouth.

Approaching from an angle, Isaac thought he recognized the gesture, an extension of the impatience of the Young Bundists. Had teenage Alter scooped food that crudely at the Kaufman family table his mother would have slapped his wrist. Isaac, however, was no stickler for manners. He bent low, the hem of his suit touching the edge of the silver-gray pot, "Altie?"

The man looked up with blank eyes.

"It's me, Itzhak."

"Itzhak?"

"Your brother."

Forget three years of lager life; nine months of freedom made an enormous difference. Here they were still skeletons, but Isaac had a little excess flesh and a little counterfeit cash. The thought occurred to him that maybe the War wasn't over in Czecholslovakia, or maybe that it was, but the Germans had won here, and the borders were only permeable in one direction.

The fellow shared Isaac's difficulty, working to fill the frame that leaned over him with a personal history that traveled back all the way Before.

"Come with me." Isaac reached an arm down to lift the stranger, who was shorter than he recalled.

Alter glanced nervously—fearful of standing out by standing up. Each brother had his own notion of liberty. If it was aftershave lotion and mother-of-pearl buttons for Isaac, his older brother was still at a more basic level. "But what about the potatoes?"

"I have money now."

"But do you have potatoes?"

"As many as you could want."

"Let me just take a few. Here, you, too." Alter started shoving them into the pockets of his brother's new suit, a beige linen with matching cravat, until it was bulging out ludicrously. Isaac couldn't help but laugh.

"Hey, Isaac, what happened to your teeth?"

"I've got a dentist, now, I'll introduce you." Almost everything was suddenly better. The scent of the necropolis still suffused the atmosphere; it was a miracle that one human being had risen from the tomb.

But Altie Kaufman was different from his younger brother. Marcus had been correct about the vitality of Kaufman genes; both bore with circumstance, and came out the other side. But Alter no longer exuded the fervor of the boy with the Red flag, parading the single street of Proszowice to the market where he would shake the world. Nor was there any trace of the scar under his eye where Vilnik the horse trader had beat him. Of course! It was all a cruel joke and Isaac should have forseen the punchline. "You're not Alter."

"I am Alter."

"Not Alter Kaufman, my brother."

"I am Alter Kaufman, your brother," the man insisting, eyeing Isaac's suit and manner, the glimmer of greed in his unsquinting eyes—staring at and craving the linen prosperity of this godsend.

"Not Alter Kaufman, my brother, who has a scar under his left eye."

The man screwed up his face as if trying to peer under his own lopsided lid. A name he could claim, a relationship adopt, but a scar he could not create. It was time for his own vision of the future to crumble as swiftly as it had been established. He sighed, "No, I'm not. But I'd like to be."

"Isaac Kaufman?" the clipboard reappeared, flanked by two Russian soldiers.

"Ask him," Isaac replied bitterly, gesturing toward the new Alter, wanting to slap the imposter, to bury the dead and have done with it, feeling hopeless for the first time since the snowfall of 1944.

"Come with us."

This did not bode well. Being singled out in the lager was invariably to be doomed. These men may not have been Germans, but they had guns. The War was not over. Nor was he safe in the kitchen on Weinerstrasse.

Captured, he was confronted with the false identification he had displayed. "Fake, fake, I say," the clipboard shook her head, lying through her teeth, because the documents were indistinguishable from the real thing. The woman had been tipped off somehow. Isaac wondered if the sergeant at the border had called ahead. But the guard was insignificant. Even the clipboard was meaningless. Some other force was at work here, but Isaac could not imagine what it was. He thought of running, but there was obviously no way he could escape, yet, or ever.

Isaac was ushered inside the armory itself, prodded by the two soldiers along dark stone halls, leading perhaps to a private shower in the basement. But no, he rose up a wide, stone staircase, and was passed from one authority to the next, sergeant to lieutenant to captain to major. Each looked at his documents, and proceeded to pass him to a yet greater authority. They moved him upward in floor and rank so fast that he didn't have time to attempt to bribe any one along the chain of command. They were afraid of him. He was a human hot potato.

From a window on the staircase beneath a stained glass skylight, he could see the plaza in front of the armory. It was empty. The driver was gone, willing to forego his fee for freedom, halfway back to Regensburg by now. Perhaps it was he who had sold Isaac for a tank full of petrol from the Baku.

But Isaac was too depressed to care. Take him wherever they would, have done with it all.

Like a train's last stop at the imperial terminal, he arrived at a door designated by three initials on a plaque: KGB. Silk-screened banners with Stalin's image hung from the same standards that had once hung the previous ruler of the universe. Behind the last door, at the far end of an auditorium-size office, was an aircraft carrier of a desk, the ex-kommandant's holy of holies; behind it sat a tall man wearing a green uniform bedecked with medallions, military decorations, and a cap with an embossed hammer and sickle shading his forehead and eyes. Extending out from under the shadow of the cap, where the skin showed, there was a long, puckered scar. The man pushed the hat off his forehead, revealing a black patch over his left eye, and said, "Welcome, Itzikl."

Shocking his twin guards, Isaac sat down in an oxblood leather chair as if he was at home. "Alter," he said.

Brothers, breathing!

Isaac and Alter went to lunch in the officer's mess, a tiled cafeteria located in the armory basement. Heavy iron bars protected the windows from the feet tramping by outside in the couryard, where the three refugees Isaac had first approached were still squatting around their open fire, fishing potatoes out of the battered tin container with a bent fork. The one who had claimed he was Alter was gesticulating, lamenting his brush with fortune. If only he had had a scar under his eye. Heck, he could have arranged a scar if he had been given sufficient notice.

A Russian private hastily set the brothers' chosen table with silverware and a tiny vase with a single red flower, a nice touch by the management.

Moments later, a second private, first class in the classless society, brought two covered platters from the kitchen. These he placed in front of the only two diners in the cavernous room with all the savoir faire of a Parisian professional.

"What's for lunch?" Isaac asked.

"What do you think?"

Looking at the elegant trappings, Isaac replied, "I doubt it's flanken." The very word called up the kitchen of Proszowice, and their mother in a perpetual mist that warped the wooden ceiling above a pot that might have been the one presently outside the grade-level window.

"Correct."

"Perhaps Wiener schnitzel?"

"Not quite."

"I give up."

Alter waved the waiter away with a gesture as light as a bird's feather and lifted the top off one of the platters, "Voilà!"

Potatoes.

Isaac turned up his nose.

Alter laughed, "Fayn shmeker."

"No, really, this smells terrible."

"It is. That shows the true equality of the Russian Army. Everyone eats shit."

"Even . . ." Isaac could hardly bring himself to do more than nod toward the braids and medals on his brother's chest.

Alter gave voice to the astonishing truth, "Colonels."

"Colonels," Isaac repeated.

"I'm expecting a promotion," Alter shrugged.

"So, um, what did you do to merit such rewards?"

"Service to the People. I've always worked for the common man. You know that."

"Franco's still in business."

"Cagey buzzard. You've got to respect him."

Isaac looked at Alter. The idealism that had shone in the Proszow-ice marketplace had been burned out of him, and although he was wearing a Communist uniform, the manner in which he had accepted his plate of potatoes was aristocratic. However long he had been in this position was long enough for him to become accustomed to it.

"I thought you died in forty-three."

"I did." Alter wore the insignia of power, exuded the manner of power, but his scarred face still bore the sallow complexion of the lager.

"And how did you manage to be resurrected?"

"A little translation, to start with, once the Germans left. I was in Buna, you know, or maybe you don't, the synthetic rubber works at Monowitz, and the Russians made that a priority. The factory was operating at ten percent of capacity since the Allies bombed us. Talk about precision, it was beautiful to watch. The B-29s slid out of the sky and deposited half a dozen loads at the most vulnerable points. All they missed were the experimental labs, which still had a few thousand gallons, which the Russians needed badly. They rolled in with halftracks with four flat tires, and we had the material to vulcanize them into the Reich."

Sirens blew as a squadron of MIG fighter planes buzzed the instal-lation in advance of the troops. Then, the broken-wheeled vehicles appeared over the horizon. The ground shook. IG Farben's managers were gone in a flash, in Mercedes jeeps with real rubber tires, but the SS was determined to take their Jews home. Evacuation was called, and the prisoners began filing toward the gate, but as far as Alter knew there was no place to go besides a ditch in the woods.

He was working in the "confection room" where three enormous vats of the rubber solution were brought to a boil. Fortunately, they had started to cool once the generators were knocked out, but were still lukewarm when Alter stepped down the rungs of a metal ladder meant for janitors to use when cleaning the empty tanks. He was holding a pen he had stolen from the chief engineer's desk. Contem-plating the pit of black ooze from above, listening to the sirens, he quickly uncapped the pen, discarded the ink cannister, clamped one end of the cylinder between his teeth, and descended, breaking the skim, and settling himself on the floor with the pen barrel poking through the surface a metal reed through which he breathed.

The gradually gelling black liquid plugged Alter's ears, eyes, and nose. It seeped through his cuffs and between the buttons of his striped uniform, the first bath he had taken in years, and suddenly he was back in Proszowice, more than remembering, reexperiencing incidents of youth and early sorrow, in a barrel filled with water from the well, warmed by the sun, in a pot of chicken soup, in a featherbed that was hospitable to his innermost dreams. He was in cheder with Reb Fainshtein; then he was a teenager atop a barricade composed of chairs and synagogue benches wedged together like a beaver's dam, and he was waving the Red flag, and then he couldn't tell if the flag itself was changing colors or if a storm-laden sky was draining everything of color, for the flag changed gradually from red to purple to brown to black.

There was a crowd at the base of the barricade, and the people did not have any of the usual sensory apparatus, neither eyes nor ears nor noses, their faces as featureless as lumps of unshaped clay. Nevertheless, they were cheering. It was ideas rather than words that were somehow communicated through their minds. Alter could see brains palpitating inside the yarmulked heads over the blank faces.

"Where am I?" Alter Kaufman wanted to know, having forgotten the tub of rubber. "Who am I?" he couldn't say, the boy at study or on the barricades, or carrying sacks of chemicals into the confection room. It was only by concentrating on the bite of the pen in his mouth that he was able to grasp the tiniest notion of presence, until he couldn't do that anymore, and felt a supernatural effort required to avoid floating away from himself, and, with no conception of how many minutes or hours had passed since he had been immersed, he pulled himself out of the glop.

"I hid," he told Isaac, "in a vat of liquid rubber."

The vanguard of Russian soldiers went fleeing from the monster from a black lagoon.

Only one man remained. He leaned against the control panel that regulated the flow and temperature of the tank and watched the creature emerge, thickened black fingers blindly seeking a hold, hoisting itself over the rim of the tank and collapsing in a sticky human outline on the floor, its open mouth the sole unblackened inch of his body, gasping for air.

The man removed a banner with the swastika emblazoned on it from its hanger on the wall, and Alter felt the soft flag gently smoothing the tar from his eyes and scooping plugs of rubber from his ears. The man unbuttoned Alter's shirt and pulled the dripping bundle off.

Blinking tar, Alter was able to perceive just enough to realize that it was not Herr Lang of the Reich Monowitz command, but a tall Red Army officer. He started singing "The Internationale."

There was still enough residue clogging Alter's ears so that he could barely hear the appreciative chuckle, "My little Yidische Schvarts."

He told Isaac, "And so I had an angel. Colonel Trubetskoi, chief of staff for Army Sector 4, Galicia."

"Was he Jewish?"

"I never knew. Although since then I've discovered that the KGB is a hotbed of Yids. Pilpul seems to be good training for the profession."

"Which consists of . . . ?"

"I did a little translation, I ran a few errands. Trubetskoi liked me. And used me. We got the confection room operating, and I showed him where the tire molds were stored and we went into production. For which I believe he was exceedingly well paid. But my colonel died just as the treaties were signed, a peaceful heart attack alone in bed, that or poison. By then we had moved the regional headquarters here. I don't know where his riches went."

"What was left?"

"His medals. I put them on. You see Marxist Leninism has stood me in good stead. The second anyone looks at me, I start spouting the Manifesto. Alter Kaufman eats outside; Colonel Trubetskoi has a reserved table indoors."

Outside it was beginning to rain, but the three men sat like stones, their bare palms cupped to protect their flame.

"And the other officers? Didn't they notice?"

Major Gruber did and duly considered informing, but once Alter had donned his benefactor's uniform, he could not be dislodged without incurring great personal risk for the would-be dislodger. Who knew what power the Jew had over his colonel, whether he was the real man from Moscow, a spy in service at Monowitz until the Red Army came to relieve him. As always, it was better to leave well enough alone. Besides, Alter gave the suspicious major plum assignments for plunder until he sent him to quell a rebellion among the partisans in Croatia where, with a little luck, the major was buried on a rocky hillside. "I learned from my Bible," Alter said proudly. "Such a strategy was good enough for King David."

As for the rare visiting inspectors from the Kremlin, they had never met Trubetskoi, and did not know whether he had a scar over his nose. As long as information flowed, they had no problems.

"Nonetheless, the position could be dangerous."

"Speaking of danger, how may I ask did you get this far with a private driver?"

"And what's danger to a Yeshiva bokher like me?"

The two boys understood each other. Morgenstern was right—a Kaufman was a Kaufman through and through.

The two breathing brothers started picking at the vile potatoes, fried in lard. Nonetheless, both had consumed much worse, so they ate with relish. Isaac chewed and asked, "One thing I don't understand—Fishl. Why'd you give him your name? Or rather the name of the man outside. It must have been a terrible risk."

"For you, Itzikl."

"Me?"

"You were the only one whose death I couldn't verify. You were also the most likely to survive."

"I was the weakest."

"And the slyest. But that was no guarantee either. I just believed that you would make it. Someday, tell me how. But not today. I gave Fishl my original name hoping that he would find you. Is that why you came?"

"Actually, I heard there were Sacher tortes in Vienna."

"Rumors. There isn't a man in this army who wouldn't sell the Winter Palace for a peach parfait."

Isaac said, "Then come to Liebknecht, Alter, we own the town."

"Get a state," Big Brother whispered.

"Fuck the State. There's opportunity in the West." Isaac insisted, and he leaned over the table, and told Alter of his enterprise. He told him of the paper trade and his desire to move into currency and perhaps other goods that retained their value. He told also of their new cousin. "You should meet Marcus."

"In good time."

Meanwhile, the plates were cleared, a gelatinous pudding was served for dessert, and Alter offered Isaac a cigarette, made in Tashkent. "They're terrible, too."

"Have one of mine." Isaac opened a mint pack of Marlboros.

Neither could say who came up with the idea—their thoughts were so alike, created from the same series of genetic and Talmudic convolutions in the Proszowice brain. If Alter had quantity and Isaac had quality there had to be some way to combine resources for their mutual benefit, and in seconds they had concocted a plan. It turned out that Alter had organized the trucks of potatoes in return for the division's weekly cigarette ration. But if that ration could be better marketed in Regensburg, so be it. Stolichnas were cheaper than straw, and if they were mixed with straw the end result was cheaper yet. Voilà!

Isaac's driver was being detained by one of Colonel Trubetskoi's aides, to make sure he waited for his passenger. Later he was booked for a weekly courier route that would ship the bulk Stolichna to Liebknecht and return empty Marlboro packs to Terezín. Alter would use enlisted labor while Isaac hired workers according to the respective customs of East and West. As for the profits, they would share as brothers. Wherever there was an opportunity to transform the returns into better returns, they would.

"An idea is as good as gold," Alter said appreciatively, not aware that he had uttered the magic word.

Isaac looked around. "Speaking of gold . . ."

"Nu?"

It was one thing to discuss smuggling cigarettes where a table might conceal a microphone. All the eavesdropper might want would be a carton. It was another to mention eighteen tons of pure wealth. Alter reassured Isaac that their conversation was confidential. "What do you have on your mind?"

"There is gold there, in Liebknecht. I can't say how much it's worth. But the cube is bigger than a Torah."

"But smaller than a synagogue."

"By a hair."

"And you . . ."

"Want it."

"Let's work on it."

"Good. So are you sure you don't want to skip the cigarettes and come home with me?"

"Itzhikl, Itzhikl, are you crazy? It's better to have one of us in each of two places in case everything falls apart. Who knows what side of the line you want to be on when the next war starts."

Lines, again. Kaufmans had an intuitive understanding of lines. The maps that broke and reconfigured over Issac's kitchen stove could break apart just as easily in 1946 as 1936. In an unstable situation, the greater the chance to escape, the greater the chance to survive. Sometimes it was teeth that kept one out of the ovens, more often it was cunning or cash, and sometimes a refuge. Proszowice was no more, but each of the two remaining Kaufmans knew that they now had a second home. Alter was welcome in Regensburg if the Kremlin caught on to his masquerade, and Isaac could always slip away to Terezín if the Allied command turned up the heat. Credit was nice; power was better; blood was supreme.

CHAPTER 9

Was it only a day later, a Tuesday like most any other Tuesday in the summer of 1946, so hot that the leaves on the linden trees leading to the gate of the Liebknechtwerke shriveled and drooped like pilgrims at prayer, that Isaac was back on Weinerstrasse? Welcomed by Frau Mannheim at the door, he skipped lightheartedly upstairs and immediately strung a pair of binoculars around his neck as if life was normal, and he was just a birdwatcher in a glade, watching a gold-breasted thrush nesting, while a brother who shared his innocent hobby less than two hundred miles away was also working to devise a method for catching the rare bird.

Marcus had greeted Isaac warily on his return, afraid of failure and perhaps more afraid of success. The dentist didn't dare to ask. "Was he there?" Instead, he poured a cup of ersatz, and drummed his fingers on the blond wood arms of a Biedermeier settee they had found in the garbage in back of Count Geiger's cottage. Its two front legs were bent under like the limbs of a hobbled mare, so Marcus had wedged a copy of *Wilhelm Meister's Apprenticeship* beneath the frame for additional support.

But Isaac brought up the subject. "I have a brother," he said, "and a cousin, too. Thank you for making me go to Czechoslovakia, Marcus." For the first time since they had met, Isaac was at ease.

Embarrassed, Marcus changed the subject. "We're onto DPID's, now, you made them up that night at The Green Hen. Let me tell you, it's wonderful. They're idiots. We won't be able to keep up with the demand."

Just like that they were back in the present. It was a Tuesday like any other Tuesday in the zone. The maps that surrounded them could have been turned upside down and it wouldn't have made any difference as long as one didn't expect to follow the blasted routes outlined in red.

"Something in me says that whoever 'they' are, they are not idiots. But go ahead, Mein Herr. Explain."

And so Marcus told how the night before, when Isaac was gone east never to return for all the cousin left behind knew, he was returning quite woozily from the Vivant. He didn't say that he had been toasting Isaac's farewell in a private wake. That was sentimental and the younger man would have despised such emotion. "That little momzer who runs the place, he wanted documents for his new crew from Essen, triplets. He served me three shots at a time to make his point; I thought I had three legs by three o'clock," when he heard an army voice by the side of the road proclaim, "Dig we must."

Marcus tripped over a root that broke the paving.

The voice was singing a boisterous improvisation:

> Dig till dusk.
> Then dig till night.
> Dig with frenzy.
> Dig with might.
> Dig until the eyes fall out of your head.
> Dig dig dig, cause they're dead dead dead.
> Dig until the toes fall off of your feet.
> Dig and cover up all that meat.

Moonbeams and Kliegl lights cast stark shadows of a dart-tipped iron fence onto the road. The site of the Jewish cemetery had been expanded to include a larger population than the medieval rabbis of the region had ever imagined might make this idyllic spot their final resting place. Jews had passed through the Regensburg valley on their journey from Spain across Mitteleuropa to Poland, but that was centuries earlier. The return of eighty thousand Polish émigrés would have meant a golden age of culture and learning to the rabbis. The manner of their return now, however, was a boon only to suppliers of bulldozers and lime. A single soldier was maneuvering an army backhoe in response to the orders from a shadow.

> *Smoother on the left.*
> *Deeper on the right.*
> *Dig, dig, dig.*
> *Till the dawn's daylight.*

Marcus stood and watched and then, emboldened by the sour whiskey he had drunk, shouted over the fence, "Keep the DPs coming!"

"What?" the taskmaster interrupted his chant.

"How do you think you can bury someone without a DPID?"

"Wuzzat?"

Answer as Isaac, the inebriated forger told himself, a dummy summoning the spirit of the ventriloquist. "Man, don't you know—Dead Person's Identification. If you bury someone without proper ID, how can you know who's where?" He felt himself getting larger as a shift in the angle of the Kliegl light cast his shadow halfway to town, like a giant blockading the road. He was blinded, but he spoke more strongly with the light in his eyes. "You are in much trouble, Monsieur. Gonna have to dig 'em all up, get their fingerprints, interview them."

"How the Hell can I interview them?"

"I don't care how. It's regulations. You don't have that DPID, you got to conduct interviews."

By now the soldier was dreading more digging and a millenium of paperwork. "How do I get these DPIDs?"

Marcus recalled the "lesson" he had learned by Isaac's brazen impersonations of authority. Never hesitate. Never look back. Once the soldier repeated the same letters as Marcus, they became the new reality; DPIDs now existed. He smiled, "I'm glad you asked. Just see my associate, and maybe he can work something out. He'll be back tomorrow." The Kliegl shifted; the shadow shrank. "I'm not guaranteeing we can help you. But maybe . . . So, um, what's it worth to you?"

Suddenly, they were negotiating. The soldier had to call his HQ on the crank-controlled field telephone.

"At that hour . . ." Marcus shook his head, "but he seemed to know the chief would be awake, playing cards, apparently. All I heard from the other side of the phone was, 'Full house, Jacks over dueces.' "

"Good hand," Isaac kibbitzed.

"He won. I could also hear the chips being stacked."

"Probably fixed the deck."

"I figured it would be a generation till the bureaucracy decided, but no."

Things can move swiftly in the army—when there's a will. Seconds later the sergeant ambled over to the fence with an astonishing offer for the first two thousand DPIDs. "Quite amazing," Marcus exclaimed, relishing a moment's suspense.

"What is it—the offer?" Isaac asked.

Marcus told him.

Even the imperturbable Isaac was taken aback. "What's a truckload of ball bearings worth?"

"Hey, it's better than money."

"You're right, I suppose we can do something with it."

"But that's the beauty. We don't have to. I got a call today from another American, seven o'clock this morning, oh-seven-hundred. I had a splitting headache, who said he heard we had ball bearings for sale. He wants to buy them."

"And what currency does he want to pay in, scissors?"

"No, cigarettes."

From the entirely real to the entirely abstract and back again—the mechanism to enact such a metaphysical transformation clearly required an organization. Despite the abundance of DPs baking under the pyramidal mound of loamy Weinerstrasse earth, a sufficient number of the more common Garden of Eden–variety DP were, relatively speaking, alive. Isaac summoned Schimmel from Aspenfeld and Schimmel brought along Schmaljin, a Dutch prisoner recently transferred from Westerbork, and crazy Berger and Zimmerman, who had spent the war in the company of a family hiding in the barn of a Polish farmer who never did understand why his pig ate so much and refused to grow. The question Zimmerman couldn't answer was how he knew the War was over. It had something to do with the quality of the pig feed his third May in hiding. That week, he emerged from the sty, washed himself in water from the flabbergasted farmer's pump, and hitchiked to the nearest camp, which was Aspenfeld, where he joined Schimmel and Schmaljin. By the time Isaac's telegraph arrived, all of them had seen as many Laurel and Hardy movies as they wanted. All of them were tired of the Yankee food that had seemed so extravagant six months earlier. All of them had heard of Isaac's legendary success and were eager to join the master.

Isaac's directions were explicit. They packed what they could carry and passed under the camp gates for what they hoped was the last time.

Schimmel and company arrived on the afternoon train, bearing the leftover chits from Aspenfeld, minus some. "I gave them to Miranda."

For a moment, Isaac thought of the girl in the bright yellow dress. He said, "Why?"

"I thought you'd want me to."

"Don't think."

"I'm sorry, Isaac."

"Never mind."

"I also . . ."

"I said, 'Never mind.'" Isaac cut the conversation short. They had to set up an office in town, and Isaac already conceived of branches at camps across the zone. There were dead people everywhere. Maybe they could enlist representatives abroad on a commission sales basis.

"You know what we have," Isaac crowed, delighted, as they lay down a half dozen mattresses on the floor to accommodate the newcomers, "A gang."

"We need a uniform."

The citizens of the ex-Reich were ragged, but there were plenty of fatigues in the attics. Maybe they could dye them from brown to black, restyle them a tad, add pleats, embroider some red thread around the collar, give the ex-SS togs a Continental cowboy look.

"A tailor, I'm not."

"Tailors we got. Guns we need."

Marcus laughed, "Doesn't everybody? In the meanwhile, you want a girl? It's all the local men got to sell."

"You're almost right," Isaac corrected him. "We do need bodies, but not that kind."

They opened the tins of strange American food dispensed at the Red Cross and devoured the contents while discussing plans for the future. If the aim was to shift from Marcus's handcrafted merchandise to something more mass-produced they had to be strong in numbers. A factory needed a proletariat.

But first there were papers of their own, both real and imaginary, to guarantee their own freedom of movement. Marcus was working on a portfolio of IDs for every member of the gang. He used the last remaining heavy stock for future members, leaving the names blank so they could always sell them if the need arose.

The DPID concept had the potential to create an enormous, entirely new strata of paperwork between Jews and the world, like the Talmudic rabbis' commentary. It granted the shades a unique death certification that no one who had ever died before had while compelling the next dead person who approached the pearly gates to show his own papers or risk being turned away, like the unwanted at the door of the Green Hen, or the passengers on board the *St. Louis*. The beauty of the concept was that the boys at 44 Weinerstrasse were the only source of such papers. They had a monopoly for a minute until the U.S. government started issuing its own postvaporization papers.

"How much paper do we have left?"

"Three reams maybe."

"Not much."

"Enough for the first order."

"How big would each ID have to be?"

"Thirty-by-forty centimeters, index card size."

"Could we do them smaller, get more product per inch? Maybe twenty-by-fifteen. Sort of like a chit."

"I suppose so. But bigger is more impressive."

"Hey, the users won't mind."

"How would it look?"

Marcus mulled over the idea of design. In Dachau's Operation George Washington, he wasn't authorized to invent a three-dollar bill. For the first time, he was not copying an existing work, but creating it. "Maybe pale yellow, we can do that with a tea bath, a circular stamp, and I know what we can use, the embosser from the Geiger Grimmelshausen."

"What's that?"

"This." He reached on top of the stove to the bibliophile's instrument that had been used at Weinerstrasse as a garlic press. He squeezed it on the edge of a newspaper, and produced a braille pattern. "Signifying the roundness of life, you know. Then three lines for data entry, name of the deceased, hometown, and lager number. Then again . . ." Marcus doodled on a napkin, inserting additional lines and sketches for a logo. A tiny picture of a brick hut with a large chimney took shape.

"But that's not entirely accurate."

"Perhaps we can have different images for different methods of death. Rifle, electric wire, disease. I can see a sort of biological squiggle."

"Too baroque. We want volume. Think German."

"You're right. But we also want a copyright, or equivalent, something intricate that Pinsker can't knock off too easily."

Earlier that month the distributor of goods had moved into production, aiming to cut out the middlemen. Isaac thought of this competition, which would surely be onto the DPID scam in a flash. But the residents of Weinerstrasse had the head start and their army contract was in the bag. "Can we do a watermark?"

"Tricky on a bulk basis. Better to work up one good design, etch it, stamp it. Getting plates is the hard part, but the harder it is for us to make, the harder it will be for them to duplicate."

"The Yankees say it is playing the catch-up."

Marcus looked baffled, and went to the pantry that had once contained jars of pickled mushrooms gathered from the shadowy corners of the Black Forest during the pantry owner's spring vacation. He returned with a bottle of red tomato sauce obtained from the U.S. Army dispensary. "Ketchup?"

Isaac shrugged, "They have their language."

"And we have ours."

"Yes, paper."

Within a day, Marcus had an attractive prototype, something no

Dead Person would be ashamed to carry, and the first samples to show the soldier who Morgenstern first met singing the graveyard shift.

Suddenly relieved of his noisome cemetery duties, Sergeant Necco, "like the wafer," he said, had been mysteriously promoted to Staff Lieutenant Necco, and his sole function as an officer of the U.S. Army was now to act as liaison to 44 Weinerstrasse. Somebody up above, presumably the officer with the Jacks over deuces, liked the DPID idea nearly as much as Isaac, for orders were coming in thick and fast. Every day, Lieutenant Necco brought in a new request on the same blank forms Marcus had been forging for USO chocolates.

The first two thousand moved on out, and an order for three thousand more followed on its heels.

Word spread swiftly about the new product on the paper market, and perfectly living people also discerned advantage in a DPID, so they too were asking for it, Germans and Jews united in a desire for paper that only Isaac could deliver. It was so difficult to keep track of the orders that Schimmel was moved off production into administration.

The competition at The Green Hen stared at Isaac and his crew with new respect when they waltzed in past the mob at the door for a postmidnight snack and Cognac apertif at a table reserved for them. While the triplets on the stage dropped their spangled panties and used their talented vaginas to puff smoke rings that linked together like the Ballantine Ale sign, a narrow-chinned Belgian sidled over to order two hundred DPIDs. When he was informed that there was a month-long wait for the goods, he offered to pay double the going rate for a rush delivery.

Schimmel was ready to agree, but Isaac kicked him under the table.

"Triple," the Belgian said.

Isaac leaned forward, interested, but still silent.

"Quadruple, and that's my final offer."

Isaac nodded and Schimmel took a deposit.

"What do they want it for?" Marcus wondered as they set up an assembly line to crank out the goods later that night, Schimmel to cut, Schmaljin to notch the edges, Zimmerman to use the Geiger letterpress, and Marcus himself to fill in the gaps, after which they swirled the resulting documents around the tub stained ochre with a dozen tea bags.

"Maybe they can't get arrested if they have this," Schimmel said, passing a stack leftward.

"Yeah, only buried," Isaac replied. He gazed out the window toward the darkened camp and thought of the next step while the rest worked. Isaac didn't do labor. He was the idea man. He mused over the distance until he felt Schimmel hesitating. "What's the matter?"

"The names."

"What about them?"

"I don't know that many dead people."

"Don't strain yourself," Isaac said. "Get a list of names tomorrow and use that."

"Whose names?"

"Any names."

"All they have at the Joint is the survivors."

"Why go to the Joint?"

"I know someone there, I tried to tell you that. It's . . ."

"I don't care who it is. Get their names."

"But all they have are survivors."

"I don't care who they are. You think the army can tell the difference between Moshe Pipik alive or dead? Make the names up if it's easier. We're writing fiction here."

Paper, paper, paper, and ink, and paper.

Isaac's next major task was the acquisition of more raw materials. The sale of one transit visa or even two hundred DPIDs to the desperate Belgian flaneur did not eat paper the way thousands at a shot did. The streets were littered with uncollected rubbish, but none of it was usable, nor were the multitudes of army bulletins that were issued on slick mimeo bond.

Marcus recalled the good old days when he was an employee of the Reich. He even mulled over a return to Dachau to see if the storage closet in the lager was still stocked with regiments of Waterman pens, oceans of Lubitsch brand India ink in tit-shaped flasks with nippled droppers, and forests of rag paper, each sheet as thick as a slice of rye bread. One advantage of working for the Germans was that they respected skill and gave it access to material, but George Washington was dead, and the provisions for his production were certainly ransacked in the first days after liberation. Every bogus Spam chit on the market was made from canvas that an artist could have turned into a masterpiece.

"What about the factories?"

Marcus shook his head. "I have heard that the Papiergemeinschaft is hardly in operation." It had been bombed late in the War under the Allied misimpression that it was a brewery—some strategy to do with sapping morale—and was due to go on line again, but was no longer able to meet its own needs. The factory had already used up its private supply of paper to produce chits for the wood pulp needed to produce more chits for more wood pulp.

Worse, the cartel's end product had lost credibility, since most everyone thought of paper as money and money was diminishing in value daily. When the Jews went to the theaters sprouting up all over the zone with stolen reels of the films shown first at the camps, they paid after they left instead of when they entered, because the mark was worth less by the time the final credits rolled than it was when the screen went silver. Inflation was running at one per cent an hour. And none of the manufacturers knew that Isaac and Marcus were out there as willing customers with a finer product in mind than mere cash.

That they were in the market at all was impressive, and the logical assumption was that the purveyors of one product would be the ones to find another product when the market shifted. Someone out there needed ball bearings. Everyone needed cigarettes. To get cigarettes, they needed ball bearings. To get the ball bearings they needed paper.

"We'll move on it," Isaac said, working the phones and swapping favors to dig up another afternoon's supply on a catch-as-catch-can basis.

That was the situation when Lieutenant Necco stood in the kitchen beneath a map of Luxembourg nearly as large as the nation itself, at attention, stiff as a popsicle, with only his eyes conveying bafflement, while he waited for his daily satchel. He couldn't help but be aware that the official papers he was sent to collect were being fabricated in the next room, but his orders were explicit. He accepted the bag filled with the IDs that were still soggy from their bath in the Lapsang souchong shoplifted from the English commissary, and then called for the ball bearings, which must have been waiting around the corner because a dump truck filled with gleaming silver spheres pulled up and parked moments later.

Isaac sat on the window ledge, and fiddled with the focus dial on his binoculars. He watched while the second truck arrived, also bearing U.S. Army insignia. The first driver handed the keys to the truck full of ball bearings to the second driver, and then both of them unloaded the second truck full of cigarettes. At the end of the charade, Lieutenant Necco drove away the second truck with the precious papers on the seat beside him. The first driver walked. Where the ball bearings went was anybody's guess, and everyone in Regensburg knew that more cartons of North Carolina's finest were upstairs on Weinerstrasse. What they didn't know was that they were due for delivery to Theresienstadt a day later.

The Vivant's delivery truck had also become a regular visitor to Isaac's distinguished address, arriving at intervals strictly following the army vehicles' departure.

Without military assistance, the gang itself unloaded yet more boxes of Stolichna cigarettes, whereupon Schimmel and the boys began fieldstripping and repacking the filter-tipped American cylinders with the flaky, malodorous leaves from Uzbekistan via Czechoslovakia, resealing the packages with a process Marcus devised using hot wax. That part they kept secret from Necco. His boss, Mr. Jacks Over, might frown on the adulteration of American goods. It could give the Philip Morris company a bad name if its premium brand tasted like Asian homegrown.

Within days, the cigarettes that had come from Colonel Alter were sent back to him in a form suitable for shipment to the Kremlin, where Party dignitaries puffed on the corrupt Yankee butts as a sign of status, while the genuine Grade A leaves liberated from their original cylinders were traded to the Regensburg underworld, which mixed the tobacco with kef from Morocco for sale to the prostitutes who used it to dull their senses as they labored to excite their clients.

As for the tobacco dust that covered every surface in the Weinerstrasse kitchen with a faint brown film, it was collected and rerolled into squares of newspaper and smoked by the workers. Comics smoked best while the sports pages filled with tiny columns of football boxscores tasted too medicinal. A gray smoke haze enveloped the apartment, which had broken through the living room wall to incorporate the adjacent flat, rented from Frau Manning on a chit and a carton a week.

When there was a delay in deliveries from the east, they substituted straw, which they got from Count Geiger's stables. The horses had long since been eaten, but the barnful of forgotten hay was sufficient for a season's inhalation.

In the middle of one such mission, while Schimmel and Zimmerman were busily baling, Isaac paused to stare at the giant mansion itself, looming in silent grandeur beyond the carriage house. On a moment's inspiration, he and Marcus crawled through a gap in the untended hedge that surrounded the property and hiked across an overgrown lawn. Rope-thick vines had attached themselves to the casement windows of the ground floor library, but they pulled the vines off, smacked a hole in the glass, and climbed inside the abandoned premises. Dust was everywhere except a gigantic square which revealed where an Oriental carpet had until recently graced the room. Pale rectangles on the walls showed where portraits of ancestors once presided. From the ceiling, a tangle of wires was all that remained of a Murano glass chandelier that had illuminated the room, which was normally entered by way of two huge carved walnut doors now without knobs; they were stripped and sold for brass by scavengers. Only the books bearing the stamp of the Geiger letter garlic press remained on the shelves, because no one had wanted them.

"How did people live like this?" Marcus whispered.

Before Marcus could reply, another voice answered, "I have a book on that somewhere."

Isaac spun around to see an elderly man in a maroon velvet bathrobe standing beside the enormous, knobless door with the crooked joint of one finger raised, Roused perhaps by the sound of breaking glass, he was as dusty as the floor and might have been a mummy consolidated out of floating motes come to life. It must have been the caretaker, left with the house when the count skipped to Brazil on a hastily arranged itinerary to a compliant port.

The old man dashed aross the room, straight between Isaac and

Marcus. Incredibly agile, he climbed up a library ladder set against the huge shelves and pushed himself off the damp plaster wall. Despite the decrepitude of everything else in the room, the ladder's connection to a horizontal rod must have been well-oiled, because it shot across three columns of shelves and would have gone farther if its pilot hadn't gripped ahold of a moulded walnut pilaster and brought himself and the ladder to an abrupt stop. "Here." He handed over a purple covered volume titled *On the Origin of Species*.

Marcus passed the book to Isaac and asked the caretaker-librarian, "Do you know all of these?"

"I know all of them only I don't know what any one of them means. But that's OK. Nobody does."

Isaac glanced at Marcus when the man suddenly continued from his pulpit on top of the ladder, "Do you know what your Torah means?"

Isaac replied. "I don't have the faintest idea."

"I have several Torahs. Rare specimens, salvaged from burnt synagogues. But they're hidden." He winked as if he might also have lampshades, too, for all the enthusiastic enthnographic interest he seemed to evince for Jewish culture.

Isaac looked at the title of the book and it seemed familiar. These words had penetrated into the sthetl with the advent of the Yiddish enlightenment. His brother had spoken of them as he also spoke of Marx before he donated an eye for the sake of the proletariat's future. Isaac tried to remember a scarless Alter declaiming the theory of evolution to their father, for whom such a notion was blasphemy. Isaac could still hear his older brother insisting that, "Science is not sacrilege," in the chicken-scented kitchen and then, a moment later as the aroma changed to mildew, the younger brother was able to muster the most famous of catchphrases, "Survival of the fittest."

Marcus nodded.

"Is that why Jews survive?" the old man asked from his perch. "Pardon me, but you don't look so fit."

"Hey, you should have seen me Before," Isaac laughed. Between his Yiddish and the man's German, they managed to converse.

The old man confessed, "I've had a few bad years myself."

Returning to the original question, Isaac himself asked a question. "Did Jews survive? I don't know what a Jew is anymore. I don't think that I bear any resemblance to my father or my grandfather or some ancestor with camels. Things are different now."

The old man got a cheery twinkle in his eye, raised his finger again, and posed a further question. "Is it possible that that which remains the same is the sense that nothing remains the same?"

"That's an easy paradox. But it's not valid."

"Why not, pray tell?"

Marcus spoke now, although he was starting to feel like an interloper in an asylum, mediating between Isaac and the old man who had the manner of an inmate and the vocabulary of a doctor. "Did they really say the same things in Babylonia and after Spain? Or is there a difference in the way we speak because of what happened to us? Or is it only because it occurred now that we think life is different?"

"What occurred now?" the old man asked. There was something about the wide-eyed naivete of the question that made Isaac understand that he meant it literally.

Nearly speechless, Marcus tried to gesture to himself and Isaac, "It!"

"No," the old man insisted with such vigor that he nearly fell off the ladder, inadvertently propelling himself a few feet down the wall of books to a shelf of Goethe, Schiller, Hoffman, and other German classics concluding with Heine bound in black. "When my father was count before me . . ."

"Whoa!" Isaac shouted.

"What?"

"You're the count?"

"Why not?"

Isaac didn't say that his conversational companion was on a list of the most wanted collaborators in the entire zone. The current titleholder had owned munitions factories, established by some distant progenitor, that not merely used but actively sought and consumed cheap labor from the lager. A "Geiger slave" was known to be as doomed as any toddler directed leftward at early selection. Yet the man so was clearly crazy that even Isaac hardly held his crimes against him. He was an idiot, and he wasn't breeding. He was obviously the end of the line. That was why he allowed some thief to abscond with the bibliopress. He couldn't read his ancestors' books and did not value them. If the silly Jews wanted to empty his shelves, his larder, or his stable, it made no difference to him.

Speaking as if Count Geiger wasn't present, Marcus explained, "Like Ludvig of Bavaria. They have a tradition. Each generation produces another loony royal. But another generation nonetheless follows. Does that mean that the country is fit?"

"Amalek." Isaac murmured the lovely syllables that recalled the child on the motorcycle he had overthrown on his short passage out from Aspenfeld. The legend of Amalek was that Jew-killers were coeternal with Jews; they emerged from a single tribe that was slated for annihilation, but was allowed to survive by an innate Jewish weakness that could not fully effect the divinely mandated slaughter. Over the millenia, Amalek replicates himself once and again, reappearing in the guise of Crusader or Caliph, to do endless battle with the chosen people, to be resolved when the Messiah arrives or the sun explodes. The boy on the motorcycle, taught a lesson in survival by Isaac Kaufman, might yet overcome his shyness, and ride his vehicle into town, as if on a white donkey, to proclaim the advent of the Fourth Reich.

"Don't talk philosophy to me," the old man said. "I studied with Kant—at least I think I did—and you know what the eunuch of Königsberg taught me . . ."

"Yes," Isaac interrupted his senior. "I think I do." He was ready to call outgo from the Hen for another delivery of maiden flesh, but first he answered the question, "In any case, there is pleasure."

"Yes, that's what keeps you fit."

Marcus nodded.

Isaac said, "Call me Darwin."

"I have only one question," the count said. "What color wine does one drink with straw, red or white?"

And so the organization grew. New recruits did drudge work under the supervision of Schimmel and Berger while Marcus relaxed by studying a history of the late Middle Ages on loan from the count's library. Isaac was busy making deals at the Vivant and the Green Hen, sipping Chartreuse, arranging for girls, and contemplating the future. Money was as easy as smoke as long as paper came in one side to emerge from the other as documents, to be further transformed into ball bearings, into cigarettes, into more cigarettes, into more cash, into more paper for more DPIDs.

Between day laborers and customers, so many unfamiliar faces passed through the entrance foyer at 44 Weinerstrasse that Marcus had to develop a system of knocks to identify and discriminate among visitors, and then they took over still another apartment in the building, hungry now for space, seeking Lebensraum. One after another room fell to the gang, until the last German family stood with their quilts and silver candlesticks in a cart, packed off to stay with in-laws in Munich, blaming their dispossession correctly on the Jews, and it was only the boys and Frau Mannheim in the house that had once been home to half the local postal service.

Of course, it was a bubble, bound to burst, so that even as Marcus entertained Isaac with tales of the Dutch tulip mania, the younger man grasped the analogy and smiled.

"You need dental work," Marcus pointed out, not for the first time.

Isaac ignored the advice and added to Morgenstern's gloomy outlook, "Not to mention that these are onetime sales." There was no way to expire the DPIDs and require new ones, but the initial buyers market was so huge that they didn't worry. The Belgian picked up his merchandise and ordered more, and a call came in for more from the Yankees. Schimmel was set to tracking down individual sheets of paper lying underutilized in the bottoms of drawers from Trieste to Potsdam, Marcus oversaw the assembly line, and Isaac still thought.

Pale, mournful Fishl, his oversize head stuffed with the accumulated rabbinical lore of the ages imparted to him before the rabbis themselves departed to a better world, was a sad, solitary presence that reeked of Yiddish regret. He moped about the flat, eating the same meals the other occupants did, but with an embarrassing lager frenzy, as if the only way he could be sure that the food wouldn't disappear was to devour it. Then he stared at the plate that had replaced the battered tin mug that had been his sole possession since 1943, transformed now into a China miracle with an etching of the Alps stained by a last drop of mucilaginous gravy, which he promptly lapped up with a dog's heavy tongue.

Fishl slept on the same mattresses the rest of the gang did, twitching, ready for the cane or the lash to splinter a dream of cinnamon hair and Torah.

The others had by no means forgotten the War or their lives Before. Once, the color of the whiskey in a tumbler reminded Schimmel of his father's hat. Once, the wave of a girl on the stage of The Green Hen echoed the fluttering fingertips of another girl whom Schmaljin had last seen going off into a transport from Westerbork to oblivion. Berger remembered his jewels and Zimmerman still woke sometimes with the stink of a Polish barn in his nose. All but Isaac were subject to the whims of memory, but nonetheless they swiftly adapted to the new world, and Schimmel gulped down the hat-colored liquor, while Schmaljin summoned the inner strength to wave flirtatiously back to the girl on the stage as if the Valkyrie tart was a shy Jewish virgin. The ground rules that had enabled them to survive had changed; there were new rules in the post-War world. And just as they adhered with a fierce tenacity to life in the lager, they used that insane energy to new purpose After.

The only luxury Fishl allowed himself was the toilet. He spent hours sitting, just sitting, on the porcelain basin, his mind as empty as his bladder and intestine, until the others had to insist he take his business elsewhere. They rattled the knob and pounded on the door, infuriated when an unusually sly Fishl replied from his throne. "That's not the secret knock."

He remained sitting until he heard harmonica music that seemed to vibrate underneath him, the clear pool rippling with tidal affect, bubbles ascending from the toilet's sole orifice to break like notes at the surface. It was American jazz that traveled upstairs through the pipes before the soldiers with their transistor radio that broadcast live performances from a USO show in Munich came into sight.

Manhattan . . .
That Satin doll.

"What do we need him for?" Schimmel asked.

Marcus tried to answer with the glibness he was picking up in café society. "We have a leader, a driver, a forger. But remember, every gang needs a rabbi."

At which point their leader concluded the conversation. Isaac stepped off of his windowsill, shook a limb numbed by rest, and said. "Alter sent him." That was the ultimate answer.

The harmonica reverberated a last plaintive wail at the door, and the radio snapped off abruptly, mid-tune, although Fishl could still feel it vibrating through the bowl under his sphincter. A moment later, they all heard the special military knock, three and then two, Jacks over deuces. It was Lieutenant Necco at the jamb, point man of a phalanx of stiff-lipped recruits whose hair was shorter than the residents.

"Need a trim?" Isaac asked.

"You know what I need," Necco answered gruffly.

"How many?"

"Five."

"Done."

Isaac had been on the telephone all morning, to connections across the zone in search of paper. From Salzburg to Düsseldorf, he had scoured the area and finally arrived at a temporary, if not final, solution. "Tuesday good?"

"Monday's better."

Isaac replied, "No problem." It wouldn't do to let on that material was a big problem, and that he needed the contact to be bona fide. Once the Yanks sensed weakness, they might seek to augment their supply of DPIDs elsewhere.

"Here," Necco suddenly announced, lifting one finger up past his olive drab shoulder, signaling two of his privates forward to deposit a large tin in front of Isaac.

The tin was the size and shape of a five-gallon bucket and it was filled with an intensely pungent brown powder that immediately suffused the atmosphere with its acrid smell. Schimmel was already on his knees, his hand scooping up the powder, allowing it to sift between his fingers like sand on the beach. He didn't have the faintest idea what it was and neither did Isaac, who said, "What's this . . . for?" adding the last word lest the soldiers perceive his ignorance.

"It's a present," Necco answered. As unprofessional as Schimmel, he couldn't keep from glancing down and feasting on the powder with his eyes. "For services rendered," Necco recited the lines that had been scripted for him. "And those yet to come."

Isaac paused to reflect before answering. Then he said, "Thanks."

Necco about-faced and lead his troop down the stairs, where the harmonica resumed play the moment the private with the radio touched the tiled foyer, joined by a tremulous saxophone solo.

Take the A Train.

The soldiers were getting looser. Ever since Eisenhower had marched through the Brandenburg Gate, the only danger they had been in was from a buried mine. As for that, Sergeant Herman Weinglass said, "Chances are better you'll get reamed by a taxi on Linden Boulevard." It wasn't as weird as the Pacific, where there were stories of Japs in the woods fighting on after Hirohito went down. This was Europe. Life was good in '46. They even forgot that the Krauts had been shooting at them the previous winter.

Frau Mannheim's sheets billowed with the waves of music and a breeze from the northwest.

The landlady tried to keep clean, not easy in a world of vermin. Without a husband, lost somewhere in the east, all she had to cling to among the values of the Fatherland was detergent. Despite the tobacco dust from the factory upstairs that filtered into her soup and the keys of her mother's Bösendorfer baby grand and everywhere else, she fought as valiantly as the soldiers at Stalingrad in the re- lentless battle against filth. She looked at the Jewish tenants who provided her with the income to purchase detergent, and shook her head. She had offered to wash their clothes, but the men upstairs didn't change from week to week.

Only Fishl was clean, and when he wasn't on the toilet, he seemed to enjoy helping her spread and clip the laundry onto the line that cut across the yard from the side door of the house to a leafless aspen at the edge of the property.

Frau Mannheim checked his hands first, as if suspicious of print- smudged Jewish fingers, or perhaps wishing to compare their whorls with the pattern on a DPID card. But after a long séance on the toilet, Fishl also took pleasure in immersing his hands in the other, less-used basin. His fingers were as clean as his soul and met with the stern laundress's approval. "You are a gentleman, Herr Fishl."

He nodded.

"Not like . . . them." Frau Mannheim shook her head at the Yids upstairs.

Isaac waved from his window seat. He heard everything, saw everything. "Yes," he called down, "if we weren't so dirty, we wouldn't have needed showers."

Frau Manheim ran toward the house, trembling, for even *Der Stern* was now publishing Elizabeth Smith Moss's photos of empty showers without drains. All that was missing was an advertisement for disinfectant.

Inadvertently, she left Fishl alone to his task, but the scholar didn't mind. Hanging laundry was nearly as relaxing as sitting on the toilet. Clothespins extending from his mouth like great wooden tusks, he carefully shook out the landlady's underwear, saving the best for last, proceeding onto the snowy mound of sheets in a wicker hamper. One by one he unfurled the vast cotton squares and clipped them neatly to the line, three clothespins per item until the job was finished and he could lean back to contemplate his labors. Frau Mannheim usually kept a further watch to make sure that vagrants who didn't care whether it was dry yet didn't run off with the wash.

Inside, Marcus said, "I don't like her."

"I believe the feeling is mutual."

"Shall we kick her out?"

"La Madame serves a purpose, a cover. We protect her; she protects us. Its an ideal union, Germans and Jews working together to skin the Yankees."

The great squares of white cloth floating up and snapping back reminded Fishl of kittels, the pure white robes worn first at one's marriage, once yearly thereafter on Yom Kippur, and then set aside to be worn for the last time as a shroud if the owner should meet his own personal assignation with the eternal before the next year was out. Fishl's father and the other men of Ostrowiec wore their kittels, so different from their normal black gabardines, on the fast-slow walk to shul on Yom Kippur, as if they were ghosts gliding through the muddy streets.

Fishl saw them again in the sheets fluttering around him, more like angels than ghosts, convening in heavenly discourse. Each sheet seemed to respond to its neighbor as the wind moved them in sequence down the line, some swaying in languorous agreement, others flapping in celestial discord. Angels were an argumentative cohort, but they always wore white.

What did God wear?

A brown shirt.

A plane overhead banked away from the military landing strip outside of town.

"Nu," Isaac called down to Fishl. "Are you ready to earn your keep?"

"You have a chore for me, Isaac?"

"Yes, my child, and it's not much harder than folding linen."

Fishl turned red. He remembered his mother, arms thrust deep in a tub of scalding water. "What is it?"

Isaac gazed after the military airplane until it disappeared into the clouds, and looked back down across the yard toward the road. "You think perhaps I should tell the whole neighborhood?"

"Sorry," Fishl murmured, and started to move toward the front door when he remembered the sheets. He looked up at Isaac and asked, "Do you think I should wait until they're dry?"

Isaac used the same gesture Lieutenant Necco had used to his troops, a single finger beckoning with authority.

"Here," he said when Fishl arrived upstairs a moment later, "you are to exchange suitcases at the train station in Frankfurt. The contact's name is Lothar. He will be wearing a gray hat with a red feather. You will wear a gray hat with a green feather."

"But I don't have a hat with a green feather."

Isaac gave his trademark smile, as if he would forget such a detail. That hat was hanging on a nail hammered into the middle of a map of the Austro-Hungarian Empire. He continued, "You will each have a suitcase with a red handle. Yours will contain money, so don't let it go. His will contain twelve reams of twenty-pound bond. You do not have to confirm this, but if Lothar is not there at precisely one o'clock return immediately. Do you understand?"

"What's not to understand?"

"Here is the ticket for a return trip. You go, you come back. Take the eleven-fifteen A.M. train. It takes a long time; it stops everywhere. You should arrive at eight-oh-seven the following morning. Stand beside the information kiosk at precisely eleven o'clock and take the one-fifteen back. Got it?"

"What's not to get?"

"Don't screw up," Schimmel added, deft enough after practice to roll a cigarette with one hand.

When Fishl returned downstairs to collect the wash, the sheets were gone.

CHAPTER 10

The kitchen was filled with flies. A few heavy black bombers buzzed around the untouched pot of overcooked kohlrabi and squash, while a few with a taste for sweets perched, rubbing their forelegs together, on the nickel-plated rim of the bucket of pudding that had been made from Lieutenant Necco's brown powder mixed with sweet cream and sugar. These bloated flies weren't so bad. Far worse were the minions of tinier insects—flies? gnats? it was hard to tell—that zipped across the periphery of Marcus Morgenstern's vision like rays of black light. Sometimes he'd feel one land on his ear; he'd slap his head, spin, and catch sight of a wing crossing the edge of the map of Shinto shrines newly acquired from a Japanese military attaché to the Reich, stuck in Zone Three with the surrender, eager to move east, in need of a visa.

"Just tell them the _J_ stands for Jap," Isaac told Mr. Kazitomo as he slipped him the expired documents of the Rabbi of Bilgoraj, who wouldn't be needing them anymore.

Work on the assembly line usually paused for dinner, but nobody was hungry that first night of the flies. The squash turned soft in its pot and the fingers of the hungerless refugees kept rolling throughout the evening. More cigarettes were produced in Liebknecht that night than in Winston-Salem.

Every once in a while, the buzzing of the flies would grow so intense that Marcus would furl up a newspaper and stalk the kitchen, slamming any flat surface that served as a temporary landing field, leaving, if lucky, a pudgy black corpse and a cloud of tobacco dust. The others laughed that he was spoiled; in the schools they had graduated from, one grew accustomed to the flies attracted to the dropouts.

All the while, the workers ground their teeth, cheeks sliding back and forth on a horizontal plane. Even Isaac was susceptible to this infectious tic; his stubs rattled a xylophonic counterpoint to the sandpapery rasp of Marcus and Schimmel. Their jaws ached from the incessant motion; it felt as if particles of bone had come loose and wedged between their molars. They paused only to puff on or stub out another cigarette.

"How much do we get for these?"

"Ten marks each."

"Maybe we should use five-mark notes for paper?"

"Then we could buy marks for cigarettes to make more cigarettes to get more marks."

The flies formed a squadron of black warplanes passing across the map of the Continent behind the refrigerator.

"This stuff is contagious," Schimmel said, smacking his lips.

When Necco made his delivery, he was so awkward—a schoolboy more than a soldier—that Isaac couldn't tell if it was the officer's own recompense for the star-blessed meeting by the cemetery that had boosted his military career or a gift from his anonymous higher-ups eager to ingratiate themselves with the producers of such high-grade creative paper. Although it swiftly became clear from Necco's manner that it was duty rather than charity that led him to make his presentation, the gift itself was still a mystery.

The crew knew better than to ask questions without Isaac's OK, but when Necco finally departed, they asked each other. "What is this stuff?"

"I don't know, but he seemed very proud of it."

"Do you suppose we eat it?" Berger took a spoonful and spat it out.

Isaac wet his finger, swiped it across the surface of the tin, and licked it off. Berger was right. It was miserably bitter. He rubbed his tongue clear of the venemous residue and said. "Gunpowder, perhaps."

"No." Dr. Morgenstern said. "It is clearly organic and digestable, even if it tastes like zinc."

"Drugs?"

"Not his style," Morgenstern shook his head, referring to Necco, although who knew what the style of Jacks Over Deuces really was?

"Very nice. He left us something that we don't know what to do with."

"A spice, perhaps."

Zimmerman, who had become the staff cook at 44 Weinerstrasse, tried to mix it with kasha, but all he produced was an inedible mess.

Schimmel, usually the first to concede, said, "Let's just ask Necco."

"No, he'll think we're rubes."

"We are rubes."

"But he doesn't know that."

"Look, it's simple. If it's bitter, make it sweet."

"My mother."

"What?"

"My mother," Isaac repeated, as he dominated the conversation from his seat on the windowill.

"What about your mother?" Marcus asked.

"It's like my mother said whenever one of us was sick. If your belly's empty, fill it. If it's full, empty it. If your head is hot, make it cold. If it's cold, make it hot. So now we say, if it's bitter, make it sweet."

"That's what God said, too," Herr Doktor Morgenstern expounded, "About life . . . if it's sweet, make it bitter."

"God and my mother," Isaac smiled. "They're both dead."

It took several further experiments that smoked up the kitchen until Zimmerman contrived a simple recipe to render the bitter powder palatable for both men and flies. Not that the men were so hungry anymore, but their reflexes were honed to consume whatever was edible, especially something that appeared to be such a delicacy. If the Americans thought this was the greatest taste on earth, it behooved the Jews to try it out, to learn to love it. The only way they could acquire this peculiar taste, however, was by ladling the granular crystals into a pot with a gallon of cream and several cups of sugar and stirring until it attained the proper consistency.

The gang was uncommonly energetic that night, trying to figure out how to overcome their latest obstacle. Even with Fishl due to return from his simple-minded mission with a suitcase full of paper, the additional reams wouldn't last out the month.

They discussed this around the table as they each took another bowlful of the brown pudding.

"Could we ask the army for supplies?"

"Never."

"Necco has to know . . . I do not mean that he should be informed, but that he probably knows already."

"What he knows and what he admits he knows are different. They require a paper wall between us. Once they don't need it, poof, we're out of business, so we better be ready for the next stage."

"With what?"

"We've got to expand beyond the military orbit. Paper is bought by the army. Cigarettes are distributed by the army. We should find something that's outside the army. Something for civilian consumption. Something that anyone craves."

"What?"

Isaac looked toward the gold in the distance. One sliver of the treasure was visible where the tarp had slipped. There it was, pure wealth reduced to its most primitive essence, a block of metal with no functional value whatsoever—unless one considered its role in Continental dentistry.

But it was too early. They weren't anywhere near ready for a raid that daring. Yet Isaac had already begun to wonder: Who else might share his obsession? What other knight-errant, wearing a three-piece suit or three stars on a khaki shoulder, might be girding his loins to set off on a quest for the same grail? "We'll think," he said.

"Think, think. All you do is think, Isaac." Schimmel was growing brazen. His mouth twitched with regret, but Isaac paid him as little heed as an impertinent child.

"So go," he replied. "Do!"

Despite the lateness of the hour, they were still wakeful so Schimmel and the new recruits took Isaac's advice. They headed off for an evening at the Green Hen, while Isaac himself called in for company.

Two knocks, two girls, first rate merchandise, blonde as the sun, arrived shortly afterward, but this encounter was not to be as anatomical as others. The girls sat, slouched on the Biedermeier couch in the living room that had once hosted their acrobatic performances, guzzling the booze ordered along with them in return for the promise of a carton of smokes, while Isaac and Marcus talked and demanded talk in return. Instead of penetration, there was conversation, and Isaac and Marcus wore the girls out.

"Tell me about your boyfriends, again, dear hearts," Marcus urged with the inquisitive drone of a psychiatrist rather than a dentist demanding, "Open wide."

The dead boys of Scotch ancestry toppled as the girls told of sweet beardless youths they once knew who disappeared in the trenches of North Africa. Confession followed, from Dad's first affiliation with the Party to the girls' own infatuation and subsequent disillusionment.

"Tell me, then, how glad you are to be here, with the true master race," Isaac insisted.

"Oh so very glad," the girls obliged, and repeated until they fell asleep at either end of the couch, like human bookends, as Isaac and Marcus continued to talk.

"We need new markets."

"Our production is outstripping our sales here."

"We're buying more than we're selling *here*," Isaac gestured toward the girls.

When Schimmel and the rest of the boys returned, they weren't sleepy either. Somewhere toward dawn, when even the hardiest were used to dropping off to rest, they recommenced work on the cigarettes.

After a breakfast of more brown pudding, they passed a day of further endeavor, another night out at the The Green Hen, while another dawn rose.

All of them remained awake except Fishl, gone on his mission, dozing fitfully in a railroad passenger car, who might have been represented on one of Isaac's maps as a black mark chugging across Baden-Württemberg, en route to his liaison in the Frankfurt station.

The fact was that when Fishl left, they stopped sleeping. It was too ridiculous to attribute a cause and effect to the "rabbi's" departure, but the connection was obvious. This led to more talk, of travel, their place in the commerce of the era, and of Fishl himself.

"He's smart."

"So, what are we gonna do, start a university?"

"Intelligence is a commodity that can always be stockpiled."

"I don't like it. Does he have relatives?"

"Only dead ones."

"Him and Stalin."

"I did not say it to justify him."

"Why did you say it, then?"

"Because you asked."

"He's polite."

"A quality we could do with more."

The gang spent the day heedless of natural rhythms, continuing to talk, unable to stop talking, as Weinerstrasse's daily routine went from morning milk wagons through daily commerce onto curious nocturnal activity when enormous, dark tankers slid through the shadows like oversize bullets, heading toward some secret rendezvous at the Liebknechtwerke. Come the sun again, they ate a healthy breakfast of the bepuddinged brown powder Necco had left them.

Assuming Fishl's imminent return, the gang stayed awake into the next day, still talking, ceaselessly jabbering, as if their mouths had been sealed for three years and they had to spew forth any dialogue restrained until now, talking business, sex, and politics under a blueprint of the floorplan of the Yalta Hotel where Churchill, Stalin, and Roosevelt divvied up the world. Any maps produced after that meeting would have different-shaped shadings of pink and lime green and pale yellow, but nothing had changed at the Liebknecht center, except the residents' sleeping habits.

It was Dr. Morgenstern who first broached the health issue he thought should be of concern. "This can't be good for us."

"What?" Isaac asked, knowing full well that after his crew closed down the cafés at dawn, they bounced off the walls during the day.

"You know."

"At least a lot of work is getting done," Isaac replied, because no matter what frenzies of dialogue, the production line moved on apace.

"People are meant to sleep. People need sleep."

"Well, the Joint seems to think we're a different kind of people, maybe they're right."

"That reminds me . . ." Schimmel started.

Marcus opened the window to try to rid the kitchen of the flies. "Why are there more of these damn things inside than out?"

"Listen," Schimmel said, hopping on one foot, so eager to get the words out that he bit the tip of this tongue.

"Take this," Morgenstern said, handing Schimmel a swatter.

Isaac didn't tell Marcus that he didn't see the flies. He was too busy with his own hallucinations. Instead of Zimmerman mixing another batch of sweet brown pudding, he thought he saw his mother at the stove.

"Let's do something," Berger suggested.

"What you want to do?"

"I don't know. What do you want to do?"

"Go to America."

"Closest we have is the Hen."

"Is that what America is like?"

"Sure."

"The man from the Seventh Armored told me they can't tell the difference between the Hen and a place called the Copa."

"What I heard . . ." Schimmel started again.

"What are we waiting for?"

"Fishl!" Isaac replied. It was hard not to wonder where their courier was, but he could have been represented as a dot on the map, stalled in a railroad tunnel between Würzburg and Karlstadt.

Five minutes earlier the train had entered the parabolic mouth of the Oberlicht Passage, which had been hacked into the mountain so that the tracks bearing disagreeable wartime cargoes would avoid intruding on the nearby summer estates of Party dignitaries. Fishl had been gazing out the window, absorbed in the serenity of the landscape. Moonlit trees were emerging from silhouette to foliage before his eyes. He saw the hook-nosed profile of the mountain itself looming, and then everything went dark. The overhead lights flickered, but did not go on; the rumbling of the wheels echoed in the enclosure. He could sense rather than see the granitic walls of the tunnel an arm's length from the side of the car, and then the train halted. The silence was immense. If he had been claustrophobic, it might have seemed like a coffin.

"Come on," Isaac said.

"I don't know."

"Let's see."

Like a group of American teenagers bored by the same Friday night routine, they filled Berger's car—he had bought it from the Wehrmacht cadet whose pockets the keys were left jingling in when the War came to its sad conclusion—en route to the same destination as always, the only hot spot in town. Marcus drove while Isaac sat in front with him, and the other five crammed into the back. The car tilted on the cobbles beside the opera and nosed in beside the Green Hen. As usual, there was a crowd by the padded doorway under the sign of the fowl.

"Mr. Marlboro!" the doorman waved the group in past the hoi polloi as Isaac handed him three cigarettes as a tip. It was good to know one's place; Isaac felt a moment of comfort. For a second, he could forget that Fishl was six hours late and nowhere in sight.

Fishl could hear the stirrings of his fellow passengers, and the hurried footsteps of what might have been the conductor moving toward the engine room. Then duration lost meaning, and Fishl couldn't tell if five minutes or five hours passed. He may have dozed off. Somewhere between dawn and the following day, he began to perceive images that were clearly not present in the darkened train. He couldn't even tell if he was dreaming, half-conscious, or dreaming that he was half-conscious. He wasn't sure if the infrequent flickering was in the hundred-ton vehicle stalled in the Oberlicht Passage or the ethereal train of his sleep. He saw cinnamon hair, and said, "Rivka?"

The Hen was even more crowded inside, but the maître d' brought a round table from the rear and fit the Weinterstrasse Brigade into a space beside the stage, inches from the troupe performing a salute to the USA, complete with star-spangled bloomers.

"So, they finally left the Vivant," Berger said.

"That's business," Marcus replied.

The Emcee was done up in false Uncle Sam beard that reminded Isaac of a rabbi, caterwauling, "I'm a yank me doodle dandy. Born on the Furze of July," while streamers of red, white, and blue confetti shot from cannons in the background.

Plumes of more mundane cigarette smoke rose from the crowd; every puff was a mark as far as Isaac was concerned. Occasionally a shriek of hysterical laughter burst out from the undertone of convivial chat and fervent negotiation conducted across the bar, which glistened with the sloshings of beer under the lights, which strobed in synch to their own particular codes.

A moment later there was a hush that transcended the clatter, emanating from the door. Word swept like a wind that it was the police.

"No problem," the Emcee called out over the heads of the audience. "Just clean fun. Well maybe not so clean, but fun nonetheless. Join the fun, gendarmes."

But it wasn't the police, rather a different authority. It was Americans, not in uniform. It was Mr. Foyle of the Joint, and Miranda.

Isaac's eyes widened.

"What do you mean, it's closed! There are a hundred people here." Foyle was arguing with the maître d'.

"A private party, Sir. By invitation only."

"This isn't the Stork Club."

Through the smoky haze, Miranda's voice rang clear, "If they don't want us, Alan . . . ?"

"Klaus!" Isaac raised a finger to the maître d', who turned his back on the intruders and was beside the table in a second.

"I'm sorry, Sir, it is these foreigners. They do not know their place."

"They're our guests."

The maître d' spun as if on a pivot, raised his own finger, the soul of hospitality. "This way, Madame and Monsieur."

As Foyle followed by a reluctant Miranda entered the room, Marcus turned with surprise to Isaac, "You know them?"

Schimmel said, "I tried to tell you they were in Regensburg."

"Fool!" Isaac hissed through a mouth clenched shut, and the teeth clattered like castanets behind the pursed lips.

The maître d' whisked two chairs out from under lesser patrons at an adjacent table and set them up alongside Morgenstern.

"Alan Foyle, Joint Distribution Committee, my partner and cousin, Marcus Morgenstern."

Marcus stood up and shook Foyle's hand and bowed to Miranda. "And the beautiful woman?"

The beautiful woman was looking sideways at the stage, where the curtain had risen on a tableau of Betsy Ross showing George Washington a few sample flags she had designed. One was a hammer and sickle, one a twisted cross.

Marcus said, "I don't believe that I've had the pleasure."

Miranda couldn't help staring as George said, "I was thinking of something more like this," and dropped his pants to reveal star-spangled drawers. Months out of Manhattan and she was nearly used to the sight of dead people. It was the living who repelled her.

Someone bumped into the edge of Fishl's seat.

Fishl could smell something he had only smelled once in the dark the night he had been married. It was the scent of skin, and now he smelled it again, together with the aroma of burnt flesh.

A peasant a row ahead of him was cracking a chicken leg and munching. But it wasn't seared chicken Fishl was smelling. Another flicker, another flash, the dream was turning nightmare. He saw cinnamon hair cropped short and an outstretched arm with a brand. "Rivka!" he screamed in a desperate, futile attempt to wake himself.

Schimmel gently distracted Miranda from her unpleasant reverie, "Miss Karl?"

Recalled to the conventions, Miranda found the composure to answer, "Hello, Moshe. Any luck in locating your family?"

"Moshe?" Isaac clucked. He had never known Schimmel's first name.

Moshe held a wavering hand outward, but was compelled to stop when the action on the stage moved into high gear. George was spanking Betsy, declaring. "Thirteen stripes for the bad girl."

Miranda closed her eyes.

"It's just flesh and blood," Isaac said.

"More flesh than blood," Miranda replied.

"You've been speaking with my friend?" Isaac said to Miranda, signaling for another round.

"It's my job."

"Yes, but it's not his." Isaac cast a scowl at the ecstatic Schimmel.

"I told you I saw her. I tried to tell you back in the apartment, Isaac," Schimmel explained.

"Schmuck."

"Where'd you think I got the list of names from? You told me to get them anywhere. The Joint opened up here last week. She came from Aspenfeld."

"Don't be upset, Moshe," Miranda said, and to Isaac. "I was glad to see him. I like to know what has become of my clients."

"A client," Marcus whistled appreciatively.

"I am so happy that you found your relative in Theresienstadt."

After a quick, reflexive glare at Schimmel, the obvious source of this information, Isaac replied, "You do know everything."

"I try."

"I succeed."

"But you didn't know we were here."

"No," Isaac conceded.

"Or that we have been looking for you all week."

Isaac had been bouncing off the walls of the apartment on Weinerstrasse since Fishl had left. And where was he?

"Hello?" the young woman with cinnamon hair answered.

"Rivka?" he moaned again, aware that he was now talking as well as seeing and smelling in his sleep.

"That is my name," she replied in the dark.

The image remained in Fishl's head as the absolute blackness surrounded him like a quilt. If he could talk to his beloved in his sleep, that was fine. He had not had a night so restful in years. He hoped that he would never wake up, although he fully understood the importance his new associates placed on his journey. Suddenly, the train jerked forward, and gradually began to build up speed.

Forests were decimated, factories devastated. Paper of any sort, for newsprint or toilets, was hard to come by. The success of Fishl's mission was imperative. Paper turned into ball bearings, ball bearings into cigarettes, cigarettes into marks, marks into shit as inflation reached insane proportions unless the marks could be exchanged quickly for whatever hard goods were available, which could be turned into plans to snatch . . . gold. Isaac had gold on the brain. Ever since Fishl left, ever since they stopped sleeping, he could hardly track the forks and branches his thinking took, but the foundation remained the same. Gold!

"You still haven't introduced us, cousin."

Jolted, Isaac realized he had been staring at Miranda's neck, where a chain terminating in a thin gold Star of David nestled against the flesh. She was cringing as if the star was aflame, leaning back away from the brand-hot symbol, allowing it to hang and sway between her breasts. Alan Foyle still held her arm firmly.

"Marcus Morgenstern," Isaac replied, "meet a woman who has unknown access to information."

Marcus said, "A pleasure."

"A pleasure," repeated the Emcee, stepping onto the proscenium, a spotlight on his ruffled shirt, "to entertain the distinguished American representatives working so hard to assist their unfortunate brethren." Everyone knew the Joint, and the power of their cash. The Germans wished they had a Joint of their own.

Schimmel held her chair while Miranda sat down at the table, her left hand cupped over her right fist as if she was trapping a cricket at her family's country house in Connecticut, while Isaac hunched forward, trying to slow down the whirligig of his mind.

On stage, George Washington pulled down his underpants. The skit was short on character development and moved directly into hardcore action as Betsy cooed, "You must be the father of this country."

"How do you enjoy the show?" Isaac grinned.

Miranda was silent, head bravely facing foresquare onto the stage, eyes clearly focused elsewhere.

"Just an entertainment for us leisure-starved boychiks," Isaac pressed. "Better than those movies you brought us."

"I am sorry that you did not appreciate our efforts."

"Sadomasochistic fantasies are prevalent among the survivors," Foyle said, as if on a panel at The New School.

"So what brings you here?" Marcus asked.

"Everybody comes to Rick's."

Isaac met this with a stare.

"Just a joke," Foyle said.

"A reference to an American movie," Miranda explained. "But, I forgot, you prefer live entertainment."

"Have pity, dear lady. I, too, am but flesh, if you prick me, do I not bleed?"

Foyle looked baffled now.

Morgenstern told him, "It's a reference."

Miranda turned to Isaac as if the performance no longer existed and declared, "You'd bleed chits."

"Now, now," Foyle tried to calm her.

Isaac said, "We're onto bigger things, now."

This was the opportunity Foyle was waiting for. He let go of Miranda's arm and turned to Isaac. "I know," he said, "That's why we're here, tonight. I want some."

"Some what?" The Lucky Boys were confusing. Foyle wasn't military, but he was as lucky as a boy got, Jew or not. It was almost easier with the Germans. One knew where one stood.

Foyle got down to business, "Perhaps you have heard of Brichah?"

Morgenstern whispered to Isaac, "The illegal aliyah to Palestine. Some of our papers get them to Italy, ships leave for Cyprus. There's talk of a British blockade."

Despite their preferential treatment in the DP centers, and despite the Joint's desire to keep its charges manageably under wing, more and more of the refugees were leaving places like Aspenfeld and Feldafing and making their way to the cities. Ports of departure were humming. The aliyah flowed through Leghorn and Brindisi, while the fortunate few at the top of the list to Montreal, Buenos Aires, and New York headed swiftly for Le Havre and Lisbon. Those without connections stayed in the pit of the cauldron. A very few with the connections to leave chose to remain there where their knowledge and credentials were the greatest.

Isaac had heard. He waved Marcus away and said, "So you ship dead Jews to the promised land, bury them, and fertilize the desert. I've heard that bonemeal is good for the crops."

"Yes," Miranda said, "I've never seen grass as green as the lawn at Majdanek."

Isaac winked. He was glad to see that she could be as tough as he was.

"We need help," she said. "We rely on Jews to help Jews."

"Haven't you heard, we only help dead Jews."

"Call it what you want, General."

"I'm no general."

"They," she gestured to the group surrounding Isaac, "seem to think you are."

"They don't know anything."

Foyle cut to the chase. "I still need help. Certain sympathetic embassies will endorse certain less than authentic documents, *if* we can deliver them."

"Fine, we'll help you. *If* you meet our price."

Marcus sipped at a green Chartreuse. He knew that Isaac had authorized plenty of visas for Germans. So why not Jews? Or was it not the Joint? Or was it not anyone who worked with Miranda? After the drink went down, Marcus continued to grind his teeth.

The flies had followed Marcus from the kitchen to the café. He swiped at them until he noticed that nobody else seemed bothered, but he didn't dare ask if he was the only one who saw them. One landed on his nose. He threw back a double of liqueur, but he knew that when they returned home, he still wouldn't be able to sleep.

Suddenly, there was a stranger hovering beside Miranda. Isaac recognized him as a young, brown-eyed Jew with the look of the lagers who also frequented the cafés, although how he gained entrance Isaac never understood, since he clearly did not have any money or friends. He always sat alone in a corner, nursing a single drink and taking notes in a spidery, illegible script. This made everyone else nervous until they dubbed him with a derogatory nickname, Der

Schreiber. The Writer. Once, he had approached Isaac about a visa, but without money, Isaac rebuffed him. In fact, he disliked him immediately, but Miranda seemed to know him. At least, he knew her. He was kissing her hand and gushing, "Madame, thank you."

"Benya," she declared, with a shocking warmth in her voice that cut through Isaac as if she had shrieked, "Raus!"

Too enthralled by Miranda to notice her companions, he gushed, "Thank you, thank you so much. I received the visa today. I was coming to the office tomorrow to thank you, but," he paused, ashamed, "I did not expect to see you here."

"That makes two of us, Benya. There are people who simply find themselves in a place like this, who are different than those who thrive on such an atmosphere. By the way, have you met Mr. Isaac Kaufman?"

Benya faced Isaac and turned cold. Then he nodded, turned back to Miranda, and said, "Yes, when I attempted to purchase a visa from him myself. Unfortunately, I did not have the requisite finances."

"Der Schreiber," Isaac acknowledged.

Miranda was surprised, "So you know Benya's work?"

"I know that he sits here with a notebook. I must assume that we are both in the paper business."

"But do you know his book? It is remarkable."

"I'm afraid he's never asked me to read the remarkable text."

"It's called *Farmakhte Oyg'n.*" She translated for Foyle, *"Closed Eyes."*

It reminded Isaac of his own inability to sleep. Even though his mind craved rest, his feet still tapped, and he rolled an invisible cigarette between his fingertips as Marcus waved an invisible fly from his own forehead.

"It's very important."

"The book or Brichah?"

"Both."

"Wait till she meets Fishl."

"Yes, she'll love Fishl."

Miranda brushed her hair back and looked straight at the stage. "Yes, I'm sure I'll love Fishl. Where is he?"

"Fishl is on a mission."

"Of utmost urgency?"

"Utmost."

And the train shot out of the mountain tunnel onto a plateau that overlooked a valley where a quilt of prosperous farmland spread out in all directions. The instant light from the fully risen sun hit his eyes, and Fishl shut them, but not before he thought he really witnessed an apparition topped by the radiant, if meager, glow of cinnamon locks.

"I'm sure that Isaac would have helped had he known your work, Benya." Miranda leaned forward across the table, swallowed the whiskey in front of her like any sophisticated denizen of New York and confided, "It's very important, Isaac."

"And so you have helped him?" He felt antagonism rising within him.

"It's your story, too, it's all of your stories. The men from *Partisan Review* are very excited by Benya. They are going to publish an excerpt."

"Congratulations," Isaac sneered at the supplicant standing by the table.

Benya nodded modestly.

Miranda went on. "They are calling it the authentic voice of despair."

"How thrilling."

Betsy and George, spent by their patriotic coupling, were joined as their ardor cooled by the rest of the Green Hen Girls and the Emcee for a final bow while the three-piece orchestra played "America the Beautiful" and the audience continued to make deals at the bar. It was getting late, or early, and the room was less densely packed than it had been at the peak of the evening.

"It is just a memoir. I want the world to know what we went through, Mr. Kaufman."

"And Miranda here has assisted you in bringing this to the world's attention. I am glad that your memoir has served you so well."

"He deserves to be heard," Miranda declared, and then, inspired perhaps by the final strains of the background anthem, couldn't resist adding, "In America."

The mere mention of a place he had only seen on the map in the Weinerstrasse bathroom, above the brown-stained toilet, made Isaac's teeth rattle across each other at a faster clip. It was the land of opportunity, where the block of gold outside the Liebknechtwerke would be used for paving stones, where Jews wore straw hats with baseball tickets tucked into the bands, where Jewish bands played in rooftop gardens for Jewish crowds who leaned over the parapets to appreciate the golden glimmer of the streets from a godly perspective.

"And you shall judge who is suitable for the golden shore, My Dear. You shall determine who shall leave and who shall remain, who shall live and who shall die. Who shall prosper and who shall wither. You are the dispenser of Jewish justice. All hail Miranda Karlinovskivinski, Queen of the Diaspora."

Embarrassed, face red as the stripes on Betsy Ross's flag, she stammered, "Th . . . that's ridiculous."

Benya held her now as Foyle had before.

"Protect her, Schreiber," Isaac advised. "Guard the Queen who gives you paper, because mine will never, I say, never, be yours. Just remember that *I* control paper in Zone Three. She may be the Queen of the handful of living, but I am the King of the Dead." His eyes were glittering, his hands clutching the edge of the table so tightly that it vibrated and one glass clinked against another.

"I'm sure you would have helped me if you could, Mr. Kaufman."

"When Der Schreiber arrives in New York I hope that you will extend your hospitality further. Perhaps you will wait for him in your bed."

"That's it. That's enough." Miranda stood up. "It's bad enough that I have to come to this cesspool. I don't think I have to be insulted."

A stricken look flashed in Benya's liquid eyes at the word "insulted," but no one noticed.

"The nerve. The nerve she has to send this, this . . ." Isaac sputtered, seeking the words with which to devastate the poor, pathetic Schreiber, settling for "this paper pusher" who shrank beneath his fury, "to the United States." He slammed a fist down on the table, and the drinks sloshed over, and he pounded again, and when this wasn't sufficiently emphatic, he swept his arm to send every glass crashing to the floor. He rose, too, and bared his teeth like an animal uncaged.

"Isaac, calm down. Calm down," Marcus insisted.

But there was no capping the volcano. One second later and Isaac would have pounced across the barren table and throttled Miranda and she knew it and knew fear and fled, followed by the young man with the tongue of his generation.

And then, as suddenly as the storm had come over Isaac, it subsided. He was exhausted. He sank to the chair.

The room was nearly empty and entirely silent. Only the Emcee stood grinning on the stage.

"Does this mean you won't help us?" Foyle asked.

Marcus Morgenstern stared at the American representative of the Joint. He was accustomed to Isaac's moods, and was astonished that anyone could dream that when Rashi or Darwin or whatever his nom de moment was was in such a mood he might "help." At these moments, no consideration could sway him, let alone this plea for a charitable impulse that had been burned out of him as the brand was burned onto his arm, as it was onto the arm shaking Fishl from his dream on the train descending into the lush farm country outside of Frankfurt.

"What are you talking about?" Isaac said.

"About help. What are you talking about?"

"About ball bearings," Isaac replied. God, was he tired, but he knew that he still couldn't sleep. He could only think of returning to Weinerstrasse for another gigantic bowlful of cream.

And the train kept moving, but the girl standing in the aisle spoke in her own stunned disbelief, "Open your eyes, husband."

Book III

CIVILIZATION

CHAPTER 11

Men who could not yet grow a beard found women whose heads had been shaved. The delicate courtship rituals established across the synagogue barriers that kept the opposite sex at a remove for centuries went up in smoke. Whether it was the erotic charge, so vulgarly satisfied at the Green Hen and bouncing on the Biedermaier couch at 44 Weinerstrasse, that had been stifled for years, surging through the newly invigorated blood vessels of the individual members of the tribe, or a deeper will to perpetuate the species, the impulse was more than evident; it was rampant. They paired like rabbits in a cage, as they couldn't when penned in separate cages for the first half of the decade.

None of the other crew members were quite as lucky as Fishl to find girls they had known Before. Most had been too young to have wives: the few years Fishl had on them were sufficient to graduate from cheder and wed. Only Marcus Morgenstern was older, but his only experience had been with his assistant, Malka, a chubby Polish girl who granted the Jewish dentist a simple insertion after a difficult extraction. Yet they all learned the new manners of maturity and rapidly found partners—usually someone who had known Cousin Esther in the Bialystok ghetto.

"Ah yes, she was last seen on the transport to Treblinka."

"A pity. And what are you doing later tonight?"

Usually they saw a movie at the army camp and slipped into the tall grass beside the road afterward, like peasants.

The women had lost their shyness well before their virginity and shared the same desperate cravings as the men. Slenderized at Ravensbrück, some had their own table at the Vivant. Some purchased bulk cigarettes and sold them in the marktplatz. They listened to Doris Day on Yankee radio and bought wigs made from the newly opened storehouses crammed with their mothers' hair. Then they paraded their new good looks for the benefit of their future mates.

"Do you think that desire is innate?" Isaac asked Marcus Morgenstern, mystified by this sudden striving. He was genuinely curious about this, as he was curious about other human motivations he did not share. Shunning the skeletal girls of the ghetto, he still felt more comfortable with German whores.

"Survival of the fittest," Marcus reminded him.

Unfit as any couple could be. Fishl and Rivka knocked on the door of Weinerstrasse, once, then twice, then once again.

Isaac tore the door open and greeted them. "What took you?"

"The trains, the tracks, they were being repaired."

"Well it's about time. Where's the paper?"

Fishl was just as direct. He said, "I don't have it."

"Why not?"

"I'm not sure."

Three days now without sleep, Isaac was in no mood for riddles. "Explain," he demanded.

"I met Rivka on the train . . ."

"Who's that?" he lifted his chin toward the young woman with the kerchief hiding her scalp.

"Rivka . . . my wife."

"Mazel Tov."

"And you decided to take a honeymoon in the Grotto of Capri?" Schimmel sneered.

"Shut up!" Isaac snapped.

"I'm sorry it took us so long to get back, but . . ."

"Forget about that. Tell me about Frankfurt."

Despite Isaac's brusqueness. Fishl wasn't offended. He answered the question. "We were late. That was unavoidable. The train stalled." He might as well have been telling the kommandant of Mauthausen why a shipment of Hungarian Jews was late. The trains hadn't run on time since Mussolini was strung upside down in the Piazza Loreto in Milan.

"He told me that we had to go to Frankfurt." Rivka added as she inched up beside her husband. "I was going to Cologne, where I heard that I had a cousin, but we went to Frankfurt instead."

"We sent a telegram to Cologne," Fishl continued. "I told Rivka's cousin that we were on a mission."

"Of utmost urgency."

"Precisely. We met the man under the clock. That was not a problem, not much of a problem. He was not understanding. He said that he shouldn't have waited and complained that I was supposed to come alone. But I showed him the money."

"Where?"

"In my suitcase."

"Where did you show it to him?"

"Under the clock."

"Where anyone could have seen it?"

"Shouldn't they?"

There was a moment of silence in the room where the crew had been talking for almost a hundred hours straight. Isaac looked at Fishl incredulously. Then, instead of a sarcastic. "Perhaps you should have counted the notes out on the floor of the train station," he asked, "What happened next?"

"I gave him my suitcase. He gave me his suitcase. We were waiting for the train back and then it happened."

"What?"

"I'm not exactly sure."

There was another pause while Isaac furiously scooped up a bowlful of the brown pudding, his fifth, sixth, or seventh of the day. As they lost their ability to sleep, they felt more and more compelled to eat larger and larger quantities of the pudding, and were beginning to wonder how they could obtain another cannister when the initial supply ran out. The six of them who had gone without sleep had devoured nearly five gallons of powder in nearly as many days. But asking for replenishment of the addictive powder would be twice as hard when they were already begging delay on the paper end. "Try to tell me."

"Well, we were standing in line and someone stole my suitcase, the new suitcase I mean, the one the man gave me with the paper in it."

"I know what the Hell you mean. What do you mean, someone stole your suitcase? Who stole your suitcase? How?"

Isaac could see the moronically blissful newlyweds, setting the suitcase down for a second to embrace. And then ten kilograms of top quality bond, no earthly good to anyone else, vanished. Some thief observed the trade under the clock. Although he must have preferred the cash, a professional could tell that Fishl was an easier target than the man with the money and made the logical but wrong assumption that Fishl was carrying a commodity of equal value to the tempting cash.

Or maybe it was some other thief, one who didn't know what was in the suitcase and didn't care, or some idiot who thought it was underwear, and wanted underwear. They could probably buy back the suitcase for a pack of Marlboros if they could find it. But the paper-stuffed valise was probably thrown into a garbage can in disgust five minutes after it was stolen. Maybe the station janitor found it. Maybe he was sitting in the boiler room now, writing love letters to his girlfriend in Ulm.

"I don't know."

"Tell me what happened?"

"It was right next to me and a second later it was gone."

"Gone?"

"Gone."

"You couldn't see anyone?"

"Just a fellow with a big red suitcase. Mine was small and blue."

"Was he a DP?"

"A dead person?"

Isaac asked, "Can you remember the handle? Of the blue one the first man gave you."

"It was leather, cracked like alligator."

"Can you remember the handle of the red suitcase the man beside you had?"

"No. Why?"

"Because it was leather, cracked like alligator."

But no one else in the room had spent any summer vacations in Canada, and they didn't understand the art of luggage. Isaac explained, "You take a red suitcase, cut off the bottom and the handles, carry it like so . . ." To illustrate, he folded a newspaper and tore a small hole in the center. Then he cupped four fingers into the hole and continued, "and then, when you see a nice suitcase to fit underneath, you drop it on top, like so . . ." He placed the paper tent over a tea cup. Then he mimed a look at his watch and said, "Time to waltz."

"I'm sorry, but I still don't understand." Fishl said.

Marcus was a faster study. He took over Isaac's lesson and picked up the handle of the the teacup through the slot in the paper. "It was a false bottom suitcase the thief had, in the train station where there are lots of suitcases to be stolen, including a blue one with the last paper we had."

Fishl nodded. "There's a tractate about two items that resemble each other and how to determine who the proper owner may be."

Isaac picked up his empty bowl and threw it across the room. Specks of brown pudding adhered to the image of Venezuela like mountains on a topographic map.

Rivka of the cinnamon hair stood by Fishl all the while, looking at her husband's interrogator as if he was a German kommandant with the power of life and death.

Schimmel said, "He's good luck?"

Charm or jinx, Fishl, with Rivka, nonetheless took up housekeeping in the pantry next to the kitchen, the only place at 44 Weinerstrasse that rivaled their old attic for connubial intimacy. It was tiny and windowless, but it was safe and perpetually scented with cinnamon. It was heaven, and the others looked at heaven's residents with a mixture of envy and disdain.

"Look!" Berger declared one day, rushing into the tobacco works, fresh from the toilet, waving a pair of female underpants clotted with blood at the crotch.

Rivka ran after him, blushing.

The implications of potential birth were stunning.

The workers passed the underwear from hand to hand, examining the stain, bending to sniff it as if the brick red spot was holy. But holiness was not in them and they nicknamed poor Rivka: "Knickers."

Fishl grabbed the garment and stormed back into the pantry.

Fishl now had many new lessons to learn in the enchanted premises marked by the black wood timbers that might as well have been the gingerbread home of the witch that Hansel and Gretel met once upon a time, a home of scary magic. Perhaps it was because he and Rivka had entered the magical address late in their ordeal, but the evil restlessness didn't bother him. He acted as major domo to the gang's pandemonium, answering the series of different knocks at the door, fetching more cream and sugar to mix with the brown powder, the only one who refrained from the pudding and the girls and the talk.

Eager to make a swift return to the blissful pantry, Fishl closed his eyes while girls came and went, along with emissaries from the other smugglers in the zone. These men had reasons for bringing Weinerstrasse into a particular deal: contacts, connections, financing. Pinsker had moved from distribution to production, but there was also Zalman Kabishnikov, whom rumor had it had been a Kapo at Flossenbürg, Herman Kalt, mayor of Regensburg, still riding in a government car with a government driver, and the Moises Group, three Moroccan Jews, wending their way eastward toward a diadem of desirable emeralds in the Levant, leaving a trail of broken promises and bad debts. When Fishl heard their special knocks, he cringed and almost wished it was more girls from the Green Hen. These people didn't have a spot of dignity, and he feared for the contamination of his own soul as he didn't while carrying bags of cement down the pyramid-size steps of the quarry at Mauthausen. If his solemn, mournful manner irked the others, they tried not to show it for Isaac's sake. And if their glib vulgarity distressed him, he tried to not show it for Alter's sake.

For those who summoned forth enterprise from the nearly emptied reservoirs of vitality that had been drained in the contest for survival, there were as many paths to a buck or a mark or a lire as there had been Before. Some took up their pre-War occupations:

livery men assisting in the endless travel from city to city, tailors plying needle and thread as if they had stopped work on a particular garment midstitch to say evening prayers—years ago. Others returned to their studies. Wisps of sacerdotal earlocks appeared beneath bald scalps and tzitzits fringes under vests as yeshivas opened in the basements of Mayen from which the Jewish population had been expelled centuries earlier. And some, lead by Isaac Kaufman and his gang, strutted the cafés in pomegranate-colored silk as they advanced to meet the new opportunities in the post-War world.

There were already rumors of a Greek Jew, the only one of his high school class in Salonika still eating grape leaves and breathing, who had cornered the gasoline market in Hamburg and made so much money that he had to open his own bank to hold the proceeds. He was busy telexing Shell oil in London and sheikhs in Arabia, carteling to impress the Farben crowd. The man was an inspiration to his peers, but not just anyone could follow his example. One found oneself in a field and made the most of it. For Isaac's chosen path, he required money. To make money, Isaac required paper. That was his business, so Fishl did his best to help.

"One of the Moiseses wants an internal visa with naval designation. What should I do?" he begged Isaac Kaufman for guidance.

"Arrange it, don't arrange it. Take responsibility," Isaac replied, too distracted to care what happened around him.

"Yes, Sir," Fishl practically saluted. Isaac was the worst of the batch, but Fishl accepted this dictum because he had to, because Alter Kaufman blessed his brother with priviledged status amid the marketeers, and, more strangely, blessed him for them. Fishl felt as if Alter had delivered a pronouncement rather than a recommendation while they were standing on the edge of the Austrian pit that would certainly have swallowed them had the War lasted another six months. As God gave Jonah instructions ignored at his peril, Alter told Fishl to knock four times—once, then twice, then once again—so he did and bore the consequences of his welcome.

Marcus watched Isaac's daily disintegration—though there was no such a thing as a day or a night in their sleepless lives.

"It's got to be dangerous," Marcus said.

Isaac was edgy. Still searching for paper, he slammed the phone down on someone in Berlin and snapped, "Cigarettes are dangerous."

"But people have to sleep."

"They have to smoke."

"That's not what I'm talking about."

"So, we don't sleep. We're lucky, then, because we don't dream."

Teeth grinding, clock ticking, Marcus tried to sum up the situation, "We still have a few hundred thousand marks left. What can we do with them?"

"Can is the wrong word," Isaac replied. "It implies choice. We have no choice, so we have to say, 'What *must* we do with them?'" Responding to his own query, he continued, "The answer is we have to go to the army, to Jacks Over Deuces. I hate it. But to survive one does what one must. Ask Necco to set up a meeting."

Coincidentally or on cue, the lieutenant appeared minutes later, with the latest shipment of ball bearings.

There was a moment of awkwardness when the professional papermongers were compelled to admit that they didn't exactly have the promised goods in return. Necco turned as pale as a line sergeant at Normandy who's just discovered that he's run out of ammunition. Unfortunately Isaac couldn't get on the squawk box and scream, "Quartermaster!"

"Not to worry." Necco recovered swiftly, suddenly reollecting that he had been warned to expect this state of affairs, "let's just say this delivery is on good faith."

"That's good," Schimmel whispered.

"No." Isaac replied. "We just issued a chit. It's invisible, but real. We owe Jacks Over Deuces now. I want to redeem that chit before the interest grows larger than the principle." He turned to Necco and requested the face-to-face meeting with the lieutenant's superior that he and Marcus had been discussing earlier.

Now the lieutenant stood back. "Why?" he asked with a quick rabbity twitch. The man was scared of his boss. Layers of army hierarchy rewarded him at a remove as wide as the Grand Canyon.

"Because," Isaac improvised, "we have a proposal."

Marcus said only half to himself. "We do?"

Although the lieutenant stood taller in his new uniform than he had as a noncom, Isaac knew full well that Necco was a messenger without authority. He was, however, a soldier and like all soldiers he felt that he had a strategic mind. That mind now sensed weakness. If this was a battle, he would have pressed home his advantage.

In fact, Isaac agreed with Necco's unstated assessment of the situation. There was nothing Isaac detested more than weakness, yet he felt it on every front, his lines caving in under enemy onslaught. The evening before, Schimmel had handed three cigarettes to the doorman at the Green Hen, who tucked the butts negligently into his pocket along with a pack of Camels. The currency had changed overnight as goods began to flow into the country. Cigarettes were no longer for trading. They were for smoking, valuable for smokers, useless to others.

By this time, they had already learned that the smokers of Liebknecht and Regensburg would no longer smoke anything that burned. The brilliant idea to fieldstrip cigarettes and repack them with straw was no longer working. Cigarettes from the army PX were floating freely; trucks were cruising in with Gauloises from Lyons.

Fortunately, in manufacturing, they had all become addicts, and were able to utilize their inventory. Even Fishl learned to smoke. Despite the initial gagging over the unfamiliar gas in his mouth, he was able to force the smoke down and blow it back out in the shape of a cornucopia; he had always been a good student. Also, the more pudding they ate, the more cigarettes they smoked. They lived on sweet brown powder and tobacco.

Schimmel clamped a butt between his teeth and patted his pockets for matches. Frustrated, he bent sideways over the stove, and there was a sudden lightning flash skipping across his forehead, and the familiar scent of burnt hair suffused the room. "Yeow!" he jumped back.

And a light no less brilliant blinked over Isaac's head. "Everyone has cigarettes."

"So?"

"But no one has matches."

"So?"

"Let's get some."

Schimmel and Marcus looked at Isaac with amazement. That's why he was the leader.

Necco said he would forward their request for a meeting on Friday, three days hence. In the meanwhile, all deliveries from the Liebknechtwerke to Weinerstrasse were suspended.

Now Isaac had to send an awkward letter eastward for personal delivery to Alter Kaufman at Theresienstadt saying that this week's shipment would not be arriving, and that Liebknecht could offer no assurance when the next would, but that Isaac was working on a new idea, small consolation.

Isaac worried that the change in plans would disturb Alter's routine, but he never could have anticipated the response delivered back to him a day later by the Vivant driver. The man returned with a message. "He wasn't there."

"What do you mean, he wasn't there?" Isaac demanded, wondering if this was going to be the same idiotic conversation he had with Fishl. Suddenly he was repeating the questions he had not had occasion to ask for years. "What do you mean?" The world was no longer comprehensible.

"That's what they said. 'He's no longer here.' Period. I didn't pursue it further because I had the distinct impression that asking was not going to get me any answers. It was more likely to get me a few questions of my own. In fact, I felt pretty happy to get out of that castle. It's drafty and I'm not going back."

"Not for . . ."

"Not for a pack, not for a carton, not for a truckload. Haven't you heard smoking is bad for your health."

Isaac was so frantic he considered calling the Joint, but he would be damned rather than ask Miranda for help for several reasons, not least that he was convinced she would fail. Whenever he saw Miranda running an errand through the streets of Regensburg she seemed frazzled. As for Alan Foyle, the man had trouble tying his own shoes. Maybe they could organize to help find a missing person in New York where there was a governmental structure to rely upon, but they were at sea in the zone. The best the Joint could do was to add one more name to the lists upon daily-updated lists tacked to bulletin boards outside the local office. Trembling in the breeze, they might as well have been comic strips.

Isaac sent the word out through underground channels, from the

Hen to the Vivant to other cafés, announcing a reward for anyone who knew the whereabouts, etc., etc.—making Alter Kaufman the most wanted man this side of Count Geiger.

Nothing.

Alter was gone, vanished, silent. As greatly as Fishl craved his further direction, he saw that Isaac was far more disturbed by this sudden absence. The younger brother frantically made inquiries across the sector and the zone and the Continent, from London to Leghorn, where the line of Jews waiting for Brichah's leaky transport to Palestine was scanned by officials in search of a man with a distinctive scar and an eye patch.

Nothing.

Isaac tapped the KGB liaison in Salzburg for information, to no effect. Not only could the older Kaufman not be traced forward from Theresienstadt; nobody could verify that he had been there at all. "I get calls from everyone," the KGB man said as he pocketed a valuable American passport in return for opening his mouth. "There's a Swede who has half the Red Army hiding him. Him, I can find. But your brother . . ." he held out empty palms.

Nothing.

The lack of sleep made everything so hazy that Isaac retroactively questioned his memories and experiences. It was five days and counting. Five nights, too, without a minute's sleep. Was it even possible that he had imagined Alter in Theresienstadt, had sent American cigarettes off into the void, had received Russian cigarettes from the void. And if that was the case, had he simply imagined the Alter of Proszowice and Proszowice itself? Born free into the rubble, he worried that time Before was merely a tantalizing fantasy. Life began in May of 1945, and everything before that was primordial flux.

CHAPTER 12

Schimmel and Marcus debated what to do. "You tell him." one said.

"No, you."

Neither dared disturb Isaac in his window seat mourning for his newly found newly lost brother, but the hour for his meeting with Jacks Over Deuces had arrived. There was a future and it depended on the present.

"You made the appointment."

"After he asked you to ask me to make the appointment."

"We can wait for Berger."

"He'll never do it."

"Do what?" Fishl asked.

Marcus and Schimmel looked at each other. Marcus draped an arm around Fishl's shoulder and steered him to their morose leader.

Necco was waiting downstairs in an open-topped jeep. Clearly surprised that the request for the audience was granted, he made it obvious that the date was not to be missed. He didn't bother to beep, but he looked at his watch, and then at Isaac in the window.

Isaac waved.

Fishl said, "There's only one man in the southern sector to go to for help. Without him, you're done; with his signature, you've got a business. Then, maybe, you can find whatever you're looking for, or whoever." It was a new, practical language that the spiritual man spoke, and Isaac looked at him with amazement. He was about to make a crack about Fishl and Rivka's quilted den in the pantry, barely large enough for one, so how did they fit, did he think that made him a man, when Fishl innocently finished. "Well?"

"Let's go."

The road out of Regensburg toward the Liebknechtwerke was more sparsely populated than the avenue to town, but there was a steady flow of traffic, because everyone wanted something the Yankees had. At the perimeter of the base, there were the linden trees and an open field mowed by army gardeners, and then a fence with a gate.

The first building inside the camp was a PX with a line at the door that now consisted of more Germans than Jews. Half of them held coupons printed on Weinerstrasse. The line extended past the gold cube covered by the green-gray tarpaulin, which the jeep splashed as it jolted over ruts caused by broken sewage pipes. Aside from the substance under the tarp, there was no trace of the Jews who had lived and died there.

Soldiers rushed pell-mell to the accompaniment of an army radio broadcasting "Chattanooga Choo Choo" from the porch of the cottage that had once been the kommandant's residence. The base was humming, but its tune was that of routine rather than extremity. There was none of the excitement of the initial post-War discovery of the camp: no reporters, no commissions, no diplomats, or dignitaries. It was simple daily life in Bavaria, the focal point of which was a redbrick hut that had so many uniforms buzzing in and out that it resembled a hive. Necco drove straight up to the front door and parked at an angle that took up two spaces.

The first person they saw had a familiar face; it was General Smith, Hammerin' Hank in the flesh, storming out of a back room, from which the sounds of chips being stacked emerged like the castanets of a rehearsing flamenco dancer. Every soldier in the anteroom stood up to salute the general, but he ignored them and shouted over his shoulder. "I'll pay you on Monday."

A WAC secretary clad in a becoming khaki ornamented with sergeant's stripes sat at a receptionist's desk. "When on Monday will that be, Sir?"

"Noon."

"Can you make it earlier?"

"Eleven then, Jesus!"

"That will be fine, Sir. I'll mark you down for eleven, sharp."

Smith's own functionary followed in his wake. It was Hamilton, the stationer captain, with rigid tobacco brown clipboard and shiny steel clasp, inking the date and hour onto his own memorandum pad and a carbon paper duplicate.

"Put that damn thing away. We'll be here."

"With the money, Sir," the secretary added with unflappable serenity.

"We'll be here, damn it!" Smith cursed and stormed past the new entrées. The rest of the soldiers in the waiting room sat down and continued leafing through various girlie magazines, the more daring furtively raising an eye to compare the legs of the desk sergeant with the legs on view between the covers, their minds on what lay between those legs.

One soldier swatted at a lazy black fly buzzing around his head and Marcus twitched.

"You must be Mr. Kaufman and Mr. Morgenstern," the secretary said. "Someone will be with you in just a moment."

The sound of cards being dealt filled the room. Necco shrugged. "It's always like this on Friday. Payday."

Without having received any apparent communication, the secretary swiveled in Isaac and Marcus's direction and said, "This way, Sirs," pointing toward the door behind her post. They started forward with Necco beside them, but the secretary lifted a finger, and Necco froze.

So the pilgrims entered the back room alone. Three desks with three young soldiers fronted the visitors. The soldier on the left kept pushing a shock of black hair off his forehead and screaming into his phone, "Legumes! Who wants fucking legumes! I want ball bearings!" while the one on the right was tabulating a row of figures on an adding machine and the one in the center stood up and stretched out a hand. There was no sign of playing cards, but the sound of shuffling came from behind a blue baize curtain that separated the men at the three desks from the inner sanctum.

Isaac took the hand offered to him, but glanced at the curtain, which reminded him of the one that covered the ark of the Torah in Proszowice. For a second he wondered if that Torah now sat in Count Geiger's secret Judaica collection.

The soldier who greeted them was a well-tanned young man whose army shirt was unbuttoned at the neck. The atmosphere here was informal. "The corporal asked me to assist you. He said I should remind you that we appreciate beauty."

Marcus remembered his glib talk in the Vivant the night he had met Isaac.

As if reading his mind, a soft voice came from the other side of the curtain, "I heard you talking that night. I liked what I heard." The voice then addressed someone on his side of the curtain. "Your deal."

Isaac glanced at Marcus.

Marcus addressed the curtain. "And you remembered."

The soldier who greeted them subtly shifted place to stand between the visitors and the flimsy barrier. He said, "He remembers what he must."

Then the disembodied voice spoke again, whether to Marcus or his fellow cardplayers, "I tend to have faith in people, don't you? Open for ten."

"Make it twelve."

"Fifteen," the betting went around the table.

Hardly pausing, their greeter went on, "So when he heard you fellows had a project, he liked it right away."

One of the supplicants Isaac had noticed biting his nails in the outside waiting room was ushered in by the efficient WAC secretary and stood humbly before the man at the adding machine, who ripped off a roll of white paper and waved it in his face. "You call these numbers?"

"Yes," the greeter said, "Captain Necco's on the ball."

"Captain now? And he answers to a corporal?"

"He likes uniforms," the voice from the back explained, "so we got him one. Got to keep the troops motivated. Maybe we'll make him a general yet. I don't like braid myself."

"And what do you like?" There was no response, so Marcus rephrased the question to the man in front of them. "What does he like?"

"He likes you. And he likes money. That's one reason he likes you. You like money, too."

"So, for the future . . . ?"

"I'll get you the ball bearings, which you'll sell back to me as usual." Isaac noticed that the soldier had started to speak in the first person. Perhaps Forty-four Weinerstrasse was part of his territory, just as the poor fellow from the waiting room, head now sunk remorsefully on his chest, belonged in the domain of the furious tabulator and the unlucky soul with the legumes belonged to the soldier on the phone. "Since you can't trade them for cigarettes anymore, you'll have to find a new commodity."

"Feathers?" asked the thin voice from behind the curtain. "Make that twenty. No, forget that one. But find something. Do you have any ideas? I don't have any ideas, but I can't get the ball bearings myself, but I need them."

"Why?" Marcus asked.

The voice ignored him, and there was the distinct sound of cash on the table.

"You want a part of the operation?" the greeter said.

"Maybe."

"Good, first you'll have to buy cigarettes from me for five marks apiece."

"But the market is only four marks apiece."

"Don't worry, a deal's a deal, I'll buy them back from you for six."

Isaac was starting to feel dizzy, but he managed to ask. "Why?"

"Because you'll be able to take the two marks profit and buy something else. Then you can sell that to me, and I can get more ball bearings from you."

"And then?"

"That's the syndicate's way," the soldier stated abruptly, losing patience with the obtuseness of his visitors.

"What syndicate?"

Jacks Over Deuces interrupted again. "The syndicate that buys and sells things. You're the only ones who are not part of the syndicate. That's why we need you. I don't mind telling people that I need them as long as they know that they need me, too. Now, the only way you can prove that you need me is by telling me what you want.

That's why you came here for anyway, isn't it? Nobody comes here just to talk. So, talk. Tell me, what do you want?"

"Matches."

"Great."

But matches were rare. Isaac explained to the curtain that there were two components to any given match: the stick and sulfur. He didn't say that any paper source for the stick might well serve his other wares, too. What he said was that he needed official army authorization to get into the Papiergeschäft factory and requisition material. He also said that he required certain money for upfront expenses.

The curtain made a quick decision. He agreed. "You're staked."

So that was that. It was time for Isaac to ask, "One other thing."

"There's always one other thing," their greeter said, happy now that business had gone so smoothly. He had learned well from the master and spoke like an acolyte reciting the catechism. "That's a rule. What's the other thing? I mean the next other thing before the last other thing."

Issac briefly considered mentioning his search for Alter, but he didn't want the U.S. Army more involved in his personal life than was absolutely necessary. He also had more confidence in the informal network of refugees webbed across the Continent. If the student with the scar Isaac remembered or the spy with the patch he had met was alive, someone would see him somewhere. Instead, he said, "Well, there's the brown powder."

"What brown powder?" the voice asked as he extended a pale, stubby-fingered hand with five cards through the curtain, displaying a trey through six of spades and a Queen of hearts. "Make that a hundred," he declared, bluffing.

"Necco brought us a container. We've nearly run out."

"Necco!" the visible soldier called.

The captain rushed in so instantaneously that he must have been standing on the other side of the door the entire time.

"Do you know anything about a container of brown powder?"

At attention, Necco replied promptly. "Yes, Sir, we brought them some Chock full o'Nuts as a present. It was your suggestion."

"Yes, the Chock full o'Nuts."

It was the answer to the mystery, but the Weinerstrasse brigade didn't understand the significance of American brand names. Marcus said. "If it's ground nuts that's OK, but we've run out and, well, we've really come to enjoy them."

Necco said, "Impossible. That was twenty-five pounds, a year's supply, easy."

"It goes quickly with five hungry people."

"Hungry?"

"What else do you do with nuts except eat them?"

"Eat it, man?" Necco couldn't believe his ears.

Morgenstern agreed, "Where I come from, we eat nuts, yes."

At ease for the first time since he had entered the room, Necco blurted. "Where I come from, we drink coffee," and there was a high-pitched giggle from the space beyond the blue curtain.

They had been so accustomed to the sour chicory brew that passed for coffee in the lagers they hadn't recognized the real thing. "Coffee?"

"Straight?" said Necco, perhaps influencing the thought of the last remaining player behind the curtain, who must have looked at the ominous blank surface of the five cards facing him and moaned, "Fold," and tossed his own three tens onto the table.

"No, with cream and sugar."

"Good," the thin voice said, and Jacks Over Deuces raked in the pot of money. Coins clinked, paper riffled. A second later, the same stubby hand swept out from between the curtain and dropped a bill, which fluttered to the floor like a green leaf prematurely separated from its branch. "Get this fellow a pillow. He sounds like he could use some rest. Hey, maybe we should do feathers after all? Patrice, take a memo."

Immediately the receptionist was in the room, jotting down a notation on a yellow pad set upon her upraised nylon-covered thigh.

"Check out the price of down in Denmark," the greeter said, and the soldier on the telephone was speaking Danish.

The conversation moved on as the invisible deck of cards was redealt and Isaac looked out the window, pulling his vision inward from the wooden sash until he was peering through a circular pull, which dangled from the end of a braided cord attached to the shade like a gunsight.

Then, careful to speak in a tone of idle speculation, he asked. "How do they know what's under that tarp?"

"I'll call that bluff!" Jacks Over Deuces said to his opponent.

"Drat!" the other man fumed.

"What did you say?"

"Drat!"

"Not you. You!" and Jacks Over Deuces appeared at the place where the two sections of the curtain overlapped. He was a small man wearing a parachutist's pale blue camouflage fatigues that made his slight frame fade into the folds of the curtain.

"Corporal, Sir!" the three men in the room hopped to their feet in a line as straight as any West Point commander could desire.

"I asked how they know what's under the tarpaulin, Corporal . . ."

"Call me Jacks Over Deuces," he said amiably to Isaac and belatedly answered the question. "They don't unless they check."

Isaac examined his new partner. He had pale sandy hair and eyes to match that peered out from a hairless baby face. "And how often do they check?"

"Never."

Their eyes met and then they both looked out the window.

A bird landed on the tarpaulin, shat a thin stream down the sodden material, and flew away.

That night, the crew was still grinding their teeth, talking rapid-fire about anything new, bubbling over with ideas, dreaming out loud as they had ceased to dream on the floor full of mattresses. The mystery of their sleeplessness solved, they knew the house would soon be quieter than it had been since the postmen of Regensburg had sipped a midnight schnapps. The five-gallon bucket of coffee was nearly finished; the salvation of repose would come once the last bowls of its energetic, emetic substance were flushed from their innards.

"Have some extra," they urged each other now that they knew what it was and they craved it all the more, compelled to scrape the remains off the rim of the cannister in order to bounce off the walls for one last night, and sleep for a week.

In the giddy moments before utter collapse, they laughed over their mistake. "Coffee pudding."

"But you know, we could have mixed it with flour and made coffee pancakes."

"We could have ground it into patties and made coffee burgers."

"Coffee eggs."

"Coffee cupcakes! Or croissants!"

They grew alliterative. "Coffee Casserole."

"Coffee Comfit!"

"Coffee CRACKERS!"

They tossed the last of the powder around the kitchen, blew pinches of it off their fingers, coffee clouds scenting the air, staining the maps. And to top it all off, just before their eyes slammed shut with the authority of the exit doors to Europe in 1939, they brewed a final celebratory kettle of the powder, mixed it with only a modicum of milk and sugar, and felt the liquid slide down their throats. So this was the form in which normal people tasted the brown powder that was all they had known for a week. The last cup would not keep them awake. It had nill effect compared to the pounds they had been swallowing. They looked yearningly toward the mattresses.

"Coffee coffee," someone said wearily.

Isaac hardly neeeded the goose down filled bag of feathers. The moment the last drop of coffee coffee dripped down into his belly, a profound exhaustion came upon him. Suddenly the coffee was a soporific. Schimmel seemed to move in slow motion, as he, too, plodded toward a mattress.

"Good night," Marcus said, unable to rise from the couch. "Sweet dreams."

And Isaac remembered his mother, tucking him into bed along with his two brothers in the attic over the family shop. He remembered the warmth of their bodies. Israel's pudgy cheeks nuzzled into his back while Alter's stubbly adolescent chin scratched his shoulder. Whether they had ever been real, they came alive in the netherland between pillow and dream.

Fond memories turned gloomy as soon as his eyes closed. He saw Alter. bloody underpants, children, and chimneys. Then a dozen small gray mice scampered into the picture, nibbling at the wrists of the children, and he tried to shout to warn them, but the mice bit through the flesh as if the wrists were rope, and a bloodless hand fell to the floor.

While the others nodded off, Fishl set out to serve his hosts. Tucked under his arm was their last batch of bogus bills, to obtain more material.

Schimmel was reluctant to trust the sad-eyed, big-headed Jew on another mission, but Fishl's desire to redeem his failure in Frankfurt was so great and everyone else's exhaustion so profound, their ability to refuse so weakened, and the need for motion so immediate that he was entrusted with another suitcase to take the place of the one he had let slip, a bright blue-and-black plaid that he swore would never leave his hands. They wished him, "Got tsu dank."

Fishl's voyage out from Regensburg was uneventful although Isaac woke at his nightmare, paced the sleeping quarters and stared at the map of local train lines over the toilet, all the while wondering if their emissary was a dot stuck in another tunnel west from Offenbach, finding his mother this time.

Isaac needn't have worried. Fishl's only problem on the train was that he missed Rivka enormously. He hadn't thought of her once during the War, but an hour away from the texture of her hair was now torture. Nonetheless, he felt an obligation to Isaac and to the Alter who sent him to Weinerstrasse. Answering knock after coded knock at the front door, torn by his instructions to ignore unfamiliar knocks, he could not help but be aware of the privileged position Isaac's crew occupied, a position that he, presumably, shared.

This time there were no delays. The train steamed into its station, and before he could unfold one of Issac's maps for directions to the factory, a messenger approached him. It was a paunchy middle-aged man with a slight limp, who eyed the passengers and unerringly honed in on his target "Herr smuggler, please," he said. "Please come with me."

Clutching the plaid satchel filled with cash for all he was worth, Fishl entered the car chartered to transport him across the devastated landscape to the Papiergeschäft, which was located in an untouched industrial district of Ludwigshafen. The churches were bombed, the houses flattened, but the factories remained. "It was a nice city, once," the messenger sighed.

Their destination was a low-slung structure that had obviously been added onto over time. A brick portion may have been the original factory, but there was a wing of corrugated steel attached to the left, and one of gray stucco to the right, their roofs combined into acres of flat expanse punctuated with smokestacks, vents, and other mechanical apparatus. A thin pillar of smoke emerged from one chimney, but a dozen others were unused. Approaching this structural mélange, Fishl saw a stream of humanity traveling in the same direction. Some were soldiers, some civilians.

A guard had been posted at the entry to the premises during the War, but such guards were gone now, and it was easy to walk into the factory, although a middle-aged woman who looked like Fishl's chaperone's twin sister informed the masses who came to the door that there was no work. The line of supplicants reversed itself disconsolately. Fishl, however, had an appointment.

The driver nodded to the woman and led Fishl up a brick-enclosed stairway to the second floor. They walked through an anteroom with several unoccupied desks into the office of a tall gentleman reading a book. The man put the book down and curtly dismissed the driver with a nod of his wedge-shaped head and greeted Fishl. "I am Franz Gruber, the manager. Please, let me show you around. I have heard that you are an expert on paper technology."

Who knew what lies Isaac had told to get him here. Who knew what this man's expectations were. Fishl had his cash-filled valise and knew that he had to leave with another, larger receptacle full of blank paper. He blotted any other consideration from his mind and set to the task.

Gruber guided his visitor back past the vacant desks to an opening cut between the original structure into the corrugated area that contained the production facilities. This space was not divided into rooms or levels: Its triple height expanse was as vast as the sanctuary of the Warsaw synagogue. It was another world, where human beings were dwarfed by the monstrous gears and levers of enormous rolling machines that resembled steel tree stumps set horizontal to a winding slab of conveyor belt that looped throughout the space like a roller coaster. Despite its potential, however, the installation was nearly silent. Only a handful of workers stood at their positions at the different stations of the process.

Gruber said. "We have capacity to take in four dozen containers of pulp every day." He said this proudly as they stepped onto on a balcony overlooking the factory, then confessed sadly, "but now, as you see we are left with only the remnants of our stock."

He escorted Fishl to an alcove inside the stucco building. It was a library, with a dozen aisles of shelves filled with thousands of brown and purple volumes, and it felt like a library except for a branch of the Papiergeschäft's conveyor belt that rolled incongruously down the center aisle, carrying a stack of books toward further categorization. Fishl, drawn to the text like a filing to a magnet, perused the spines of the books that passed beside him, and was not suprised to recognize a sampling of Hebrew literature. He saw multiple copies of Sholem Alcichem and Mendele Mocher Seforim, and then he found Ladino poetry in volumes that dated from the sixteenth century. He heard a curious scraping sound from farther within the library, behind a shelf.

"This was a museum at one point," Gruber said as he lead Fishl around a corner where the archives of the Jewish community of Lodz took up several dozen encyclopedic volumes that a man was shoveling from the lower shelves onto the conveyor belt

"This is our curator," Gruber said, "Irving. Irving, this is Herr Fishl who has come to give us advice."

"We need advice," Irving replied without glancing up from his task. He resembled Fishl's friend, the chemist, who took other people's stories into himself. Fishl half expected Irving to wink at him, but he said nothing more; he was a human metronome, ticking back and forth—empty shovel, scrape, full shovel, empty shovel, scrape, full shovel—transferring books onto the conveyor belt, which led through a hole in the wall of the library.

"Come," the manager interrupted his guest's reverie. "We can follow the procedure. Minor though the output may be."

They ambled beside the belt, which traveled at the same pace as they did, as the books led them back into the factory. "It is easier," Gruber said, "to keep the process going at the lowest possible rate than to shut it down, so we search out raw material and feed it through to keep the wheels turning, but you know this."

One thing Fishl knew was that Isaac in Liebknecht required quality rather than volume. A single pure ream was enough for a hundred passports. A suitcase was enough to change into enough cash to purchase a factory. A trunk was his goal. Paper enough to produce one day's edition of the *Frankfurter Zeitung* would secure Weinerstrasse's place as the printers of record for the rest of the decade. Fishl had his mission, and the material was there, and if it was not enough for the papiermeister, it was more than enough for him.

Fishl nodded and the man continued. "During the War, we ran overtime. twenty-four hours a day, three shifts. We produced memorandum pads and requisition forms. You wouldn't believe how much paper the army used." He sighed at the recollection of glory.

Together they watched the process from a catwalk, which lead to the control room.

The books moved along until the conveyor belt looped underneath itself and the books dropped off the edge in a fashion that reminded Fishl of the workers at Mauthausen. They joined heaps of Hebrew books in a large steel vat while a crusty pipe extending over the edge dripped a clear liquid down the wall.

"Hydrochloric sixteen," Gruber said.

"But I know this," Fishl replied as the acid hit the covers and turned them to a mash the consistency of oatmeal, and he felt his heart clutch. He could almost feel the release of the words within. "Shma Yisroel" rising from the pulp to the heavens as the same words had risen from the owners of those books as they were placed into a different processing center.

A gate opened at the base of the vat and the semiliquified books flowed sluggishly into another container. Large wooden paddles sloshed the brew around, and the letters floated off the surface of the pages to the surface like the noodles in alphabet soup. Plots and characters from one book entered another, and languages were scrambled into a polyglot urtext. Mendele's *Mare* was created on day five of Genesis while Maimonides's gloss commented on works that wouldn't be written for another four hundred years. Ansky's *Dybbuk* inhabited a story written in English by the young American author, Schwartz, culled from *Partisan Review* by the diligent librarians of the Reich for future reference.

Fishl, reverent for text, was appalled, but the fact that the stuff was to be made into more paper to be covered with more words was a comfort. It was part of some universal go round, like the water cycle, rain from clouds into seas, evaporating to form rain for clouds.

The German manager looked at him as the books of prayer and poetry dissolved, but Fishl watched dispassionately, disappointing the man if he had expected terror or regret.

Isaac tiptoed past the slumberers to his private room, to his private bed, where he dropped quickly back to sleep. There were no more dreams of mice and severed limbs, but he twisted his sheet in a clenched fist as Miranda appeared to enter his bedroom in a diaphanous red blouse. "Here are your papers," the dream girl said.

"Here are your papers," Isaac repeated, turning to deliver them to his sister Chaia, but Miranda was standing where he thought Chaia should. But Chaia was dead, and the only paper she could use now would be a DPID. Disconcerted, his teeth started grinding and the molars ripped through his pillow, and feathers seeped out and billowed up in a faint breeze to snow down upon his sleeping figure.

"This," the manager said, "is the most vital portion of the installation." He ushered Fishl into an octagonal control room raised on stilts in the center of the premises. Only a single engineer regulated the entire factory from a large console of switches, gauges, knobs, and levers. "Mr. Keller," Gruber introduced the man who shared his perch with two huge sluices that led down from two enormous tanks marked with chemical designations. "This is where the most delicate solutions are mixed and deployed."

Fishl tripped, sprawling against the giant chute, fingers inches from the "solution" that would have turned them to the same stubs as Isaac's teeth.

The chute angled inches to the left. Acid sprayed over the side, and Mr. Keller's glasses fell to the floor and cracked.

Gruber gasped, "Oh my Gott!"

On a busier day in a livelier season a dozen thick asbestos mittens would have reached out to rectify the problem. Today, the acid flowed like water, steaming and hissing, burning a hole through the floor like a hot coal in a snow bank. It pooled about a wire, and the rubber tubing disappeared, revealing a copper filament, which started to glow. The filament ran beside a stack of Hebrew manuscripts waiting for distribution.

The conveyor belt jerked to a halt, pamphlets flew off the side, and the librarian with the shovel appeared on the balcony across the way.

"Um," Fishl said, as the brittle folios caught. Their transformation was different from what was intended. It was not paper to liquid to paper, but paper to smoke. Flames licked upward, toward the control panel.

Anyplace else, the fire would have been just a fire. Here it was harder to extinguish. The man behind the controls pushed a lever from an upright position all the way down, but sparks leapt from the table. The wires to relay the console's instructions to a valve were writhing cinders. Instead of shutting down, the flow of acid increased, and the tank sent yet more acid cascading down the chute, sloshing over the edge, and smoking, and the room was suffused with the scent of hard-boiled eggs.

"Let's get out of here. When that hits the saline solution . . ."

"What?"

"The volatility of the mixture, the availability of the fuel!"

"You mean the paper?"

"The fuel. Combustion. Hurry."

They barely made it to the exit, where three workers were having lunch on the steps, when the doors were blasted off their hinges. A plume of smoke rose. A flame leaped out of one chimney, and the bricks crumbled off the edge. Starting with cigarettes, aiming for matches. Fishl didn't know that he had inadvertently helped Isaac to make one final leap in his dream logic.

Miranda was arguing with him in his head. "Start with the people," she said.

"You mean consumers," he replied.

"I mean people," she insisted.

Miranda didn't smoke, but in the dream, she took a cigarette from her red blouse pocket. She lit it, and the tip of the cigarette touched her blouse, which began to burn like an empty cigarette paper without any tobacco to impede its movement. Isaac felt curiously unable to help, but, more curiously, she didn't require help. She simply stood while the blouse turned from cloth to ash and started to flake off, revealing specks and patches of flesh, which joined together like pieces of a jigsaw puzzle. Eventually she stood naked, with two red nipples left and right while three red buttons that crossed them remained eerily intact on a vertical axis as the fabric that linked them disappeared, and the fiery filter of the cigarette glowed between her lips. "You don't know where to start," she said.

"No," he argued. "The start is given. It's the end that's unknown—but that makes it a matter for choice." One commenced with the raw material, the elemental truth. Start with one cigarette, say, then sense the fingers probing into one's vest pocket for one match, touching the head of the match for one teardrop of sulfur compound, but first dig into the ground for the raw material.

Under the ground. There was no way to break through the gate to get into the army base at Liebknecht, but one could go under the gate, under the ground.

Isaac was more than halfway there, but he had to figure out how to take the last step, from cigarettes to matches to sulfur to gold, when Fishl answered the question, "Explosives," at the moment the Papiergeschäft blew off the map.

SABOTAGE! the paper's banner headlines blared.

They sold out immediately, not because of the remarkable news, but because so few copies were available. News, good then bad, had been abundant for years, but recently the paper had begun to carry the "Katzenjammer Kids" to boost circulation. The comic strip starred two pudgy eightish-year-old brats and their violent relationship with a father figure called The Captain. Pirated from the USO daily paper, translated from a transliterated German accent into the native tongue, the antics of "der boyze" sold more copies than any ongoing reports from Nuremberg.

"Ach, dos vellose!" Der Kapitän screamed as the rascals interrupted his daily nap by lighting firecrackers under his hammock.

"Oops! Ve iz in big trouble, again!" one of the kids informed the other as they hightailed it away from the furious adult, and anyone who wanted to follow their exploits into the final panel had to move fast before the slim edition disappeared entirely.

There was not enough paper in Frankfurt to produce even a short run of the *Zeitung* since the explosion at the plant in Ludwigshafen wiped out production capacity and the resulting fire destroyed the storage yard behind the factory. Three sequoia-size rolls of printless paper had to be borrowed from the Mainz *Konstitutionell* and hauled from Mainz to Frankfurt on a flatbed truck to save the *Zeitung*'s face, if not satisfy its advertisers. The headline would have been a scoop, but in return for the loan of the paper, the *Zeitung* was forced to cede its rival exclusive rights to Elizabeth Smith Moss's dramatic photos of their own catastrophe, and that was galling.

The famous photographer had returned to the States after her series on the liberation of the camps, but she found D.C. so tedious that she wrangled a commission from the *Saturday Evening Post* to do a photo essay on The New Europe. Back in the zone, not an hour off the plane, her shortwave set to police frequency told her of the fire, and she was there, catching Fishl's shocked expression as flames appeared to leap from his ears. Retaining American rights, she sold the original negative to the *Zeitung*, which was compelled to trade the dramatic shot to Mainz for sufficient paper to run their daily installment of the K Kids.

"Perhaps ve von't see dinner diz eefning," one kid moaned to the other as the Captain dragged them off by the earlobes.

"It ought to be illegal," the other said.

"Yesterday afternoon an explosion at the Papiergeschäft obliterated the one remaining factory . . ." the staid newspaper report continued opposite the comics. "Fortunately, the perpetrator was captured at the scene of the crime. A Jew . . ." the news continued. This was the copy which landed on Isaac Kaufman's breakfast table.

"Where is he?" Isaac wondered, before he read the paper, back on Weinerstrasse. The apartment was a wreck. Half the crew was still catching up on its sleep, the other half staggering around with a caffeine hangover and a craving that couldn't be satisfied by all the beans in Brazil. There was no coffee left and neither money nor paper to make into money to obtain more. The premises, scrubbed for generations by Frau Mannheim and her former tenants, was filled with the detritus of their industry and the filth of their habits. Every surface was coated with tobacco dust or covered with cups and bowls crusted with dessicated pudding and the floor was dotted with puddles of dried Scotch hard as shellac. The only one who ever cleaned was Fishl; without him the place was a sty.

Marcus, no longer disturbed by imaginary flies buzzing around his coffee-addled head, swatted at the real things that buzzed around the leftovers, and stamped angrily on a cockroach which slid out from under the stove. "Gregor Samsa, I presume."

"What?"

"Nothing."

"Where is he?" Isaac repeated. "He should be back."

"Gregor's not coming. Neither is Franz. Nor Rabbi Akiva."

"I meant Fishl."

"Oh, him. Yes, he should be back," Marcus agreed.

"So why isn't he?"

"I don't know."

"What do you know?"

Everyone was testy, and the rent was past due. Schimmel said. "At least we can eat now."

"If . . ." warned Marcus

"If what?"

"If we had any food."

"You want food. Damnit, I'll get food." So proclaiming, Isaac went to the door, and opened it just as someone on the other side was about to knock. It was Der Schreiber, still thin and undernourished, hair grown into a shock of white pasted over his sweaty forehead. His hand was raised with his air of perpetual uncertainty.

Did he know a special knock, the one for traitors, that rat-a-tap-tap of a machine gun at midnight? "Go ahead, punch me," Isaac laughed.

"So sorry," Der Schreiber apologized, lowering his fist as if it wasn't quite attached to his wrist.

"Did you bring any eggs?"

"No."

"Potatoes?"

"I could have."

"But you didn't."

"No." The young man looked at Isaac. Shy, he was still self-possessed. "I came for a reason."

"What else is new?"

"Miranda sent me."

"Of course, the Queen of the Diaspora. And you are merely the court mailman. Or is it the court jester?"

"I'm sorry about the incident the other night."

"I don't remember it."

"That's very gracious of you."

"That's what I'm known for."

"I have, here . . ." He had the Mainz *Konstitutionell* tucked under his arm. "She asked me to give it to you."

Without a glance at the dramatic front-page photograph, Isaac thrust the paper under his own arm and said. "Thanks for keeping us so well-informed," and shut the door.

Assuming that the writer himself had an article in the paper. Isaac ignored it until he sat down to enjoy the "Katzenjammer Kids" an hour later. It took a moment to absorb the connection between the headline of the *Zeitung* and the garish photograph of the *Konstitutionell,* but as soon as Isaac noticed Elizabeth Smith Moss's credit beneath the photograph it made sense, as if every ring of the chain had to be linked and the finger pressing the shutter was the solder.

"Come here, Marcus," he demanded. "You, Berger. You," he kicked a body on the floor. "Everyone." Then he held up the paper to explain itself.

"Not again," Schimmel moaned.

"Fishl's been arrested." Marcus spoke the obvious truth, noting the size and prominence of the photo.

"What should we do?"

"Perhaps we should just wait and see."

"But we need more information, don't we?" Isaac led the discussion. "Getting this paper was a fluke. We need to get every paper, every day. We need a source in the courthouse." His mind was racing. "Then, once we know what has happened, we will know what course of action to take. But first we need to know, and there's only one person who can help us."

"One already did," Marcus muttered, referring to Miranda, but Isaac had already reached for the telephone.

"Quartermaster's," a voice answered

Isaac heard the familiar clacking of poker chips and the ringing of other telephones in the anteroom to the back office on the army base, less than a thousand yards to the west, less than a hundred feet

from the four-foot cube of gold. "Kaufman. Weinerstrasse," he identified himself. "Let me speak to Him."

Isaac tapped his foot. He wouldn't have been made to wait a week
ago. His status was evaporating.

Finally, the familiar voice picked up the phone with cheery exu-
berance. "Good morning! Make that twenty. Need any feathers? The
truck will be leaving for its daily pickup as soon as it gets gassed."

"We're not going to have the next delivery for the pickup," Isaac
blurted. "There have been . . ." He paused, then resumed, "unforseen difficulties."

"Raise you ten."

"What?"

A voice in the background upped the bet to, "Fifteen."

" 'Unforseen difficulties' sounds pretty vague. I prefer explicitness,
specificity, numbers, details. Make that twenty-five. What's happening, Rashi?"

Isaac also preferred specificity. He didn't blame Jacks Over
Deuces for his clear discontent, but for the first time he realized that
the War was over and the worst that authority would do was by no
means the worst that could be done. Gas was for trucks now. He
gained strength and said, "I need information."

"What sort of information?"

"For now, I believe that newspapers will be sufficient, daily delivery, every paper in Zone Four. But I might eventually need court
documents from Frankfurt."

"Moving around, aren't we?"

"Will you get them?"

The other voice in the distance announced, "King high straight."

"Will you get them?"

"Mine's to the Ace."

"Damn, friggin' son of a bitch. Next time I play with a noncom
we play on my field," Hank Smith bellowed.

"Will you get them?"

"What am I, Reuters?" Jacks Over Deuces scoffed as he stacked
poker chips in front of him.

"Will you get them?"

"Sure." Cheered by his winnings, Jacks Over Deuces agreed to relay any information he could obtain, although by the time he did so, Issac was grinding what was left of his teeth again. He thought of Fishl, the fool, no-good, ne'er-do-well, nebbish. He couldn't imagine what his brother had seen in the fellow, but he couldn't ask Alter, who was gone, too.

"Your deal."

Whether this was addressed to him or not, Isaac never could tell. Nevertheless his request had been granted. Mission accomplished. "Thank you," Isaac said.

And the information service Isaac relied upon provided him with the unfortunate truth. Not two hours later, Necco pulled up as per schedule, with the usual truck full of ball bearings and cigarettes. Unlike his usual routine, he didn't take any of the cigarettes out; he just left them parked in front to taunt the residents. Nor did he stay to chat. "Newspaper delivery!" he called and tossed the wrapped bundle against the front door with a single harsh thump.

"Whose knock is that?" Marcus asked as Schimmel retrieved the paper, which told of Fishl's incarceration, complete with photo, and showed the Katzenjammer Kids in yet another scrape.

Fishl, dazed by the flashbulbs, was hauled off to the local jail. The car that transported him was the same model as the one that had taken him to the Papiergeschäft one day before and the policeman at the wheel resembled his first driver. Even the jail resembled the central brick structure in the preexplosion Papiergeschäft down to the attached Quonset hut, and the prisoner felt that he was reliving Monday rather than experiencing Tuesday until he was dragged out of the car and thrown into a cell.

History was repeating itself, but without a hope of blowing up the prison and setting Fishl free with Elizabeth Smith Moss there to record his newfound liberation. Lightning strikes but once. An hour later, Fishl sat inside an eight-foot cube.

Served a penitentiary mix of rice and scrambled eggs, he contemplated his past and future. What kept him awake was wondering where Rivka was. He who had slept through coffee mania ceased sleeping. His own days and nights melded, and he hallucinated that two nasty little boys were setting fire to his earlocks as he hovered in a study over a centuries-old illuminated manuscript that turned to cigarette paper before his eyes and burned with the same flame as the crematoria. Smoke rose and he sat upright, rubbing his eyes. A priest was in the room, his face shaded by a peaked black cowl. Fishl tried to make out the face under the cowl and thought he was still dreaming.

At that same moment, when he had ceased to be news and the only reason to purchase a newspaper was the comics, Isaac said. "We're a family. We have to get him out."

Without coffee to stimulate the flow of ideas, the brain trust sat sullenly in the slovenly living room pondering any course of action. "How?" one young man who had found his way from Feldafing to Weinerstrasse the previous month asked.

"How?" another responded in the Talmudic back and forth the once-upon-a-time Yeshiva students automatically fell into.

It took every ounce of Isaac's decisiveness to turn despair into action. "You ask how to get him out of prison. Why not ask how they can keep him in prison? You think these amateurs know how to run a prison. Hah!" Isaac was getting furious. For half a year there were rules. No more. No rules and no Alter, no Fishl with no paper, no dollars. They were even running low on marks and half-straw cigarettes and Frau Mannheim was starting to make an ominous clicking noise in the back of her throat whenever she heard anyone coming off the street, a noise like a cash register opening, awaiting the ring of deposit. Isaac did not enjoy having to tiptoe past this guardian of the threshold. Whether rescuing Fishl was the right thing to do or not, it was surely the only thing to do. "I'll tell you how, we'll break him out."

"Out of prison?"

"No, out of the Tivoli Gardens. What do you think? Is he in prison? Then we get him from prison."

"How?"

"That's what I asked before."

Marcus admitted, "A little coffee would help."

Isaac at the window said, "No, a truck would help," and a moment later came the daily thump of newspapers, information that still arrived without coffee, without cigarettes, without regards. Isaac grinned horribly and said, "God provides."

Marcus stood beside Isaac. He put a hand on the younger man's shoulder. "No."

Ignoring the wise voice of restraint, Isaac leaned out the window and called as seductively as he could, "Oh, Caaaaptain?"

Necco looked up, his beefy head sinking into his shoulders. Aggressive and doleful at the same time, he announced, "It's sergeant again," as if it was Isaac's fault, forgetting that it was Isaac who led to his stripes in the first place. Life in the military hierarchy was a yo-yo. As Isaac's stock descended, so did the value of those whose misfortune it was to rise with him. Only Jacks Over Deuces remained content as a corporal with the power of a king.

"Sergeant," Isaac corrected himself, commiserating sweetly for the soldier's demotion, "we do have something here for you after all."

Resigned—and curious—Necco tramped up the stairs. Facing the blank door, he gave the Necco knock.

The door opened and a pillowcase dropped onto his head.

"Oomph. What the . . ."

As the blinded noncom reached for a gun, Schimmel placed him in a hammer lock, while the boy from Feldafing wrapped a bathrobe belt around his waist.

"You're crazy. Hey, hey! Kaufman, do you hear me!" Necco shouted.

Isaac calmly foraged in the pockets of the struggling noncom for the keys to the truck. Pulling forth a ring attached to a spent bullet shell, he said, "Yes."

"You're crazy. Help! HEL—"

Frau Mannheim or her cat might have heard the soldier's cry, but it was cut short by another belt cinched into the gap in the pillowcase where the mouth was trying to make itself heard.

Isaac addressed the bundled bag of military insignia. "Take my word, Sergeant, this is just a temporary condition, I assure you, necessary due to unforseen circumstances. But have no fear, your stripes are in the mail. We believe that we shall have your keys, your freedom, and your paper by tomorrow. I hope that you will not be missed."

"Oomph."

"Are you crazy?" Marcus repeated Necco's query.

"Just as long as the truck is gassed up, we're fine. It should take four hours to get to Ludwigshafen, and we'll figure out what to do when we get there. In the meanwhile, you vellose tek gut care of Der Kapitän, I mean Der Sergeant." Turning to those he wished to accompany him, Isaac said, "Hop to it, boyze. Der car iz vaiting."

Easing onto the big cushion behind the wheel that alleviated the pain from Sergeant Necco's hemorrhoids, Isaac veered and made a U-turn on Wienerstrasse, just missing a cement truck. Seconds later, Isaac, Marcus, and Schimmel were northward bound. Moving at sixty, seventy, ninety, one hundred thirty kilometers an hour, past hitchhikers and stalled vehicles, zigzagging around the bomb craters that the cement truck was supposed to repair, they approached Ludwigshafen almost as rapidly as a train had delivered Fishl a week before.

"Keep an eye out," Isaac said.

"For what?"

"For whatever we need to break into prison. You know what prison is? Look for dynamite. God will provide."

Marcus groaned but he looked.

Isaac hummed along with a song on the truck radio set to the Voice of America.

> Zip-a-dee-doo-dah.
> Zip a dee ay.
> I've got a feeling
> That will last all the day.
> Mr. Bluebird on my shoulder.

God did not provide dynamite, but a construction site on the outskirts of Ludwigshafen looked promising enough to pull off the road to examine. It must have been a government project because there was a guard booth, but the sentry barely glanced past the Yankee green of the truck's hood; if he had any doubts, the last army documents Marcus had shaped from the scraps of their paper horde provided easy entry past a skewed sign that read, REICHSTATION 5.

On the other side of the guard was a surprisingly large compound, with an internal roadway system that led past enormous piles of cinder blocks and heaps of sand and mortar that might have served if

Isaac wanted to build a jail rather than break into one. He cruised at random until he stopped beside the skeleton of a building, presumably Reichstation 5, that had ceased construction years ago. Its exposed steel beams were rusty and the empty structure had a forlorn, abandoned look, but hanging from the second story was a steel cable set to help hoist pallets of cinder blocks and buckets of concrete. "There," Isaac declared.

After a little creative disassembly involving the combined knotwork knowledge of the three lawbreakers (so far guilty of conspiracy, kidnapping, grand theft auto, and speeding), the cable was duly organized, and wrapped around the rear fender of the U.S. Army vehicle filled with regulation ball bearings and cigarettes. Schimmel was beginning to get into the spirit of the adventure. "Next stop, Ludwigshafen Prison."

Marcus was punctilious, "Estimated time of arrival, two A.M."

Isaac looked at the cigarettes in the cab and said, "Open a carton. I could use a Lucky right now."

The sentry saluted as the truck exited the compound.

Huffing smoke, adrenaline substituting for coffee, they drove the final miles to their destination, a municipal prison marked on Isaac's map by a miniature rendering, while Isaac planned ahead. Prisons may take many forms, and he didn't know what to expect, but assumed that between paper, steel, and the power of his will he could deal with whatever pitiful excuse for a lager the post-War authority thought fit to use to detain one of his gang.

Indeed, the actual jailhouse was almost laughable, a simple stone box with the barred windows a child might expect giving onto a small courtyard and none of the additional protection that Reichstation 5 merited. A single light shone from a room beside the front door, and a guard slept behind a desk with a copy of yesterday's *Zeitung* open to the comics page on his lap.

Parking behind the building, Isaac found a half dozen windows, and sent Schimmel to explore.

"Fishl," Schimmel hissed under each window.

"Shut up, I'm trying to sleep," a gruff voice answered from the first, and there wasn't another response until the last of the row, a faint "Yes," from the sleepless prisoner imagining his wife's chestnut hair.

"He's here," Schimmel said.

"And where else would he be, the Grotto of Capri?" Isaac stood on top of the cab of his stolen vehicle and looped the cable from the fender around the bars.

"Wait," Schimmel said, but Isaac was already in the cab, gear set to reverse, left foot to the brake, right to the gas, gunning the engine. He lifted the left foot and the car shot backward; there was a clattering racket, and the fender flew off the body of the car, and dangled from the bars.

Marcus said, "A little trickier than we thought."

An alarm went off.

"Shaddup, I said!" the far prisoner yowled.

"What's going on?" another prisoner shouted.

A light across the street went on.

"Let's get out of here," Schimmel cried.

But Isaac put the truck into forward and rammed straight ahead and the wall caved in, nearly smashing the head of Fishl on the bunk in the corner, who thought it was just another apparition.

Unfortunately the cell was built below grade, so although the wall had collapsed, the opening created was still seven feet from the base of his cell. "Come on."

"I can't climb that high."

The alarm was louder and there was a siren of an approaching police car.

"You've got about three seconds."

Fishl took a running leap, his hands flopped to the outside, his belly barely wedged up below the jagged surface of the newly created sill.

Marcus and Schimmel each took one arm and tried to pull him out, but it was only when a black-cowled priest appeared behind the prisoner and pushed that Fishl came crashing up to ground level like a trout yanked out of a stream.

"Who's that?"

The figure spread the cowl back to reveal his face and all Isaac saw in the moonlit cell filled with tumbled stonework was the scar across the man's forehead and the patch over his left eye.

"Bless you, my son," Alter made the sign of the cross.

"Come with us."

"Not now, mein bruder." In the harsh flashing light of the approaching police car, the priest swept his entire cape in a flourish and disappeared. The cape lay empty as a shadow on the floor, and the door of the cell burst open to the furious jailer.

"Excuse me," Marcus tapped Isaac on the shoulder, and the four men rushed into the truck. Its good strong military engine still roaring, they skidded past the police car, rumbled over bits of brick and plaster and broken fender and drove like the devil, ball bearings clinking in the back like a cache of silver coins, until they were well out of Ludwigshafen, across the zone and back into Regensburg by dawn.

Idling in front of 44 Weinerstrasse, Isaac said, "Schimmel, ditch the truck."

"Where's a ditch?"

"You don't know the Yankee slang by now? Lose it. Dispose of it. Get rid of it. Park it in the Vatican garage and walk home for all I care."

"Walk?"

Isaac emptied his pocket of his last bogus bills. "Here. Take a taxi. Better yet, steal a taxi and bring the cash back home. We have an appointment at the base tomorrow at four."

"All in good time," Marcus yawned. "I'm sleepy."

"I've heard that before."

Isaac and Marcus and Fishl stepped down from the jeep and waited until Schimmel drove away.

"Nu?" Isaac said. "Nu?" he repeated, louder, jarring his dazed rider.

"Huh? I'm sorry," Fishl answered. "You said?"

"I was about to say," Isaac turned philosophical, "What have you learned?"

"What do you mean?"

"We learn something from everything. Don't we?" He saw Frau Mannheim's silhouette behind the first-floor window and turned his back to the building as if contemplating the roadway. "Explosives, for example. We start with cigarettes, we move, or try to move into matches, but we suddenly understand that a match," he scratched one across the brick face of the building as if it was Frau Mannheim's face, and lit one of the Luckies he had taken from the jeep. "That a match is no less than a tiny bomb. So we move from matches to munitions. By blowing up a factory . . ."

"I didn't mean it," Fishl cried

"I don't mind it, dear boychik, because we learn from experience. You see, we suddenly understand what means we can use to obtain a certain end. We move from munitions to minerals."

Marcus was attentive and anticipated the direction of Isaac's thought. "Specific minerals."

"Yes," Isaac nodded. "Valuable minerals."

"Gold."

"Gold."

Fishl, almost forgotten in the colloquy of peers, still didn't understand and interrupted with his own dismay. "But there's one problem."

Isaac refrained from saying, "You!" when Marcus quite mildy asked, "Yes?"

Fishl sobbed, "I lost the suitcase."

"Don't mind," Isaac laughed. "We don't need money anymore. We need bombs."

"And guns," Marcus added.

"Yes, our goal is no dinky jail. It's is a U.S. Army base. You're absolutely right, Marcus. We also need guns. That's why I made an appointment tomorrow afternoon with the quartermaster's office."

"Tomorrow?"

"Tsk, tsk, how frail of me. You're correct again, Herr Morgenstern. I meant today."

"Today?"

"Time does fly."

CHAPTER 13

Money had bought the Weinerstrasse gang the privilege of lethargy. Now, lack of money turned privilege into a necessity. Deprived of their income, the gang moped around the apartment. Most reread old newspapers from the days of Fishl's incarceration, laughing at their fiftieth examination of the "Katzenjammer Kids" with hollow familiarity, while Marcus perused more rarifed material semipermanently borrowed from Count Geiger's library. He was midway through a private folio with supplementary "How To" on anti-Semitism commissioned by Pope Otto IV in 1508. It was a lovely handwritten manuscript bound in hammered brass with a keyless clasp that he ripped off with a monkey wrench.

But contemplation has limits and a life of leisure ceased to satisfy most of the would-be-racketeers. They were bored and testy, devouring the last few tins of army surplus rationing as if it was lingonberry jam. Without coffee, they slept, but sleep was the universal luxury; without money, they were poor.

Only Schimmel had discovered a new gimmick. In an age of transaction, time was important, but the clock atop the Regensburg town hall had still not been repaired so watches were popular that season. A good Yankee Timex was worth its weight in gold, but Schimmel purchased broken ones for a hundred marks each, scooped out the works, and replaced them with bumblebees. When a German buyer tried to determine if the timepiece was working without waiting for one of the hands to make its stately go round, he usually held it up to his ear, heard the reassuring buzz and paid a thousand marks. By the time the bee died, Schimmel was long gone.

Isaac immersed himself in his maps, comparing mileage charts and deciphering the symbols that distinguished population centers from provincial capitals in India, examining topographical gradations of the Andes, following a stitch representing a rail line, charting his own path from Proszowice and extending it in his head to the subways of New York. He had received a map of the latter from an American soldier in exchange for some Moroccan pornography involving veils and willing he-goats.

The soldier had kept the map in his pocket as a talisman of home, but no longer needed such a token once he was rotated stateside to ride the underground in person. This map, folded so many times that its begrimed creases took on the clarity of the printed matter, particularly intrigued Isaac. He spent hours poring over the turns the A train took on its path to a seashore resort called Far Rockaway located at the farthest extremity of the municipality whose streets were paved with the precious mineral he coveted.

With a name as exotic as Far Rockaway—and no Near Rockaway in sight—it must have been a mountainous landscape, facing the Manhattan skyline in one direction and the ocean to Europe in the other. Crowning the tallest peak, amid the outcroppings of granitic schist, sat a multiturretted castle with a pink slate roof that reflected the sunrise. The castle was guarded by crimson-uniformed hussars whose helmets sprouted soft egret plumes as they stood at attention, stiff as a dukeling's lead toy infantry. Isaac imagined a princess imprisoned in the dungeon. Her image was unclear to him—manacled to thick walls in damp, crepuscular doom—but her predicament was vivid, and the only way to help her was by taking the A train which sped under the swamps of Brooklyn, making stops at such lyrically named spots as Hoyt, Throop, and Van Siclen. To save the princess, one had to embark upon a journey that was as trying as any fairy-tale third son's quest, to a Gothic haven far from the synagogue of Proszowice and the apartment on Weinerstrasse. Isaac shifted scales and pointed to the site of Far Rockaway on a map of the world, his forefinger covering half of the Eastern United States, and said, "That's where I want to live."

"Tell me when you get a map of Australia," Marcus answered, and for the first time he considered going out on his own. His intellectual curiosity had also reached its limit; his patience was frayed. "That's where I'd go."

"Why don't you?"

"Inertia." He flipped a page in the church manuscript, from black magic to blood sacrifice. "I am subject to the same forces as nations and galaxies. A body in motion tends to stay in motion. A body at rest tends to remain at rest."

"Subways never stop," Isaac said.

"Only friction slows anything down. Of course, too much friction leads to fire."

Though he would never dare to mock Isaac, the newly successful Schimmel felt free to put in his two cents. "No friction here since the Green Hen girls refused to come if they didn't get paid."

Berger said, "They came; they just didn't want to give you the satisfaction of knowing that."

Schimmel threw a pillow at him.

"Subways," Isaac continued, ignoring the others' antic remarks. "Imagine if there was a subway right here."

"Great, we could go straight into Regensburg," Marcus replied. "What a thrill."

"Go to Regensburg," Isaac repeated and then commanded. "Go to Regensburg. I said, 'Go!'"

And despite his eroding authority, with neither goods nor paper to back up his command, Schimmel obeyed. Berger followed less reflexively, and so did a pair of twins recruited by Isaac in the marketplace several weeks earlier. They had been standing like bookends flanking a pushcart filled with shoes, none of them paired, when Isaac ambled by and was struck by the mirror image faces on either side of the heap of random footwear: left boots, right opera shoes, and stray pumps, slippers, and wingtips. Isaac was as amazed by the twins' strange dual form as the German Doktor who had kept them under observation until it was too late to kill them, and then he offered to purchase the entire cart. Between offer and payment, however, he took them in as tenants, who quite naturally fell into the routine of Weinerstrasse and contributed their stock to the group's own Canada. Like Schimmel, the twins followed directions well. The only one who didn't budge was Fishl. He sat cross-legged in the shade of the empty refrigerator, searching his mind for a particular passage from the decisions of the Sanhedrin.

Fishl had joined a group that gathered together for weekly study, assigning themselves a portion of some given text. Their problem was access to material, but Fishl became their library, reciting the pages he had committed to memory, summoning tractates from his childhood. He was the blank slate on which his peers wrote their commentary. This group, not quite as odd as the Weinerstrasse confederation, was culled from the same pool of recruits, self-selected by those with a more theological bent. There was a young rabbi from Vilna, an insurance man who had grown up in Regensburg, and even Der Schreiber attended the group's farbrengen. They met in the Joint's assembly room and in the park and once on Weinerstrasse, but never again since the scribbler's famous altercation with Isaac.

"This is a business, not a school!" Isaac raged as he remembered the yeshiva of his own youth, gray wooden shingles loose as the walls of the lager and crowded just as fully with youth endlessly flipping the pages of the holy writ, as Fishl flipped through the texts in his head.

Only the voice of Alter, wherever he was, permitted the incompetent Fishl to remain and continue to re-create the vanished world out of his head as he failed once and again to fulfill his mission and inadvertently blew up the Papiergeschäft. But Fishl's ideas entered Isaac as unbidden as a subway to a tunnel, and sometimes infuriated him. "Go, damnit!" Isaac shrieked. "Get out of my sight!"

A hurt look swimming in his eyes, Fishl prepared to leave, though he had to ask Rivka's permission first.

"Why?" Berger asked, "Do you want to sell her red knickers to the paratroopers?"

But Fishl couldn't have done this if he wished. Rivka's undergarments were as clean as Frau Mannheim's sheets, and Berger was jealous.

Whatever life force had gone to creating the flow that stained was put to more particular use now, yet the Jews were too ignorant to understand what was happening, even after other symptoms become evident. Nausea was common among them, and so was an exhaustion that had been waiting for years to reveal itself with impunity. Only when Rivka's belly began to expand did they begin to realize the biological process that was as inevitable as War was in August 1939. Just as plans hatched in the Reichstag set the due date for September 1, so a different timetable had its absolute end point.

Inside Rivka's swelling abdomen, there was a baby struggling for Lebensraum, breathing room.

The announcement of Rivka's pregnancy had been made to great celebration, but that, too, was forgotten over time and "knickers," her humiliating nickname, remained; nine months was forever in a world without consequence, duration incomprehensible after the pure immediacy of the camps. But the inexorable growth of Rivka's belly continued until it was unavoidable. On the infrequent occasions when she left her nest in the small room off the Weinerstrasse kitchen, she bumped into people because she didn't realize how much space she occupied.

Passersby in a world where figures could only put on weight by eating thought she was voluptuous compared to the scrawny prostitutes of the Green Hen. Even among the Germans, there were virtually no births during the first half of the decade. Weight could only mean food, food meant money, money meant freedom, so sheer volume was a sheer value, clear and erotic and measurable as life itself.

The idea that weight would emerge into its own being was as extravagant as resurrection.

"I don't feel good," Rivka sighed, lying in bed, fingers creeping across the mattress and clutching at the tattered coverlet.

Fishl smoothed the damp hair off her forehead, and stared at the dome of her belly with astonishment. "You're looking pale today."

"My child," she said.

"Our child."

"Not him, or her. You."

"Me?"

"Isaac wants you to go, so go. I'll be all right."

"I don't have to. I can get you a glass of tea. We still have tea."

"Time enough for that." Rivka turned into the covers, and her hair spread across the pillow.

The ragged group that had once had wheels when others hiked keenly felt the degradation as they tramped on foot, and Fishl remembered a parable about a rich timber merchant from Bialystock who lost half of his fortune in speculation and was reduced from four horses to two. The local rabbi gave him enough money for two more horses, but his students responded angrily to this gesture. "Here, this man still has two horses, when we have none, yet him you give charity."

"You don't understand," replied the wise man. "He feels the loss of the two worse than we feel the lack of any."

Tugging the pensive Fishl along with them, Schimmel and a few of the swollen-footed new members were sent out without a benevolent donor to pound more pavement in common labor. "Remember," Schimmel said, "Arbeit macht frei."

But try as he did to mimic Isaac's cynical authority, it came out glib and vulgar.

Fishl looked at him with pain.

Schimmel sneered, and said, "This way," veering off The Carlsbad Road to the post office, a stumpy limestone cube hewed from Protestant values when the town was founded by a band of Martin Luther's acolytes in the sixteenth century.

In the absence of Herr Mannheim and his coworkers, the U.S. Army insisted that the municipality of Regensburg hire Jews for any available jobs whether as hospital attendants, sanitation workers, or postmen. Hospital labor was generally preferred, because aspirin and bandages could slip out the door of the supply closet, but Isaac insisted that his men apply for the postal positions. The hospital was acquisition, the post distribution. That was where the power was. Isaac never worked himself, but his gang used the route to sell tins of food from the commissary along with the aspirin others liberated from the hospital as well as back issues of *Screen Star Magazine* they acquired from soldiers at the PX in Liebknecht. Paid a salary by the government, they toted yo-yos and English-language primers and occasional fruit cakes door to door in their canvas bags. When there wasn't enough room for both merchandise and mail, they tossed the mail into the sewer.

Mail floated in the sluggish current under the Regensburg town hall to the Danube, bobbing among the townfolks' shit and random waste products. Stamps came unglued and drifted off envelopes and washed up on foreign shores while the mail itself—love letters, dunning notices, party invitations and suicide notes—was swept to some vast Sargasso, swirling among the lost communications of the ages— cuneiform tablets miraculously buoyed by the salt water along with illuminated manuscripts, papyrus, parchment, and telegrams conveying President Wilson's regret that your son won't be coming home for Xmas—consigned to the dead letter office in the blue.

Unfortunately, since Fishl's debacle at the Papiergeschäft, Weinerstrasse itself might have been lost in the Sargasso. Its ability to deliver the most desired commodity, paper, transformed through the judicious application of Marcus's skills into a skeleton key that could open other doors, was curtailed. Worse, they wouldn't have known what paper to deliver instead of the mail. So many refugees were floating back and forth beyond the ability of any army to contain them that all borders were essentially open.

Even those most stationary of Jews, the dead ones, no longer needed their DPIDs since the military government had dispensed with such documentation. It had taken a while, while the Jews in question built up like a barricade around the perimeter of the camp at Libeknecht, until the Fifth Army's chief medic called on his own authority to set the stalled bulldozers moving again. Confronted with a steaming pile of flesh, he quite rationally declared, "It's typhus or names."

In just as long a moment as it had taken to adopt DPIDs, they were rendered useless. So even if Issac had paper, he did not have a crystal ball to tell him what to imprint upon its virgin surface.

Thereafter, they tried to stick to cash, but even so they couldn't keep up with the inflation. Denominations that were too huge to be cashable on Tuesday were picayune by Thursday.

Once dealings shifted back from identification to currency to produce, bulk came into the picture. No longer able to carry the company's stock in a briefcase, they needed muscles to load and unload whatever left shoes they were selling that week. Nobody bought their watches anymore.

It was up and down on a tiny chart, minor coups, major defeats. Once Isaac and Marcus bought eggs at the Gymnasium, all of them, every egg for sale, cornering the market. They didn't eat the eggs, though—they were too valuable. Instead, they traded them for boots, full pairs, triple EEE width stuffed with newspapers to take up the slack, marched to buy more eggs that they held again to trade far beyond their useful life, despite the sulfurous taint of embryonic decay that issued from their mail bags. Eventually, they traded the mailbags themselves for more fresh eggs. For a week, they felt as if they had reattained some position.

Then they were summoned to deliver eggs to the mayor's office. Expected, they were ushered into the executive chambers and greeted not by Herr Uhlmuth himself, but his son, a young man Isaac's own age, with black hair recently grown out of a style familiar from posters and postage stamps, brushed off his forehead, commencing to curl behind his ears.

Standing over a single burner hot plate in his office, the mayor's son cooked the egg in a pool of boiling tap water, counting the seconds on a military chronometer. Then he opened his father's desk and took out a spoon marked with the Reich's eagle. Noticing the insignia, he shrugged, "Old habits die hard, yes?" and rapped the dome of the egg until it broke into a jigsaw pattern. He plucked away several of the shards and then he plunged the spoon into the heart of the oval.

He ate the egg, its solid white and congealing orange-yellow clearly done to perfection, in two gulps, smacked his lips and said, "That was no good."

"No good?"

"Nein," he said, and rubbed the spoon smooth on a municipal dog license before replacing it in his father's desk. "You should be glad that we don't arrest you for selling tainted edibles."

Schimmel started forward, but Marcus restrained him.

"Your friend has a problem?"

"No, Sir."

"Good, so you will leave the rest of the eggs as evidence, and perhaps you can return when you have better quality. Say next Monday."

"Perhaps."

"I'll put it on my calendar. That should fall just prior to the annual inspection of all provender suppliers."

"Sounds convenient," Isaac agreed, but as they were stalking down the front steps of the town hall, he said, "We could beat him up."

"No," Marcus said, "we work, we achieve . . ."

"And then they kill us, the same as always."

"Perhaps."

"What do you suggest, that we tell his father?"

But the second Isaac made this comment a stadium of fathers appeared in his mind. Tiers of fathers rose to a sky dotted with constellations of fathers and spread into a firmament of fathers, kind smiling fathers, grim studious dads, evil sires, benevolent progenitors. Father upon father filled the horizon and the empyrean—all of them dead. Isaac looked at Fishl, who was going to be a father himself one of these days, on this earth, and said, "Go!"

Occasionally, after he sent the troops off on their errands, Isaac paced the streets of the town he had briefly owned and felt worthless. He felt this most sharply when he approached the café outside of the Green Hen, where those who had proven to be wiser manipulators than himself were sitting in the shade of blue-striped umbrellas set into holes in the center of round tables set on the sidewalk. They were the ones who had anticipated the change to oil and real commodities that retained value best. The only papers they dealt in were invoices, receipts, and notes exchangeable on demand. Lesser manipulators eagerly accepted their crumbs, gleaning those deals too small for the highfliers' notice.

The Weinerstrasse gang's previous history at the club might have gained them passage through the velvet-roped passport control, if not a sympathetic shot at the bar, but Isaac forbade reliance on the kindness of strangers. "A debt is a debt. Until it can be paid it should not be incurred."

Marcus looked up and said, "Really?"

"Paid, or ignored." Isaac clarified.

"Some debts can't be ignored?"

"A few."

"Well, look who comes to visit. Long time, no see."

At their last visit, Pinsker, resplendent in regimental tie and tweed suckered off a British major, offered to hire Isaac's organization to smuggle motor oil, hidden in kegs marked BLUE NUN wine from the Rhine valley. It was a deliberately degrading offer, but "Hey," Pinsker smirked, "it's a parnoseh," a living.

Pinsker collected people. Beside him were several of his lieutenants, who might as well have been named Pinsker II and Pinsker III for all the variety and individual character they showed, smirking along with the boss, but he also had Der Schreiber slouching cozily in one of the woven rattan seats at the table, sipping carbonated water.

Der Schreiber said, "Their wisdom lags behind their pocket."

Marcus observed, "One can be entertained by a pet parrot, but it will still shit on your table."

"My skeptic," Pinsker agreed, happily accepting the writer's abuse as he snapped his fingers for another round. But it was clear that if Isaac accepted Pinsker's parnoseh, he would not be allowed Der Schreiber's freedom; he would be Pinsker IV, a human trophy to please Pinsker I.

The waiter went to fetch the wine that had been smuggled in kegs marked MOTOR OIL, and sounds of hilarity seeped out the padded door to the interior of the club.

Inside, the same show as Isaac first saw ages before entertained the usual dissolute batch of soldiers, visitors, and bums. The same slack girls were on display. Hair coloring at a shortage, crow black strands emerged from their prematurely gray roots, and hung down upon costumes threadbare with innumerable puttings on and takings off. Still, they were the only game in town. The routine at the Green Hen had gone stale, but stale bread was the staff of Regensburg's life. Only a captive audience and lack of competition kept the place alive.

"Skeptics sometimes speak the truth," Der Schreiber said.

"You see, you need someone to keep you honest, Kaufman." Pinsker said. "That was your mistake."

"Pride," Der Schreiber agreed with his patron this time. He wasn't on anybody's side; he was the disagreeable voice of integrity.

"How's your book going?" Isaac asked.

"I must admit, I'm proud of it." Der Schreiber saw vanity wherever he looked, even in the mirror.

Isaac knew how far down the evolutionary ladder he had slipped when he noticed himself peering at an unusually long cigarette butt on the street. A year ago it would have been a treasure; six months ago a carton would have been beneath disdain. Now, long since finished with the cache from Necco's jeep, he didn't pounce, though he was tempted to stoop. It looked good, hardly crushed by street traffic, a filter with lipstick, a Bulgarian brand mixed with real Turkish tobacco. Isaac was theoretically free to ignore the enticing remnant, but his desire was obvious.

Pinsker noticed Isaac's yearning and generously called out, "Hey, have one of mine."

"No thanks, I'm trying to quit."

"Too expensive?"

"Haven't you heard, they're bad for your health."

"Sick or healthy, I'm always on the lookout for good help." Pinsker repeated his offer of a job, as he poured out another glassfull of bubbling white wine.

"We'll think about it."

When there was no way in Hell they would.

"The offer may not last forever."

"Neither will you," Marcus said, reaching out one finger like a pen to paper and tipping the fluted stem glass onto their would-be employer's lap.

Pinsker jumped up, sputtering, "You'll regret that, Morgenstern," as the other Pinskers, but not Der Schreiber, wiped frenetically at his spotted crotch.

That was why Isaac and Marcus Morgenstern lived so well together; their relationship was forged by willpower. Acting against self-interest was the ultimate indulgence, but it was all that remained to prove their worth.

"What happened to inertia?" Isaac asked.

Marcus shrugged.

In addition to the friendships that were determined immediately in the chaos, more ties were established daily. More gangs were formed, more cousins of cousins discovered, tenuous family connections serving to replace those closer genealogical links that had been broken, and more marriages consecrated by U.S. chaplains who joked among themselves that they might as well be stationed in Las Vegas.

Elsewhere in the zone, Rivka's state was echoed in the swelling waist lines of women who started to replicate, and then the DP camps heard a sound that had been inaudible since the very last Hungarian roundups of '44. The difference was that these new squawls were hushed differently than those of '44, not with a gunshot but the satisfied burble of life at the breast.

The Joint began to order infant formula, as well as teething rings, baskets, and bales of diapers.

Since establishing its regional headquarters in Regensburg, the Joint's space had doubled, as a flood of donations poured in every time one of Elizabeth Smith Moss's photographs appeared in the American press, and the front room was filled with young do-gooders at desks, on telephones, arranging food, medical supplies, and transport. Unlike the papers generated in the bathtub on Weinerstrasse, bona fide visas started to remove a boatload at a time from the Continent, starting with those who had relatives in the states willing to sign for them. The plan was to depopulate the camps gradually by sending the last remaining, most misbegotten orphaned wards of the tribe to cultivate orange groves while learning the language of their ancestors in Palestine.

"Our object," Miranda said, "is to put ourselves out of business," as she also worked to put Isaac out of business.

"Eighty million Arabs and and a desert: Who needs it?" Isaac said as envy or—he would have insisted—mere Chance drew his path to the door of the Joint.

"Shall we?" he pretended to ask Marcus.

"Can't be any worse than the Hen."

"Sure it can, but shall we?"

"After you."

"No, after you." Isaac let Marcus thread their way through the clusters of milling refugees. It reminded Marcus of the PX at the army camp, without the backroom poker. Perhaps this hubbub was the American style. As usual, Miranda was a one woman flurry, looking over this one's shoulders, checking that one's clipboard, until she noticed the unexpected visitors. Her eyes widened, then narrowed. She smoothed the lapels of her blouse, and her hands fluttered down to clamp upon the outlines of her waist.

"Busy?" Isaac said.

"There's a party," she replied.

"Oh, goody, let's have fun!"

Miranda ignored Isaac and addressed herself to Marcus. "It's two weeks from Sunday. I received an invitation for myself and one for you."

"Me?"

"All of you. I'm just a mailbox."

"Why didn't you send Der Schreiber. He's very good at such tasks."

Miranda continued. "I just received it yesterday. I would have sent it over this afternoon. Here." She handed Marcus a gilt embossed form, with a watermark of a jackal.

YOU ARE INVITED TO A RECEPTION
ON BOARD THE *ANUBIS*.
DRESS FOR THE SAKE OF DECEPTION.
PIER 14.
THE BOAT WILL DEBARK AT MIDNIGHT.

No name was given and no RSVP required.

"Pretty mysterious, huh?"

Isaac couldn't tell if she was sarcastic or serious; she could have been either. The *Anubis* was a forty-meter yacht that had appeared a week earlier, a sumptuous teak-and-brass apparition come downstream from God knew where, although it was rumored to be the former Reich's Minister of Propaganda's "playboat," commissioned from the subworks in Hamburg, but never used because the Danube's gentle current made the boat's master queasy.

The boat docked at the municipal pier on the edge of town from which temporary port its crew, clad in naval bellbottoms, black T-shirts, and matching berets, had come into the square to purchase supplies. Whatever currency the merchants desired, they had. Whatever the price of whatever luxury, they paid. But when the local shakedown artists led by the mayor's son appeared to collect docking fees, the captain, a tall, rubber-hued Indonesian veteran of the South Seas, laughed, and said, "The plank is only wide enough for one person at a time. Who wants to be the first to step on it?" and took out a pistol.

Except for the crew who went about their errands with strange, silent rectitude and did not, as any normal sailors would, so much as check out the Vivant or the Green Hen, the boat remained virtually still in the small cove for a week until the mate, a saturnine Alsatian who only appeared on board with various nautical instruments and charts for five minutes at dawn and at dusk, issued a summons for local carpenters and painters. These lucky craftsmen were set to work erecting canopies and banks of terraced seating over the prow. They labored in three shifts around the clock and were paid fabulous wages that were the envy of the town. Clearly an occasion was in preparation, but no one could imagine what it was despite the ardent speculation ashore. Then the invitations appeared. They were a sensation at first, and the recipients displayed them proudly until it became apparent that everyone of any consequence in Regensburg was invited. Whoever had composed the guest list knew the elaborate social pecking order of the zone, and had included soldiers, smugglers, bureaucrats, and the mayor and his son. Let them make of it what they will. No RSVP was necessary, because there was no doubt that everyone would come.

"Nice paper," Marcus commented, genuinely impressed by the rare bond even as he feigned even greater enthusiasm to distract Miranda while Isaac backed up to a Gestetner machine and slipped a ream of mimeo paper into a pocket sewn into the back of his jacket for the purpose. The paper would be good to have, but the theft was a reflex, and hardly provided enough raw material to be worth the tea to steep and stain it in; besides which, the forms changed faster than their ability to counterfeit them.

"How's Rivka?" Miranda asked.

"What do you mean?"

"I mean how is the young woman who is going to have a baby feeling?"

"How should she be feeling?"

Miranda rolled her eyes, signaling their dismissal, and Isaac was too chagrined to do anything but slink out the door.

A moment later, when Alan Foyle came from his clean back office, Miranda was arranging work on her desk. "What were they here for?" he asked.

"Just stealing paper."

BOOK IV

CELEBRATION

CHAPTER 14

Once upon a time, many years ago, a young girl named Cinderella watched her mean, snub-nosed stepsisters ready themselves for the castle ball, a gala affair to which all the likely young ladies in the kingdom were invited. The castle itself was just like the one in Far Rockaway, its gleaming turrets overlooking a fertile quilt of small farms abundant with sweet potatoes and sugar beets, which were harvested and brought into the castle by singing peasants in wooden spoked carts, hauled by teams of dappled mares. Inside the castle walls was a bustling square, like the one in Regensburg, where happy citizens met to exchange goods and chat at the local soda shoppe. There was also a tiny theater in which The Passion of St. Mark played perenially, a gingerbread factory that produced toys in a golden haze of lathed larch wood dust, a gas chamber, and the prettiest little fountain topped by an apple-balled cherub who peed an endless stream of bubbling Rhinevasser into a clamshell basin, glittering— even these days—with the coins tossed in by those who believed the boy's urine was lucky. Despite the outward serenity, however, all was not well in the kingdom.

The prince needed a wife, the land an heir, a leader, a future. That's why the dance was being held, to find the prince a mate, and all the eligible young women were summoned to pass under his rod, to be deemed fecund as the farms or returned to their flock. Oh, the fussing and primping that went into their toilette with an eye toward reaping this precious reward, from satin buckles on their shoes to hair ribbon and beads.

In one smaller castle, Cinderella's two stepsisters engaged in a frenzy of last minute preparations, ordering Cinderella to shine those shoes for the fourth time, take up this hem just a quarter of an inch, make every single final adjustment to perfect their attire. Poor Cinderella was so busy assisting her demanding stepsisters that she couldn't iron her own modest pinafore and clean her own fawn-colored saddle shoes and couldn't possibly attend the ball in her shtetl rags.

Finally, the sisters went off to the ball, and Cinderella was left alone, weeping by the hearth that inspired her humiliating nickname, until the shimmering, glimmering figure of an elderly female took shape, hovering several inches above the flagstoned kitchen floor. "I," she said, "am your fairy godmother."

Wiping the tears from her eyes, Cinderella asked. "What's that?"

"I am that I am," was all the transparent woman's enigmatic reply, but it was sufficient.

Genie, wraith, spirit, hallucination, she was benevolent and almost omnipotent. A wave of a wand like a leather riding crop and, voilà, shebang, metamorphosis, a pumpkin turned into a carriage, mice to footmen, rats into six noble white steeds, Cinderella's rags to a stunning, floor-sweeping gown that revealed healthy cleavage—even the girl's breasts grew larger with her fairy godmother's help—spider webs to strands of pearls strung from her hair and neck and the Tseno U' Raenah into an embossed, watermarked party invitation. Cinderella was a vision, newly beautiful as she was eternally good.

But as the delighted girl raised a single delicate glass-shod toe to step into the coach that the ex-rodent footman held open for her, the fairy godmother had one single caution, "Nu, dearie, the magic will disappear at the stroke of midnight. You got that?"

Cinderella nodded and promptly forgot. She arrived at the ball, caught the prince's eye, danced, and lost track of time until it was too late. High atop the castle, a deafened lackey wielded an enormous padded mallet upon the suspended copper bell.

Gong. Gong. Gong.

Only the sound of midnight's chimes brought the fairy godmother's warning to mind.

Gong. Gong. Gong.

Cinderella dashed for the door.

Gong. Gong. Gong.

"Hey, wait!" the handsome prince cried out for her. "I don't even know your name."

Gong. Gong.

The door was locked. Cinderella didn't have passport, a visa, a boat ticket to Far Rockaway.

Gong.

The magic disappeared in a flash. Her gown turned to shreds, her prince to a poor yeshiva student, the castle to a shul, and the colorful court orderlies to panzer troops.

Blitzkrieg. The glass slipper slipped off and smashed into a thousand shards, and Cinderella was barefoot, bleeding.

Anubis: Egyptian God of death and funerary procedure, master of embalming, enshrouding, and burial skills. From the baked mud brick bottom of the Nile to the celestial oasis, the jackal-faced deity keeps the measure of time alloted his human tenants. Whether or not they acknowledge him, pray to him, and seek his blessings, he confers or withholds those blessings on beings from Luxor to Liebknecht and everyplace that has ever been mapped in-between.

Liebknecht: an imaginary village, latitude 48.7, longitude 12.9, where real people would have been killed had they the misfortune to live anywhere nearby—if their faith had been the faith of those who once suffered in the domain of Anubis and his earthly avatars, the pharaohs.

Liebknecht: a small village of death outside of Regensburg, a real city, in which imaginary people now roam, on their way to a fairy tale appointment aboard a yacht named *Anubis*.

The day before the party, the residents of Zone Three were abuzz, frantic with last minute anticipation. Hairspray was in great demand and the shelves of the PX were empty of Brylcreem, Aqua Velva, and Kiwi brand shoe polish necessary to look one's best for the event of the season. The ointments and lotions were easy to come by, but the "dress for deception" line in the invitation was taken to mean "costume" and that was more difficult.

In a sense, everyone in Zone Three dressed in costume, be it military uniform or rags pending the resuscitation of a textile industry or the lime green spats of the flamboyant black marketeers. In order to deceive, however, the party invitees were required to swap outfits, and that was the first, most natural path of deception. American marines exchanged their stripes for Pinsker's gang's pinstripes, while others sought a playful sexual turnabout. Wacs wore slacks and Alan Foyle of the Joint begged to borrow Miranda's yellow dress, her mascara, and perfume. Nylons were hard to find so Alan had to make do with a less delicately woven mesh that stretched taut over his elegantly molded thighs.

Marcus Morgenstern knew costumes from his days of urban life— he recalled the bloodred gown an actress who played Lady Macbeth wore with particular vividness—but the only experience the less urbane of the Weinerstrasse crew had with costumes dated from antediluvian Purims, when their shtetls would go wild with the shrieks of miniature Hamans, Mordecais, and Esthers. By 1947, the holiday that recounted the miraculous salvation of Persian Jewry was noted ironically rather than celebrated effusively, and nobody was dressing as the biblically righteous until today. Still, there was an abundance of more indigenous Jewish costumes in Liebknecht's Canada, and these were the special favorites of the German invitees, duded up in Hasidic gabardines and wide-brimmed, fur-lined hats. One young fraülein wrapped an embroidered prayer shawl around her crotch, exposed midriff and bust—a Halakhically inspired bathing suit.

Others responded to different cultural images. Some high-ranking American soldiers, pleased to recollect the days of their childhood, patched together costumes in the tradition of a Winesburg Halloween, burnt corks simulating the kind of chin-rubble army discipline forbade, mops cut down to create fright wigs, and one major dressed himself in a black sheet sketched over with bones of a phosphorescent white paint otherwise used to delineate airplane landing strips.

For those who had come from the new world on seaborne convoys, the party began early. Breakfast at the PX consisted of scrambled eggs and Jax beers (General Hank Smith's favorite) that sloshed onto the green felt table along with the cards that deposited the usual leavings in front of the usual faces to nobody's surprise or suspicion.

"What, me again!" Jacks Over Deuces cried with pretend amazement, spreading five hearts in a fan.

"Flush with flush," one of the other players said.

Raking it in, the corporal changed the subject and asked Necco for a costume. "Party's tonight and I don't have a thing to wear. How about my borrowing your uniform, Sergeant. It will be a step up in the world."

"Yes, Sir," Necco saluted.

"So how 'bout now, boy?" Hank Smith said. He was losing big and seemed to need to show his authority, although it also looked as if he was afraid his own stars might be requisitioned by the corporal who already had all his cash.

"Now, Sir?"

"Now. Let's see what the corporal would look like with a promotion. Drop trou."

"Here?"

"And now!"

"Yes, Sir." Embarrassed, Necco stripped as a new hand was dealt. A tattoo of a roller coaster appeared on his bicep as he shed his pants and shirt.

"Thank you, Sergeant, that will be all. Ten to open," Jacks Over Deuces said, and Necco left the quartermaster's office in skivvies and a fierce expression that dared anyone to notice his temporary lack of proper military attire.

"Think he'll wear that to the party?" Hank Smith guffawed and met the corporal's bet, bound to lose once again.

Marcus was dressed in his pre-War occupational getup, that of a dental surgeon in white smock, with a holster full of dental instruments strapped to his waist and a coal miner's lamp set upon his forehead to illuminate the mouths in which he sought gold that had not already been mined and refined and stored in public display.

Schimmel was dressed as a Nazi kommandant, complete with riding crop with which he slapped his boots with pleasant, authoritative whacks.

Fishl didn't dress up, but he might have been the parody of a reufgee in an ill-fitting sack of a sweater and baggy pants. He and Rivka, inclined to sit at home like a pair of sad-faced Cinderellas, were urged to come.

"You must," Marcus said.

"Why? I don't like parties."

"Have you ever been to a party?"

"No." The ineluctability of the logic failed to convince him. "But I don't have to do everything that I haven't done before."

Marcus said, "Fishl, we were invited. It would be rude not to attend."

"And why do they care if I attend?"

"I don't know." They all paused to contemplate the mystery.

"It will be a place where things will happen." Isaac the seer read the future, then insisted that it was determined by the past. "As long as Alter has placed you with us, you will do as we do, and we are all going, all of us."

"But . . ."

"Perhaps you can stuff a pillow into that scarecrow belly of yours and go as Rivka."

Appalled at the suggestion, Fishl conceded the larger issue, "I'll find something else."

"Good."

"And what about yourself?"

But a costume involved too great a leap of personal transformation for Isaac to imagine. Before donning an outfit, he tended to a more economic view of the party. Where there was a demand, there was a place for a supplier, so he managed to pocket a few stray marks trading wedding veils, and took in more substantial profits with a boxful of Venetian Carnevale masks rushed in from Trieste. Then he discovered that the real vein was already in Regensburg, ready to be tapped by the miner able to perceive it. Like the purloined letter, a heap of random costumes were sitting in plain sight on top of the trunks backstage at the Green Hen. Isaac swapped these to the same girls who wore them daily for chits for sex.

"Our own gear," one bitched.

"Just because you wear them does not mean you own them," he

said, brandishing the bill of sale, done up to his specifications by Marcus the night before—but who would know the difference?

The girls were scheduled to perform at the party, but they wanted something more elegant for the rest of the evening, to mix, mingle, and, with luck, catch the eye of a prince with a one-way ticket out of the zone.

"It's a trade," he said. Each girl had to sign an IOU for herself and her friends. In case one caught typhus or fled, her chit could still be exacted of her cosignor.

"It's not really unfair," Isaac explained to Marcus. "They wear what they would wear anyway, and they do what they would do anyway."

"And so do you."

"It's a zero-sum game."

"Except your pockets are a wee bit fuller."

"Call me J. P. Morgan."

The girls had hitched a ride with an Italian sailor, who dropped them giggling at the door of Weinerstrasse. Frau Mannheim scoffed audibly from behind her door, but even she was excited about the party, and followed them up the stairs.

"The rent's not due till next week," Berger said.

"And who's asking about the rent? she barreled past the entry into the living room, where half a dozen girls were swamped amid their possibilities that looked so different here than they had twenty-four hours earlier in the dressing room of the Hen. "My what a lovely dress. I was thinking of something like this." Mrs. Mannheim lifted a green brassiere up to her substantial chest, like a stamp celebrating some national park to a manila envelope.

"*You* were invited?"

"*I* was invited."

And why shouldn't the landlady to the postal service merit such honor?

Everyone was invited, but no one knew the capacity of the *Anubis*. Nonetheless, it seemed the party givers were confident that the boat's nether regions could expand as much as necessary to accommodate whomever found eternal abode beyond its obsidian gates.

"Any advance billings, luv?" asked one of the girls Isaac had taken on the kitchen table ages earlier, as she chose a sleek black number with conical breasts built outward in a wire mesh framework.

"Give it time."

"Sure you don't want to use a chit right now?" she persisted, rolling a stocking far above the knee onto her mottled thigh, but Isaac withstood the temptation. He had other things on his mind.

Schimmel, though, indulged, and took two girls upon his beswastikaed arms. Flushed with pre-party drink, he gazed upon the four available legs and proclaimed, "It's a new world."

"Funny," one girl said, tipping his black visor backward, "it looks just like the old one." There was the combined aroma of sweat and a dab of pre-War perfume as she lifted her arms and dropped them on Schimmel's shoulders.

"You'll owe me," Isaac warned Schimmel.

"I'll pay you," Schimmel promised.

"I'm not feeling good," Rivka said, retreating toward the bedroom, unwilling to see those who did the same thing she had (at least once), without the obvious consequences.

"She going as a virgin?" the raven-chested girl laughed.

Costumes sold, even Isaac was in a jolly mood, and offered everyone tea. If they weren't going to be staining passports, they might as well drink the stuff, or whatever else was available, and by the time the witching hour approached, they were all spiked with the dregs of Scotch left about from better days.

Feeling pleasant, Isaac sifted through the underwear the girls had left behind, and in a moment of inspiration he saw his own costume. He took two pairs of tights into the bathroom along with a pair of scissors and a prop from one the Hen's most popular shows. "The Woodsman and the Wolf."

"Getting on midnight," Marcus the timekeeper announced and Mrs. Mannheim offered her car in a transport of booze-induced affection for "de girls" if not their companions. Unlike the *Anubis*, the car was not infinitely capacious, but it was convenient, so they jammed in, girls giggling on "de boyze" laps, Mrs. Mannheim acting as chauffeur and chaperone.

The whole town was deserted, the Green Hen and the Vivant both dark for the night. Any poor slob wandering the streets without an invitation was hardly a human being. The Germans looked like mice slinking along the perimeter of the square, as the mice came out to feast on the meager leavings of the market, and no one turned them into handsome footmen, although from a sidelong view beneath the breasts of his lap-rider, Issac did think that Mrs. Mannheim bore a distinctly rodent expression during their merry passage from Weinerstrasse to the pier.

Once the carpenters put the final touches on the seating, tacking elaborate egg and dart mouldings to the edges of their bleachers, painters set to rendering garlands of flowers on every surface in sight. It didn't seem to make a difference that their faux florals were to be obscured by masses of fresh orchids trucked in for the occasion from the last operating greenhouse in Milan.

Excess was the only principle. Electricians strung cables and sound men fiddled with microphones on the flower-strewn stage. Below-decks the kitchen staff labored overtime to produce the kind of feast that hadn't been seen in Regensburg since the rallies of '36. Sweetbreads were simmering, oysters shucked, cubes of elk and venison skewered while pastry chefs iced three-tiered angel food cakes and an army of assistants molded a vat of marzipan into a topographic map of Mitteleuropa from Copenhagen to Trieste, marked with different shades of food coloring to delineate the different Allies' spheres of influence.

A string of Japanese lanterns swayed gently in the breeze, and a dozen more stationary lights made twin lines down the wooden dock over the dark water. At the point where the path lead onto the boat visitors passed under an arch of wrought iron letters that read, WILLKOMMEN. And a butler costumed in the style of Louis XIV announced the names of the guests to the empty dance floor.

People started to arrive at eleven and by eleven-thirty the boat began to ride slightly lower in its berth. Cars double-and triple-parked and still more partygoers streamed aboard. Figures with plumed hats that brushed the lanterns walked the gangway in front of men covered neck to navel with military insignia. Aside from the setting it might have been opening night for a new show at the Green Hen or the Copacabana. Hookers and generals, rabbis and gangsters, anyone in the zone with any claim to clout was there, done up as sultans, Roman senators, William Shakespeare, or wearing each others' clothes, civilizans as soldiers, soldiers as rabbis, rabbis as hookers, hookers as close to ladies as they could get.

The only one who hadn't made an appearance yet was the host. All the interior cabins were still locked, and nobody knew what lay behind the brass hardware. Guests cruising the eight-foot aisle tried to peek between the slats of the blinds, but could discern no more than light.

Isaac took a place at the rail, pinching loose the two pairs of tights he wore, one on his legs and the other over his head with jagged holes cut for his eyes and mouth, as he contemplated the lights of the town. He turned and watched the partyers strolling by him, avid to explore the fabulous yacht. In addition to the array of exotic but human costumes—princesses, ballerinas, Churchills in homburgs and cigars—there was a domino cut from a cardboard box and the mayor had gotten himself up as an anarchist's bomb with a round black papier-mâché body, a fuse glued to his head, and, inserted into his belly, a clock that ticked. The mayor's son waddled behind him as Humpty Dumpty, a fat egg in the same shape as his father.

Back under the WILLKOMMEN sign, there was an awkward moment when a human tree created from cardboard tubing used to pack bombs, painted brown and ornamented with sprigs and branches of assorted foliage, tried to present a fake invitation to the party. From Isaac's vantage point, the card looked like a fine simulation that would have fooled half the passport controls in Europe, but did not meet the majordomo's standards.

"I'm sorry, Sir," he said. "There seems to be something, er, wrong with this invitation."

"Nah, nothing's wrong with that." a thick Romanian accent spoke from within the foliage.

"I'm sorry, Sir, I cannot admit you," the majordomo turned a large shoulder to the tree as a crowd of Red Army generals swept through with the most cursory of his notice.

"What about them?" the tree complained.

"Their papers are in order. Yours are not." He held the card aloft.

The tree reached out a limb, but the announcer let the card slip between his fingers to drop below the gangway and the portholes beneath, onto the surface of the Danube. Despite the ostensible universality of the guest list there were clearly those who were not welcome, and there would be no exceptions. Two ominous black men in sailor suits that were uniforms not costumes emerged from the shadows to affirm physically the majordomo's decision, and the tree slunk back to the shore and disappeared into the woods.

A flash of light recorded the tree's ignominy, and Isaac recognized the photographer immediately.

Elizabeth Smith Moss swiveled and took a picture of Isaac, too. An executioner, wearing a black hood and black tights, holding a double-edged axe, was reflected in her lens. She had been there to record those wide eyes' first encounter with the world After, so she recognized him despite the hood. That shouldn't have been a surprise; Miss Moss never forgot an image. "Ah, my smiling man. Liberation has been kind to you, I see."

Isaac was damned if he would confess his desperation and glibly reminded her, "That's because I hoard my credits."

Miss Moss was dressed as a cowgirl, in leather jodhpurs with lasso, which she twirled idly up in the air by the funnel of the *Anubis* as if looking for a heifer to rope, as she used her camera to capture human heifers in the wild. She knew what he was referring to and was pleased to acknowlege it. "A credit given is a credit earned. I still owe you, boy, and you know where to find me."

Isaac nodded. "Front page."

"Above the fold."

Then the funnel gave a low mournful hoot and a cloud of dark gas puffed from its opening. The two Negro sailors who had frightened off the tree prepared to haul in the gangplank.

It was ten to. Almost everybody was long since on board, because they somehow knew that whoever had issued the invitation meant it, and that one minute after the hour, you would be left, fashionably late, by yourself on shore. At one minute to the hour, however, a black sedan pulled through the parking lot to the edge of the dock. The driver lept out of the front seat and opened the back door, and a shadowy figure strode up the gangplank seconds before the sailors lifted it. The majordomo said, "Welcome, Doctor," and the engines came to life from somewhere underneath, a low vibrating hum like a cat's purr.

The mud of the Danube bottom churned into silver patterns like ghostly fingerprints, and a school of fish fled from the whirls as the boat severed its connection to the shore. The lights receded swiftly, a glittering necklace that blinked out gem by gem as the *Anubis* rounded a bend in the river.

Regensburg disappeared, and the lights on the deck went out, too, to the squeals of the girls, more than one of whom was pinched by a stray hand taking advantage of the blackout, until a course of fireworks shot off the upper deck, drizzling down in purple and red. By the time the last streamers descended, an eight-piece band stood, waiting for the conductor's baton to drop and signal them into life.

Parachuting down, the figure of a man seemed to emerge from the last fading fireworks—Orion come to life—although he may have been shot from a cannon ashore or dropped from a mail plane cruising past in the darkness overhead.

Whether it was deliberate or not, the parachutist's path floated in front of the ship's approach, as if timed to topple into the funnel.

Projecting the trajectory, the crowd stood stunned by the inevitable. The angle of descent was too perfect to deny.

Clad in white jump suit, the daredevil swayed lower with each delicate arc until the cords attached to his silk umbrella got tangled and the chute collapsed into a crescent. He looked like the moon transformed into a falling star, plummeting. He tugged at strings left and right, but could not subdue the force of gravity. He picked up speed, flailing, as the ship picked up speed, and the two objects rushed to meet each other. The squeamish averted their eyes, but they were few.

Rivka buried her face in Fishl's shoulder.

Immaculate planning or good fortune, a second before impact the funnel blew a deep bassoon blast of hot air. The steam held the visitor aloft, scorched maybe, but safe as a Ping-Pong ball over a lottery machine.

"Look," shouted the dominoes to the dice, soldiers and sandmen, bathing beauties and cab drivers who broke into spontaneous applause.

Smiling at the people above whom he hovered, the chutist grinned and waved. The audience could almost feel the currents of air lifting his feet up over his head and tumbling its human cargo. He somersaulted while biting the cords that fluttered from toggles on his chest, and severed all connections to the chute; it floated up and off behind the boat into the Danube, landing like an enormous lily pad from space.

Isaac watched Elizabeth Smith Moss finger the trigger on her camera, but she was suspicious and the finger remained suspended. She usually took shots of images that were not created for the benefit of her lens, and didn't know if the air ballet was premeditated or extemporaneous.

Then, abruptly, the giant bellows beneath the deck ceased, and the man dropped, one shoulder bumping the edge of the funnel, catching ahold of one of the rungs attached to its side.

The crowd applauded more vigorously and a girl from the Hen rushed up with a kiss as if the chutist was Lindbergh arriving in Paris. She was there, at the base of the funnel, while he climbed down the rungs to the deck.

"Nein. Nein," he shouted with an Oklahoma accent, twitching at the sky.

"Yah. Yah. Go und get him, Bessie," cried a voice from the opposite stage. It was the Emcee from the Hen, who had appeared in his own circle of spotlight.

The parachutist swiveled left and right in manic despair, while the bird-chested girl closed in.

The man ripped a pair of heavy rubber-framed goggles off his nose and spread his arms wide, revealing a black cape with a curious red-and-yellow insignia resembling a missile in flight stitched to the lining.

The girl paused.

"Yes, tis I," he declared. Dashing and leaping over the heads of the revelers toward a farther deck, he shouted midair on his own propulsion. "Rocketmann shall return."

A crew of waiters swarmed out of the open doors to the galley, bearing dozens of trays filled with white fish, sausage, and glazed peach canapés and scores of fluted glasses bubbling over with freshly poured champagne.

"Rocketmann. Rocketmann," the gossip ran through the crowd. The fellow who fell from the sky was legendary in a place where legends were hard put to contend with actualities. It was a world of heroes and villains, all larger-than-life. Nonetheless, Rocketmann was as famous as the Katzenjammer Kids. He was, they said, a U.S. soldier who romped through the zone in search of his own esoteric notion of fulfillment in the form of magical rocket formula.

"Fucking loose cannon," Hank Smith said.

"You think they hired him just for this?"

"Should haul him up on a court-martial."

"Guy doesn't blink for less than a grand."

Everyone had heard something; nobody knew anything except that the mystery man was at large on board.

"I heard he was Dresden."

"I heard he was killed in Dresden."

Fact mingled with fiction; it was all too strange. There was no sense, no proportion. Tears formed oceans here and oceans shrank to teardrops. Crimes were committed from means without motives. Distance meant nothing. In Paris, Sartre claimed that Nothing meant something.

A rabbi, dressed happily in sneakers and a baseball player's outfit he borrowed from a Jewish second baseman in the regimental league, sipped at champagne, and said. "Sometimes. I think it was a dream."

"Nightmare," Der Schreiber corrected him. Of course he was there, too, scribbling who-knew-what notes in his head: images, ideas, prayers.

"No," Isaac said. "Neither. You don't wake up and find that you've imagined it. The rest of our life is the dream. Turn over, blink, and maybe we're all back in the lager. Raus."

Der Schreiber pinched himself with fingers as long and bony as a compass. Then he said, "I guess we're still here."

"Thank God," the rabbi said.

Isaac said, "Who?"

The rabbi drifted after a waiter bearing a covey of partridges skewered live, plunged into honey, suffocated and seared, and Isaac found himself alone at the rail with Der Schreiber. The younger man was dressed in a pewter armor plate, so that Isaac thought he was a medieval knight until his companion raised an arm to point at some shadows on shore and three additional arms followed in synch. Der Schreiber had black tubing cleverly sewn into his side, or thorax, and hanging by threads from his topmost, fleshy appendage, so that for all the world he appeared to have four left limbs.

When Der Schreiber saw Isaac's confusion, he raised his right arm and revealed that it too had four limbs. It was not chivalric armor he was wearing, but entomological; he was dressed as a cockroach.

"Very urban," Isaac complemented his companion.

"Yes."

"Kafka? Marcus has told me about Kafka."

"No, just a kitchen creature, not one for the library." Trained to Talmud, tainted by the rabbinic fantasies of Nahman of Bratslav, Der Schreiber had undergone a crash course in High European Modernism. After he was discovered by the visiting intellectuals (also on board, done up as a troupe of marionettes with oversize papiermâché heads), he swallowed great heaps of the Hermit of Prague as well as Joyce, James, and Proust. Influence or affect, Der Schreiber's education took. He was an apt pupil, so his teachers adored him, but Isaac did not.

For all the animosity between them, the two men had a lot in common. Both expected the worst of any given situation, Isaac with cynicism, Der Schreiber with sorrow—as did Fishl with resignation, and Marcus analytically—but each also had the sense that he was able to weigh the odds subtly in his own favor. Their reflexes were honed to make decisions at each fork in the road—instantaneously, for to pause was to invite doom—to volunteer or not to volunteer for a "work detail" that might conclude with a crust of life-sustaining bread or a death march, to stay with one brutal master or shift toward another who might be more lenient or more lethal. Each maintained an inner compass directed toward life at every crossroad bar none, for ninety-nine out of one hundred was not good enough. Given the knowledge that every diverging fork was decisive, they had, through chance or prescience, taken the series of alternative routes that had led here. That alone separated them from the human dust that settled over the Continent, onto the ruins of the Reichstag and the Leipzig Soccer Club second-place trophy on the mantle, whisked clean and buffed to a silvery glow by a hausfrau of Berlin before she sighed and took it to the market to swap for her own crust.

Perhaps that was why neither Isaac nor Der Schreiber could stand the countryside; there were fewer diverging paths. From ancestors in the Fertile Crescent through the Pale of Settlement, they inherited the intuition that agricultural destiny was relentless. The sun rose; crops failed: the old God died.

Neither man felt comfortable outside the city gate. In a city, any city, Babylon, Venice, Amsterdam, or Newark, the rootless cosmopolitan could study, scheme, and wander freely. The city was an outlet for their congenital nervousness. There, cheek and jowl by neighbors and strangers, the juices of Jewish life could flow. That was why the rumors that Jews were draining swamps and planting trees in Palestine were so disconcerting. Only mildly ameliorating this intelligence were additional rumors that newspapers and cafés were sprouting in the oases.

Outside the city, the forest was a house for the darkness of the soul. No matter how vulgar the antics of the Green Hen, how petty the market economy, how rarified the theological disputation, how hysterical the speculations of the cellar eschatologists, the terms of their debate or the shape of their humor, their very inflections were comprehensible. Cruising between the banks of the Danube, Isaac and Der Schreiber both felt the inhospitality of the woods. Nature had no call for them.

Nature was amoral. There was no such thing as beauty in nature. There was sublimity composed equally of awe and terror. God might reside in a burrow in a cave or a garden, but Good was the prerogative of man. Of course, the trade-off was Evil.

Redemption was not to be sought on plains but plazas, not in caves but tunnels, not upon mountains but buildings, even churches erected by the heretics of the chosen people. Then the Teutons confused matters. They took the lessons of the forest and transported them to the ghetto. Then they took the Jews who had never learned those lessons and transported them to the lager built out of pale pine fibers cut and milled into planks. And now the boat steered between twisting branches to the left, hollow trunks to the right, yet Isaac and Der Schreiber were at ease for the *Anubis* was a floating metropolis, jammed as a Warsaw synagogue or a Manhattan subway. Strings of pearl-shaped lights went on, and music burst from the interior cabins.

Isaac was suddenly glad that the costumed tree had been refused admittance. "Look what they've done to us," he said, apropos of nothing.

"How can you forget?"

"How can you remember?"

The two men stared at each other until Miranda approached. She was dressed in a cardboard outfit with three dozen plus letters, numbers, and typographical symbols attached to the chest, starting with Q W E R T. She was a typewriter.

"I would love one of those," Der Schreiber said. His fingers twitched with hunger for the keys.

"In Paris," she replied.

"Paris?" Isaac repeated.

"He didn't tell you? Benya is going to Paris next week. He's been invited."

"Invited?"

"Yes."

Der Schreiber offered no further explanation, but Miranda couldn't contain herself. "The Académie Français saw excerpts from his book and asked him to speak at the Sorbonne."

"You go everywhere you're invited?"

"That's why I came here."

"He's going to teach a seminar."

"Perhaps you will teach us something."

The gloomy cockroach raised his palms and eight limbs and sighed. "I have nothing to teach you, Mr. Kaufman. I was rather hoping you could teach me."

"I'm not a scholar," Isaac sneered.

"That's why I thought you would know better. I seem to be able to describe, but I still can't understand. I guess that I can survive. I have, like a . . ." He raised both arms to display himself. "But I need help. The problem is that life is not a book; I think you know that." As he plead, Miranda moved closer to him, and seemed ready to hug and comfort him.

Tears brimmed in her eyes and she knew that she couldn't remain much longer. Her visit to Hell was nearly over, visa expired. She didn't know where to get a new one. It was her first and last boat ride. The reflection of the ship's lights blazed on the water.

The cockroach seemed ready to scurry for the nearest damp shelter and Miranda looked at Isaac.

"Send my best to Paris," the executioner said, and slipped into the crowd, furious without having the faintest idea of why he felt such fury.

"Temperamental," Der Schreiber said.

"How do you remain so calm?" Miranda asked him.

"It is because I have nothing left inside. Temperament may be a strange form of emotion, but it shows the ability to feel."

"But your work is so . . . so feeling, and so real."

"Ah," he smiled, and Miranda could not help but notice how different his teeth were from Isaac's. Der Schreiber's were gray and decayed from lack of nourishment, but nothing like the cruel range set within the smuggler's cheeks. He said, "The work may be real, but I am not."

Miranda paused to consider this, and leaned backward onto the cool brass cylindrical rails. She felt the delightful summer breeze off the Danube and inhaled the scent of earth and tadpoles, and could not begin to place this scene on the East River of Manhattan. It was her room with the pink dresser and frilled curtains and a twenty-five-dollar Madame Alexander doll whose porcelain face overlooked that other river in her place that were unreal to Miranda; the thought of returning to that cold island was intolerable. She saw Alan Foyle saunter by, awkward in her dress and high heels, and she heard the sounds of revelry from the deck, where the Emcee from the Green Hen was introducing his show after the unexpected interruption.

"Ladies and yentlemen. Ladies, ladies, yentlemen," Spotlight illuminating his white mask of a face, the Emcee called out in a sideshow barker's chant. "Ve haf been commissioned to our best show for the happy people here. Und so I am happy to present Berta."

One girl came dancing out and struck a pose beside the Emcee.

"Nora."

Another girl slipped out from between two Oriental folding screens that delineated the backstage dressing area.

"Helga und Heidi. The twins. Heidi's my favorite. Yodel for me, Heidi."

One of the girls let rip with a wild "Yodellayeeehooo!"

"You know, we could have brought girls from Paree, or the Côte d'Azur, but they say that the homegrown girls are the freshest." At the last word, he reached his thumb and forefinger up between the thighs of the nearest high stepper.

Heidi yodeled again.

Isaac moved indoors.

The Emcee sniffed his fingers and feigned a swoon, caught by his troop. Lolling on their outstretched arms, he drew the spotlight to the tip of his pinky, snapped his fingers, and the light blinked off. "I luff this setup," he cackled, the lights went on, and in his place the three girls stood alone, left profile, right profile, and center.

> *Bei mir bist du shame*
> *Means you are to blame.*
> *Bei mir bist du shame*
> *Means that you're bad.*

Wagging fingers, the trio continued,

> *You could say guilty, guilty,*
> *Could say wunderbar.*
> *The only way to explain is*
> *t'was just a faux pas.*

Miranda saw the army bureaucrats she hassled for supplies guzzling at the waiters' obsequiously lowered troughs, and the local Germans dressed as soldiers joining the soldiers dressed as burghers, clinking glasses, and she saw some of her clients, too.

Fishl and Rivka were in full flight from the deck, his arm wrapped across her shoulders. What a pair, Jack and Mrs. Sprat. Rivka was composed of a preponderant belly under the pathetic balloon of a gown she wore to try to satisfy the dictates of good cheer, denied by the distress on her face. "What's the matter?" he asked.

"I . . ."

Miranda stepped forward, "What's the matter?"

"I . . ."

Der Schreiber said, "That's not a costume, is it?"

Miranda glowed with the empathy of universal motherhood.

Der Schreiber answered himself. "No, nothing is, I suppose," and he wrapped his eight arms around his carapace and shivered as Rivka's skin dimpled and her mouth opened soundlessly.

"She needs to rest."

"Come, we can find a bed."

The interior of the *Anubis* was vast as a hotel. There were ballrooms hung with crystal chandeliers that shot tiny rainbows across the walls and salons with green velvet settees under swags of blue velvet bunting and there were galleys fore and aft spilling more suffocated partridges and strips of marinated seal onto the deck as fast as the chefs could produce them, and fountains gushing wine between bars stocked with Russian vodka, Scotch whisky, English gin, Kentucky bourbon, and French brandy. Clowns and magicians hired to entertain the guests circled the room, only to be confused with guests dressed as clowns and magicians.

There was a confusion of Madame Pompadours of both sexes blocking Miranda, Der Schreiber and the Fishls's path as they sized up each others' hair and gowns, but the typewriter pushed her way through the brocade bunch. One wrinkled her nose and sneered, "Peasants."

Behind the trio, flanking panting Rebecca, the Emcee was warming up his audience, "So what did Hitler say to Mussolini when the Italian premier paid him a suprise visit?"

Pause.

"If I'd known you were coming, I would have baked a kike."

Miranda winced and helped Rivka forward, but she was halted at the round window in a teak door. Something in the glass moved; it was a fish. Half a dozen goldfish drifted at the bottom of the window and one slid through a patch of seaweed fluttering up past a tiny porcelain sea-wreck inhabited by a tiny porcelain diver from whose breathing apparatus a stream of bubbles aerated the minature sea. Peering through the water, Miranda felt as if she was in the Battery Park Aquarium, but instead of gigantic, wart-faced groupers and hammerhead sharks with gills apulse in their sandpapery flanks, she could see people on the other side, laughing and drinking. She expected to see air bubbles floating upward from their open mouths.

The stateroom on the other side of the door was a casino, and the second Miranda opened the door, she heard the clink of coins. A large roulette wheel dominated the room and there were half a dozen other tables set up for games of chance and skill. Fields of green felt muffled the clatter of dice and the slapping sounds of a dozen decks of cards decorated with the *Anubis* emblem. Not content to impose the image of the jackal upon the backs of the cards, the management had redesigned the faces of the royalties to incorporate the snout of the jackal. The Knave was obvious, the Queen a bitch, and the King was a shepherd adorned with a crown as well as a collar.

Although employees of the boat dealt the cards, the house took no cut, its rules established for the innocent entertainment of the guests. There were one dollar tables and ten dollar tables and a single no-limit table on a raised platform under a stuffed borzoi hung from the ceiling by fishing wire.

The tenants at the low-risk tables murmured with mock Monte Carlo refinement, but the dialogue at the no limit table where a fortune changed pockets with every hand, was as raucous as it was at the army PX, logical since the players had come directly from the base, military Klaxons blaring across Regensburg to the *Anubis* pier. Churchill and Stalin were at the table along with Pinsker the black marketeer in a pretentious ermine stole that reminded Isaac, peering over his shoulder, of the cards he held, contending against Jacks Over Deuces, humbly costumed in Necco's sergeant's stripes and General Hank Smith, bellowing and guzzling, in a diaper. Charmed by Sergeant Necco's morning disrobing, the general had opted to regress for deception in an army mess tablecloth that swaddled his bottom and was held together by safety pins. He made some baby, pendulous hairy breasts hanging onto the card table as if he was preparing to give rather than receive succor.

As in the PX, the cards fell the way the cards always fell.

"Why," Pinsker asked the flaxen-haired corporal in a sergeant's outfit—such a modest deception—with the largest stack of chips in front of him, "do you play when there are so much larger games that you play?" Pinsker was there to make connections and do deals, and his impatience showed. He was careless and lost, because he had no inherent interest in the game itself; it was the stakes.

One eye to the table, one to the questioner, both eyes flickering to the ticker tape machine in the corner, Jacks Over Deuces said,

"Winners win. That's what we do. In the market, you've got to wait for your investment to make a difference. Here that happens immediately. It's nice that way." He hungrily eyed the tiny stacks in front of the other players, eager to accumulate all the chips.

For a second, the corporal glanced at the newcomers to the room, but Fishl and Rivka were never going to become players and Miranda played her own games. He looked past them, through the aquarium door, which worked like the lid of a music box—whenever it opened a crack a snatch of song from the outdoor stage slipped inside.

> Way down upon the Wansee River
> Far, far away.
> That where the Hebrew folks are playing
> That's where I long to stay.

Unable to see the show that accompanied the routine, all they heard was laughter and some beery sing-along from the crowd. Then the door shut, and it was only the sounds of the game room again. Isaac turned away from the typewriter, the cockroach, and the refugees weaving between the tables toward another door at the far side of the room, to listen to Jacks Over Deuces finish his statement.

"You know what a poker game is, it's an environment that I like. But why do I like it?" he went on in his Socratic mode. "The felt is nice, but so is the green, green grass of home—if there's cards dealt. The companionship is nice, too—as long as there's cash there. Take the smoke . . ." he inhaled ambient fumes deeply and turned to Necco. "Gimme a stogie," he ordered the sergeant, who was sadly attempting to deceive by wearing his old captain's uniform, tossing the uncomfortable noncom a ten-dollar chip for a tip, sure that it would eventually boomerang to its home in his pocket.

"It's smoke, too" he said, igniting Necco's cigar with a thousand-mark note that would have been an evening's play at the lesser tables. Waiting till the banknote had shrunk to a cinder light enough to float away, he grew poetic. "As long as smoke hangs low over the cards, and what do the cards represent but smoke, winning and losing, losing and winning." That satisfied him. Done, he puffed contentedly and turned to Isaac and asked, "And how you doing, boy? You owe me, you know?"

A party was a party, but business was business. Pinsker wasn't alone in his concerns; he was just unsubtle.

"I know," Isaac replied. For all his early success, he was still not nearly as good at the new world as he had hoped and once been. Gallingly, he was clearly not as good as Pinsker, but he explained his new scheme, "We're still selling cigarettes, but you know we're moving into matches. Of course, we had a small setback."

"Yes, I heard you had a bad time in Ludwigshafen." Jacks Over Deuces looked at him, folded two pairs before three kings, lost another tenner to a Churchill who made the vee sign to another Churchill across the casino in identical vest and homburg. Ignoring his own temporary setback, he said, "But they're free, the matches."

"If you can get them."

"So you'll charge?"

"No," Issac replied, pleased by his cleverness. "We'll print ads and get whoever wants their message out there to pay."

"Hmm," the corporal liked this. "Of course, you're doing our job then, disseminating information. It's OK for now, but just wait till we have any conflict—Whammo." He looked Isaac in the eyes and said, "Then we'll kill you."

But Jacks Over Deuces had made a mistake. In America, where there were rewards, death made a difference. In Europe, death was no threat. Desire and despair were emotions Isaac might be familiar with; fright was not. Now he was out of the wilderness, into the city, back on the gray, gray sidewalks of home. Kill him, they might, or must, if the situation as urban competitors required, but that was a given. He nodded.

And for the first time, the corporal was nonplussed when his threat proved useless. "How do you get them?" he asked, folding a flush before a full house, losing a pair of twenties to Stalin, who said to a pair of shaved-head Lenins cheering him on, "It is part of my five-year plan."

"We buy them."

"From who?"

"Sources." Isaac felt a need to be cagey.

"I mean, can you make or manufacture them instead? What do they consist of?"

"Consist?"

Marcus came in off the deck just in time to explain the question and Isaac answered, "They are produced somewhere, out of paper, not good paper for visas or IDs, but recycled wood pulp, that and sulfur, I believe. There's some element to stablize the explosives and something to . . . ignite them." It was not the first time he had conceived of matches as miniature explosives and a familiar fuse lit in his head.

Increasingly frustrated, Jacks Over Deuces folded a straight in front of a flush on the other side of the table. He lost nearly a hundred dollars to Hammerin' Hank.

"Losing your touch, Corporal?"

Jacks Over Deuces signaled to the dealer to shuffle faster, but Isaac's mind was moving more rapidly than the cards that fluttered onto the table. He had moved in a blink from cigarettes to matches to sulfur to gunpowder.

"When I was a child," Hammerin' Hank said, "my brother used to make tiny little bombs. He'd sit for a week, cutting the heads offa matches with a big old toenail clipper and stuffing them into a cylinder. Tin was better, but the tube from toilet paper would do."

Marcus explained to Isaac what toilet paper was in America.

"Anything to keep 'em packed and aimed in one direction. You know the force of ten thousand match heads in a toilet paper tube. Used it for . . ."

"FUEL, Damnit!" Rocketmann materialized in the game room. His cape with the bright emblem fit in with the attire of the other players.

Jacks Over Deuces surveyed the maniac calmly. "Deal you in?"

"FUEL, I say!"

"Did he say 'Fool'?"

Stomping about the periphery of the table, tripping over his cape, Rocketmann muttered half aloud, half to himself, "Got to keep looking, keep moving, aerial reconaissance. Didn't want to hit that damn funnel, damn girl chasing me down, felt like a coon among the hounds." Rocketmann's eyes twitched furiously, expecting assault at any moment. "But there's fuel on board. I can smell it."

"Fuel for thought," Jacks Over Deuces said, but it was Isaac's mind that was racing. Fuel. Matches. The explosion at the Papiergeschäft.

"What happened to your brother?"

Marcus wasn't asking him, but Isaac twitched at the last word, and lost his train of thought.

"Yes, what happened to your brother?" Jacks Over Deuces asked the diaper-clad general, as he folded a flush before a full house and lost another hundred. In the time Isaac had been at the table, Jacks Over Deuces's stack had shrunk to insignificance. The American was beginning to think that the Jew was a jinx.

"Tell us," Marcus said. He wanted the theatrical resolution. He craved the end of the story.

Isaac felt the churning of the *Anubis* engines all of a sudden, and the darkness of the riverbanks hemming them in from the outside. "You want stories, ask Der Schreiber," he said and lurched from the table in search of a bathroom.

"Something wrong with that boy?" the general laughed in his good-luck mood, scratched his butt, and said, "Think I got diaper rash, damnit!" and continued his story. "Flamethrower, made one 'bout every two weeks, that was how long it took to get the material. Worked good the first couple of times. Then one of them blew off his left hand. Bled to death. Raise a hundred."

Jacks Over Deuces was coming unglued, and let an ace slip from his hand to the table, jackal face up. He tried to pretend that he had done it on purpose, but the assembled heads of state could smell his weakness. They folded and let him collect their antes.

The dealer shuffled.

Past the casino, through the corridors hung with prints of hunting dogs, into the labyrinth of the staff quarters off the steaming, oil-spattering pandemonium of the galley and out again, Miranda drew the panting Rivka, as if they were running from Germans in the sewers of Warsaw. Finally she opened one door and knew the room she wanted, because it had a bed, a narrow one compared to the luxury of the rest of the ship, but covered with an eiderdown quilt that puffed eight inches above the mattress, nearly up to a niche in the wall containing several books and a brass chronometer under a porthole that looked out on the water, which reflected the lights of the party above.

For a second Miranda expected to see poker players through the window.

"I can't go any farther," Rivka gasped.

"You don't have to. Here." Together the typewriter, the cockroach, and Rivka's husband eased her onto the bed, propped pillows behind her, and gathered chairs to the edge, where they could watch the sweat pour from her pale forehead.

"Eat," Fishl said. He had learned something from his companions, and swiped a miniature frankfurter from a tray in the kichen during their swift passage.

"I don't think this is kosher," Rivka said.

Unaware of the extreme forethought of their hosts who actually hired a thin rabbi with a thick beard to certify that everything that came out of the kitchen was prepared according to the ancient dietary laws, Fishl took Rivka's objection seriously, pointing out that the obligation to sustain life outweighed the Levitical prescriptions of kashrus. Presumably that was why she was not merely allowed but compelled to swallow whatever slop she had been given for the past five years. Gently he reminded her, "You have eaten treyf."

Rivka sat up and threw up, and then relaxed. "I'm not sick now, I'm . . ." she trembled and then yawned.

"Tired?" Fishl filled in his wife's unfinished thought.

"Very tired," she agreed.

"Farmakht di oyg'n," Der Schreiber whispered.

Miranda looked at him. The title of the book that was going to take him to Paris was *Farmahkt Oyg'n*. She repeated it in English, *"Closed Eyes."*

"Sounds like a lullaby," Rivka sighed. "Can you sing it?"

Upstairs, another song wafted over the speakers:

> *Jews are my sunshine.*
> *My only sunshine.*
> *They make me tremble*
> *When skies are gray.*

Fishl buried his head and wept.

"Please," Rivka said, "make it go away."

Miranda looked at Der Schreiber. "Do what she says."

Speaking firmly to blot out the Emcee's obscene cackle, Der Schreiber began his own lullaby to soothe and distract her, "Sing . . . of the tracks . . . of people . . . in the sand . . ." His voice was low and solemn as he found each succesive phrase to create a picture. "Of caravans . . . marching . . . with bags . . . of purple . . . and spice . . . for the Temple . . ." Not only was he a scribe, recording, but a seer, creating pictures of his own.

And in a minute, the gentle rocking of the *Anubis* gave way to that of a procession of camels in the wilderness on the far side of the Red Sea, heading inexorably to the revelation on Sinai.

"We're there somewhere," Rivka hallucinated from the description, and grasped for her husband's bony fingers.

"Yes," he said.

"Such a good story."

"Yes," And Fishl, the man without stories, silently listened to Der Schreiber's rendition of the Bible while silently adding his own commentary. Sinai was the place where the Jews thought they had been given the covenant by God, but what it really meant was that their home was consigned to paper or parchment or baked mud tablets, whatever surface could retain the tongue of the Jews, since their feet were banished forever from the earth. They were condemned, like Adam and Eve, to wander homeless, creatures of the word and the air, luftmenschen.

"Go on, please," Rivka asked, "I want to know what happened." But even though she was in a state that made shyness ludicrous, Rivka could not admit that what she really wanted to know, but was too afraid to ask, was not what already happened, but what was going to happen. The terror of the past was tolerable; the future was ineffable and therefore more painful than the pain she knew.

Passing from Babylonia to Rome to Spain, sometimes tolerated, sometimes despised, inevitably expelled, Der Schreiber recited the travels and travails of the chosen people until they arrived at the fertile lands of Mitteleuropa. Jews lived in Cracow for as long as they did in Palestine; Jews embraced Kultur in Berlin, reading and memorizing Schiller, Goethe, and Heine, without realizing that it was also the language of Hoffman's Sandman who ate children's eyes, and then, in a decade that might as well have been a millisecond or a millennium, sent the Jews back into the air as the plume of smoke that once led them through the Wilderness, and flakes of burnt flesh.

"Enough!" Miranda sighed.

"No, you must know everything." Feeling the same upheaval in his belly as Rivka did, he wasn't going to be stopped until it all came out. He followed the gentle path of German literature until history split wide open. It was 1939.

Rivka sat up, body bent double, and shrieked.

The three leaned forward. The typewriter took her hand, the cockroach wiped her brow; the husband swayed back and forth like an old man in prayer.

"I'm fine," she sighed. "Tell me more."

"Are you sure?"

"No," she gasped. "But I'm here."

From '39 on, Der Schreiber's story shed its panoramic scope and began to focus on one shtetl boy whose passage echoed the generations before he was born, from the words of the commandments to those of the kommandants, from the wandering in the wilderness to the death of the father. He told of a march from Gross Rosen to Sachsenhausen where he was so hungry he ate poison ivy.

Miranda chewed on her knuckle and remembered a party in '39. Her father had rented the rooftop at the St. Regis and invited his legal friends to celebrate his daughter's coming of age. Some of the gentile partners sent generous presents to fulfill their social obligation, but the place was packed with beautifully soused people amid the kind of floral extravagance she hadn't seen from then until tonight. Glenn Miller played and the affair made the society column.

It wasn't Glenn Miller's vocalist singing upstairs, but the Emcee and his girls who sang:

> *Pardon me goy . . .*
> *is that the concentration choo choo?*
> *Yah yah,*
> *Track 39!*
> *Goy, you can give me strychnine.*

Can you afford to board concentration choo choo?
I got my fare
and just a trifle to spare.

You leave the Budapest station 'bout a quarter to four.
Read a bit of Talmud and then you're in Geppersdorf
Dinner in the diner
Nothing could be finer
Than to have your lox and eggs in Bratislava

When you hear the whistle blowing eight to the bar
Then you know that Ebensee is not very far
Travel all a'callin'
Gotta keep it rollin'
Ooh ooh, concentration there you are.

When she heard the obscene variation of her own memory, Miranda realized that Der Schreiber had stopped. He did not come to the moment of liberation and did not picture himself in the bowels of the *Anubis* telling his story. Modestly, he did not acknowledge his place as the voice from the mountain, or, in the urban vocabulary he spoke, the chimney.

Unable to enter the last chapter of his own saga, Benya's low voice faded and Miranda looked at the heavy lids droop over the soulful eyes, and thought: Und Der Schreiber's Oyg'n Farmakht. "Sweet dreams," the American girl wished him.

They sat there, in silence broken only by Rivka's heavy breathing. She felt as if they were not cruising down a narrow Bavarian river, nearly able to pluck leaves off the trees on shore, but on a boat midatlantic, with not a speck of land in sight, a continent removed from everything, not only the tombs of her grandparents and the tombless, disembodied souls of her parents, but from history itself. Her memory was washing away with the waves.

The others hardly realized they were moving, but Rivka felt the lapping of the water, the swell of it rising and pouring over the decks, sluicing down the corridors, following her path from the stage through the casino into the labyrinth, under the shut door to her tiny chamber, into her bed, which was wet.

"What's that?" Fishl asked.

"I peed." She was raised to be shy, but personal humiliation had long since been forgotten.

"No, I don't think so," Miranda hesitated.

"What's this then?" Rivka lifted the sheet off to display the sopping wet sheet.

"That's not . . ." Miranda blushed to refer to bodily functions, and blurted out. "Your water broke."

"So?"

"You're going to have a baby."

Fishl patted Rivka's belly with a smile. "We know."

"I mean now."

"Now?" Neither of the parents-to-be really had the faintest idea of the biological procedures they were about to embark on. It was all just supposed to happen.

"Now!" Miranda shrieked. "Oh my Lord . . ."

As if responding, Rivka's belly contracted, she bent forward, and another great gout poured out of her, puddling onto the floor. Miranda jumped back, immediately ashamed of her response. "I've got to get a doctor," she said to nobody in particular. "This boat has to have a doctor."

Fishl said, "Marcus was a dentist."

Miranda snapped, "She doesn't need help with her teeth," and regretted her sharpness. "That's good. Yes, I'll get him, or someone." She jumped for the door, touched the knob in the shape of a jackel's snout, and paused. "Will you be OK?"

But nobody in the room had an answer. Rivka just sat, composed as the ark afloat on the waves approaching Ararat. Finally she took pity and allowed Miranda to pursue her chosen task. She waved an arm and gave her own order, "Gei. Go!"

As soon as Miranda left the room, and they could hear her feet pattering down the hall, like the sound of an Olivetti, Rivka's pain eased. The American girl meant well, but there was some relief she could not grant. Rivka stretched out a hand to Fishl.

No more than children themselves, they were at sea, on the way to the new world.

Doctor or no doctor, nature would have its way. In the meanwhile, Rivka had a chance to examine her surroundings. Although the boat

272

was built to gargantuan scale, the room was miniscule, barely large enough to contain the narrow bunk and the chairs on which her companions sat, yet every appointment was perfect. Rivka had been a seamstress before the war, and she noticed that the stained comforter had an ornate pattern more glittering than the finest sofa of the richest banker in Lublin; there appeared to be threads of solid gold embroidered in the shape of a jackal's head that stuck out from under her thigh.

Der Schreiber meanwhile was examining the small row of books on the shelf above Rivka's head. He couldn't figure out what was odd about their perfectly aligned spines until realized that they weren't books at all, but a single leather box ribbed to resemble individual volumes with a half dozen incomprehensible German titles in gold ink.

Soaked, Rivka turned to Der Schreiber. He had woken when Miranda left, and knew that it was appropriate that only the survivors were alone when new life was set to enter the room. They might have been alone as she said, "That was a lovely story."

"No," he said.

"Yes. You must continue to tell it."

Fishl looked at Der Schreiber and thought of his friend, the chemist, who had also taken into himself the particular history they lived through, and then died, as if he could not bear it once the War seemed ready to end.

If Salidano was here he would have dressed as memory if he could have figured out how. But if he had figured how to embody memory—perhaps as a book, or a scroll—he wouldn't have died; he would have been here to sip champagne and breathe the river air. It was as if history itself had ended and there were no stories left to tell.

Oh, the world would seek them out, and sit agape. Safe, suburban, American Jews would listen to these tales from the abyss, clucking vows to do better next time. They'd cry and decry the atrocity, with all of Miranda's heartfelt empathy, and though Der Schreiber claimed that she must know, he lied, for she couldn't. Nobody else would ever really understand, only the Jews who had been there. And, of course, the Germans.

Der Schreiber considered himself a creature of the page. Born with a literary predilection, he might have left the shtetl anyway, moved to a garret in Warsaw, shaved and drunk coffee, consorted with journalists and socialists, and written modernist poetry, but instead he was gifted with the most powerful story of the pre-Messianic age. He was wrong to dress as a cockroach; he should have been a human fountain pen, his nib sucking the blood off the ground and spitting it back onto sheets of lined foolscap.

As if she was not the center of attention, Rivka asked Der Schreiber again, "Please tell it."

"No," he said. "I can't." He thought of his room in Regensburg, overlooking the market, and the paper he filled with recollection transmuted into narrative. He still didn't believe the strange response to his imaginings. Fighting to compel the story to make sense, and being told that he did so, he lifted all eight of his arms over his head and sobbed, "Failing, failing utterly."

Isaac staggered into a WC in which Nero would have felt at home. There was a huge marble tub topped by a spout in the shape of a jackal's head, and hieroglyphic carvings that told the saga of the ancient god's trip to the netherworld. The space was so vast that, heaving over a jade-green basin, Isaac didn't notice that he wasn't alone. Somebody came up behind him, grabbed him by the shoulders and ordered, "Get away from there."

"What?"

"I lost something," the crazed parachutist said. It was Rocketmann. Up close, he had a thick, pasty nose and bloodshot eyes broken into a hundred red rays.

"In there?" Isaac pointed at the toilet.

"What's it to you?"

"Why were you hiding?"

"I thought it was that crazy bird girl again. I can't get rid of her."

There was a frantic knock on the door. Then a pounding. It was Miranda, but they didn't know that.

"Hush," Rocketmann whispered, his whisper echoing off the room's arched ceiling. "If you give me away, it's curtains." He pretended to rip a knife across his throat, but whether he was implying homicide, suicide, or somehow referring to Isaac's costume, the executioner couldn't say. He could hardly hear who was out there anyway, the distance was so great, the door so solid. He thought he heard a female voice with a familiar foreign accent and maybe she was asking for a doctor, but he wasn't a doctor anyway, and he still had to throw up.

When he turned back to finish his business, Rocketmann's hand was plunged into the toilet, snaking along the hidden channels to the interior of the bright green fixture, an operation similar to a surgeon's navigation of the chambers of the human heart. "With the right fuel, you can put a garbage can in space."

"Why would you want to?"

"I dunno. To get where you got to."

"What's the fuel?" Isaac laughed, "Methane made from dreck?" He remembered one camp where the prisoners' shit was carted to experimental laboratories in the hopes of extracting precious natural gas from human waste. Who knew, if the experiments had been successful, the Germans might have kept the Jews alive, and fed them better to harvest their droppings. Once again, he thought of matches, munitions, fireworks, explosives, to what conceivable end he didn't yet know.

"No, that's not what I'm looking for, this is personal. I think the fuel is at Liebknecht."

Isaac knew every inch of the lager, and said, "Nonsense. There's just barracks and storerooms and all they have is dirty magazines." He didn't mention his own aspirations for the site.

Rocketmann twisted his face around and stared at Isaac while he struggled to wedge his shoulder more deeply under the rim while he groped in the liquid darkness. "Oh, I can feel it. Damn, slipped away. Another inch. But you only know what's above the surface. Nothing valuable is ever in plain view."

Isaac didn't dispute this, but he began to understand that Rocketmann was doing more than coining a metaphor. "Are you saying there's something underground at Liebknecht?"

"The place is riddled with tunnels. It's Swiss cheese, man, a maze."

"Where?"

"Everywhere. Every inch."

Anubis, God of the underworld, ruled in his domain, but the Jewish dead who should have been buried at Liebknecht were in the air so the paths of the underworld were vacant and unguarded. If there were tombs or tunnels at Liebknecht the army hadn't gotten to them, and if they were everywhere, they might lead where he wanted to go, and out.

Rockets exploded in his head, pieces of the puzzle consolidating, starting to shape all of his stray bits of information into one coherent plot involving Rocketmann's tunnels, Jacks Over Deuces's munitions. Of course, he'd require a vehicle and an hour. But when could they get underground, he wondered, and answered himself immediately: "While di Oyg'n hob'n zikh Farmakht."

The Emcee lay on a bed, warped for the stage. A normal-size bed looks abnormal on a proscenium, so the theatrical bed is shortened and widened. This one was backed with an ornamental board shaped like a fan, piled high with fluffy pillows and stuffed animals.

He was pretending to wake up. His bright red mouth was a puckered scar in a field of white makeup, smudging his fine sharp teeth as he declared, "A dream, just a dream, not so nice as the dreams with soft kitties and pink-cheeked cadets. Not so nice as the fleecy herd that accompanied me to dreamlandt."

The same three girls who opened the show reappeared, each wearing no more than three white cotton puffs, strategically placed. They scampered across the stage and hopped over the foot of the mishapen bed, circled behind the bedboard, and hopped again.

Grinning gleefully at the audience, the Emcee slid a riding crop out from his under his pillow and held it horizontally while the girls continued to jump over it. "How lovely," he sighed, "but all dreams must come to an end. We wake and it didn't really happen. Call me Rip van Winkle. Was it really a thousand years?"

The girls stood up and ranged themselves left, right, and center.

"You know this is a place of fun and the imagination, and if we really work hard to pretend that It didn't happen, Voilà!" He gave a cheery smirk, "It's true, because we can make it so."

The girls struck a pose, the one on the left placing her left hand on her left hip, the one on the right with her right hand on her right hip, the one in the center crosslegged with her hands on her companions' hips.

"But now we are awake and we must get to the business of really entertaining our customers." The Emcee grinned, "Always willing to oblige our customers' idiosyncratic tastes. The more idiosyncratic the

better. Und zo . . . for the sake of idiosyncracy, we present "The
Shepherd and His Flock." But first we need, what's this, am I anticipated, is this intuition, are you a volunteer?" He leered at a woman
from the audience who was clumsily climbing the stage, having a
problem with her boxy costume.

"No, no!" the human typewriter said as she pulled her space key
over the edge.

"Yes, yes! Velcome, ve haf a volunteer," the Emcee cried out,
extending a hand toward Miranda, his fingernails painted black, skin
fish white.

"You're disgusting," Miranda said, as she grabbed desperately for
the microphone, "We need a doctor. Is there a doctor there?"

"A doctor?"

"I'm serious. There's a woman on the boat, she needs a doctor."
And although there must have been doctors on board, even if they
were dressed as King Solomon or the Queen of Sheba, none heard
her or answered her if they had.

"A doctor?" the Emcee repeated. "Vat a coincidence," he declared, lifting a black satchel out from the bed. "I am a doktor."

"No!"

"So, OK, I vill be the patient, a patient patient I am." He plugged
the earpieces of a stethoscope into his ears and listened to his own
heart. "Good news, it's still ticking."

"That's not funny!"

"Not so much fun listening to oneself either. Heidi. Komm sie
her."

Marcus Morgenstern had left the poker room after Isaac, and gone
up to the deck for a breather. He watched the show with professional
curiosity while one of the three sheep, the girl with a pimpled face,
sallow from lack of vitamins, hobbled around the edge of the bed
and stood calmly as the Emcee took his stethoscope and began mas-
saging her breasts.

"Stop that! Stop that, I need a . . ." Miranda gave up; she looked
around her at the performers, at the upraised eyes of the audience,
and ran off the stage.

The Emcee said, "Ah shame, she left, a pretty girl like that. But
that outfit," he put his palm to his forehead. "Why couldn't she wear
a nice yellow dress?"

"Got it," Rocketmann cried and pulled a small object from the drip-ping waters. Crusted with brown ordure, it was as silver as a dead fish, but more rectangular. The maniac cradled it to his chest, and then, perceiving Isaac's eyes upon him, dashed for the door. "It's mine!" He fled.

Inspired by the performance or the scent of rutting frogs in the mudflats off the portside, couples started dancing to "De Svingin' Sounds of Der Bund Bandt" after the girls left the platform, dancing that swiftly moved beyond anything the rabbis had ever seen, men and women writhing as if on a griddle. Even the girls still dressed as sheep joined the dancers, although it was harder for them to dis-cern levels of status here than in the club. There, they could always recognize a well-lined pocket by the pocket's exterior, but here, where dress was to deceive, they had to rely on an intuition that had failed them every day since 1933. One found herself waltzing with Alan Foyle, who was saddened at being spurned by men who could distinguish better legs than his.

And dancing, as ministers of all ages knew, led to other things. Hands slipped down beneath straps, and worked themselves up un-der hems. Two complementary dominoes found each other, and linked, six dots to six dots, and adjourned to the nearest lifeboat. They crept under the tarpaulin and set the boat that hung from pylons rattling and rocking as if it was loose in a squawl.

One ballerina's neck burrowed into a hussar's uniform and only the monkey beside them told Miranda that the scene wasn't occur-ring in the Rostov mansion in nineteenth-century Moscow. If Mi-randa, jostling her way through the crowd, didn't know better, she would have thought it was a real ape, so dense were the clusters of hair, so authentic the curled toes.

"Doctor? Doctor?" she pleaded, and the ape wrinkled its brow and raised one elongated limb to hang from the arbor.

The hussar grinned at her over the ballerina's head and said. "He says he's a vet."

"Monkey sausage and durians!" called out a waiter with a precar-iously balanced tray of sizzling meat that sent the ape scampering toward the rigging while those whose cravings lead to gluttony plucked at the tidbits and toppled the tray to the dance floor, grinding the chunks of pale pink flesh underfoot, while those of more sedentary appetite seated among the wilted flowers wiped the grease of the fifteenth course from their chins and waited for a sixteenth to appear along with yet more of the liquor that flowed as relentlessly as if a magical pump sucked Danube bilge water out of the *Anubis*'s hull and transformed it to any variety of potent beverage.

In the card room, money flowed like liquor.

Miranda tried room after room, until the people began to recognize her carriage and call out before she had a chance, "Doctor!"

She got lost in the labyrinth inside the *Anubis* that seemed impossibly larger than the shell that contained it, and it occurred to the girl on her fruitless quest that so did any infant seem to outsize the boundaries of its mother's belly, and she even ran into the huge bathroom that Isaac and Rocketmann had already left.

At the rail, the night was misty, sultry, the deck glistening, lamps glowing with a nimbus, stage lights an iceberg at the foredeck.

Isaac saw the same driver who had carted goods for the Weinerstrasse crew from Regensburg to Theresienstadt, dressed as a pack of cigarettes, a large Lucky Strike target on his chest, real cigarettes tucked behind his ear and poking out from his pockets. He was talking with Marcus, which set Isaac's plan to percolating as he started to fit together the images in his mind with the need for transportation. "Hey, Mac," Isaac interrupted, "you want to make one more trip?"

The driver said, "I was just telling this gentleman that I plan to make one more trip. Aliyah."

Aliyah was the ancient Jewish return to Zion, and for the first time since Exile, it was a widespread reality. The Jews were finally finding their way out of Europe, and one path, preferred by some, merely accepted by others, was southwards on a scow to Cyprus and from there, who knew how, to destination Palestine.

For Isaac, the whole idea of a Jewish state was nearly as foreign as a forest. The idea of Jews on beaches was preposterous. The next thing you knew they'd wear sunglasses and sport suntans. They'd eat crabmeat, drive German cars, and have myocardial infarctions under the palms. For a second he saw a vision of Far Rockaway.

Marcus bent forward in his medical manner. He was interested in how the driver would accomplish the same goal. "How will you do this?" He might as well have been saying, "Where does it hurt?"

"Brichah, the organization. If we can move cigarettes back and forth, why can't we move Jews?"

"I hear that it's hot."

"The weather is not a major consideration."

"I hear the Arabs are not so happy to have Jews immigrating."

"Can they be any worse than the Germans?"

Marcus nodded. "A hard life."

"And whose is easy?"

"Yours, maybe," Isaac interrupted, insistently returning to his single-minded desire. "We need one last trip. I can pay."

Marcus refrained from asking, "How?"

That didn't make a difference to the driver. He wouldn't go over the line again. Things were settling down. Laws were passed and enforced. Anyone who violated them was placed in prisons that you couldn't penetrate. Any day, the heap of gold at Liebknecht would be placed in the central reserves of the newly established national bank in the name of stabilizing the currency and encouraging the rehabilitated German people to join the West in its looming battle against the new enemy just eighty kilometers to the east. The anarchy on board the *Anubis* was a last gasp before the return to normalcy.

Isaac waved a document in front of the driver's face. It was one of the last bona fide visas to Portugal, where ships left steadily for the States. Precious as it was, he had the nagging feeling that this was the night he had to piece together his plan and was ready to use every resource at his disposal. A visa was nothing without the money to use it. With enough money, another visa could be bought.

"More paper?" the driver scoffed.

It was outrageous that a damn driver disdained his product. "Paper is life."

But the pack of cigarettes had learned other lessons. "Not good enough," he said. "Life is only as valuable as you make it." And he took the paper Isaac offered and, in the giddy spirit of the night, flung it overboard.

Before Isaac could lean over the rail, he heard a ferocious snapping sound. When he looked down he saw the snouts of half a dozen crocodiles below, placidly chewing on the visa as if it might be the passport to whatever reincarnation they sought.

"Did you see that?" Isaac was shocked. Crocodiles for God's sake. The whole strange scene was starting to get to him. Poker-playing potentates, Miranda, the sex show, munitions, Rocketmann, rabbis, tunnels, mirrors. He was beginning to lose his grasp. The rebuff of the driver should have been irrelevant, but he suddenly felt as if he could no longer reach and grab his rightful inheritance.

Marcus tried to soothe his self-defined cousin, the only family he had. "They're just normal fish dressed for deception. Or maybe men in crocodile suits."

"But why are they white?"

"It's a trick of the moonlight."

Miranda rushed up, all her coolness gone, so glad to see someone she knew dressed in a surgeon's white smock that she cried with relief. "Marcus, come with me."

"Why?"

"Rivka. I think she's going into labor."

"I was a dentist. And even that was a long time ago. I have no surgical skills, unless she needs root canal."

"You have more than anyone else. Come," she ordered. "Now!"

She hadn't even noticed Isaac, whose fragmenting composure had returned the moment he saw her. "Is that an order?"

Miranda turned furiously to the smirking executioner. "You idiots. You think you know everything, but you are . . . unfit. Ignorant, rude, inhuman. You know nothing."

Isaac and Marcus looked at each other, and shrugged. The crazed passion of the American was baffling. She was angry, but there was something funny about her fury. She was like a child stamping her feet when she didn't get her way.

"Nothing! Nothing!" She ranted. He didn't even know what coffee was. Strutting and dominating his tiny corner of the universe, he didn't know what the shabbiest dirt farmer in Proszowice knew. He could still recite chapter and verse from his earliest memories of cheder Talmud, but he had long since forgotten what his ancestors texts really meant. He knew the letter but not the spirit of the law.

"Oh no," he said, raising a glass with overt good cheer. "I know very well what spirits are."

She looked at him with disgust. "You don't know what meaning is."

"What, you want me to study?"

She stopped raving and answered the question. "No, I don't want you to study. I want you to live, Mr. Kaufman."

Isaac was quiet.

Then Miranda remembered her mission. "Live, like a baby, a baby, you idiots. A baby, born . . . here," and she started crying.

That's when Isaac felt the old fury rise in him. Weakness was death, tears its harbinger. He knew everything he needed to know. "We know she's going to have a baby."

"Now!"

"Now?"

"I had better go with her," Marcus said.

"You go," Issac turned red, "And . . ."

"And what?" Was it a threat. Go and don't return. He had lost power, strength, believability. His costume was a sham, his self a fraud, just another D.P.

"Nothing," Isaac muttered peevishly. So Marcus was abandoning him, too. So what! He was solitary, self-reliant. He survived enemies; he would survive friends.

"Come on," Miranda pulled the dentist's arm, and together they left, leaving Isaac contemplating the crocodiles that swam beneath him.

The band was swinging now, a saxophonist letting an archipelago of notes loose, like an anarchist flinging a handful of marbles under a squadron of police horses' hooves, and the dancers gyrated wildly until dessert arrived on a Viennese table that even the most frenetic paused to admire. It was covered with pots of mousse, piles of exotic fruit, kiwis and lingonberries, apricots, blood oranges, and raspberries that bruised if one so much as glanced at them, and pies with butter-sodden checkerboard crusts baked in the *Anubis*'s own oven. The centerpiece was a three-tiered cake that represented the stages of cultural development on the Continent, commencing with religion, followed by the fine and concluding with the practical arts. It was wheeled in by the Emcee, who was done up for his service in an incongruous admiral's uniform of crisp white ducks, gold braid, naval blue trim and a row of Pacific campaign ribbons.

The first level, like the base of a ziggurat, was a large square temple complete with niches with spun sugar statues of the virgin. Atop this lay an aesthetic archive with tiny violins made of chocolate and shelves of almonds set in a row to simulate a library and shrunken versions of the most famous paintings from the Louvre, Prado, Hermitage, and other museums, from *The Night Watch* to *Mona Lisa* painted on in dabs of food coloring framed with squiggly gilt icing. On the topmost level, were plows and a cannon, spears, and muskets made of intricately carved marzipan with flags of cotton candy that fluttered in the breeze. When the Emcee put a candle to the cannon's mouth, a tiny puff of cinnamon smoke emerged.

"Where have I seen that cake before?" one of the American puppet heads wondered.

"Eat, eat to your heart's content," the Emcee cried. "But do not forget to save a little room for the stag hearts that will be served in brandy sauce. "And if you can take your eyes from your plates and your glasses, perhaps we shall give you something to entertain the other senses. On ze rear deck, starting in ten minutes, vor your pleazure, an athletic competition." Looking around the crowd, he called for, "Mr. Bukiet?" He pronounced the name with the accent on the final syllable, to rhyme with "To bet" or "Who get."

"Did he say Bukiet?" The buzz went swiftly around the deck, and downstairs, too. As far as these people were concerned, a fancier name could not have been uttered. Bernard Bukiet was the undisputed Ping-Pong master of the zone.

There was no Ping-Pong in the shtetl, but the bored Jews of liberated lagerland took to the sport with all the enthusiasm of modernity. It was the perfect game for the refugees. Anyone with decent reflexes could play, and as far as the warders were concerned, it kept the natives occupied. Soon even those camps that the Yankees had not blessed with regulation green tables had makeshift ones. All it took was a sheet of plywood propped on twin sawhorses. "Rackets" were also cut from the plywood, and the only things the players couldn't supply for themselves were the marvelous balls, puffed with a gas that made them bouncier than the rubber stuffings of golf or tennis balls. At first, such balls were rare, but a shipment of a hundred gross disappeared from the army PX and materialized at large, and the stakes at the PX poker game increased that week.

Still, some took more naturally to the sport than others and there were champions. That was where Bernard Bukiet came in. A short, thickset man, he had been a streetcar conductor Before, but the second he grasped the handle of a racket in his hands he knew he had arrived at the place he was meant to be. For the first time in his life, he was a winner, and he swiftly discovered that he also knew how to make the most of his skill. He would amble into a camp and pick up a game, for a small wager, usually winning by slimmest possible margin, two points, until it became obvious that he beat everyone by two points no matter what their level of skill, as long as their dollar was on the table.

Eventually though Bukiet's fame preceded him, and he became as legendary in the zone as Rocketmann. Unfortunately, there was one way he could always be identified. Whenever a stranger stepped up to bet at a table, the first question asked of him was "Number?" because Bukiet's clothes could change, but not his brand, 175,663.

When it became obvious that he was unbeatable, he started putting on exhibitions. These were organized by the Joint as entertainment at the USO center. Bernard Bukiet would play the local champ, left handed or alternating hands with alternate shots, and then, when the game came to its foregone conclusion, he would do tricks, bouncing the ball off every surface in the room, hitting it behind his back, under his legs, juggling moreso than playing. For the culmination of his act, he slammed the ball across forty feet of air into a Coke bottle. It wasn't only the aim that was stupendous—the trick was greater than that. Once the ball had landed in the bottle, he'd hand it around, and show that although he could get the ball in, nobody could get it out, because the neck of the bottle was narrower than the circumference of the ball.

It figured that, sparing no expense, the *Anubis* would hire Bukiet along with the Green Hen entourage and the great chefs of France for the party to end all parties. The *Anubis* picked up speed. It was 3:00 A.M.

The saxophonist held a mute to his instrument and continued to play in the background while the Emcee finished his anouncement, "We are pleased to present Bernard Bukiet, playing the game of his life." Hinting broadly, he winked and said, "He'd better," and then added, "Will the guest dressed as an executioner please report to the rear deck? His assistance may be required."

Isaac was already inclined to see the exhibition. He needed entertainment, anything to take his mind off . . . everything. He had been thinking of Miranda in that idiotic box—and she called *him* an idiot—and he considered using one of his chits to summon the Green Hen girls when he heard himself paged over the loudspeaker. It reminded him of other loudspeakers that called whole barracks to a different executioner not dressed so medievally.

As the cake of European culture crumbled, two of the ship's Negro stevedores moved a Ping-Pong table to the center of the deck while two more moved the gangplank to the prow, delicately anchoring one side while extending the other out over the protuberant nostrils of the Danube crocodiles who ate Isaac's last visa.

The Emcee told their story, "These primitive beasts were captured last week in the Nile valley where the *Anubis* has its permanent home. But we have not been good zookeepers. In fact we have not fed them in that week. As some of the less fortunate here tonight have had to do without, they know what ravenousness is. But perhaps these sad creatures will be fed. Now . . ." He dropped a thigh-size slab of meat over the side, where twin spotlights played upon the ripples in the water, and the crocodiles' prehistoric jaws lept and snapped from below the surface, tearing the meat to shreds, leaving a bloody slick.

"Und that's yust the appetizer. These creatures need a meal, Bernard," he addressed the Ping-Pong master, who was nonchalantly rolling a Halex 4000 top-of-the-line ball over the nubby surface of his racket. "Here's the wager. Free passage to anywhere in the world if you accomplish your tasks, and if not, well," he giggled. "That's why we have requested the kind aid of the guest executioner, to help feed the pets."

Isaac was standing in the rear, and those around him made a small circle to give him room while Bukiet stepped up, and started his round of tricks. He began by bouncing the ball up and down, and then hit it so that it skimmed across the top of the taut mesh net and returned to him. He sent it ricocheting off the twin funnels of the boat and back again. It was his usual grab bag of tricks, which he performed with a bored sneer that led one observer to say it would be harder to get the ball between his lips than into the cola bottle. He curved the ball so that it looped wide, and landed in the Emcee's champagne glass.

In his privileged spot, Isaac was growing dissatisfied with these tricks that served no purpose but the display of technical facility for its own sake. He pressed his thumb against the edge of his axe.

"Finally have a job suited for you?" Necco said. They hadn't spoken since the Papiergeschäft debacle that led to Necco's demotion.

"Nice wings," Isaac replied, fingering the sergeant's fake medallion, wondering if there was a market for the fabrication of American military insignia.

"Thank you."

"What you planning to do with them?"

"Fly away."

For a second, Isaac thought that this one was also heading for Palestine, that Necco, revealing a prior act of remarkable deception, would drop his trousers and say, "See, I'm Jewish, too," but the soldier sipped at his beer.

Antagonism and resentment fully evident, the two men nonetheless shared a curiosity about the machinations that brought them together. And Isaac couldn't help but wonder about Jacks Over Deuces's rise to the top of his real profession while remaining in the lowest ranks of his putative one.

Ignoring the Ping-Pong master's virtuosity, they began speaking about their mutual acquaintance. Necco explained the legend as he heard it. First, there had been a plain sale of sanitary napkins from the WAC warehouse for the bleeding women of the Reich, earning a plain profit, but as the prices rose, so the profit rose. A lesser man might have pocketed the windfall, but Jacks Over Deuces just naturally parlayed. He was as adept in his field as the Ping-Pong player was in his. From then on, the corporal went from strength to strength, arithmetically then exponentially, from Ping-Pong balls to bombs, with nary a glance back at where he had been.

"Yes," Isaac murmured, "I've been thinking about munitions."

"How the Devil are you going to get munitions?"

"I thought you just said that He deals in them. So they should be at the base."

"Actually," Necco said, "The base at Liebknecht is out of ordnance."

Isaac couldn't believe it. "The army base is out?"

" 'Fraid so."

"But, how?"

"He sold them."

"To who?"

Someone dressed as a Soviet general—or maybe it was a Soviet general, because there was something in the man's manner that said that he was not dressed to deceive—walked by with red stars. Necco shrugged his head in that direction. "World markets are coalescing around uncharted fields of enterprise."

Incredulous, Isaac clarified, "He sold American munitions to the Soviets?"

"He's a patriot. He wouldn't give it to them."

"But . . ."

"Besides, if he didn't someone else would."

"Who?"

"There're a hundred like him, well maybe a half dozen, but there're a hundred would-bes. But that's all besides the point, now." He explained that the change had come when Jacks Over Deuces had sold a crate of muffins in Malta for less than he bought them in Crete, and discovered that he made more money that way.

Isaac might just as well have asked how the ball fit into the bottle.

Necco continued to parrot the official guidebook. "That's how the syndicate works." The quartermaster's housing at Liebknecht was the point on a pyramid that was more like a volcano, surging up from beneath in response to the manifold needs of its myriad constituents. "Which was where you came in."

Before Isaac could ask what Necco meant, Schimmel and several of the lads from Weinerstrasse came barreling down the aisle.

"Where have you boys been?"

"They had movies set up on the C deck."

"Not *Oliver and Hardy at the Biergarten* again?"

"No, this time it was *The Three Stooges Go to the Reichstag.*"

"Yeah, the Russians arranged it. Nyuck, nyuck, nyuck," Lefty rubbed his fist against Schimmel's head.

They were about to squeeze themselves into the front row, but Isaac crooked a finger and called them back. "Kommt her. You have something to learn from this young man."

Necco bowed his head modestly.

"You were saying?"

"Actually we're trying to move out of products altogether, into financing, facilitating, you know. Nowadays it's all information, trans-portation, communication, the service economy."

The word "transportation" evoked images of pipelines and con-duits and the truck Isaac required and train cars thoroughly washed and scrubbed, the concentration choo choo come to choo choo them home.

"Trade in labor, too," Necco went on. "No warehouse, no flucta-tion. Look, today a mark represents a pair of shoes, tomorrow a cigarette, the day after tomorrow nothing at all. But an hour of labor is still an hour of labor, same time, same sweat. You've got to move into abstract values. As things become unreal, abstractions become reified. Unless of course, you've got a uniquely valuable commodity."

And Isaac's mind leapt toward the cube of solid gold.

Necco said, "What are you looking at?"

"The way out."

"Not that way," Schimmel said, pointing at the crocodiles canti-levering themselves above the waves on huge primitive tails like surf-boards.

"No," Isaac agreed as he led the topic back toward transportation. He knew that he couldn't use the driver from the Green Hen any-more and speaking to Necco he realized that what he desperately needed was an army truck. "What about the one we had for Lud-wigshafen? It would have been perfect if only we hadn't disposed of it. Drat!"

"Well . . ." Schimmel said.

"Well, what?"

"We do in a way."

"What do you mean?"

"When you told me to get rid of it . . ."

"Yes?" Isaac was ready to pick up Schimmel and hang him over the edge where the crocodiles would snap at his nose, unless he answered immediately. "Tell me, damn it!"

"I think I can get it back."

Cowering with fear lest his disobedience be punished, it reluctantly came out that Schimmel hadn't "exactly" disposed of the truck as instructed. Instead, he held onto it for later by parking the vehicle in the shed behind Count Geiger's mansion. "I'm sorry," he blubbered. "I just couldn't . . . I mean, that it was too good to . . . I mean . . . I did cover it with hay."

"Never mind," Isaac said.

"You mean that?" Schimmel was still afraid that this was just a mean joke and that his punishment still lay in wait.

"Dear boychik." Isaac almost kissed him on the cheek.

"Good idea?"

"It never pays to follow instructions." Knowing that Necco wouldn't understand him, and eager to tell someone, he said, "I think that when we return we have a viable plan."

Necco quoted the daily comics. "Ach, dos boyze."

Just then, the crowd that had been watching Bukiet's warm-up with murmurs of appreciation and small scatterings of applause, broke into sustained cheers. The master had accomplished his trademark trick by placing the ball inside the bottle, but he had one new trick that the Emcee announced "has never been performed in public before."

Starting on top of the ruins of the cake and moving to strategic locations across the deck, Heidi, Bessie, and Helga lit a half dozen stubby wax Shabbes candles.

From a perch on the rungs of the funnel he had once descended, Rocketmann tried to discern the figure the six candles formed, like a reverse constellation.

"Vis one shot he will snuff zem all out," the Emcee declared. "Vis one shot . . . or . . . " he glanced backward over the railing.

Bukiet prepared by withdrawing into himself, blocking the crowd from his mind, concentrating on the exact position of the six candles. Regulating his breathing until it was as metronomic as a clock, feeling the weight of the ball, the grip of the racket, he assumed a stance that was half crouch, racket held above his shoulder, ball at eye level, and the drum rolled. He tossed the ball several inches into the air and brought the racket down so swiftly it was a blur that came to rest on his thigh like Wyatt Earp's gun in his holster. Immediately, the ball passed a quarter of inch over the wick of the first candle, leaving a tiny plume of smoke. It snuffed out the second and the third in a direct line as well. Nobody had seen the deft spin Bukiet placed, but the ball suddenly veered to the left as if it was entirely independent of all human initiative, snuffing the fourth, and then veered spasmodically to the right to wipe out the fifth. The fifth was the hardest and Bukiet sighed with relief. One more candle remained only several feet dead on from its predecessor, and the audience watched as the ball seemed to arrive at the wick in slow motion. It touched the flame, but it no longer had any impetus left. It hovered there, like Rocketmann over the *Anubis* funnel, and the gas inside caught and exploded in a giant flare. The explosion ought to have rendered the candle dead, but it didn't; the singed shell of the ball fell to the deck; the single flame remained.

"Oh, I'm so sorry," the Emcee's lips turned down in exaggerated distress.

There was a hush, broken when the Emcee addressed the corner where Isaac stood with Necco, still thinking trucks and trains. "I know dis is an interestink converzation, but vill the guest dressed as an executioner please report to work detail. Ve need his assistance."

The Emcee drew Isaac to the edge of the plank where Bukiet already stood, chagrined by his unaccountable failure, ready to pay the price.

The door to the interior of the *Anubis* opened again and Fishl swam forth, just to breathe for a moment before turning and returning to wherever he had come from, and a door opened in Isaac's mind. He remembered Fishl's arrival at Weinerstrasse with Alter's knock.

While the Emcee affixed a blindfold and bummed a Lucky Strike from the Vivant's driver for Bukiet's last cigarette, Issac couldn't help looking around for someone with a scar or an eye patch. Everyone else was here. It was obvious that if Alter was anywhere in Europe, he was on board, but unless he wore the deceiving headpiece of the wild boar, its tusks frivolously teasing at the puffs of cotton that barely covered Helga's breasts, he wasn't identifiable.

"Und now . . ."

Without a pause, Isaac called the announcer's bluff. He wasn't going to perform, wasn't going to succumb to the audience's desire for suspense. He looked at Bukiet poised on the gangplank, and, without so much as a blink, he pushed.

There was a splash in the water, and the boat itself tilted as the entire crowd rushed to the starboard rail to watch, but as the bubbles came to the surface they revealed themselves to be a thousand Ping-Pong balls that bobbed peacefully in the ship's wake.

Coffee was served for those who were growing tired as the boat clock chimed four bells, and coffee pudding for those who needed a real jolt to keep from nodding off and missing something. The last hand had been dealt, not because it was deemed the last hand and not because it was dawn, though rosy fingers were beginning to poke through the gloom, but because the narrative of any poker game leads inexorably to one moment that will define that session's winners and losers. Understanding this unwritten rule, the players fidgeted as they scrutinized their cards and then furtively or brazenly, with cool dispatch or hot gusto, peered around the table. It was nice to have a nice hand, even nicer when one's opponents had minimally less nice hands, best of all when one's opponents had brilliant hands just a wee less brilliant than one's own.

The game was five card. There was a bet and a draw. No one took more than a single card.

"How much?" said the tall, quiet stranger at the end of the table. He had been anteing and folding so regularly that Isaac, returned from the deck in time for this ultimate game, hadn't noticed him, or mistook him for the dealer all evening. Both wore tuxedos, but the visitor's was clearly custom made in the style of the last century. He held a silver-tipped cane and, now that he was engaged in a hand, he placed a monocle in his left eye to examine his cards more closely. It might have been the "give" that unconsciously revealed his hand to the table, but without a history of prior betting, it could have been the bluff of a give. He spread the five rectangles in his hand infinitessimally apart.

Stalin held up five fingers, and the stranger nodded. "See and raise."

"See and raise again," Churchill harrumphed.

"Well I'll be," Hammerin' Hank declared. He sucked at a beer and crushed the can in his fist. "See and raise again."

Pinsker gulped without beer to wet his throat and repeated the phrase as if it was a mantra. "See and raise again."

Jacks Over Deuces smiled and pushed his stack of chips to the center.

No more chips on the table, dollars emerged from pockets. Pockets emptied, IOUs were signed. The rhythm of bet, raise, bet, raise continued as gawkers accumulated, eyes as stunned by the heap of ribbed wooden chips and scrawled paper chits in the center as if it was a glittering pile of diamonds, as the engine of the *Anubis* purred and the water churned from the immersed machinery.

Isaac knew how the game would end, and turned to Necco, who had accompanied him indoors, and said, "You hate him."

"Sure, he hates me," Jacks Over Deuces said, pushing more and more and more money into the center of the table, reveling in his role and his hand.

"Sure, I hate him."

Hank guffawed, "And they all hate me, that's what I get paid for." He, too, pushed his all into the center. It was the hand to kill or be killed by.

They all hated each other, and that was why they dressed as they did. Churchill hated Stalin and glowered as he signed a chit good for the British crown jewels, only to be seen and raised by Stalin's presentation of the Tzar's household chachkes.

"And yourself?" Stalin addressed the man in the monocle.

"Hate is invigorating. Germans can't hate the Jews anymore and that's why they lost the war. They had guns, they had men, they just ran low on hate." The man spoke in a cultured middle-European accent as he calmly scribbled his name at the bottom of a series of elaborately watermarked certificates that represented shares in the Prussian railroads.

Hammerin' Hank picked them up and squinted to make out the name. "Baron Something Something de . . . what is this?"

"Rothschild." Of course. Who else would sit down so easily with Churchill and Stalin. Who was deceiving whom?

Sitting cross-legged under a Christmas tree in Topeka not much more than a decade earlier, still wearing closed-toe pajamas, shuffling the deck of cards Santa Claus had given him, the future corporal would not have been in the least surprised to find himself at this gathering, at this moment. He had been unaccountably losing all night, but every penny he had put onto the table had reappeared multiplied, and he had no doubts whatsoever where that lovely pile of cash and credits was going to land. "Call," he said.

Jacks Over Deuces relished the moments when the pathetic Stalin, whose moustache fell onto the pile as a last offering, opened his own Jacks, three of them, over his own deuces, an additional pair, and proudly said "Full house" only to be met with Churchill's austere glare and the Englishman's proud Queens, three of them, over threes, an additional pair. "Not full enough."

It all made no difference, because Hammerin' Hank had four sevens, and slapped them down so hard that the ash from Churchill's cigar fell off the tip.

Three players were left, and their eyes met. Pinsker blinked and opened his own slyly described, "Two pairs. Eights and eights," but Rothschild accepted the challenge and laid down a beautiful fan of hearts, a straight flush, two, three, four, five, six, one of the best hands possible.

It was the corporal's turn. He could forget Churchill and Stalin and Pinsker, the ruler of the Regensburg cafés. He could certainly forget Hammerin' Hank, whose ass the corporal had been whipping throughout the European campaign. He could even forget the Baron with his precious mien. The noncom felt sure of the five cards that lay face down in front of him. He had seen them once, and hadn't peeked again. Far better than the straight flush to the six, he had the royal to the Ace, *the* best hand possible. He was ready to sweep the table, when he glanced up and saw Isaac Kaufman.

A full house was a full house, but Churchill and Stalin were sunk in misery and the bones of Wild Bill Hickock lay in the ground with a bullet hole in his skull. Likewise the value of four of a kind depended on what kind there were four of. Royalty lived well in castles on mountains, but Queens and Kings were both subject to the depredations of prelates and peasants, witness the head of Louis XIV rolling about in a wicker basket beneath the guillotine. The perfect hand was only perfect if the rules were obeyed.

Suddenly, there was a wild card.

For a quarter of a second, there was doubt in Jacks Over Deuces's mind, and before he unfolded his royal flush, he looked at Isaac and made him an offer. "Half my hand for half of yours."

From the Kremlin to Whitehall, from St. Peter's to Wall Street to 1600 Pennsylvania Avenue, among all the homes of power, it was the lager that reigned supreme and turned herrings into heroes. Omnipotent at the poker table, Jacks Over Deuces felt impotent before the Jew, not the Jew of Jerusalem, not the Jew of Vilna, not the Jew of Mainz, Grenada, or New York, but the malnourished, mistreated, branded, and beaten Jew who still stood breathing the Hellfire of Auschwitz, the Jew now, After.

Munitions, Isaac thought. Mines, he thought. Trucks he thought. And revisiting his vision somewhere on shore, he thought of the cube of gold formed from the broken teeth of the broken covenant that was damn well going to come to rest far from the green felt table, tucked securely as a black cotton yarmulke in the breast pocket of Isaac Kaufman's vest.

The others looked at the man in the executioner's mask. Stalin and Churchill would have offered their hands, too, but they knew that no matter how brilliant the cards they held, they were just not in the game, doomed. Both their Empires would shatter under the battering ram of history. Even Rothschild would have to content himself with the meager consolations of the Paris bourse, as would Pinsker with his own reduced version of that domain. Hammerin' Hank had nothin' to offer. The corporal waited for an answer.

Isaac smiled, and a chip off another tooth fell to the table. He flicked it away with the ball of his thumb and the fingernail of his forefinger and smiled his executioner's grin, "No, I'll play my hand by myself."

So even as Jacks Over Deuces raked in his winnings he mourned the killing he couldn't share. What he didn't know was that Issac had one weak spot. There was one thing he'd trade his hand for, pay his profits toward, but it was the one thing Jacks Over Deuces could not find on the world market to buy him and deliver, a brother with an eye patch, because the one thing that had more value than gold was blood.

"You'll never catch me!" Rocketmann cried, a good bet since nobody was chasing him. He turned to the room. Then he extracted a shiny silver object from his breast pocket and brought it to his mouth.

Isaac gagged back his disgust, but even his knowledge of where the object had been found was forgotten when he heard the sound that emerged from the thing as Rocketmann's lips slurped back and forth across the ornately etched silver surface: a raucous carnival melody that mixed one note into the other like a meat grinder pulverizing a chunk of filet mignon. Chord overlapping chord, it was irritating and exalting at the same time, a divine harmonics of the gutter.

A black soldier dressed as a white soldier with talcum powder smeared across his face grinned, and took his own harmonica from a breast pocket to join in while Rocketmann wailed the blues. A moment later, the two instrumentalists were joined in a dirge sung by the heretofore silent stevedores of the *Anubis.*

> *Sweet jazz and jism.*
> *Gettin' out of prison.*
> *After twenty long years*
> *I got the Lonesone Devil Blues.*
>
> *Talk about your fission.*
> *Nuclear division.*
> *Sweet jazz and jism.*
> *Got the Lonesome Devil Blues.*

The wailing of the harmonica came to a stop, and the soldier whose whiteface was turned into zebraface by the sweat pouring off his forehead stood upright again. The stevedores moved off to their nautical duties.

✿   ✿   ✿

In the corner two men were rubbing hips together, and one of the girls from the Green Hen was fingering herself on a couch, murmuring, "Sweet jazz and jism."

Everyone in the room swayed under the influence, with one exception. Frau Mannheim was a stolid, ungainly presence who had spent the hours since her arrival turning her head from one loathsome display after another. She had felt the fury building in her, like rocket fuel heating, prior to combustion, and she was ready to explode. She marched up to Rocketmann as if there was a trumpet in her head, when something about the material of his getup drew her to touch. Immune to the influence of music, she had always had a love for fine fabric, and her fist unclenched, her fingers stroking the strange design sewn into the cape like metal inlay in a rotten tooth. It was parchment, or sheepskin folded and unfolded so many times it had the texture of parchment. But then, when her own fingers unfolded the image, she stood back. "The service!" she gasped.

"You know?"

"My husband." She swiftly corrected herself, "my dead husband."

"Your dead husband?"

"He was a carrier."

Shapes have meaning, and the secret emblem of the postal universe that Rocketmann was dedicated to taking from the Pony Express to the speed of light was comprehensible only to an initiate. Frau Mannheim's musky emanation enveloped the room as the brittle fabric that encased her split down the middle like molting snakeskin.

In a second, Rocketmann's tights were down at his ankles, exposing the bony protruberances of his knees, his skinny legs and hairy thighs, and the dangling member that was commencing its own slow rise, like a V-2 on the launching pad, as she echoed the words he had uttered when confronted by the lesser creatures of the Green Hen. "Nein, nein," she moaned, "Not so brazen my . . . my . . . carrier," but he could not hear her, or if he did he knew that she didn't mean it, because everything meant its opposite. Time itself was turned around. The new physics delivered rockets to places they could not rationally travel.

"Yah," she cried. "Yah, I do. Yah, yah," and then as Rocketmann swept his cape over the head of his beloved in an act of tender modesty, Der Schreiber emerged from the bedchamber, overheard and muttered, "Joyce."

A coming screamed across the sky.

"Isaac, we need you." It was Der Schreiber, speaking so peremptorily that even the poker players looked up to see the cockroach, out of place in the posh casino, demanding that the man who turned down the offer that any of them would have jumped to accept accompany him—who knew where, who knew why.

"Oh?"

"Now."

"And if I don't?"

Der Schreiber repeated the litany of his vocation. "I am just a messenger. I can guarantee only that the message will be delivered, not that it will be understood or obeyed. Sometimes I think that I can guarantee the opposite."

Isaac looked at the cockroach disavowing all effect, and wondered if Der Schreiber was sly enough to convince him by pretending that he had no chance of convincing him. It wasn't shame that Isaac felt as his toes inched forward; he refused to acknowledge shame. Perhaps it was curiosity.

"This way," Der Schreiber said, and Isaac followed the cockroach through the labyrinth belowdecks of the *Anubis*, as if through a crack in the wall.

"Sure did find a private place, didn't you?" he said. Griping every step of the way, Isaac was led from room to room to room, each sunk a few steps beneath the last, descending to the ship's most abysmal chambers, which must have been beneath the hull, if not the bed of the Danube, into the cramped cabin, where Marcus and Fishl and Miranda had been joined at Rivka's side by the queer Count Geiger whom Isaac had once met in the decayed mansion off Weinerstrasse. Of course, the count would have been invited to the party to end all parties, but the fact that he had managed to come and leave his decayed house was somehow amazing. He certainly didn't take the "dress for deception" dictum to heart. He wore the same bathrobe and slippers he had worn in his library. Indeed he sat in the tiny room with the same composed unconcern with which he had greeted the burgling refugees.

There was blood all over the place, not the blood Isaac was familiar with, leeching the life's energy from bodies without count, but blood meant to harken in a new life. This blood, smearing the sheets bunched at the juncture of Rivka's thighs, still wet, was disconcerting.

"Something the matter?" Marcus said. His tone surprised Isaac. There was nothing of deference. It sounded like an interrogation.

"No, of course not."

"What did you expect?" Der Schreiber demanded.

"Nothing. I said 'No!' "

"Nothing?" Miranda insisted.

"He said 'No,' Fishl declared. And that was the end of the discussion.

"Thank you," Isaac said, but the second he acknowledged the small favor Fishl had done him, he resented it, for the reprieve, like the assault, like the blood, were all the reverse of the world he thought he knew. "So, why do you want me?"

Whatever crisis had led to Isaac's summoning had subsided, and they waited for the next. There would be more cries and moans, but again they would not be the cries that had filtered into their lives for the last half decade. That was then; this was now. That was During. This was After.

"It's not the Konzentrationlager here" the count said, reading Isaac's mind and proving that he had some knowledge of the real world. These were the first words he had uttered. Five minutes earlier, he had walked in as if there was nothing unusual about the situation and relaxed in the armchair beside a standing lamp with a purple-fringed shade. As soon as Isaac was ushered forward, however, the count stood up to peruse the shelf of false volumes. "No books, here," he said. "Nothing to read. Nothing to learn. Nothing to regret. Nothing to forget. Nothing to remember."

"Something to see, though."

"Oh, do you mean . . ." and with a disparaging sweep of the hand that took in the whole *Anubis*, from prow to anchor, he said, "this."

"I'm not sure that I did, but I suppose that I could have."

"This is just the ancestor's."

Isaac was unsure what Geiger meant, but there was something about the man's use of the word "the" that struck him. He thought of his own ancestors, hounded from the Middle East through Rome and Spain, through France and Germany, into the fertile valley out-side of Cracow, where their children were prohibited from owning land, and therefore sold seed to the farmers, who resented them and killed them for the fun and to pay them back for their privilege. Then the Germans came. Five years later, five hundred years of Jewish life in Poland was gone, like magic, in a puff of smoke, dis-sipated in the wind. Take a deep breath and inhale a Jew.

It was Marcus who understood the count. "Is this . . . ?" he ges-tured toward everything that surrounded them, from the jackal-decorated quilt to the sounds of the party. "Yours?"

"Mine? Well, yes, I suppose so."

This was the host.

Der Schreiber whistled.

But Geiger was modest. "Actually, I was referring to the original count."

"Who?"

"You're interested?"

"Yes."

"A man from the mountains, heavy boorish type from the looks of him, one portrait survives. Mud-on-the-boots kind of fellow." Geiger was no dandy, but he did glance at the overlapping alligator-skin scallops on his own slippers.

"And . . . ?"

He grew garrulous. "It's a family story, maybe apocryphal. Maybe the successors didn't want to acknowledge the ancestor's intelligence, preferred to see him as a kind of lucky boy. He was in the mountains, a lonesome picnic with a ham sandwich, very good luck that sand-wich, should be on our coat of arms, sliced pig rampant on a pum-pernickel field. He put it down and a squirrel, brazen nibby-nose, grabs a piece of meat. He turns, says, 'Ach!' Squirrel runs; he follows. Chases the squirrel for hours, up hill, down dale. Finally corners the little beast, who slips into a burrow. Fellow reaches a hand in, lucky his finger wasn't bitten off, lucky the squirrel wasn't rabid, lucky he lived to spread his seed, well maybe not so lucky, look what's become of us . . ."

He seemed to await a response, but when none was forthcoming he continued the saga of the original count. "Grabs ahold of some-thing in the burrow, thinks it's the sandwich, this part doesn't ring so true to me. A slice of ham, it's soft. He grabs something hard, pulls it out, holds it to the sun. That's it . . ."

The audience of four waited for the punch line, but the count was finished. He hadn't spoken at such length for decades. He was exhausted.

It took the curious Schreiber to ask, "And then? What was it that he found?"

"Oh, that. It wasn't ham. It was gold."

Isaac nodded.

"You've heard of the mines, very close to here, little town called Liebknecht, just down the road, not wide but deep, one pure vein, enough to establish the ancestor in the royal court, proverbial overnight success. From there, investments, you know, real estate, factories, railroads, always liked mines though. Sort of a hobby. Did some excavation in Egypt."

"But the house you live in. It's so deteriorated."

"I've left the house—it's yours. Take it."

"We will."

"Oh, good," the count said, "Nine generations in the same place is enough. Anyway, it's not the same place anymore." He lit a pipe.

Suddenly calm, Isaac focused on the end result of nine German generations that had made their own pilgrimage, not geographically as the Jews, but occupationally from Geiger the First's mine through Geiger the Ninth's lager. Isaac immediately knew that this man had owned camps from Swabia to Serbia, producing mattresses and toothbrushes from the hair of Isaac's mother's head, and he did it without leaving his home, probably without knowing, surely without caring. Isaac wanted to wrap his hands around the old man's throat and squeeze until the miserable line came to an end.

Again, the count seemed to anticipate Isaac. "No children," he said.

It didn't make a difference. Isaac wanted vengeance, but instead he asked, "That mine, is there a map?" but he didn't get an answer, because Rivka screamed, and the conversational portion of the evening was over.

Marcus was doing his best, but it didn't seem to help. He knew teeth, and the swollen female body he tried to decipher was nothing like a bad case of periodontis. He sweated as much as Rivka did and bit his tongue to keep from joining in when she screamed again. Miranda flitted nervously and Der Schreiber ran his eight hands across his forehead. Only Fishl was calm.

Geiger asked, "Is she sick?"

Miranda said, "Look, if you don't mind, we can't find a doctor."

"Oh," Geiger replied, "Why don't you use the ship doctor?"

"Ship doctor?"

"Wonderful man. Just found him when we docked in Vienna. Exactly what we'd been missing."

He maundered on, but Marcus interrupted. "Why didn't you tell us?"

"You didn't ask."

Miranda stared at the man and bit her lips to keep from screaming louder than Rivka. Count Geiger was as ignorant as a baby although the wrinkles on his forehead were as convoluted as the map of Europe his family had written. She took his shoulders and looked him in the eyes and said, "I'm asking."

"Oh, certainly." He picked up a contraption with a mouthpiece set into the pattern of a jackal on the wall and simply commanded, "Ship's doctor to level five, master stateroom." His voice boomed out across all decks, obliterating the clink of cash in the card room and the voice of the Emcee who was crooning lullabys to the tired revelers.

"This is the master stateroom? It's smaller than the broom closet."

Geiger shrugged."It's cozy."

Rivka sweated and screamed, and, between screams, she panted, "For three years, I didn't make a sound . . . not when they shot my father . . . not when they dragged away my mother . . . not when I dreamed about what they did to my sisters . . . Now . . ." Again, her cry shook the room.

Miranda clutched Isaac's arm, and he could feel her nails through his taut black costume.

The placid Geiger perused the spines of the mock books on the shelf, and said, "I didn't know we had this on board. It's fascinating. Oh, but here's the book you were asking about." He removed one of the volumes from the shelf and gave it to Isaac. It was Maimonides's *Guide for the Perplexed*. Isaac put it on a desk top.

Then another voice said, "Make room, please," and a figure

dressed in a severe black suit was inside the cramped room, too, bending over the bed with such authority that Marcus fled to the wall with relief. The man took Rivka's wrist, measured the pulse, eased a pillow under her spine, explaining everything he was doing, "It looks uncomfortable, but it will ease the passage."

Isaac remembered the way the stevedores had greeted the last arrival to walk up the gangplank in the seconds before the ship disembarked.

"Doctor?" Miranda nearly moaned with gratitude.

The man didn't answer, but turned. He looked at Miranda, Fishl, Der Schreiber, and Isaac with his one good eye. The other was covered with a patch.

Isaac started forward, but the doctor brushed him aside, and said, "My bag," pointing to a medical case on the floor. It looked like the same bag the Emcee had taken the stethoscope from, and maybe it was. Isaac handed the bag to his brother.

Doctor Alter removed a hypodermic, squirted a tiny geyser of liquid to eliminate any air in the cylinder. Thumb at the top, two fingers holding the point of the needle in place against the soft flesh inside Rivka's elbow, he said, "This will ease the pain." He plunged the needle into the vein.

"You," he said, to Miranda. "Can you say 'Push'?"

"Push?" her voice was a whisper.

"No, PUSH!"

"Push," she attempted to impart a little vehemence into her voice.

"That will have to do. I want you next to this woman's ear. Wait until she has a contraction. Don't ask me when; you'll know. Then say 'Push' and mean it."

From her first contraction shortly after midnight until dawn had been almost five hours, and there had been minimal progress. According to the doctor, she was only one centimeter dilated, but from the moment he arrived, she widened visibly. Within fifteen minutes of heavy breathing, back-breaking contortions, and pushes that seemed more likely to pop Rivka's eyes than her straining belly and loins, the crown of a child's head appeared through the distended opening.

Suddenly the lips closed shut with a vacuum sound and the skull retreated, willfully it seemed, back into Rivka. It was either a sign of the child's modesty or the first reaction of a princeling to the sense of his realm, a lethal, shabby domain composed equally of lunacy, misery, pandemonium, and pain.

"Next time," the doctor said.

"Always next time. When does it stop?"

"Never. It goes round, history does. What this child will see, will it be different from what we saw?"

There was no time for anyone to answer him. Whether it was the drug he had injected taking effect or the sudden revving of the boat's engines that induced further activity, or whether the child's time had simply arrived, there was another splash of red stain, and this time an entire head burst out of Rivka's vagina. The doctor gripped it brusquely and would not allow it to return. Left hand under the knob of a chin, he placed his other behind the neck, like a shoehorn, and tugged. Suddenly one arm and then the other appeared, and everyone in the room started counting fingers. Before they could reach ten, however, the child's own belly and the thick pulsing cord that bound it to its mother curled free, and there were the child's muscular thighs and the child's own ten toes.

In a second, the doctor lifted the body into the air, and snipped and clamped the two foot length of gory human rope, and a minute later the liverlike placenta floated out onto the linen.

The child of suffering was coated with blood and a fleshy transparent membrane, like the white of an uncooked egg.

"A caul," the doctor said, "It's considered fortunate." Then he removed a delicate blade from his bag and sliced the membrane from forehead to navel, and peeled it back like an ermine cloak from the newborn's shoulder blades.

There was a sour odor and Isaac held his breath as he stared at the creature. He had smelled worse, but the frank, disingenuous aroma of newborn stunned him.

The doctor lifted a palm to whump the child on the back. There was a hiss of breath, and then the squawl of life. Still holding the child, he noticed a clock on the wall. Unlike Cinderella catching a glimpse of a different hour, he said, "I've got to go." He handed the burden to its mother.

"What?" Isaac started.

Alter packed away his medical equipment, the scalpel and the clamps and the hypodermic tucked into·individual pockets of his case.

"Will you return?"

"Once more, when you need me, for the last time."

"When will that be?"

"Soon," Alter said, "In the meanwhile, read your book."

"Look," Rivka said. Forgetting her own pain, she cradled the large, bulging creature.

Even Isaac looked at the veins pulsing on its forehead and the beatific smile on Rivka's face. When he looked up, however, Alter was gone.

"Read your book," he had said. Isaac grabbed the book he had left on the desk and opened it. There were no pages. Der Schreiber had already noticed that the "books" were phony; they were containers not for words, but objects, and might once have held cash or jewelry to be hidden on a shelf in plain sight. *Guide for the Perplexed* had a single piece of paper folded into sections. Count Geiger was right; it was the book Isaac wanted. The paper was a map of the Liebknecht mines, rendering in perfect twenty-foot scale every inch under the camp.

The *Anubis* had turned around, cruised upstream, and docked back at the Regensburg town pier. It was well past dawn and the yard workers were already at labor. Two stubble-chinned men sat on a half-painted rowboat, rolling tobacco and watching as their gray-faced betters wobbled down the gangplank, flanked by the team of black stevedores, untouched by the gaity since their moment of musical communion.

Costumes long since stained, torn or shed, disgarded in a fit of passion or pique at their inconvenience, or just turned back into rags, or shmattes, the party was over. Beads, sequins, and feathers littered the path.

Drivers who had been waiting all night signaled to their fares, who stumbled into the backseats that were still warm from the drivers' own slumbers and instantly fell asleep so soundly that they weren't even woken by the horns as every car in the lot simultaneously tried to squeeze out the single-lane exit.

The Emcee said, "Zis way, ladies," lively enough for a breakfast show, as he twirled a cane to prod his trio toward a Volkswagen bus like a shepherd maneuvering his flock.

Hammerin' Hank shoved his driver into the passenger seat of his jeep, took the wheel himself and roared over a berm.

Churchill and Stalin hugged and bid each other a sleepy farewell.

Holding enough IOUs to satisfy Croesus, Jacks Over Deuces glanced at Isaac Kaufman with regret and envy.

Some pockets were emptied at the card tables, others filled. Deals had been made, promises broken, lies believed, truth affirmed and denied over the residue of partridge bones and chestnut puree and vodka and coffee that clotted the teak floorboards and tarnished the brass rails.

Alan Foyle, wig askew, mascara running, lipstick smeared, yellow dress stretched beyond recognition, took Miranda's reluctant elbow. She, too, looked longingly at her partners in passion from the tiny master chamber, but Marcus waved and she left. Der Schreiber went with her.

Isaac waited for Fishl, Rivka, and the youngest partygoer to join the group intending to motor toward Weinerstrasse in Frau Mannheim's car. The vehicle was there, but unfortunately Frau Mannheim and her keys were not; they had disappeared into the ether with Rocketmann.

"What do we do?" Schimmel whined.

Marcus turned to Isaac, but it was Fishl who gave the obvious answer, "We walk."

If Miranda or Elizabeth Smith Moss had remained in the empty parking lot, she would have insisted on assisting, but the refugees did not need any help. Fishl reached out to carry the newborn, swaddled in a pillowcase bearing the face of the jackal, but Rivka refused to relinquish her burden. A trickle of blood dripping out from her under her dress onto the gravel, she placed one foot in front of the other, and the rest of the crew kept pace.

They were used to walking and, besides, time for contemplation suited their leader. Isaac Kaufman had a lot to consider, for he had learned a great many important things during the course of the night. There had been the revelation that Schimmel had not discarded the truck, the discussion of bombs and explosives at the poker table, Rocketmann's information about the tunnels, Count Geiger's map of the mines, and Alter's statement. Put them all together and the plot would had been evident from the first page. It was time for Isaac to consummate his plans and he knew precisely what to do now. He was going to bring to parturition his own brainchild, not animal, not vegetable, pure twenty-four carat mineral, eighteen tons worth.

Issac didn't look back to see the *Anubis* floating away. He was sleepwalking when he was roused by the cry of the baby.

Book V

REPARATION

CHAPTER 15

Most of the bones were gone, plowed under, ground to bits. Occasionally a jagged shard was scuffed to the surface by an army boot, like an Indian arrowhead from a lost civilization. Less frequently, an intact tibia could be seen, gnawed in the shadows of the base pharmacy by a piebald dog whose own ribs looked ready to pop out of its emaciated chest. There were of course a few perfect skulls kept as souvenir paperweights on the desks of the former Reich and perhaps an entire set, complete down to the three tiny components of the inner ear—hammer, anvil, and stirrups—strung together with wires and hung upon a rack in a laboratory or a folding valet in a wardrobe.

Besides bone, however, there was skin. Despite the elegant lampshades that diffused the illumination of Siemens's bulbs onto the pages of Hegel's texts, most of the skin that remained from Before was mobile, its carriers rotting at a level far beneath the numbers seared onto their forearms in a blue script that varied with the brand-writing of their individual signatories. More recently, they had grown accustomed to new numbers assigned them by the Joint and stamped onto crisp new passports issued by the Allied forces to keep track of the refugees.

All of Isaac Kaufman's old passports were invalid.

Alan Foyle originally suggested reusing the German numerology, because it was already in place and would save effort, but Miranda said, "Yeah, and maybe we'll start with a number one on your forehead," and stared at him with such ferocity that he fled into the bathroom and tended his eyelashes. They had grown curly with the damp river air, contaminated by proximity to bearded Ashkenazim, so he worked vigorously to straighten them before the damage was irreparable.

Besieged in his own domain, Foyle primped in front of the mirror that he had obtained through the good graces of the army quartermaster, and then he peeked back into the office. Miranda was still on the prowl, so he shut the door, and paced the tiny room, two steps, reverse, two steps reverse. It reminded him of a dance step, but the tiled square was not the herringboned cherry wood at the Copa. Desperate to escape, he climbed onto the toilet tank and began to inch himself through the tiny window that ventilated the room. He paused on the ledge, however, because a cluster of DPs stood outside, next to the yellowing lists of the genuinely dead.

Fewer and fewer of the refugees still searched for lost family, so their conversation had less to do with the old lists than new ones that determined when they would board transport that lead to America rather than Auschwitz. Over thirty percent had already received their papers and Foyle looked forward to the day when the Continent was truly Judenrein. In the meanwhile, however, he hovered, upper body in midair, toes en pointe upon the toilet. Though he had never mastered their guttural Yiddish, he could understand the men below him now, because they had learned English or the native language of whatever nation they hoped to be dispatched toward whenever their number reached the top of Foyle's list. Many held pocket grammars and practiced foreign vocabularies.

"Excuse me, Mister, do you know the path to the train station?"

"Yes, Sir, it is only a single one block to the vestvard."

"Thank you very muchly."

"You are velcome."

Transportation was the obvious and natural topic, so their conversational exercises were peppered with references to schedules and terminals. Everyone was moving out. No longer worried about raging infections, the army had lifted most barriers to "domestic" travel, and, no longer impressed by the advantages of their situation, the twins split for Hamburg. Singularly unbound by even the mildest strictures, Der Schreiber boarded a sleeping car for Paris. Amid of a flurry of ooh-la-laaas from the French intelligentsia for his "voice from the ashes," he still managed to find time to send Miranda a series of letters on blue stationery.

Isaac Kaufman's paper was no longer special.

Regensburg itself was subject to the torpor of the season. Since the *Anubis* had left, the only excitement occurred when barracks of army troops were sent home. There were rumors that aside from a small garrison, the rest of the base would be dismantled by summer.

Miranda knew that she, too, would leave eventually and worked as diligently as Isaac once had to produce visas for her constituents.

More surprising, Count Geiger disappeared. Schimmel discovered this when he was sneaking behind the mansion to retrieve the truck he had hidden in the overgrown forsythia. Stumbling among the bushes, he wondered why it was so hard to see, until he realized that the light that had always cast a dim glow from the library was out. Inside, the telling sign of the count's departure was the absence of his slippers. Whether the degenerate scion of the Liebknecht Mines had just floated downstream with his yacht, or what, Schimmel didn't know, but the house was surely vacant.

"Yes," Isaac said, bored. "In fact, he gave it to us."

Back on Weinerstrasse, the crew discussed the idea of moving into the abandoned mansion, but they were too stunned by lassitude to act. These days, however, inaction was wise. Return to normalcy had led to a crackdown on the black market. The government was desperate to stabilize the wildly fluctuating currency. There were a series of arrests that led to serious imprisonment in cells not as easily cracked as the one Fishl had left in Ludwigshafen. Even Pinsker was talking about going legit, opening a store. So rather than contend against a less military, more constabulary presence, it was better to wait on any one of a hundred lines: for food, for information, for consolation, in the damp weather, gray outfits turning grayer, except for a single green feather in a Tyrolean hunting cap. It was a time of tedium, alleviated by Ping-Pong, gossip, and the occasional movie.

Abbott and Costello Meet Anschluss played at the town cinema.

* ❁ ❁

The one important change at Weinerstrasse was held in Rivka's arms beneath her swaying breasts, their tips white with crusted milk. Rivka's comely muliebrity was as shocking as the madonna in an opium den and the child's cooing interrupted the usual raucous discussion.

Schemes were developed now with an eye to the child's welfare. Even Schimmel was suddenly interested in trading cigarettes for baby food at the market and swapped one of the last bona fide visas to Denmark for a pair of plaid booties. Only Isaac didn't notice. Instead, he was rather glad that he was no longer the focus of attention. If anything, he yearned for yet greater solitude to mull over his plans. Hoping to get rid of everyone, he suggested they go to the movies.

"What?"

"Gei avek."

Fishl raised his eyes to Rivka to implore her to save him from such entertainment, but even she thought he needed some leave from the hourly feedings, and said, "Go."

So Schimmel and Fishl had decamped for the Guttenberg Cinema, seeking release from the drabness that would have been heavenly two years earlier. "We've seen this before," Schimmel complained, as a newreel preceding the feature flickered onto the screen. It was highlights from the Olympics of '33. Jesse Owens was running flat out, but—ah, the magic of editing—history was changed. At the last moment, when the American runner's broad black chest was just about to break the tautened finish line, a blond young man emerged from the pack to snap the ribbon with his own Aryan musculature. The scene dissolved to cheering crowds from the Nuremberg rallies.

"We've seen everything before," Fishl replied.

"Can you believe that it's been two years?"

The time spent at large in Europe was now, according to the laws of temporal duration, longer than the time spent in the lager. But the weight of differing time spans was relative. Barbed wire circumscribed their souls. The two years in captivity would endure forever, unless, of course, one assumed that they never happened.

Already the French referred to Der Scheiber as "le chroniqueur de l'ère concentrationnaire as if it was as long ago as the Cretaceous

Era and he was the last neanderthal, sipping espresso, regaling sophisticates with tales of his life in the cave. On the other hand, the two years in Europe from May '45 to '47 were but a blink in the waiting room for the next stage on some imponderable journey: destination Palestine, Australia, America, anyplace.

More so than the film, Fishl recalled the scene at the door. It cost fifty marks for the first show, but Schimmel elbowed past the cashier, who shrugged. The gang from Weinerstrasse might have lost its power, but the Germans didn't know that. Cowed, the German workers didn't dare question Kaufman's boyze. Anyway, they didn't care. By the end of the first show, the sign for the second show said seventy marks.

"But the price was fifty when we entered."

"But we didn't pay."

"They did."

"So?" Schimmel smiled.

"So, now its seventy. How could the price have gone up in two hours?"

"Inflation."

"I don't understand."

Schimmel gave an elementary lesson in economics. "In a country with nothing to buy, people will fight to spend the money they have. Prices will rise. Money will be worth less every day than the day before until there are new products to suck up the marks. It is now officially cheaper to light a cigarette with a ten mark note than a match."

"But we don't have matches."

"Right!" It was a sore spot, because the day after the party on the *Anubis*, Jacks Over Deuces had gone to work. By the end of a phone call, he had traded the Fourth Army's entire supply of chocolate pudding for the only match factory in the zone. Then, rather than sell the matches, he had the heads removed, like Hank Smith's brother, to produce explosives. He never knew when they might come in handy, and in the meanwhile Weinerstrasse's new product was off the market.

They were just killing time and might have sat in the cool dark of the theater until the reels changed again, and films taken the week before at the Nuremberg trials segued into footage from the Olympics of 1973. Instead of a black man, there were men in black masks, while the scenes of electrifed crowds remained the same.

"Marcus says that doctors say that cigarettes are unhealthy."

"So, we need to provide new products."

"Yes?"

"Do you have a spare Mercedes?

"No."

"Nu? So we went into the cigarette business without cigarettes."

It was ordinary life, but instead of organizing a crust to sustain life, it was a packet of cigarettes or a packet of paper that occupied them. Back at Weinerstrasse, the crew played cards for insignificant stakes that seemed to grow more minor as the game proceded. This was inflation made specific. In the moment between "raise" and "see" the value of the bet had diminished. Logic therefore dictated that every bet be called. If you didn't have more on Wednesday than you did on Tuesday, or at eleven o'clock than at ten o'clock, you had less. History worked the same way. Fishl didn't say what he thought he had seen in the theater and Schimmel didn't seem to remember.

"What good did it do us? We're still playing for bubkes."

Playing for "bubkes" or beans had new significance. One would rather have a potful of beans than a pocketful of marks. Army shipments still ferried bulk food to the Continent, but farmers were beginning to plant and harvest again. The Marshall Plan had already designated the Ludwigshafen Papiergeschäft as a suitable pilot project to resuscitate German industry on the theory that if people were working and earning decent wages, it would provide the greatest bulwark against Communist propaganda from the East. All the administrators who were taking the place of generals wanted was "business as usual."

But business as usual meant a different kind of activity in the quartermaster's office. After Alan Foyle slipped down the wall of his office, much to the amusement of the men swapping vocabulary, he had fled to the base at Liebknecht, as if he would be safe from Miranda behind the barbed wire.

Sergeant Necco, relegated or raised to the role of doorkeeper, welcomed Foyle as an old customer. "Coming in for shoe polish, Sir?" he commented on the bureaucrat's scuffed wingtips.

"What? Oh . . ." the head of the Joint squatted to wipe the dirt from his toes while real customers walked in and out of the small building. The most suprising were not the men in Stalin masks that Jacks Over Deuces had played cards with, but real Russian officers, so high up in the Soviet hierarchy that they wore suits.

"Nice material," Foyle murmured, "London cut. What are they doing here?"

"Oh, them," Necco was nonchalant. "They're here for weapons. Armaments. We've been moving into explosives. You know, the kind of surplus our soldiers don't need anymore."

Horrified and afraid of being overheard, Foyle whispered to Necco, "But they, the Communists, they're the enemy now. He can't give them weapons." *He,* of course, did not need to be named.

Necco was humored to answer the same questions Isaac had asked on the *Anubis.* "Hey, he doesn't *give* them anything," Necco said. "He trades."

"For what?"

"Airplanes."

"What's in the airplanes?"

"What difference does it make?" Parroting the master, Necco went on, "Look, you know the story of the two guys during the Blitz, in London, when the generators were bombed. Without electric light, candles became valuable. One of these guys comes up with a box of candles and sells it to the other for ten pence. This usually goes for two pence. Well, a few days later, prices have risen again so he buys the box back for twenty pence and later that same day sells it back again for thirty. This goes on. They sell the box back and forth. Fifty pence, a pound, two pounds, ten pounds. A hundred pounds. A thousand pounds. This goes on until the price hits a million pounds, and then one of them opens the box and discovers that the candles don't have wicks. 'Hey, these are no good!' he complains.

'So what does the other say: 'Idiot, there are candles for lighting and candles for trading."

There was a pause while Alan Foyle absorbed the lesson. Then he asked, "So what's in the airplanes?"

"Explosives."

"What!"

"There's the beauty. It all connects. Hey, you think those guys with the candles are Jews?"

Isaac mused on the nature of transience and the transient nature of value as the heap of chits he had amassed poured out of his suitcase. Some were scribbled on napkins, some typed, invoiced, notarized. Each one was originally good for something.

Marcus examined the stack of paper and said, "It means as little as mine."

"Are you kidding?" Isaac picked up one chit at random and read, "For a very good time, redeem with Bertha."

"Sorry," Marcus sadly explained, "It's just a promise."

"What else is money but the promise of value, sworn to by a central bank?"

"And look how well that has held up." Marcus took a thousand-mark note from his wallet and ripped it into long narrow strips.

"We make up value together. We collaborate, but one of the partners has failed to fulfill his portion of the bargain. The system remains solid."

Marcus began cross-shredding the strips into tiny squares. "You are reading fiction, young Isaac."

"No, money is poetry."

"They had poetry in Warsaw, you know," Marcus said as he sprinkled the cash confetti about the room. "I used to go there to purchase dental supplies. Poetry and plays. In English, you know, the word, 'play' has two meanings." Marcus had been taking language lessons in the alfresco classroom outside Alan Foyle's bathroom window. He described the alternate definitions for "play" and said, "They had both in Warsaw."

Isaac considered the difference between art and reality. It was time to put the final deal together. He looked back on the gang's change from street urchins to financiers and back again, and was ready for the final transformation. He remembered Fishl's half-assed attempts to deliver paper, until by the time he finally succeeded, the market had collapsed, and they tried to move onto matches. That, too, had proved galling as Jacks Over Deuces now used the match factories to trade their explosive elements to the Russians for the airplanes to ship the explosives to the Russians. But even the vision of the quartermaster's office had not perceived that there was yet one more leap to be made, from the paper that represented money, more shabby daily, to the cigarettes that also fluctuated in value, to the money itself, to the element that by common consent gave the money its value.

For a second, the past receded and then the clouds parted and a ray of light burst from between the seams of the canvas tarpaulin at Liebknecht, and the dead heap of glimmering gold smiled.

"But hey, cousin, we do have each other. Blood is thicker than water."

"And gold is thicker than blood."

Isaac thought of all the food those teeth had eaten: the kugel, the derma, the rolls with onions embedded in their crust, the hard-boiled eggs cut into slices, each a pale yellow disc surrounded by a white corona, a whole school of herring, tender and lightly salted, sold whole or deboned, that arrived at the Kaufman breakfast table straight from the nets of the Baltic Sea, and, finally, the pots and pots of cholent, succulent with meat, barley, beans, and potatoes, baked overnight in the town oven, stoked before sundown on Friday night and still warm to the touch by the time the mothers of Proszowice retrieved their vessels the next afternoon to serve their loved ones lunch on Shabbes, the weekly holiday that celebrated the creation of the world.

Awake, Isaac was oblivious to the leaves in his hair and the first dusting of snow on the ground. It was the early winter of '47, but he couldn't have said what day or what decade it was. He was more exhausted than he had been since the episode of coffee-induced sleeplessness.

All he thought about was the sheaf of papers he carried everywhere in a loose-leaf binder stolen from the storeroom of Hiram Hamilton, Officer of Office Supplies, Secretary of Secretaries for Zone Three. The binder was covered in a rugged Annapolis blue weave, but despite the military specifications it met, the edges were growing furry with fingering. Inside were Count Geiger's original blueprints, some graph paper charting vertical and horizontal topography against velocity and shock waves. A mass of notes to himself was scribbled on scraps attached at the corner with a paper clip. The paper that Isaac would have once used for documents was now covered with calculations.

At night, Isaac tucked the folder under his pillow and clutched it like the tin bowl he had been assigned at Aspenfeld, without which he would have been denied soup and doomed to starve the next day and die the day after.

Asleep, Isaac dreamed of the satchel's contents: maps and diagrams of underground train tracks, calculations of weight per square foot of earth, notations of directions that an explosive impact should follow and contingency escape routes should the impact fail to obey the laws of thermodynamics. There were also boat schedules, charter fees, and the names of half a dozen skippers out of three alternate ports, hotels in four separate destinations.

Isaac Kaufman's every minute was consumed by ongoing planning for the operation. The extent of preparations rivaled the Allied landing at Normandy. It required logistics, communication, transportation, financing and, above all, timing. It had to happen soon. One of the most marked pages in Isaac's notebook was a calendar, but no matter his own personal emendations, he kept returning to the single date a month hence that was already printed in red when he acquired the calendar. It was Christmas.

For one moment, Isaac took pleasure in the poetry of his plans. But even when he forced himself to consider them from a tactical rather than an aesthetic point of view, logic had to concur with poetry. If there was one day when the crew was least likely to meet with interference, December 25 was it. X-Day.

He remembered the way the Yankees celebrated the last anniversary of the birth of their Lord. First there was dinner: turkey, mashed potatoes, and what the soldiers called "trimmings." During the meal they drank creamy egg nog with rum, and then, after dinner, the egg and cream were dispensed with. Straight shots ensued. Eventually the rum led to recitations of adorable letters from Little Tommy back in Des Moines.

"Dear Dad, Mom and Uncle Arnie are reading the paper in bed and wondering when you're coming home . . ."

"Why you stopping?"

"Who the fuck is Uncle Arnie?"

This led to endless maudlin renditions of "Jingle Bells" before the weary carolers sank into Nod.

Dates, diagrams, numbers. So exclusive was Isaac's concern that he hardly focused on the gold itself or what the wealth of the mouths of Europe might mean in the world. The others at Weinerstrasse thought differently. While Isaac desperately attempted to create the reality of their plot, their thoughts were pure, self-indulgent fantasy. They spent hours imagining the beaver coats they would wear, the sealskin collars that would caress their necks, the kid leather wallets they would tuck negligently into their pockets.

"Ah, pockets!" Schimmel sighed, because he still couldn't tell which was more wonderful, "leather soft as a German boot" or "a pocket."

In some way it was still 1943, and what they really wanted for Christmas was a truth they would never believe, that it really was 1947, that it wasn't 1943, the year that would last forever.

Some dwelled on the meals they would eat, "noodles, thick with cottage cheese." Others dreamed of where they might go: the opera, the ball games they heard on USO radio, the theater.

It was 1947 and the truly amazing thing was that such decisions *were* theirs to make. For the first time since '39, choice was possible. Escape was possible. Travel was in the works. Everyone was on the move. Besides Geiger, besides Der Schreiber, most U.S. troops had already been sent home.

Unfortunately, as opportunities to leave the vicinity grew greater, reason to remain declined. With the shrinking of the military presence, the industries that serviced it began to shrink. Less food and shoe polish was required on the base, which meant that less filtered out of the base. Less liquor was required, and fewer outlets for sexual release. The girls at the Vivant grew slovenly as cobwebs grew between their legs. Even that was better than the situation at the Green Hen, which announced its final performance and prepared to reopen as a supermarket.

The place was owned by Pinsker, gone respectable, a proprieter now instead of a manipulator, with a market of his own. His gang all wore aprons over their suits and were busily unpacking boxes of tinned meat and crates of vegetables that gave off a rank agricultural aroma.

"Alas," the Emcee sniffed, wiping away tears caused by a pyramid of onions next to him on the stage, "My good friends, who haff been such good friends through the difficult times we have had. I am sorrowful to announce that you are all welcome to join to bid myself and Heidi and Helga and Bette Farewell, Auf Wiedersehen, Adieu."

Drinks were on the house, because there was nobody left to buy them.

"The age of abandon is over," Pinsker said, "we're into nourishment."

"Life grows tedious here," the Emcee continued. "But do not pity us. There are other interesting places. Ve shall storm the barns. India is pleasant; I haff a gig on a houseboat in the Kashimir. All the world's a stage."

It was a doleful crowd, and the mixture of smoke and onions created a dreamy Arabian mist. For the last time, the kohl-eyed girls tossed their heads back, goose-stepped forward and performed for those who would remain after they were gone. Soon to be exiles from their native land, they were still cheerful, ever-hopeful, looking to the horizon.

The Emcee shared his parting words with the audience. "Come and see us in the new year, at the Kitty Katmandu Klub. Adieu, Bon voyage, Farewell."

Also departing that afternoon was Frau Mannheim. A flatbed truck with the image of a missile stenciled on the hood arrived to pick up all of the Weinerstrasse landlady's possessions. At first the movers started to load the truck in the most efficient way possible, but the frau objected. "No," she screamed. "The chair does not go beside the breakfront."

There was a moment of hesitation until the movers agreed to arrange the furniture on the truck as it had been in the salon, chairs and hook rug in perfect configuration, standing lamp with fringed shade in the corner, magazines on the coffee table, each crystal ornament carefully glued in place along the precious breakfront.

They even unhinged the door with the hole for her to peep

through and set it into a slot on the edge of the truck. Now all that was missing was the walls, and for a second it seemed as if the moving men were considering how to dismantle them and reconstruct them on the truck, but their boss, Rocketmann, made his peace with that small lack. Last of all, he hoisted Frau Mannheim's bulk over the threshold, and positioned her in the chair on the hooked rug on the truck like a manequin in a natural history diorama labelled "Homo domesticus, Female."

The landlady said, "I'll miss you, boys," and waved a white handkerchief.

"We won't," Berger muttered.

Rocketmann sat in the driver's seat, the back of his small head nuzzling the back of Frau Mannheim's and drove his human cargo away.

"Where'd they go?" Isaac asked. He also had highway routes delineated in his notebook, sections of the new Autobahn, paved and unpaved. Miles per hour. Rest stops. Gas stations.

Marcus laughed and said, "Far Rockaway," the epitome of ambition, but Isaac had to think for a moment to place that fabulous place beyond the boundaries of the map he now held flat on the table, corners tucked under salt shakers. None of the old maps on Weinerstrasse walls had meaning any longer. Isaac saw beneath land, into the labyrinth of spent mining tunnels that honeycombed the earth.

As the image of Rocketmann streaked off, another figure entered the room, but Isaac didn't even notice Der Schreiber.

Fresh from the Champs-Elysées, the young man they had known in tatters arrived, glad to be shed of the company of journalists that had dogged him for months, their pads and pencils at the ready to memorialize any further dispatches from Hell. Time had ceased to work for Der Schreiber. He had escaped from the tyranny of the hour, but carried the lager with him wherever he went. Like Kafka in Hollywood, his eyes bore the sign that made it unnecessary for him to roll up his sleeves and display his arm. His past and his present were inseparable.

"What are you doing here?"

"Miranda has good news."

"And you've come all the way from Paris to deliver it?"

Der Schreiber ignored Isaac and continued, "She has three visas to Palestine for . . ."

"How much?"

"For the family."

For a second Isaac didn't know who he was referring to. Then he understood. Everyone at the table turned to Fishl.

Der Schreiber answered Isaac's first question, "For free."

"Congratulations," Isaac addressed the lucky man. "This is good news, but I warn you, someday one hundred million Arabs are going to make the Germans look like . . . like . . ." Isaac struggled to compose his curse and then blurted, "Englishmen."

"I don't want to hear this." Fishl cringed.

Isaac loomed. "You must know everything."

"Zakhor!" Der Schreiber intoned, and there was a hush. The Hebrew word for "remember" had particular resonance not merely as a verb, but as a command, a biblical injunction to the people of Israel.

Isaac sat down and asked, "For how long? How long do you remember? How long do you mourn?"

Der Schreiber thought out loud, "It took, what, the last three thousand years to arrive here—then maybe we mourn for the next three thousand."

"Nonsense. You'll forget it all in thirty. They . . ." he lifted his chin to the rest of the room and, by extrapolation, the rest of the world, "will surely forget in three."

"And you, Isaac, how long will it take you to forget?"

Isaac smiled, "Forget what?" His mourning would end on Christmas.

But Der Schreiber ignored Isaac and went on. "The only difference between us is that I look to the past and you to the future."

"Insignificant," Isaac shrugged.

"The point is," Der Schreiber continued, "that neither of us lives in the present. This reveals a hidden capacity for abstraction or idealism."

Isaac turned to Schimmel and the rest of the reduced Weinerstrasse Brigade. "Anyone here notice my capacity for idealism?"

"Nonetheless it is there," Der Schreiber insisted, "Thank God."

"Who?"

"Our Lord in heaven as He is on earth."

"On earth?" Issac repeated. "On earth?" He pretended to look around, at Pinsker's men unpacking vegetables, at the last glimpse of spread thighs on the stage of the Hen. "Our God, on earth?" He was angry again. Theology was too high falutin'. So was memory or nationality, or any idea, any abstraction. Riding on the ship of the doomed, he had decided to get off. Christmas was coming soon and he was determined that his stocking would be stuffed with eighteen tons of gold. Then time would stand still. Then he would live in the present. Then Der Schreiber's analogy would be finally and ultimately disproved. They had nothing in common. In the meanwhile, he turned on Fishl. "Go, go to the goddamn Holy Land. I don't care. I need someone to go to the base with me. Now! This minute." He was raving. "Now who's going with me?" He stared around the circle.

"I will."

It was the one person in the room he wasn't speaking to, the one who could have declined, the one who, as of five minutes earlier needed nothing from Isaac, the one with a visa off the Continent, Fishl.

Isaac and Fishl entered the base shortly after dusk the following day. Just as Isaac didn't notice the chill in the air or the leaves fluttering down from the linden trees, neither did he sense the changes in the atmosphere behind the barbed wire. Soldiers stood together in anxious knots. The smooth flow of operations had been disrupted and there was no telling what was going to occur next. There was a nervousness to the place not entirely unlike that faced by the previous occupants of the camp, though clearly without the drastic repercussions. Everything was in flux, particularly the quartermaster's office from which all order had once emerged. Even the poker game lost its verve since Jacks Over Deuces's culminating moment on the green felt of the *Anubis*. The corporal stood at the door of his brick hut, waving a pale green sheet of paper as if it was on fire. He had received marching orders.

"What is this?" he demanded.

Alan Foyle had inadvertently become the bearer of bad news when he stopped by the radio room and intercepted the message on his own way across the base. Thinking to please, he offered to deliver it. "It's your release," he said to the surprisingly displeased corporal.

"Release from what?"

"This," Foyle spread his hands wide to signify the camp, the army, the Continent.

"I don't want a goddamn release."

"But everyone . . ."

" 'No!' I said."

"I'm sorry," Foyle cringed.

Holding a blueprint, Isaac paced out measurements, calling numbers to Fishl as they crisscrossed the pebbled terrain, attempting to trace the pathways of the tunnels below the frost line, until they arrived a few meters from the front door of the PX. Everything depended on the accuracy of Geiger's blueprints. If they were off, a severe reconsideration would be necessary, and if they were the fiction of some warped Teutonic prankster, well, Isaac wouldn't know what to do. Pray, maybe.

Foyle glanced over his shoulder at the two Jews with their maps and their tape measure, but was too stunned by the unexpected fury of Jacks Over Deuces to focus.

The corporal was ranting. "This is ridiculous. Absurd. I refuse. Absolutely. Categorically."

Foyle tried desperately to comfort the disconsolate NCO. "But all your friends have gone home."

"I don't care. I want to stay." Suddenly the ruler of Zone Three was reduced to a childish victim of unfair authority. His wisp of usually well-groomed hair fell over his forehead, and a cowlick sprang up on his crown. He was nearly crying.

This was the worst thing that could have happened to Jacks Over Deuces. Glancing at Isaac, his mind caught fire at the idea of changing names, and identities, sending a refugee home in his place, but just as swiftly dampened when he realized that his parents back in South Bend might object to receiving some bald, tattooed bag of skin and bones instead of their son. Now he was whining, "What do you mean my term is up? I want to reenlist."

"Sorry, it's a peacetime army now, specialists only."

"But there're fortunes to be made here. Its borders and languages, vive la différence. It's history and catastrophe, we've got nothing to compare to that in Indiana."

"I'm sorry, Sir."

The corporal looked back at Isaac and Fishl and their tape measure. For a second, he wondered what the Hell they were doing, but he couldn't concentrate. All he could see was that they were allowed to remain when he was compelled to leave. Sadly, he declared, "I envy you boys."

And Isaac almost understood him. He could see that same envy in Miranda and the pack of journalists who stuck to Der Schreiber like lichen; they, too, wanted to have confronted the blackness and emerged, to have the inner strength to survive despite the odds.

"Do something, for Godsake," Jacks Over Deuces begged Foyle.

But the American citizen's capacities were limited. He tried to explain. "I can only get some people out. I can't keep anyone in."

As if Foyle was referring to the building rather than the Continent, the door opened on cue. It was Sergeant Necco, straight from the telephone. "Good news, Sir. Ball bearings."

"Huh?" For the first time anyone could remember, Jacks Over Deuces was at a loss.

"We finally located the additional ball bearings you wanted. The factory that made them for the Panzer tanks was in Portugal all along."

"Damn the ball bearings," Jacks Over Deuces cried. The objects he had been searching for for months were finally available, but it wouldn't make any difference to him if he was in America.

"But they're on the way," Necco said. "Eighteen thousand gross. They're arriving in the morning."

"And I'm leaving in the afternoon. Or some afternoon." The corporal stared at the green slip, but didn't seem able to read it. "When?" he demanded.

Foyle answered, "January third."

"But the ball bearings, Sir. What should we do with them?"

"Shove them up your ass!"

The corporal took his tantrum back inside the hut and Foyle wandered off in search of shoe polish. Isaac was left with Necco. It wasn't the ideal situation he had in mind for a particular discussion, but the refugee was flexible. He replaced his blueprints and took out the pages from his green binder that contained his thermodynamic calculations. Come X-Day they would need power, and this was the right moment to arrange the transfer of explosives that hadn't already been sent to Russia. Bearing in mind the exchange he'd just overheard between Jacks Over Deuces and Alan Foyle, Isaac knew that the market value of any remaining munitions had just plummeted. He intended to buy low and use high. Sky high.

It was a little awkward approaching Necco, whose truck the Weinerstrasse gang had, after all, stolen, but Isaac was prepared to make his peace with the demoted soldier. "How's it going?" he opened.

Although Necco still mourned the loss of his stripes, he had effectively been reinstated to a position of stature if not rank. Jacks Over Deuces was brutal, but he was also compassionate. "I learned a lot," Necco replied sullenly. Then, before Isaac could move the conversation in the direction of business, Necco began to chronicle his trips all over Europe from the new republicans of Sofia to the upstart drug market in Barcelona, trips that might now come to an end. "You see, the more information I brought back about the needs of our constituents, the more important the information itself was, and the less important the constituents and their needs were. Look, if you've got to get a load of beer to Athens, you've got to get a truck and a driver."

"I know."

"And the beer."

"Of course."

"But if you just use that information, if you're generous and allow others to benefit, and you just take a few points from someone else for, well, arranging matters, you can do well. And if you make the arrangements and they happen to fall through when you've already shorted beer on the market, you do better." He didn't add that the information they processed had recently become even more abstract. The quartermaster's office was maintaining surveillance over the airwaves, selling codes, cyphers, cryptograms.

"It's a career," Isaac said.

"At least it isn't money," Necco replied. "But you don't need a truck. You still have ours." He rubbed it in.

"How do you know?"

"I just told you. Information." Having learned from his boss, he didn't care what people did as long as he knew what they did.

Information held different meanings for Isaac. Today it meant the location of underground passages that might lead to salvation, but it also meant a secret cellar in the ghetto, no longer secret, an SS Klaxon at midnight. Information meant betrayal, and Isaac ran down a list in his head to determine who might have told Necco about the truck.

It could have been any one of the gang, and the logical suspects were the twins, who had left in such a hurry—the traitors—but Isaac knew in his belly that this particular piece of information hadn't come from Weinerstrasse itself, but rather someone who had visited there, but did not live there. He had no proof, but he knew that it had been Der Schreiber who ratted.

It didn't make a difference. Only one thing mattered now; it was less than two hundred feet from Isaac's shoelaces, and the laces were untied and all of his early advantages in the race were gone. All he had going for him now was the information inside his binder and the passion inside his heart. If Isaac had leapt into the world during the moment of curious pause that followed liberation, the world had caught up with him, and now he could not afford to rest. Once again, the Germans had the minerals that were free-market manna. Soon others might eye the gold and dream of a gigantic calf.

Suddenly, it was not only appropriate, not merely convenient, but absolutely vital that the Jews act on Christmas, before the New Year. If Isaac's thoughts automatically centered on the cube of gold, he knew that the last move Jacks Over Deuces would make—whether he realized it yet or not—would be to take that cube with him, or try.

The cube was a magnet. It drew obsession as a lodestone does metal, fascinating the strong and the weak, the faithful and the heretic, as the magnet does not discriminate between nails and coins, iron crosses or six-pointed stars. It drew the ascetic as well as the mercenary. Even as Isaac Kaufman and the American corporal each drew up their plans, Fishl brought up the business to hand with Necco. There were explosives to be procured. "What about . . ." he gestured toward the inside of the hut, from where Jacks Over Deuces was still raging. "Him? Is he OK? Can we rely on prompt delivery?"

Necco shrugged. Sometimes it was necessary for the subordinate to take the reins of leadership. Fortunately, the corporal had taught Necco well. He had established an organization that hardly needed his guidance. And he would do well in Indiana, too. Especially if he had enough gold to open his own Fort Knox.

"When do you need it?"

"The day before Christmas."

"And the conveyances?" These were the papers necessary to ship goods across boundaries, a snap compared to visas. Necco didn't know that he was trading the explosives to get the gold for the documents that Jacks Over Deuces hoped to use to transfer the gold.

"The day before New Year's."

Isaac knew the American calendar well. "You'll have them," he said, and thought, "In the mail."

The time had come to see how real Count Geiger's diagrams were not theoretically, but actually, underground. According to the dimensions Isaac and Fishl struck off a central point, there ought to have been a track running directly below the cube of gold and, after many a branching, a path that led beyond the border of the camp.

For a second Isaac thought about what would have happened if someone had been aware of this passage during the War. He looked at the barracks. If anyone in those wooden deathbeds had known about the trail, there wouldn't have been gold on the premises today—those teeth would have walked—and that was why he and Fishl had to verify the accuracy of the map. He was determined to make the breakthrough from the surface to the substrate.

But here the map did not think to offer help, because the entrance to the defunct mine, the point from which all of their measurements were taken, was obvious, a great parabola-shaped opening in the mountain, collapsed under an avalanche of stones, boarded over with blackened timbers. Isaac and Fishl lingered beside the entrance, examining it for a chink, but the massive struts had been in place for so many years they looked to have petrified.

There had to be some alternative access or emergency egress. "We have to get in," Isaac insisted.

"The explosives will take care of that," Fishl suggested.

"Good idea," Isaac replied, dripping sarcasm. "We'll just blow this place up, waltz around, check to make sure everything is OK and come back two weeks from now to execute the plan."

"I'm sorry."

"You don't have to be. Look." Isaac pointed to one small mark on the blueprint, the symbol for a ventilation duct.

Night fell, and there were no longer guards to protect Axis prisoners or Allied property. The presence of the gold tormented Isaac. He felt as if the house on Weinerstrasse had a view of the rainbow's end, and the green-clad American soldiers were an army of leprechauns who had abandoned their mission to protect their pot of gold. For a moment he wondered if his gang could simply lift the treasure onto the truck, but it was best to proceed as planned.

Isaac paced out the markings on his blueprint, and found that a small building had been erected just over the spot where the ventilation duct was supposed to exhaust fumes from the mine. It was a shower house, not a mock installation that led directly to the crematoria, but a real shower that had been used by the SS officers to scrub themselves of the human tissue that stained them during operations. And there was somebody inside, a thick shadow behind the milky white translucent glass, bellowing:

> In a mountain,
> in a canyon,
> excavAAAAAting for a mine.

A mist covered the tiles, collected, and sluiced into the drain.

"There's nothing here," Fishl whispered.

"Let's go in."

Hammerin' Hank was naked, soaping himself, and singing like a bull in heat:

> Oh my darling,
> oh my darling,
> oh my darling, Clementine.

Isaac stared at the drain underneath the naked general's bunions. It was the size of a map of a Warsaw sewer system. The water was going somewhere. X marked the spot as well as the day.

Hammerin' Hank stepped out of the shower, looked at them, and whipped his towel idly at the grate, crushing a waterbug that dared poke its antennae out from below. "Largest fucking cockroaches I've ever seen. Make the Texan ones look like itty bitty mites." He repeated the end of his song:

> *You are lost and gone forever,*
> *Dreadful sorrow.*
> *Oh my Darling Clementine.*

Then he left. Isaac and Fishl were alone.

Fishl worried, "What if someone finds us?"

Isaac took a page from his notebook and a pen. He swiftly drew the image of a skull and crossbones and wrote:

WARNING

POISON

and posted it on the front door. Just to be sure that no one would interrupt them, he removed the single lightbulb from its socket, and slid the bolt on the door home.

They were alone in the dark, amid damp, sweaty odors and slippery stubs of soap, with the only light coming from a faint luminous square of window high on the wall above a row of hooks. But Isaac had brought a flashlight and let its light rove around the room, onto the hooks, where some soldier had inadvertently left a pair of BVDs. He focused the beam down at their feet. "Crowbar," he said.

Fishl reached inside the pack he had shlepped from Weinerstrasse and found the appropriate tool.

Kneeling, Isaac prized up the slippery grate of the shower, revealing not a rat-size pipe chase, but a hole large enough for a man. "After you."

Fishl inched his legs over the edge and immediately found rusted rungs set into the foundation, and lowered himself, not more than seven feet until he touched earth. Isaac put the light in his back pocket and followed.

"Bingo!"

They were standing on a track in an arched tunnel. Water from the shower trickled in the direction of least resistance, disappearing toward the main that would empty into the Danube. Peering that way, Isaac said, "Let's go."

They found an old cart, wheels rusted to the tracks. Together they put shoulders to the rim and pushed. The cart creaked. Rust flaked off the wheels, and the vehicle started to rumble down a slight incline. They ran after it, the walls echoing their footfalls and the clanking of the wheels on the bumpy track, rats scurrying madly to escape. It made an unholy racket, but the earth itself muffled the noise. The light of Isaac's torch flared off extrusions and heavy wooden supports. The wall itself glinted, as if bits of gold were still embedded in the jagged outcroppings.

Finally the cart came to a rest in a trough between inclines. Pausing to make sure that no one had followed them, Isaac pored over his blueprints, so long wrapped up that they were as permanently scrolled as a Torah. He took out a surveyor's tool and by the dim light of the torch, he measured. The tunnels were precisely as Count Geiger's maps delineated. They were perfect to the last turn. Moreover, if they had seemed abstract in the open air, they were as specific as a city map within their domain, with streets, avenues, and boulevards detailing the route by which the wealth of the earth worked its way out of the earth until the mine was tapped and a new installation for a different mineral purpose was erected above.

They stood at a crossroads between gentle hills leading to precipitous slopes. If Isaac was correct, the left-hand road lead into the camp and the right to the woods.

Left. Right. Right. Left. The turns reminded him of Selection. It was his first day in another camp. The line of Jews trudged forward, toward the small man with a branch he had whittled to a point. Left. Right. Right. Right. Right. Right. Right. Left. Right. Left. Right. Right . . .

Isaac was sent to the left, but he knew that both directions led to death; the only difference was how long it would take to arrive at one's destination. For every survivor, the journey had been unaccountably delayed.

As Isaac did not care for the surface world when poring over his blueprints for the underground, now that he was below the surface, he felt the reality of the block of gold up above. By opening a chasm, he would create a mouth to swallow that wealth, and there, already in place, were the teeth.

He ground his own teeth and savored the pangs that shot from the exposed nerves to his brain. And then, for the first time, he knew what he would do with his share of the loot. He would hire the best oral surgeon on earth to rip every single stub from his jaw, and wouldn't even bother to replace them. He would drink milkshakes forever.

"Isaac?"

Right. Right. Right. Right. Right. Right. Right. Left. Right. Left. Right. Right . . .

"Isaac!"

"What?"

"You looked sad."

"Forget that. We have work to do." All business now, Isaac ticked off the requirements in the damp, dripping gloom while Fishl replied.

"Truck?"

"Check."

"Gasoline?"

"Check."

"Maps?"

"Check."

"Explosives?"

"Check."

"Gold?" If Isaac was correct, they were directly underneath the cube.

Fishl paused, looked up through the layers of rock. "Check."

Somewhere inside his binder, in addition to the figures and the maps, Isaac had thumbnail character sketches of his various crew members. Talents. Disabilities. Who was a good driver. Who could be relied upon in a pinch. Who claimed to have knowledge of weapons. For Fishl, the entry read, "Fuckup. *See under:* Papiergeschäft." But Alter had sent Fishl for a reason and this must have been it. It didn't surprise Isaac that Fishl had been the only one to volunteer to accompany him on the mad quest. "Men?"

"Check."

Isaac thought again of the food that the gold consumed. The food was transformed into blood, and the blood further alchemized into gold and the gold heated to molten fluid that could assume any form imaginable: an ingot, a cube, a calf, a tooth, a soul.

CHAPTER 16

Fifty years later, wealthy and surrounded by grandchildren and the fruits of a long, mostly happy life, one survivor would say: "If I had been offered a deal back in '44: Ten years of life, any life, and then a bullet in the head, sign here, no lawyers, no loopholes . . . I would have signed the contract in a second." He scrawled an imaginary signature at the bottom of an invisible document and then rubbed his finger joints. Not for a second back in Majdanek could he have imagined arriving at an age when arthritis was more of a threat than Zyklon-B.

Waiting is not a uniform activity nor duration a uniform quality. It varies according to the occasion. Would you rather be given ten years to live with a guaranteed death sentence, no chance of commutation, or the possibility of a day, a decade, who knows what? And what sort of false bargain is that? One thing is for sure—the end.

The poles are not finite and infinite; they're finite and indefinite.

Waiting rooms in a dentist's office, deco lounges at the train station—all of premessianic history can be construed as a waiting game with this world just the anteroom to the palace of eternity. Unfortunately, the foyer needs cleansing. Maidservant, wipe those nasty blood spots away. Dirty Jews.

Waiting also differs for different people, some anxious and impatiently tapping their toes, cracking knuckles, checking their gold watches every second, others sanguine, blithe, secretly philosophical, immersed in contemplation of their past or anticipation of their future. Those are the ones who see the simple difference that depends on which side of the bludgeon one inhabits—whether your hand holds it or your head knows it.

Manservant, sweep away those bodies. Bury them and burn them if there isn't enough ground. Danke schön!

Of course, waiting is also different for the same person in the same situation at different times. All of the tedium had been thrilled out of the wait at Weinerstrasse once X-Day was set for 25 December. The circumstances of Isaac Kaufman and Marcus Morgenstern and Schimmel and the others' lives were no different from what they had been a week before—their groats and whores were the same mealy consistency—but now there was a date, beyond which all would be different. December 25. Santa Claus was coming to town. If L'ère Concentrationnaire had extended past VE-Day, through the Russians' march to Berlin, this was the end, the period on the first sentence of their lives.

In preparation, Isaac sat in a hard-backed kitchen chair set in the center of the living room floor, a sheet wrapped around his neck, about to have his hair cut by Marcus.

Scissors or scalpel, hair or root canal, were all the same to the dentist. "A little off the top?" he suggested.

"No, more."

"How much more?"

"All of it."

"All of it?"

"That *is* what I said."

So Marcus put down his scissors and picked up a razor. In five smooth arcs, he swept all of Isaac's newly grown locks from his skull to the floor, where they mixed with tobacco dust.

Time turned backward, and Isaac was back in the labor camp outside of Proszowice. His hair was on the ground there, too, together with his father's beard and his little brother's payes. After the haircut came the selection. Right. Right. Right. Right. Left. Right. Right. Right. Right. Right. Right. Right . . .

"Next," Marcus said. "Get ready for the Year of Their Lord, nineteen forty-eight, A.D."

"Not A.D., anno Domini," Isaac whooped, clasping hands, bowing his head as if a priestly cowl weighed down his scarred and newly reshaven pate. "A.G., you dodos, After Gold!"

The only ones who didn't really care were Fishl and Rivka. They had been through the wait for miraculous transition before. They, too, had known the awe of the "due" date, but their countdown was not for several weeks, but nine months. Now they were out of synch, because they lived on the far border of the waiting room. For them the door to eternity had opened, and on the other side was a doughy child, blessed and cursed as surely as if it had been born in Bethlehem.

Regensburg itself was as much of a backwater as Bethlehem. The entire town had reverted to the sleepy fairy-tale village it had once been when the only event to rouse the populace was a bear from the forest who wandered into the square to paw through the market vegetable stalls at dawn. Streets were repaved, asphalt shingles recovered the holes opened in the slate roofs by shrapnel from the sky. As far as foreign journalists were concerned, Zone Three no longer displayed the photogeny of devastation. There was even talk of repairing the town clock, a masterpiece from the age of early mechanical engineering. In front of the great, milky white, Roman-numeralled face, two figures revolved on a track that led in and out of the housing. A delicate girl dressed in a green copper skirt and blouse to contain her budding iron breasts had preceded a boy wearing suspenders and short pants, by inches, hour after hour, forever.

Rolf and Judy's endless chase had come to an end in 1939. For three hundred years the ball bearings had kept Judy fleeing in circles, with Rolf right behind. Every hour on the hour for three hundred years, Judy had rung the tower bell in alarm, but in 1939 she stopped. In 1939, Rolf caught Judy. Several years later, a bomb hit the steeple and the twin statues spun on their axes, and the side of the girl that had never been seen revealed itself. Upon her sleeve, Judy wore a yellow star.

The town seemed to be shrinking in on itself. The gang's empty house was no longer a rarity. Mrs. Mannheim had gotten out just in time. It was gold that built her house, the industrialization of death that revived it, and two years of post-War authority that arbitrarily kept it rentable. Why did the Allies use Liebknecht for headquarters rather than other spots? Maybe Hank Smith liked the waters. But Hank was going home. The waters had run dry. No one died at Liebknecht anymore.

The Green Hen had closed down, and the black market was withering with the dismantling of the base. Even the mayor had given up his sinecure to join a Marshall Plan commission in Bonn. The man who knew corruption from the inside dispersed Western largesse to programs that submitted financial assistance applications for his approval; his son was the bag man. It was business as usual, but not in Regensburg. All the gold was tapped; all the Jews were dead, and all that they left was their gold, and that was going, too. Anyone with half a brain was leaving town.

Even Alan Foyle prepared to depart. Trunks packed, he dreamed of nights at the Copacabana and the Stork Room. Sadly, the Joint's chief's dream turned nightmare. He knew he couldn't dance anymore. His toes had lost their talent and the stink of Europe would remain on the soles of his patent leather shoes no matter how he scrubbed. After remaining aloof for his entire stay in Zone Three, he had suddenly become the product of his surroundings. After a lifetime of clipped bureaucratic jargon, he spoke the profane vernacular of Jacks Over Deuces, whose language he had learned instead of Yiddish. He might as well have taken lessons along with the refugees in the market. "Excuse me, Sir, but do you know the way to the train station?"

"Yeah, to the fucking right. A mile and a fucking half."

Of course, he spoke the tongue of the Little Corporal to everyone except his instructor, a crimp on his new expertise. He spent most of his time genuflecting at the brick hut, and as Jacks Over Deuces pushed him, he pushed Miranda. "What's happening with those transfer papers?"

"I don't know."

"Then you're the only fucking one."

Word had already begun to seep out of Zone Three. Rumor had it that a rumor had reached Eisenhower whose only comment on the gold was, "Christ, that's enough to ruin the whole financial market of the West!"

The corporal said, "Just think of the opportunities." Then he turned to press Foyle on the transfers, who pressed his subordinate further. "We need those fucking papers," he screamed at her. "If he doesn't get them immediately, we're all in deep shit."

But such documents were not in the Joint's domain. The organization dealt with people, not objects. "What does he want them for?" Miranda asked.

"Don't ask. Just get what you're told, you cunt."

Never, never, never had anyone spoken to her that way. She felt like her Madame Alexander doll had been dropped out of her bedroom window into the East River. She didn't know whether to sob or scream back; instead she held her tongue and started walking toward Weinerstrasse.

She could have called—phones were working—but the mission ostensibly required a meeting. What was clear, if not to her, was that she couldn't keep away from the place.

What drew her to the shabby living room? It was the baby. Rivka sat in the chair that Isaac had just vacated, peaceful among the busy plotters, like the blissful victim of a vampire, sucked dry, and ecstatic at the process. Miranda couldn't stop staring at the child's round cheeks. She felt her own breasts grow heavy and milky, but that was impossible.

Isaac was there, too, but Miranda had to steel herself to address him. Instead she turned to a more sympathetic Marcus. "Imagine what the infant doesn't know."

"Or what it does," he replied. "Love, need, satisfaction, frustration, faith, fury."

"And it can't utter a word."

"Lucky." Isaac spoke.

Miranda spun around. "What? I mean why?"

"Because I know the first word it will say, and then it will be doomed."

"What?" She couldn't help it. She knew that she didn't want to hear his answer, but she was curious. "What?" she repeated.

"Jew."

Miranda sighed. After two years in their midst, she still didn't know what the word meant. She didn't begin to understand how the sad, sensitive Der Schreiber and Isaac Kaufman could exist in the same universe, or how she could share anything with either of them. Only the baby seemed familiar. "Jew," she repeated.

As if summoned by the word, the child's father appeared. Fishl had been reworking Isaac's calculations in the back room. "There's a legend," he said, riffling through all the lore in his head to apply to the situation. Not Sinai, for none of the generation of the Exodus lived to reach the promised land. Not Masada, for all of the rebels against the Romans had killed themselves rather than surrender. Not Cologne, for no one emerged from the fabulous auto-da-fé. Not Cracow either. Not Warsaw. Not Vilna. Not Lublin. Not Radom. Not Lodz. Not Bialystok. Not Sosnowiec or Poznán or Prozowice. "The legend of the last Jew."

Isaac imagined the infant coughing, imagined it dead. He imagined it on Xmas eve, destined to transform the world.

"Once upon a time," Fishl began, "many years from now . . ." Confusing past and future, he went on, "when all the Jews had been converted to Christianity, as also every Moslem and Hindu and Buddhist subscribed to the faith of Rome, when it was said that every last savage in New Guinea and Greenwich Village atheist reaped the benefits of the one universal faith, there was true harmony."

"Like Poland," Schimmel quipped.

"Hush," Isaac said. "I want to hear this."

And Fishl told of a shoemaker in Grenada, the ancient Spanish city that was just one of the provincial capitals of Christ. Although the shoemaker's family had lived in the sunny, vineyarded region for over half a millenium, his ancestors had been forced to hide his faith during the bad days of the Inquisition. Yet even as that early Agosto underwent a mock Baptism and disclaimed his ancestors, he made his children swear a solemn vow to retain their Jewish heritage in secret. This they swore, and so their children swore, and theirs, too, in a rite carried through time. Even as an age of tolerance came upon the land, and the great synagogue of Grenada reopened, the family maintained its faith in secret. This was wise, because history is a pendulum and once more the synagogue was shuttered, and the Agostos were the only family to remain safe, because they were unknown. Elements of liturgy and lore were forgotten, but the essential remained.

"So it was," Fishl said, "from generation to generation, until there was a knock on the door of Arturo Agosto, unmarried shoemaker, a man without offspring, the last of his line, one common Sabbath eve.

"It was a priest, together with his elderly parents, come on a pilgrimage to the city. Their car had broken down beside the shoemaker's cottage and they sought help. The shoemaker invited the people inside. He made telephone calls to a mechanic and offered the strangers tea while they waited for repairs.

"But as the mechanic was delayed, and the Spanish night descended, the simple Jew took a silver cup and candlestick and frayed prayerbook from his blackened oak cupboard. In front of the astonished guests, he poured himself wine, sang himself a weekly hymn to creation, and sipped. Then he muttered a set of incomprehensible syllables over a loaf of bread and tore a chunk from its heel.

" 'Excuse me,' the priest asked politely, 'but what are you doing?'

" 'It is the Sabbath and this is the way I welcome it. Please, won't you have some dinner. The shoemaker had a roast chicken in the oven, and proceeded to set the table while the guests pondered his response.

" 'But the Sabbath is not until Sunday,' the priest insisted.

" 'Oh, but the Jewish Sabbath is now.'

"And so the priest discovered the last remaining Jew, no longer secret, simply private, who conducted his solitary faith without shame and without the fear his forefathers ought to have more strongly inculcated.

"The priest's elderly parents stood back and would not eat a bite from the treyf table, but the priest leaned forward in astonishment. 'Is this true?'

"The shoemaker nodded, the mechanic arrived, and the evening ended.

"Several days later, the shoemaker was summoned to the local diocese. The archbishop asked about the situation the priest had hurriedly informed him of the afternoon after his discovery.

"It was true. So the naïf admitted.

"The archbishop was a vigorous, black-bearded man with a full plate of purple calf's liver in front of him, 'You do not understand,' he explained. 'There are no more Jews. Our missionaries from

Burma, from Patagonia, from Yemen have guaranteed this. You cannot be a Jew.'

" 'Alas, but I am,' the humble shoemaker replied.

" 'So I see,' the archbishop said, not really certain whether he was hallucinating. Then, whether it was a fiction or a man he was addressing, he withdrew a long, scrolled parchment from the breast pocket of his robes. It read, 'I, Arturo Agosto, of my own free will and determination, do hereby renounce the faith and being of the Jews, and humbly request to be granted admittance into the congregation of Christ triumphant.' The archbishop said, 'Please sign this.'

" 'But I cannot.'

" 'Why?'

" 'Because it is not true.'

" 'I see,' the archbishop said, and the audience was over.

"Word sped upon the ecclesiastial highway, from Grenada to Seville, from Seville to Madrid to Paris, from Paris to the Holy City of Rome, which duly sent an emissary to bring the Last Jew before the Supreme Pontiff, Vicar of Christ on earth, nearly triumphant.

"Unlike the Grenadan archbishop, the pope was a frail, elderly man who did not appear very comfortable in his ornate vestments or expansive chambers. He chose to conduct his own interview across a small folding card table with the remnants of a game of solitaire still spread across its humble surface. This delicate pontiff, whose universal domain was called into question by the Spanish shoemaker, reviewed the situation to confirm everything he had been told, had a pleasant theological discussion with the shoemaker, and concluded, 'You, Sir, are a gift, a sign in the flesh. Together we have an opportunity to enact a drama that will echo forever, as your final absence will harken in and define the age of purified humanity. We must make an example of you. We must display the obduracy of the last Jew on earth, and celebrate the moment of your departure . . . ' he placed his fingers together, 'one way or another.'

" 'The five.'

" 'The five what?'

" 'The five of hearts. You can move it to the six of spades.'

" 'Oh, thank you.'

"And so the shoemaker was caged and sent on tour. His cage was mounted on a wooden-axled cart lead by four gray horses and drawn through the streets of every city on every continent so that the people could witness the last stubborn vestige of his kind, the last of any kind but theirs, until he was finally returned to Rome, to prepare for his ascension.

"The shoemaker was weak from starvation and humiliation, battered by the rocks that the crowds lining the route of his transport threw between the bars of his cage. 'Are you ready?' the pope asked as they stood together in the great plaza in front of St. Peter's, surrounded by the multitude of the righteous.

"What specific fate the Church in its majesty had in store for the Jew was never to be revealed. 'I am ready,' the shoemaker said, meaning that he was more ready than anyone could have imagined. Indeed, he could sense the approach of his final moment that would not await the Church's benevolent assistance. Throughout the tour, he had kept himself alive by sheer willpower sufficient only to reach the Holy City and make one last statement. 'I asked myself many questions on these recent dark travels. First, I asked why you were doing this to me, and then I understood that it was in your nature that you must do this to me. Then I asked myself why no one would help me, not you from whom I cannot expect but what I receive, but God. How could God allow this to occur? But I did not ask for his help, just his answer. Then I understood this, too. We are chosen to be eternally bereft. God must help others. If he helps the Jew, he denies the Jew. Only then, refused by God, does the Jew truly become other. And if I am not myself, who am I?'

"Posing this one final question, the shoemaker sank to the marble floor."

"What happened?" Berger asked.

Fishl sadly explained, "The last Jew expired."

"It doesn't have to be," Miranda said, shyly unaware that she had spoken at all. Then she shivered and watched Rivka wrap the baby deep within her shawl, so that only a tiny nose peeked through. The icy truth of Fishl's tale had penetrated the cracked windows loosened from their frames during the bombardment of '44. "It's cold in here."

"Still cold . . ."

"I said it was still cold."

"It's always cold."

"But you don't notice it."

"No."

"That's because you're cold."

Every one of the gang except for Isaac leapt to discuss the temperature and the weather, and not one of them said a word about Fishl's story.

"Of course," Fishl provided the inevitable addendum to any Jewish tale, "There is an ending beyond the ending. In every city the shoemaker had been seen, so it was told, the seeds were planted, the faith renewed. First it was individuals, then groups, cadres, gathered together in secret, and then in public, to read the Hebrew Holy Books, to worship the God who would not save them. The last Jew became the first Jew, the new savior, born again in the minds of men."

Explosives were delivered and set in place, strapped to the upright supports with duct tape. A series of old barrows were rehabilitated, wheels greased, made ready to move outward with their cargo. Measurements were all confirmed and reconfirmed. Down below, the gang made copies of Count Geiger's charts and gave names to the underground avenues so that no one would get lost in the maze of mines. The main route that lead toward the surface gold was called Far Rockawaystrasse.

"So what are you here for?" Schimmel asked resentfully.

"I don't know," Fishl said.

"Not you. Her," he pointed to Miranda.

"I have messages for Mr. Kaufman." Desperately wishing merely to bask in the glow of the baby's cheeks, the girl was thrown back on her mission.

"Messages?" Schimmel emphasized the plural.

This surprised Miranda, because her interrogator's implied question contained an implied answer; she did have one single message that she was delegated to deliver. Schimmel's syntactically aroused suspicion was wellfounded. It was as if he already knew the score. "Yes," she said. "Private messages."

Isaac looked at her and Schimmel looked at Isaac, awaiting an order to evict the intruder. Instead, Isaac said, "Then maybe we should speak privately." He opened the door with mock-gallantry and ushered Miranda onto the dimly lit landing. "My office."

The shadows were filled with fumes from the cooking of squatters who had occupied the premises since Frau Mannheim's departure. Miranda wrinkled her nose and without a word they went outside.

The weather was warmer than it had been, and the first dusting of snow had begun to melt. "Now," he said.

They stood on the lopsided porch while Miranda relayed the first notice from Foyle. "It's about the transfer papers."

Isaac already knew that the quartermaster's own plans for a minor eighteen-ton eighteen-carat extraction were in development. He didn't know what methods they were planning to use, whether explosives or plain manpower, but fortunately they relied at least in part on Isaac's papers, which were going to be delayed at least one day too late. Still, Isaac was worried. Jacks Over Deuces was not one to leave anything so vital to chance. He looked at her, "Now why would you need to know that?"

Miranda was no idiot. The scent of money had permeated her family's apartment in New York, and she knew when the chase for a hot stock market issue was intensifying. But all she said was, "Others also know."

"Who?"

Suddenly she knew the second message. "Benya."

"Benya who?"

She sighed, "Der Schreiber." She hated calling Benya by his nickname. She didn't know why it was derogatory, but it was, and she didn't know why the other refugees disdained him. He was their voice. Was it because the author of *Closed Eyes*, whose eyes would never close again, was, despite his wisdom, more of a boy than Isaac would ever be that the latter was so maddened? Was that why Der Schreiber was bound to betray the younger man, and was that why she was betraying Der Schreiber? She was supposed to help them, not intervene.

"What about him?"

"I don't know. Something he said. It made me think that he made a deal with . . . I just want to say . . ." She paused as a tram pulled up in front of 44 Weinerstrasse. These vehicles were new presences on the new roads of the vicinity, meant to transport workers to their jobs to revive the nation. "I just want to say . . ." The tram's doors hissed open. "That you should . . ." The tram sounded a sharp clarion blast. "You should watch out!" Miranda cried and dashed for the tram, fleeing from Issac and everyone else at Weinerstrasse, even the baby. Suddenly, she couldn't stand it anymore. Everyone was going home and she wanted to retreat to Beekman Place where it was safe. She clambered up the steps as if it was the Madison Avenue number 4 bus, flung a twenty-mark note into the receptacle as if it was a New York Transit token and collapsed exhausted into a curved wooden seat. She felt a shadow. She looked up.

"Thank you," Isaac said. He had run after her, and sat down beside her.

The tram rumbled along the road, past Count Geiger's empty mansion, toward town.

Isaac remembered other trains. They had no windows except in the engineer's cabin; this one was the opposite. There were windows for passengers, while the conductor was locked into a tiny booth behind a windowless door with a slot through which he accepted the fares.

Isaac looked at the other passengers. The women wore bonnets and the men had shined their shoes. The day before Christmas was a holiday and the tram was taking them on an outing. There were well-behaved children who sat beside their parents and carried wicker baskets that smelled of hard-boiled eggs. The volk couldn't resist the opportunity to picnic. One minor thaw, green peeking prematurely through the snow and winter was over as far as they were concerned. Isaac remembered the boy with the motorcycle by the picnic grounds outside of Weimar.

"Any other messages?"

"Why should there be other messages?"

"There should be other messages."

"There are."

"Yes?"

"I have a visa for you . . . to America."

"Oh." Isaac felt curiously neutral. Two days from now he would be able to buy America. He didn't need any visa. "So the system works. Channels come through."

"Well, not exactly."

"I don't understand."

"This visa didn't arrive through the system. You don't qualify for a normal visa."

"Why not?"

Miranda was embarrassed. Isaac was on a state department list of undesirables, along with Nazis. She smoothed her skirt and he noticed the knees that stood out like a baby's cheeks. She explained in a murmur.

Isaac laughed with delight. "Maybe I'll go to Paraguay instead. I hear Germans are welcome in the jungle." He looked around at their companions on the tram. "I'll be right at home."

"I think you'd be at home anywhere." She looked around at this strange world she had willingly adopted a year and a half earlier. Indeed, though she held Isaac's visa, together with a boat ticket, in her pocketbook, black leather with a gold clasp, she didn't know how he would react to the new world.

"Tell me about America."

"Well, I suppose that the first thing you'll see is the Statue of Liberty. It's just . . . beautiful." Misty, Miranda didn't know what was happening to her, espousing a patriotism she had never really felt. The statue was a gift from the French people to the United States, she said, a great woman as tall as, taller than, the Regensburg clocktower. "She holds a torch and a book, although I don't know what book it is, and there's a famous poem on the pedestal, written by a Jewish woman." She quoted:

> Give me your tired, your poor,
> Your wretched masses yearning to breathe free.

Tired and wretched well described Isaac, but he was damned if he would land in the home of the free poor. He would arrive with his gold, establish himself as he wished. He'd buy a palace, with a chapel that he'd never enter. The pews would be carved from ebony inlaid with ivory and, yes, gold, studded with porphyry and jewels, and all of its ritual objects would be made of brass or crystal and its floor would be a carpet woven to his specifications in a pattern of endlessly repeating yellow stars and twisted red crosses. But it wouldn't have a door; the chapel would be sealed like pharaoh's chamber in the pyramid. Those carpenters and jewelers and glassblowers and other craftsmen who built it would be locked inside, to pray and starve until the strong ate the weak until one was left. And he'd starve unless he was able to eat himself. "What about Far Rockaway?"

"It's beautiful," she lied, and described New York's outer borough as if it was placid and sanctified Judea, and the Ferris wheel down the shore at Coney Island was the dome of the Jerusalem skyline.

"So if not normal channels, how?"

"Why must you know?"

"One must know everything." He would let nothing go. Miranda's incomplete story required an ending. He would get everything out of her, until nothing was left.

"When I couldn't . . ." She didn't dare to admit that she had paid for his visa and ticket with her own money. She was afraid that he might refuse the gift that had cost the equivalent of a German worker's annual pay, or, in her own domestic terms, a week's allowance, or a night at the Copa. It was to atone for her shabby mission for Foyle. "I met a travel agent."

"What?"

She tried to explain. "Not a secret agent. Someone who arranges things, an intermediary."

This was interesting. Isaac thought he could use such a person. He was learning on the tram—not just words, but customs, the inner language of civilization as well as another, strange bodily grammar. Miranda's breath tickled his ear.

He ignored the ebb and flow of passengers, and was trying to parse this new language when she mentioned the agent's "eye"—singular. She couldn't even recall precisely what she had said, but it was part of a description that neither of them was paying much attention to.

Isaac forgot everything else. He spun in his seat and said, "Which eye?"

"What?"

Furious, he insisted, "The left or the right? Which fucking eye?"

Other passengers immediately looked away. Perhaps it was the native delicacy that was afraid to confront their own brave blind and crippled soldiers.

Hurt, Miranda remembered Foyle's insult. Then, just as she had stifled her pain before, she acquiesced to Isaac's desire. She described the travel agent. "I think it was the right. Yes, he wore a patch over the left. He looked a little like that doctor on the *Anubis*." She didn't know that he surely also resembled the priest at the Ludwigshafen jail, and the KGB colonel in Theresienstadt.

"Where was he?"

She decribed the makeshift office with a single steel desk covered with brochures to exotic islands and raggedy train schedules. Word by word, the place came clear.

"Where was it?" Isaac nearly shook her. "Let's go there."

"But it's closed. Closed for good. I was his last customer."

"How do you know?" But even as he asked, he knew it was true. If the man did not wish to be found, he wouldn't.

He hardly heard as she explained, "I asked him, 'Will you be working after Christmas?' "

"Tell me," Isaac begged.

There was something about Isaac's desperation that made Miranda hesitate, but he would tolerate no evasion. She knew that he had to know everything. " 'No.' he said. He said, 'I've done enough work for now.' He said, 'I'm going back to Poland.' Isn't that strange?"

"Poland?"

"That's what he said."

"Then that's what he meant." Isaac wondered if this was a veiled message meaning that he, too, should go back to Poland, but the papers Miranda placed in his hand conveyed a stronger message. If Alter had gotten him the American visa, to America he would go. But he wouldn't go like the others, as a supplicant, throwing himself on the mercy of the community of those who did nothing Before and During, and now sought to assuage their guilt and absolve themselves in the endless After. He would go to the Far Rockaway of his own and Miranda's creation.

"Next stop, Poland." It was the voice from the conductor's booth. They had been so absorbed in conversation that they hadn't realized that everyone else had left the tram. They were alone with the disembodied conductor.

"What did he say?"

"Zoland. It's a suburb."

"No, he said Poland. Let's get out. Quick."

Isaac was in such a hurry that he leapt the last few stairs. Miranda leapt after him, but landed awkwardly, twisting her ankle and stumbling into his arms. He had never felt anything so soft in his life. The tram pulled away.

They were surrounded by trees and a single bench beside an upright bus sign. Isaac looked around nervously.

Miranda giggled.

He had never heard such a sound, the sound of bubbles and lavender. He looked down at her face as if seeking the origins of that acoustics of heaven. He saw her mouth and she saw him see her mouth and closed her eyes.

There was a moment of waiting, but all moments of waiting have their own predetermined span that can range from the finite through the indefinite to the infinite. Then the Regensburg clock rang, on time for the first time since before the War. Judy was running again. One would hardly have known the War happened.

Woken from the strange strange pause, Isaac drew back, and held Miranda at a distance. "I have to get some sleep," he said. "Tomorrow is a busy day. Let's go."

"Yes, let's," Miranda replied, sure that she would never be able to giggle again.

It was the end of the route. Alone, in the tiny, windowless booth, the tram conductor removed his patch and rubbed the empty socket.

CHAPTER 17

Silent night. Holy Night.
All is calm. All is bright.
Round yon virgin, Mother and Child.
Infant Jesus, so tender and mild.
Sleep in heavenly pee-eee-ace.
Slee-eep in heavenly peace.

The sounds of soldiers a cappella drifted from the mess tent at Liebknecht while a silent, unholy army invaded the base. Dressed in black pants and jackets, faces tarred over by shoe polish, the gang from Weinerstrasse took their positions. Some waited with the truck in the woods beyond the gates where the rear entrance to Der Geigermineh had been all but excavated; the rest sped around the one lonely lantern hung from a pole in the middle of the yard.

The drill had been practiced until it was as punctual as the renascent Regensburg clock, and they hardly glanced a hundred feet off toward the dark cube. Several men were dispatched to the shadows to keep a careful eye on the Yankees while the rest headed for the shower room. Each man knew his task.

Unlock the door.

Lock the door.

The shower was empty, the floor dry. As a final precaution to make sure that no dirty soldier decided to cleanse himself for the holiday, they had cut off the water supply to the room the night before, positive that no Christian plumber could come to repair it before X-Day. They had crowbarred into the tiled walls where a labyrinth of pipes converged and then smashed the pipes with a tender sledge and jammed every towel and blanket in Weinerstrasse into the cavity.

"How much can this take?" Schimmel whined as his own blanket followed the mass of tablecloths and antimacassars Frau Mannheim had inadvertently left on the clothesline.

"Keep stuffing," Isaac said, sending a couple of men out to one of the emptied barracks for armloads of additional army blankets. It seemed that an acre of woolen fabric disappeared into those pipes, but eventually they clogged, and not a tear's worth of water dripped from the shower head. Then they reset the tiles.

Now, inside the familiar cell with the useless pipes, Schimmel and two helpers were set to keep a watch on the watchers outside from the shower room's single filmy pebble-glassed window.

Pry open the grate.

Isaac wiggled a toe to secure a place on the first rung of the ladder beneath the basin.

"Good luck," Schimmel said.

"No such thing as luck," Isaac replied as he found the rusty iron bar and descended into the mine. Marcus and the rest followed.

After the first turn from the bottom of the ladder where the faint moonlight from above shed a dim cone on the rocky floor, they were in absolute blackness. Isaac found it a comfort as they scurried as efficiently as beetles in a dungheap, sensing their way through the subterranean passages until they reached the spot where torches made from mops doused in gasoline had been left in readiness. He tickled through his pocket for a match, the last pathetic remnant of another grand enterprise that was picayune compared to the new adventure. This was grand. This was deserving of the darkness. He was almost reluctant to light the torch, but he followed the plan to the letter.

The torch flared to life, casting spiked shadows across their daubed foreheads.

"Let there be light," Marcus said, and each man took his own torch from the crude rack they had hammered into the wall and lit it from the first. "The shammes," Marcus said, referring to the way candles were lit for a different faith than the one currently being celebrated above.

"Don't get Jewish on me," Isaac snapped.

"I didn't *get* Jewish. I *am* Jewish."

"You know what I mean."

"If God helped the Maccabees, he might help us."

"God has nothing to do with it."

Nobody replied and they hastened farther along the dank avenues as quietly as the rats that were the permanent residents.

The rats, accustomed to midnight rehearsals, were no longer surprised by Isaac and his crew, but they would be surprised when the explosives were finally lit. Nasty little scavengers. Serve them right. Expose their lair to the air and destroy them, their homes, families, libraries, and shuls. God had nothing to do with it.

The explosives were waiting, strapped to the proper supports. Timers were checked. Fuses were checked. The row of carts to carry the gold were rolled into place beneath the giant yellow X Isaac had personally marked on the arched roof of the tunnel.

Flakes of damp earth fell down like black snow. One last time, the tunnels were checked. No obstructions. No intruders. Nothing was left to chance.

They waited. Not a sound could penetrate the layers of sedimentary earth. Isaac could hear himself breathe, but gradually he felt as if he could also hear the songs from the mess tent and the ether beyond Liebknecht. All over Zone Three, victors and vanquished, Allied and Axis, Americans and Germans, Christians reunited after a slight aberration of history, sang their praise to a Jew who had been dead for nearly two thousand years.

All across the globe they sang. There were Georgian chants at midnight mass in Rome and Mexican, Coptic, Polish, and Greek Orthodox melodies at cathedrals and churches on every continent. Calvinists in Zurich sang in communion with Lutherans in Stockholm. They sang from Canterbury to Kiev; they sang in Seville and Chartres. Beside the Presbyterians, Episcopalians, and Baptists, the last renegade Anabaptists and Huguenots sang. Unitarians sang with Trinitarians in two part harmony. In whitewashed chapels the size of shower rooms, they sang on a hundred Greek islands. In Jerusalem, at the Church of the Holy Sepulchre, the priests and the pilgrims sang together. The only ones who did not sing and could not hear the songs were the Jews themselves, steadfastly quiet as their own God, underground.

Marcus's walkie-talkie crackled to establish contact with the other groups. Schimmel was in charge of the shower room and Fishl was in the woods. "Upper control?" Marcus said.

"Check," Schimmel replied.

"Outer control?" Marcus said.

"Check," Fishl answered, but there was another sound coming over the speaker.

For a second Isaac couldn't recognize the static gurgling. Then he realized—it was a baby's cooing. He knew what it was, but he demanded confirmation, "What the Hell is that?"

Before he could receive the answer, he heard another voice, singing a Yiddish lullaby.

"What's Rivka doing there?" Isaac shouted, although, of course, he knew that, too. The mother was where she belonged, with the child.

Fishl tried to explain, "The baby was wakeful."

"So you brought it, you . . ."

Before Isaac could provide the expletive, a third voice interrupted, "So they brought it."

"Who the Hell is that?"

"I had to come," Miranda answered.

"Shit." Isaac stamped his boot and more flakes of earth drifted from the gigantic yellow X.

"Oh, don't worry. There's no one else here."

"Why not? Why not invite the whole fucking Joint?" He was furious and wanted to make her disappear, but they were separated by a mile of tunnels and a million tons of earth. Still in charge from Lower Control, he made the only business decision he could under the circumstances. It was against the plans and detestable to have to deal with women—one of them an outsider, no less—but worse to have that dizzy American dame traipsing through the woods. "Welcome!" he snapped the walkie-talkie shut.

Up above, the soldiers strung popcorn and empty cartridge belts on the tree that newly repromoted Lieutenant Necco had personally selected from the woods outside the base the week before. The evergreen was a six-foot beauty, with symmetrical branches spreading from a hooped skirt to a single apex—there had been two, creating more of a forked effect, but Necco had severed the lesser limb to enhance the glory of the greater—on which the officer placed a single military star loaned to the troops for the occasion by a jovial General Smith. It was lovely.

Under the tree, the soldiers opened presents wrapped in festive red and green packages that had been sent from homes in Dallas and San Diego and Minneapolis and Tallahassee and Providence via the same emergency aircraft that had been incapable of delivering a Christmas bombing on the train tracks to Oswiecim. They sang,

> *Angels we have heard on high,*
> *singing sweetly o'er the plain.*
> *And the mountains in reply,*
> *echoing their joyous refrain,*
> *Glooooooooooooria.*
> *In excelsis De-o*

In the shower room, Schimmel uncorked his own bottle and took a swig, shuddering down the liquid fire. Despite the thaw, it had turned seasonally cold again, and his own Christmas wish was for just a splash of hot water. Instead he made due with another shot of liquor.

Their moment of contemplative sobriety over, the soldiers grew more festive. WACS had been brought in from Zone Two to share the night with the last boys on the base, and there was an enormous pink ham to serve them, its haunches glistening with honey sauce. The beast's marbled eyes pensively considered the scene.

Then there were libations. Jacks Over Deuces, dressed in a Santa Claus outfit, had arranged eggnog at a small profit to the quartermaster's office. "Step right up, ladies and gents," he said, ladling spoonfuls of grog. "Ho! Ho! Ho!"

The liquor flowed and the suckling lost its porcine bulk slice by slice until only its bones and its eyes remained. Still the moment seemed melancholy. It was the soldiers' last Christmas in Europe, and as homesick as they were—all those vestigial childhood sentiments evoked by rum-soaked eggnog—for many of them the War was the best time in their lives. Half a dozen years earlier, they had unwrapped toy tanks and now they had ridden real tanks to win the most immense conflict ever. They were the conquerors, not only of Germany, but the world. They were the victors of history, resplendent in ribboned and bemedaled olive khaki. Going home to one girl and Levittown, to the Long Island Railroad, to a job selling insurance or refrigerators, or repairing refrigerators or tabulating actuarial tables, was not as exhilarating as battle for young men with bona fide carbines slung over their shoulders. Christmas in Pawtucket or Portland was not the same as Yule under the magical Black Forest sky. Toasting themselves and their youth, they drank as much in sorrow as joy, as much in consolation as congratulation.

Marcus was tired. The preparations for X-Day had exhausted him more than his labors throughout the War, or during the first years After. It was the sense of conclusion that made him recall the holidays of his own childhood and start to contemplate the future. "Where are you going with your share, Isaac? Next Year in Jerusalem?"

"What is this religious frame of reference, Herr Doktor Morgenstern, first Hanukkah, now Passover? What do we get next, Tisha B'av?"

"It just makes me think."

"I suggest that you attempt not to." Isaac didn't know if he should tell Marcus about his visa, didn't know if Miranda had told. The thought brought back her image, bundled in the truck cab with Fishl and Rivka and the child, and rekindled his anger. Still he stifled that anger in anticipation of a greater reward.

Lights in the mess tent went off. Several couples kissed under the mistletoe or snuck away to more private conjunction. Only one candle was left burning on the tree, a single guiding star. It was nearly as dark above as below.

The watchers outside would signal those in the shower who would relay the signal to those below when the soldiers reached the bottom of their bowl—their mood altered from melancholy to hilarity—and began to reel from the mess tent, their songs changed in the brisk air from "Silent Night" to:

> *Walking down Canal Street.*
> *Knock on every door.*
> *Goddamn,*
> *Son of a bitch,*
> *Couldn't find a whore.*

Schimmel took another shot of whiskey before he completed his role and reported, "Upper Control to Lower Control."

Marcus flicked the switch on the walkie-talkie. "Lower Control here."

"All clear."

"Then let's do it," Isaac said. He stepped toward the tiny plunger attached to the wire attached to the sticks of dynamite bored into the rock.

"But . . ." Marcus said.

"But what?"

"Shouldn't there be a . . ." It was difficult to explain, but Marcus felt they ought to be ceremonial.

"Nonsense."

Marcus argued briefly, but the most he could coax from Isaac was a countdown. That was practical. They needed a few seconds to press themselves against the walls. Despite all their calculations, there was no telling how the rock would crumble and fall.

Isaac began. "Tzen. Nine. Acht. Ziben. Zeks. Finef. Feir. Dray. Tsvay . . ."

"Let's stop right there."

The Jews were trapped. For a second, they thought it was Germans whose steel-blue weapons reflected the light of the torches. The mine was filled with soldiers in a V formation that cut the cluster of terrified plotters in half and pinned them to the wall like butterflies on a matte. Standing at the point of the V, however, was the unmistakably American bulk of Hank Smith.

"What are you doing here?" Marcus asked, a dumb question.

"Well, now, I could be askin' you the very same thang, but I won't. Let's just say that the answers to both questions are pretty friggin' obvious."

Above ground, Schimmel and his companions at Upper Control were resting quietly, tied to the benches in the shower room with lengths of nylon cord. Upper Control was neutralized and so was their first rank of watchmen, whose shadowy haven had not been secure enough to hide them from the Lucky Boys.

Hammerin' Hank and the men he had chosen for this mission had drunk enough at the Christmas party to allay suspicion, but not a drop more. He knew they were being watched. They left the party in ones and twos and met at a predetermined rendezvous behind the army garage. Hank may have been a boozy, vulgar buffoon, but he had also been first in his class at West Point. He knew strategy and tactics. It was easy to sneak up and lasso the men outside. The shower room, however, was a trickier objective since it maintained contact with the force below. Hank pretended to weave across the yard, and built up a good head of steam, angling as if to give a wide berth to the little structure, but he veered at the last second and crashed through the shower room door before Schimmel could sound the alarm. In seconds, the walkie-talkie was in American hands, and another ten soldiers were in the room, five guns aimed at each Jew's head. Prepared to unarm the Jews, Hank was surprised to discover that they had no weapons. Some plans. "Fucking candy from a baby," he jeered.

"But . . ." Isaac said. "How did you know?"

"Shit, boy, how stupid do you think I am? For the last month I couldn't take a shower without you looking up my ass. I must admit, I wouldn't a thought you had the balls to do this, or the brains to do it now. Nice timing," he complimented Isaac.

"Thank you."

Then, cutting the cordiality crap, Hammerin' Hank continued, "I mean, do you stinking little Yids think we beat the Krauts with nothing but guns? Got to know where to aim them guns. Got to strategize. Got to allocate resources before you attack. Just remember, boy, we won the War. You lost. And it looks like you just lost a teensy-weensy skirmish down here, too. Now, if you'll just back away from that there

357

device, I probably won't shoot off your pointy little Hebrew head."
He extended a massive pearl-handled pistol into the hollow under
Isaac's jaw and reached back with his other hand to scratch the seat
of his pants; it had been tight squirming down the shower steps into
the ground, and it had been scary in the kingdom of the Jews until
he got his bearings—thanks to the street signs that had been so
obligingly placed, "Might as well have painted cha-cha footsteps. One
two. Turn. One two. Turn."

The general swung his bulk in rhythmic delight, while Isaac pondered the situation. There went Far Rockaway. But just as he felt
his dream dissolving, he realized that he didn't really care. It was just
like when the War ended—so what? He felt empty as a mouth without teeth responding to the tongue's insistent probe. After was the
same as During, and Before didn't exist at all, not even in the mind.
Before was as far gone as baby teeth. Issac had no blissful recollec-
tions of home the way the soldiers did. That was why they were
vulnerable and he was free—even if they had won and he had lost.
One game was over, but another would undoubtedly begin.

"Just one moment, General." Swift as that, another game began.

The voice came from another tunnel. It was a husky woman's voice,
as Texan and twangy as Hank's own, but filled with the more sophisticated allure of Scotch and Gauloises. It was Elizabeth Smith Moss,
wearing a pair of strange black goggles that made her look like a bug in
the dimness of the mine. Her own chosen weapon, a Leica F, compli-
ments of Berlin Optik Haus, which she and an empty duffel bag had
personally liberated, was slung over her shoulder. She removed it, but
Hank didn't budge. It was a lesson he had learned at West Point; always accommodate the press.

Isaac was baffled. He thought he was alone and now it seemed
that the only ones who weren't there in the Geigermineh were the
rest of the El Paso Traveling Rodeo. Next time, he would remember
the difference between solitary and group action. He told himself
that he was just learning another lesson. He told himself that next
time it would be different.

"Just one photograph for the *Stars and Bars*, General," the journalist requested, and lifted her camera to her face, and focused. Her

thumb and forefinger spun the lens with the deftness of a prostitute slipping a condom onto a customer, or a rabbi rewinding a Torah scroll.

"Bitch," Isaac cursed. "You owe me."

"Then close your eyes," she said sweetly. "Now."

Isaac closed his eyes and she shot.

There was a flash, but it was nothing like the million minor blips of light that happy Dads were creating in a million living rooms across the States to record their little one's delighted reactions to the chachkes stuffed in the socks under their trees. Attached to Miss Moss's German souvenir was a special high intensity bulb, trade name "Lightning," cooked up in the Kodak labs to take pictures in outer space. Missiles weren't able to leave the earth's orbit yet, but Kodak knew as surely as Rocketmann that they would, and the corporation was ready to bid the contract. There was a blinding ray of light, not meant for human eyes. Simultaneously, the general and all of his soldiers and all of the Jews, too, cried out. One gun went off, but more dropped to the floor as the incapacitated armies clawed at their faces.

Although Isaac had had a second's advance notice, his closed eyes were suddenly holes through which fire was poured into his head. It expanded there like a gigantic white-hot balloon in his brain, pushing the borders, about to burst his skull apart. The walls of the tunnel were glowing.

Elizabeth Smith Moss strapped an extra pair of goggles over Isaac's eyes and the light just perceptibly began to dim. "Sorry, I don't have any for your buddies, but they'll be all right—later. Say, Tuesday." Then, calm as if she was stepping through a battlefield for a good angle, the photographer strode forward, flashing again, left and right, each shot ricocheting off the walls with incandescent brilliance. She took special care to boot Hammerin' Hank's sausage fingers away from his face and flashed again directly into his exposed features. When every last soldier as well as Marcus and the rest of Isaac's crew were crashing into each other in their blind panic and flying apart like the cosmic debris the bulb was designed to record, she turned and said. "Elizabeth Smith Moss pays her debts . . . In full. Now, let's have one for the rotogravure." She switched bulbs and took a normal photograph of Isaac in his protective goggles. Then she said, "Your move."

Isaac nodded and pressed the plunger.

There was a buzzing from within the rock, as if the molecules of slate and sediment were vibrating. Then, for a second, there was pure silence. Having hit its pitch, the rock rested. Even the screaming soldiers were suddenly hushed. They ceased rubbing their eyes, and stood still while the ground above them trembled, and their sense of that motion in the absence of their sight told them what had happened.

Time held still. Then everything shattered.

The ceiling came down in a gush, and in the fraction of a fragment of time that Isaac had to wonder, he thought, "Water?"

The map did not include sewer pipes.

Three substances came down: masses of rank military waste that had been dammed inside the Liebknecht sewage system by the Weinerstrasse gang the night before, the earth, and the gold.

Four feet on a side, sixty-four feet cubed, the nuggets from approximately thirty million teeth, from approximately six million mouths, collected, melted, and recast so not the trace of an incisor remained, returned to the mine from which they had been excavated to fill the mouths of the ghetto. They tumbled ingot over ingot, as if plunging from the gaping hole of sky over Liebknecht.

Still blinded, the soldiers and gang members scrambled for the safety of intersecting tunnels, but Isaac stayed where he was, covered in brown fermenting ooze. It made no difference; along with shit, blessed gold came down in a pell mell crash of bricks that landed an inch from taking off his head directly onto the cart in place under the X that was no longer there. At least some of his plans had worked.

From then on, plans were beside the point. If Isaac had expected his men to push the cart slowly down the tunnel to the woods, he could no longer rely upon them. Nevertheless, the cart started a slow roll of its own. It was the water, sloshing about its wheels and Isaac's ankles, deepening by the second as the massive truncated pipes continued to pour a cataract into the mine, that set the cart inching in the direction to which it was gravitationally inclined.

Elizabeth Smith Moss, sheltered under an outcropping marked

"Har Zion," took a series of photographs that would make splendid copy the next day. Front page. Above the fold.

Hank Smith, back upright, flailing madly, began shouting orders. "March, men. Hup. Two. On your feet. Court-martial. Court-martial!"

Isaac easily eluded the staggering general by wading in the knee deep pool that was still increasing as the two foot tap above showed no sign of diminishing. He was under a Niagara of pristine mountain water mixed with urine and confetti streamers of sopping toilet paper.

"What the fuck is going on?" Hammerin' Hank yelled, as he was hit by an enormous four-star turd, possibly his own, backed up in the system and suddenly let free. "This place reeks."

Isaac sloshed away from the General, and saw the cart commencing its own movement away from him. His problem was solved by the water. Even if the men had had the slope working for them, effort was going be needed to shepherd the gold to the exit. The water provided that power and more. It came sluicing down in an endless spate that started to push the carriage. Isaac reached a hand to pause the iron bucket with the immense mound of golden ingots heaped atop it, but had no more effect than a fly crashing into an Alp. He was pleased. No effort at all was going to be needed.

Like a hobo catching a ride on a slowly moving freight, he hoisted himself onto the edge of the vehicle, and then clambered aboard the cargo of gold, heels pressed against the rim of the cart, head inches from the ceiling of the tunnel as he cruised into the shaft, away from the blind, drenched pandemonium, as stately as the *Anubis* upon the dark waters of the Danube.

But the water created another problem. Just as it eliminated the need to start, it gave no help at all in stopping.

Gradually the cart picked up speed, and the gentle cruise accelerated, though it was still pleasant to Isaac, at first. Then the combined effect of the water and wheels spinning in their iron trough, grew less pleasant as the ceaseless jet propelled him downhill. The walls ripped past him so fast he couldn't make out the signs. The torches singed his scalp a second before the water extinguished them, and then they were past the place where the torches had been set, and back into the pitch. Surfing forward, he tried to find a notch in the slippery surface of the gold to grasp. Cheek to the cold metal, he was washed clean as the detritus sank to the bottom of the flood and the pure cleansing fluids drew him forward and down, down, down, down the endless tube.

He pressed flat as he could, feeling wind ahead, waves behind, and hearing the clacking of wheels on the track. He knew the path well; he had staked out every inch, making sure it was clear right up to the final wall. Weeks before, they had taken picks and shovels and narrowed that wall where Count Geiger's topographic map said it came closest to the surface in the woods. They had deliberately not pierced through, because they didn't want to expose an opening, and they hadn't thought to determine whether the wall was an inch or a foot thick. A stick of dynamite was going to take care of that last obstacle at the last minute. But Isaac was not going to be able to leap off the speeding cart and outrun it, and light the fuse. He was going to crash.

It was the last train he was ever going to ride, and it might have been a cattle car pulsing with scenes of its last passengers, all Kaufmen. Suddenly, in a flash of panic, Isaac saw his parents boarding that other train from Proszowice to nowhere. Guarded by a handful of Germans and a helpful Ukranian cohort in front of a jovial Polish crowd, they shuffled up the ramp into a small windowless shack on wheels. He saw the rest of his family boarding the same train, and his neighbors, and his friends, and the people he had once thought were his enemies, until he met real enemies in black uniforms. He saw every Jew in Eastern Europe on that same train. The shack was adequately built to serve its original bovine passengers, but not at all secure for human traffic. Isaac could hear the Jews' murmurs from within; they were wondering where they were going, when he knew damn well and wanted to shout out a useless warning.

There were tiny gaps between some of the warped slats of the cattle car. Isaac could see his parents' fingers emerge from between the slats. They were waving "Good-bye," their fingers scratching the air. After the train had left, all that remained were the scratches of those fingers on the air, tiny rents in the fabric of being.

Where the tunnel turned, ingots of gold flew off the cart and where it narrowed they knocked chunks of rock from the wall, but hardly slowed in Hell-bent momentum. Accompanied by the roar of the water and the screech of the wheels going faster than ever intended, Isaac rode the flood from the sewer main. He was borne along on a raft of gold on a tide of shit.

He clutched the surface of the shattered cube, and his own fingers seemed to penetrate the metal. Suddenly it was not gold beneath him, but a golden liquefaction that he desperately struggled to keep a grip on. The mineral was turning soft and coalescing into a different, animalistic shape beneath him. But it was no golden calf that he clung to in the whistling, roaring blackness. It was more generous than the idol from Sinai, more like a living calf, but softer still, and then the new golden form seemed to speak to him, in a voice he knew, to say, "Not so rough."

It was a woman with golden hair, and those were the sparks of her soul as she banged the walls. She had golden skin and golden toes, golden calves, and golden thighs that wrapped around him. Isaac pushed into her golden midsection, as they hurtled through the absolute blackness.

The cart rattled around a final bend, and there was a light, a real light, coming from six tiny pinholes in the shape of a star. It was the end of the tunnel and their excavation was deeper than he remembered. In the gang's energy, they had turned the rock wall into a porous rock screen.

The woman was Miranda.

Isaac pushed deeper into her, and everything in the faint illumination was a blur, except the onrushing conclusion. He closed his eyes underneath their goggles and shouted at the silent gold figure to which he was conjoined hip to hip, loin to loin, soul to soul in their final moments together, "Hold on!"

There was no moon, but it seemed bright outside compared to the darkness of the tunnel.

A truck was waiting. It was facing the mountain, and its lights were parallel cylinders. They were the beams that Isaac had seen through the pinpricked mountain before the rushing cart filled with eighteen tons of teeth blasted out of the earth into the open. Fishl sat behind the wheel.

Isaac lay on the ground, aching everywhere, unable to lift a finger to brush aside a single blade of glass scratching his cheek. He blinked as the truck emptied. That was good. The men from Outer Control were collecting the ingots which had flown all over the field and lay like pieces of a shattered sun.

Isaac blinked again and found Miranda hovering over him. "We made it," he said.

"Yes, we did."

She reached down to remove the goggles.

Strangely selfless, Isaac thought of the scene he had left behind. "The others, they're still in the mine, with soldiers, but I think they'll be all right. They'll need guidance. They can't see for a while."

Fishl the ineffective had already taken charge. He sat in the truck's cab, ear to the walkie-talkie. He leaned out the window and said, "Yes, when Upper Control stopped answering our messages, we grew worried. I've already sent some men over there to get them."

"Good. And what about . . ." Isaac was woozy and couldn't complete his line of thought.

"Take it easy," Miranda said, stroking his filthy forehead. She was softer than gold.

"It's over," he gasped.

"Not quite," another voice chimed in. It was the only voice yet unheard that night. It was Jacks Over Deuces, who said, "I've been waiting." He had removed his Santa Claus costume, but a few wisps of white cotton fluff stuck to the stubble on his chin.

Another platoon of soldiers stepped out of the woods. There were green uniforms everywhere, with their own flashlights that crossed the truck's steady beam, and their own guns.

"It's just like poker," Jacks Over Deuces said. "Sometimes you don't win a hand all night, but if you keep some chips in reserve, and wait, if you're patient, that last hand that's dealt before dawn will be yours. You know what I mean?"

Isaac nodded.

The corporal couldn't resist continuing his excursus according to Hoyle. "I knew you'd leave Hank back in the mine somehow. It wasn't the next to last hand I wanted anyway. It was the last one. You had an ace, but I had the joker up my sleeve. Playing it straight, you lose every time."

"But . . ."

"Something just rubbed us all the wrong way, I guess. The transfer papers were taking too long. Never any unusual delay before. 'So why now?' I asked myself. And then I answered myself. 'Don't underestimate these fellows,' I said. They haven't had your advantages, but they've had others. They've grown sly these last few years. They want the same things you want. We could have gone in and taken the gold yesterday, but, thanks to Hank, this is even better. The general thinks you've got the gold, but you don't. I do." He glanced at the truck with a silent Fishl sitting behind the wheel and a reconstituted cube sitting on the cab. "Everything all packed up, nice and tidy. Don't forget that one over there," the corporal gestured behind his shoulder, to Lieutenant Necco, as if he could see backward.

Of course, Jacks Over Deuces couldn't see backward, because if he could, he would have seen more than one last ingot. He would have seen the Regensburg tram bouncing along the rutted fire lane that he himself and, several hours earlier, Fishl and Outer Control had come by. One last card remained undealt; one final twist to the tunnel of plot lay unturned.

Isaac recognized the tram. "Alter?" he sighed, blissfully certain that everything was going to be all right. His eyes were closing and he was willing to pass himself along to destiny.

Miranda recognized the tram, too, but unlike Isaac she saw the figure behind the wheel. She said, "Benya?"

Isaac opened his eyes again, and Jacks Over Deuces squinted.

The tram pulled onto the hard flat ground between the fully laden pick-up and the circle of soldiers and captives. Miranda was right. The truck's headlights clearly illuminated Der Schreiber at the wheel of the tram.

"Friend of yours?" the corporal asked.

"I thought you knew him," Isaac answered, awake and sure now that Miranda's warning had been accurate and that here was his betrayer to gloat. "Come for your thirty pieces of silver?" Isaac croaked.

Der Schreiber apparently had something else in mind. He spoke from the loudspeaker in the tram's front compartment. "Don't get too close."

Taunted by his warning and undaunted, the phalanx of soldiers began approaching the vehicle, led by the intrepid Necco. "I know who that is," he said. "He came by the PX this week. He bought . . ." Suddenly Necco knew the next twist, and tried to avoid it, like an infantryman who's stepped on a mine. "Wait!" he shouted at the soldiers.

But it was too late. Der Schreiber pulled the lever that opened the twin doors to the tram with a hydraulic hiss that was immediately drowned out by the sound of an avalanche of tiny round pellets, thirty million of them, rolling out of the tram, bouncing down the stairs and covering the open expanse where the soldiers stood.

"Ball bearings!" Necco cried, the first to lose his footing. Soon all of the soldiers, as well as the men from Weinerstrasse, were slipping, arms windmilling, feet flying up over their heads, incapacitated as surely as if they were blind.

The only one with neither desire nor ability to rise, Isaac began laughing. Yet even as he laughed at the slapstick, he realized that this was his last chance. He lifted his head from Miranda's lap and shouted at Fishl, "Get out of here!"

For a second, Fishl was paralyzed, too. He was supposed to wait for the rest of the crew to join him.

"Go!" Isaac screamed as urgently as if he was giving the same advice to everyone who had lined up for the last train out of Proszowice. "Take the teeth and go!"

And finally, for the first time in his life, Fishl didn't screw up. The engine roared to life.

"Shoot him," Jacks Over Deuces cried.

A hundred bullets pinged off the body of the truck. One shattered the rear window. Others chipped off pieces of gold the size of a tooth. A six-pointed pattern entered the engine block without hitting a vital organ.

Obeying Isaac or protecting Rivka, Fishl put his foot to the gas, and the vehicle's wheels turned, spitting a fountain of ball bearings out from under their mudflaps, and started moving and disappeared into the night, while from the radio of the stationary tram someone was singing:

Jingle bells. Jingle bells.
Jingle all the way.
Oh what fun it is to ride in a one horse open sleigh.
Hey!

CHAPTER 18

There was a trial, of course. It was delayed initially by jurisdictional wrangling, since the alleged theft occurred on an American base in the British Zone, closer to France than either Great Britain or the States, with some dubious assertion involving interzone conspiracy by the Russians. Everyone wanted a piece of the action. Even the Germans timidly hinted that if they were to be truly rehabilitated, they ought to be able to try Jews—those who deserved it, rat scum filth.

A court was convened in all due majesty, but before the opening arguments were heard, it was obvious that the new judicial system was under an entirely unexpected kind of strain. Whether it was enthusiasm for due process or mere voyeurism, crowds circled the Regensburg municipal building, and measures had to be taken to provide for security and the serenity that justice requires. Military cordons blocked the building. Only those who belonged were admitted at the checkpoints.

First among equals were the defendants, ushered past the crowds as large as those of the neighbors who watched them post off five or six or seven years earlier from Proszowice and Osnowiec and Posnán and Cracow and Bialystok and Lodz and Warsaw by lawyers grudgingly provided by the Joint, and their opposing members of the prosecution, as small in number as the gentlemen in black boots from

Munich and Frankfurt and Hamburg and Cologne and Berlin who had organized the Jews' earlier incarceration and extermination. There were even a few lawyers from Nuremberg on a busman's holiday. Hauling Jews to the docket was quite interesting; they could imagine the defense. The challenge appealed.

Isaac arrived from the hospital on a gurney, strapped-in lest he tumble, borne horizontally through the crowd eager to catch sight of the face that Elizabeth Smith Moss had made famous. Marcus came on foot from the jail across the square, and Der Schreiber in a car from the Joint's headquarters where he'd been allowed to remain in Miranda's custody. A chair was left empty for Fishl, and Marcus dubbed it: "Elijah's Seat."

"Shut up," Isaac said, healthier than his multiple casts and bandages might have suggested. On council's advice, he had avoided the appearance of full recuperation, the better to garner sympathy, but his every expression revealed his disdain.

Der Schreiber was hardly more sympathetic, scribbling his impressions of the proceedings in a blue notebook, ignoring the petitions on his behalf circulated by readers of *Partisan Review*.

A few lucky members of the public were admitted in the name of full disclosure, but they had to show the authorization cards that were already traded on a black market starved for goods in a city starved for excitement. Those cards might have provided a temporary sideline for people who dealt in similar documents, but there was no longer anyone in Regensburg with the requisite skills, at least no one who was not currently under indictment. Marcus leaned back and sneered at one of the cards held by a local butcher who had slept in front of the courthouse for three days to obtain the coveted paper. Marcus, who could have duplicated it in the dark, spent his time at the table designing more foolproof identification.

The press was also admitted, in strength, led by a woman with a camera. Debt paid, she leaned over the balcony to snap a viciously unsentimental photograph of Isaac sneering. His teeth, so pathetic two years before, were bared under the curl of a caged tiger's lips. Penitence never crossed his brow.

The prevailing sense of the crowd was that the arrogant Juden deserved hard labor, but that would be up to the judges, since no jury of peers was available. There was one French, one English, one

Russian, and one American judge. The Germans would just have to wait, at least until the verdict.

Unfortunately for those who had already convicted the three defendants as well as Fishl, in absentia, there were other, more severe problems with the case. First there was the question of the witnesses; there weren't any. None of the soldiers who had been alternately blinded or physically immobilized knew why they were in the mine or the woods. To a man, they responded in a phrase they had heard elsewhere: They were only following orders.

As for those who gave the orders, they, too, were struck dumb on the stand. General Smith, wearing sunglasses, heaved his bulk onto the witness chair and said, "Shit, I was just taking a shower when the whole place exploded. I thought it was a backed up hot water heater."

As for the corporal, he looked the judges straight in the eyes and swore that he was nowhere near the explosion. "I was playing cards when I heard the noise. Had a good hand, too, Ace high flush in diamonds. Ruined the whole game."

The last remaining figure of authority, Colonel Necco, insinuated by the defense to be the real mastermind of the crime, had been transferred to a small atoll in the Pacific.

"But, Sir . . ." he had complained the week before the trial when Jacks Over Deuces told him of the sudden reassignment.

There was no room for error in the organization. The quartermaster looked at Necco with ineffable disgust and said two words, "Ball bearings." And the former noncom was gone.

But Necco did well—the man had learned the lessons of the master. He started trading coral and moved quickly to bauxite. In Bimini he was able to wear boxer shorts and teach the natives how to play poker. He became known as Kings Over Treys.

Back at the trial, the judges had other questions. Thorniest, was that of ownership. Whose teeth were stolen? Since nobody could track the first holders of the gold, there were legal questions about whether a theft had occurred at all. How could something be stolen if there was nobody to claim title?

Indeed, nobody could verify that it was gold—or gold-painted lead—under the tarpaulin, which was all that remained after Christmas Eve, Exhibit One.

Neither did Exhibits Two through Twenty-two, the tram, the cart, the ball bearings, the stick of dynamite that never exploded, the torches, the maps of Far Rockaway and the mine, and the rest of Isaac's incriminating computations do much to provide that philosophical imponderable: proof.

The defense romped across the playground of uncertainty, winking, leering, since everyone damn well knew the truth. Forty years later, a junior counsel became a name partner in an international law firm and defended a denier.

Daunted already, the lead prosecutor seemed to give up the ghost after a short chat in the halls with the unhelpful Jacks Over Deuces during lunch break. At first he was angry that his witness had recanted his initial testimony, but the corporal shrugged his shoulders as if he was folding a bluff that had been called, and leaned forward to whisper something else. It was a promise—in return for a performance. Why the corporal was suddenly concerned with the welfare of the defendants, the prosecutor could not imagine, nor would the corporal say. He simply made his offer, something about a position back home with the Attorney General's office.

Forty-five minutes later, the prosecutor returned to the bench to say, "New information has led me to conclude that this case may not be as strong as the state originally thought."

Ultimately, the four judges looked at this thicket, and at the defendants, sitting like three brass monkeys, Der Schreiber all eyes, Marcus all ears, Isaac all teeth. Fishl, all nose, was nowhere to be seen.

They removed themselves to chambers to parley in multilingual dialogue.

"Merde," the French judge said.

"No shit," said the American.

"The voice of the people says forget it," said the Russian.

"I concur," nodded the Brit, making it unanimous.

Clearly there was no charge that anybody wanted to argue, and that was that. Over and out. Roger wilco. After a few days in the docket, Marcus, Der Schreiber, Fishl, in absentia, and Isaac, miraculously able to walk again, were freed. Case dismissed.

✸　　✸　　✸

Had Isaac observed Jacks Over Deuces's hallway overture he might have understood why the corporal approached him several weeks later on the street. They were both waiting outside the Green Hen. A final sale of the cabaret's fixtures was scheduled for noon before the supermarket opened in its place.

"Congratulations," the corporal said.

"For what?"

"You won the game. You're free and you've got the gold. How come you're still in Regensburg?"

"Maybe I like it here."

Isaac kept his hand hidden. He didn't tell the American that there had been no word from Fishl since he fled Liebknecht with his truck full of Christmas goodies, not a phone call, not a postcard, just endless infuriating absence. At first, the rest of the gang assumed that Fishl was being cagey, lying low, waiting for the furor to subside. Then they decided that he was smart, suspecting a trap waiting to be sprung when he thought the coast was clear. But the coast was clear and the fuss was ended, and Fishl was nowhere.

"Well, you can afford to go elsewhere, although gold can be an illiquid commodity."

"Yes . . ." Isaac said noncommitally.

"Luckily, there are ways of liquifying just about any commodity."

Isaac thought of the way the gold had changed shape under him as they hurtled through the darkness of the mine.

"There's trading, and there's fencing."

"Fencing?"

"Outright purchase, at a moderate discount from market value, because there is no market, except for . . . me."

Isaac understood. Furthermore, he would have understood why Jacks Over Deuces had lent his delicate assistance to their legal cause. In jail, no deals could be made. As long as the gold was loose, it was available. As long as it was available, it could ultimately be his.

The corporal leaned close and made a discreet offer for the bullion. "That's eight zeroes," he said.

Too stunned to realize that if this man offered eight zeroes, the gold was probably worth nine, Isaac confessed the truth. "I don't have it."

"But you can get it."

"No, I can't. He's stolen it, damn it."

"You mean the quiet guy in the truck, Fishl?"

"That schmuck!"

"Not such a schmuck, apparently." The corporal could always appreciate a well-executed scam.

Isaac pounded his left fist into his right palm.

Jacks Over Deuces stepped back to consider the situation. He prided himself on his ability to read a man's hand as if the cards were marked. Jews were tricky, but he had enough recent experience to make him confident in his judgment. There were no odds to dissembling. If Isaac had the gold, he would at least consider shopping it. If he had already sold it, he wouldn't be in Regensburg. Therefore he hadn't sold it, and he didn't have it. Therefore he was telling the truth. Unless one of them could track down Fishl, the game was really over. On the spot, he shifted gears. "Hey!" he whispered, now really conspiratorial.

"Yes?"

"Wanna buy some cigarettes?"

"That's where we came in."

"I can get you one-hundred-percent Virginia leaf."

"No, thanks." Unlike the corporal, Isaac wasn't in the game for the sake of the game.

"Then that's where we leave off." As far as Jacks Over Deuces was concerned, one deal or another would be made. Some were bigger, some smaller, but the shape of the transaction remained and so did the satisfaction. He entered the supermarket, looking for Pinsker, chits good for a trainload of Lucky Strikes tucked in his pocket. Once he moved the cigarettes, he was ready to retire to California. There was a bankrupt dude ranch near Palm Springs that he was interested in, and he had already wired a deposit to the broker. He had also made a deal with the former Emcee of the Green Hen and his girls to fly in from Katmandu.

For the Jews, too, there was nothing more to do in Germany. There were no games left to play. The Marshall Plan was fully operational and the black market disappeared under the boom of the laissez-faire economy. Regensburg was back to routine, to work, to church.

The tram, returned to the Municipal Transportation Authority, ran on time and the town clock rang out every hour.

Some still spent their days trying to track down family from before the War, and every time Isaac sent one of them to dispose of their last stock of spurious documents in the markets of Linz or Mainz or Salzburg, the fellow took a sidetrip, to stand in lines at the remaining DP centers, to ask if anyone had seen a woman named Malka or someone from the Tucker family. Invariably they met with disappointment. Most everyone the Germans failed to eliminate had been shipped off by the guilt-ridden Allies, whose own shores were suddenly swarming with refugees as the Fatherland was approaching an ideal Judenrein state.

Isaac was the only one who never asked. He knew the Kaufmans were all dead, except for Alter, who would be found only when he wished. Instead, Isaac exercised the muscles that had been torn in his flight from the Geigermineh by lifting a pair of barbells that had been left behind by an Allied soldier, recalling the stack of books he had carried to and from cheder every day back in Proszowice. That was exercise for the body and the soul. Once he had been tripped by a Polish boy and nearly spilled his huge, annotated Tanach. He had stumbled and barely managed to right himself while the Polish boy laughed and imitated the Jew's funny dance. Though tempted, Isaac did not confront his tormentor, because it was forbidden to set the sacred book on the profane earth. Later, he was told that he had fullfilled a holy obligation, because the volume he had saved was a world in his hands, but he had always suspected that this was a Midrashic justification for cowardice. From then on, the daily weight had been too great until he was told there was a world in himself, too. Now no weight was too great to bear.

The house on Weinerstrasse, haphazard in the best of times, had the stagnant air of a way station. Trunks were heaped in the hall with color-coded transit tags looped around their handles. Only Isaac had delayed packing, but even he had begun to untack maps and fold them into his valise with underwear. The house itself was slated for demolition by the new Housing Authority since it was "structurally unsound." Bulldozers, freed from burial duties, hired to commence work the following day, were parked on the lawn.

Under these circumstances, the gang gathered for a last pathetic reunion and farewell. Except for Fishl, they were all there, Isaac and Marcus and Schimmel and the few others who had not left the city and the Continent yet, also Miranda and Der Schreiber, welcome now since his strange heroism on Christmas.

It was a quiet party. The gang was tired and dispirited. As Marcus said, "Might as well be Crusoe, washed up on shore."

Der Schreiber, reading the canon of Western literature to which he now seemed to belong, quipped, "Call me Friday."

Schimmel, bored out of his skull, asked, "Why not tomorrow?"

"Why not yesterday?"

"That bastard," Schimmel said, and they all knew who he was referring to.

All they had to do was to rehash the events of the famous night again and again, wondering where they went wrong. The answer was always the same: "Fishl."

"Son of a bitch."

"Where are you going?" Marcus asked Isaac in order to change the subject.

Miranda peered at him anxiously.

Isaac took down another map and answered, "America."

"When?"

"Soon."

"I've heard that you have to study the history of the nation to obtain citizenship."

"What's to know? George Washington lived when the Baal Shem Tov lived. Thomas Jefferson was their Vilna Gaon. You just have to think in analogies. They had slavery there. Do we know slavery? Must we study the meaning of the word?"

Miranda said, "There's a visa for you, too, Marcus." She was pleased that she had taken care of each one of her constituents. She took it from her pocketbook. "Here."

Marcus examined the paper. "Almost as good as mine," he said. Then he handed it back to Miranda. "Give it to someone else. I don't need it."

"What?"

"I'm staying. I'm too old for a new language, a new culture. Besides, the German Bureau of Engraving needs designers for currency. After the trial, a fellow offered me a job, a salary, government housing in Bonn."

Der Schreiber had been listening quietly but he suddenly commented. "You've already experienced the splendors of German government housing." He sounded like Isaac. There was a bitterness in his voice that had not been in *Farmakht Oyg'n* when he merely recounted history. Now he was judging it. Sadness disappeared under rage.

"Nonetheless, I remain." Marcus said. He didn't feel like talking about himself. "What about you?" he asked Schimmel.

"Aye, Matey, G'day," Schimmel imitated a cheerful young man he had met at the Australian consulate. "It's the land down under for me."

"Like the mine?" Der Schreiber would not relinquish the floor. Whatever anyone did, wherever they were planning to go, he saw doom.

"No," Schimmel explained unnecessarily. "Australia. Kangaroos. Koala bears. Eucalyptus trees. Good for the sinuses." He had been enticed by Marcus's own abandoned aspirations.

"Why not?" Der Schreiber shrugged. "Botany Bay. Once a prisoner always a prisoner."

But Schimmel didn't get the reference. "How about you?" he asked Der Schreiber.

"Paris. I've been there. They like me. I know a bis'l French." The writer leaned back and braided his fingers behind his neck. He had earned his place here and felt more comfortable in this room than the Café Deux Magots.

But there was one question nobody had asked him. Now, wrapping things up, there was no reason for secrets. It was Isaac who asked what they had all wondered, "The ball bearings. How did you get them?"

"You heard the sergeant that night. I bought them."

"With what?"

"I sold world rights to the book. Or rather swapped them. To that odd corporal. We drew up a contract. Lawyers and everything. He owns *Oyg'n* and I own the ball bearings—or rather, owned, since I guess they're anybody's now. It took a while to shovel them into the tram through the windows, but I thought they might come in handy."

"But what does the syndicate want your book for?"

"I don't know. They're trying to corner the market on history. They can have it."

"But you could have taken the gold yourself."

"I didn't want it."

"But they would have given you a lot more than ball bearings if you'd just helped them get away with the gold."

"I didn't want them to have the gold either."

"But . . . us?"

"Better you than them. Besides," Der Schreiber shrugged, "it makes a better story."

"So, Fishl's got it all to himself."

"Who would have thought?"

They spent more endless, fruitless hours, stewing about Fishl and his horde. They had developed the plot, discovered the mine, charted its underground depths, organized the dynamite, set off the explosives, evaded half a battalion of soldiers below and the other half above, and their man had escaped with the prize. All that remained was to divvy the loot whenever he returned, but he didn't return.

"He stole it, the momzer. He's never going to return."

"Enough!" Isaac finally declared. "Leave it alone. Don't you have anything better to do."

"Actually, no," one of the sullen, newer recruits said.

"Well you should. What was was. Things are no different than they ever were."

"Right," Der Schreiber agreed.

"What do you mean?" Isaac insisted.

"No different at all."

Marcus interceded before an argument could flare up. "Isaac is right. Not about history. At least not necessarily. What I mean is there must be something better to do."

But Isaac was in no mood to be placated. He reversed position to demand, "Like what?"

"Well," Marcus paused as he looked over his own bundles set aside for the short train ride to the new German capital. The only item that he wasn't going to trust to the baggage department was an alligator satchel containing his dental instruments, a set of slim tools wrapped in a felt cloth. He had been allowed to carry the satchel through the War because he told the Germans he needed it for his work for Special Projects. "Forger's tools," he said. They didn't know an etcher from a drill. He didn't know why he held onto the tools so fiercely as he learned the new occupation that had served him so much better than the old. He didn't even know if he still had his dental skills. "Your teeth," he said. "Let me do your teeth before we say 'Good-bye.'"

"O.K."

Marcus halted at the last answer he would have expected. Was it really that easy, as easy as waving a line of Jews toward a shower room without any water. "O.K?"

"It is what they say in America, is it not?"

Miranda nodded.

Immediately, before Isaac could recant, Marcus placed him in a chair in the center of the room and dragged over a coffee table. He plugged in a desk lamp and shone its beam directly into Isaac's face. He leaned Isaac's head back onto the neck of the chair and cushioned it upon a folded pair of trousers since Weinerstrasse's towels had all been used in the mine. Then he commenced to unpack his satchel. He hadn't looked inside in years, but his fingers knew the path to the various compartments, and he lay a row of instruments side by side on the coffee table. He took out a hand mirror and offered it to Isaac, "You may hold this if you wish."

"No, I'll wait."

"As you say. And now, some minor preparations." He extracted a small brazier from the case and set it atop a tiny burner attached to a tiny gas cannister that hissed on as if it had last been used the day before. He adjusted the flame downward and scraped something granular from another small jar into the bowl. Then he removed several small vials of novocaine and a hypodermic needle tucked into a flap in the side of the satchel and filled the needle with the clear liquid and leaned over Isaac's face. "Open," he commanded.

"What's that?" Isaac said.

"Anesthetic, so you don't feel anything."

"I don't need it," Issac said.

"But . . ."

"No."

"As you wish." Marcus was not going to argue, particularly not now that he had Isaac in the chair, but he kept the hypodermic ready, though he knew that Isaac Kaufman never changed his mind. "Open," he repeated, and this time Isaac revealed the full extent of the damage.

Marcus had made many covert professional judgments about his "cousin's" teeth during their years together, but now he inspected them one by one. His thumb pushed Isaac's lips back while he inserted a tiny mirror on the end of another silver stem into his patient's mouth to examine the view from the rear. He took a finely calibrated set of miniature pliers from the cloth and said, "I believe that we can save four of them. In order to build a bridge, we need to save four of them. I'm going to take out the rest."

"I didn't ask you to tell me what you were going to do. I authorized you to do it."

"Fine. Hold onto the arms of the chair then."

Instead, Isaac clasped his two hands together on his lap as if in Christian meditation, and Marcus set to work.

Miranda winced and turned away. She sat in Isaac's window seat, overlooking Weinerstrasse and could not imagine it turned into Beekman Place back in New York. She remembered the hours she spent watching tugboats on the East River, and she did her best to create that scene for herself for the hours that passed until Marcus said, "End of stage one."

Isaac's chin and chest and Marcus's fingers were covered with a bloody sheen, and the table was covered with small bloody stumps.

Marcus had to rest. He was sweating, but Isaac remained calm. He said, "Ou remin mih ob da dahdor aw da Addubith," through his empty jaw as drool and tiny gobbets of torn flesh spattered outward.

"Yeah, he taught me everything I know." Marcus said.

"Mih, doo," Isaac replied, but they didn't understand, not his enunciation and not his meaning.

"Let's get back to work. I can begin to make a bridge. You know, this should be done over a six-month period."

"Who haff tum?"

And so the work continued. Marcus anchored tiny steel pylons into the exposed bone of Isaac's jaw and stretched thin wires between them to establish the boundaries of the wall between Isaac Kaufman and the world as efficiently as a German engineer overseeing the construction of a lager. All that was missing was a motto hanging across the great red opening to Isaac's mouth, ARBEIT MACHT FREI. Finally he turned to the tiny fire that had been simmering all the while, mixed it once as if it was stew, and said, "Ready."

"Wha tha?" Isaac asked.

"I saved a portion from before. I didn't have any chance to use it until now. But it doesn't go bad, and I believe we have just enough for this job. It's gold."

Another hour passed, marked only by the grunts of pain from the observers in the room, and another hour with only silence from the chair. Finally Marcus wiped his forehead with his sopped sleeve one last time, peered across his work with the tiny mirror, shaved one last ridge of new tooth, and stepped back. He took the larger mirror and handed it to Isaac. "What do you think?" Then, before he could stop the sentiment, he added, "I'll miss you."

"But you'll have a cousin in New York." The words came from the new mouth with clarity as the blood dripped.

But there's a difference between saying and meaning, and this time there was no doubt in either's mind that they would never see each other again.

Isaac hadn't looked into a mirror in seven years. He angled the silver left and right. The teeth were there, but he couldn't see the rest of his face. All he saw in the angling of the mirror was the living room, a few last unpacked maps, the ghastly pale expressions of his companions, Marcus nodding with pride in the professional accomplishment of his career, Der Schreiber taking notes, and Miranda, still sitting by the window, gripping the sill beneath her, knuckles white, staring at him, and her tears fogged the glass.

"He's just a boy," she thought, just like those Yalies in tuxedos her father liked to see her dance with on the roof of the St. Regis. His gold was visible while theirs was in their pockets, or their fathers' wills. No, there was a much greater difference. Insulated from life as her prep school dance partners were, they were aware of their privilege. No matter Isaac's experiences, he could never look at them from the outside. And she could never look inside.

"How did you survive?" She had been meaning to ask this of all of them as long as she had been in Europe.

"The same way everyone who survives does. You find the opportunity that you need, you never look behind you. What was was."

"And what will be?"

"Good things, of course."

"Of course." Then she scribbled an address in Manhattan across a piece of paper and walked across the room and gave it to him.

"Is it near Far Rockaway?"

"Near enough."

"How far?"

"Oh, about as far as from here to the other side of Regensburg, the tram stop they call Poland."

"Oh, really. I thought it was as far as . . ." Isaac looked at the map of Europe, burnt at the periphery over the stove. Then he stood—shakily, but he stood—and walked across the room, and stood at the map and pulled one pin from a bottom corner. For a second, he thought of Fishl, and stuck the pin back at random, hoping that it would serve like a voodoo doll to locate and puncture the traitor's heart. It landed somewhere in the southeastern quadrant of the real Poland. "Here."

There was a knock at the door; then there were two more knocks. Then one more.

Everyone looked at Isaac, who said, "Let him in."

When Fishl entered the room, he looked as dumbfounded as he had when he first arrived. Perhaps he was surprised that they were no longer fieldstripping cigarettes, dabbling in currency. He who compared everything to something in Torah could not understand change. Things don't go full circle. Wheels spiral outward. This time, half a dozen hands were hugging him, patting him on the back. This time, there was delirious joy at his arrival.

"Fishl!" they screamed, "Fishl!" they danced, and if Frau Mannheim had still been in residence she would have pounded the handle of her broomstick against the ceiling below to hush them, and they wouldn't have cared. "Fishl's here."

"He's back."

Schimmel said, "I told you he'd return. Good old Fishl."

Marcus was too weak to join the celebration, but he too was grinning. Although he found the professional aplomb to continue wrapping his tools, he turned to Isaac and said, "Who next, the Messiah?"

Isaac asked, "Where's Rivka and the baby?"

"By the station. We're going to Palestine."

"Good."

"She has a cousin there."

"Good. Where's the gold?"

"Yeah, yeah," the others jumped, "What did you do with it?"

"I buried it."

"Good. Good."

Isaac asked, "Where?"

"Sacred ground."

Isaac stopped for a second. "What do you mean?"

"It's in a cemetery."

Isaac was relieved. "Good, nobody would think to look there. When can we get it?"

Fishl was exhausted. He staggered into the room, and collapsed into the chair Isaac had vacated, ignoring the sweat and saliva and blood. He, too, had seen worse, recently.

Isaac moved forward, and turned the desk lamp on Fishl's pale face. He repeated, "When can we get the gold?"

"You don't understand, Isaac. It's all that's left of them. They're buried, now. You can't unearth the dead."

"Why not?" Isaac was already thinking of logistical problems. "We get some shovels. Explosives if necessary. We've done it before. How far down is it?"

"That's not the point, Isaac. They are in sacred ground."

"If you don't mind, I must say that I can't understand a word you're saying. Explain."

And so Fishl described the scene. He thought of the chemist who was once his friend and felt he was telling his story to that shadow.

It was dark driving north and east, wherever the turns in the ruined Autobahn took him. He could not control his direction, as if the load in the back was being dragged toward a gigantic magnet. The going was slow since the truck was weighed down by its obscene cargo. At forty kilometers per hour, he drove through the night, and without knowing it he crossed into the Russian sector. But no one stopped him. The truck was invisible. He drove over the gentle western foot-hills of the Carpathians and crossed the Polish border. As soon as he entered the nation of his birth, he recognized the fields of sugar beets under the steady cultivation of the peasants. He continued to drive without stopping as the gas gauge slid slowly toward empty.

Fishl had been born in central Poland, but he had traveled more during the War than he had before or since. He hadn't known where he was being taken as he was randomly transferred from lager to lager, but he could tell from the smell miles away that he had been in this place before. Then he saw train tracks in a shallow trough by the side of the road, and he followed the tracks the rest of the way through a sleeping village until he recognized a long, low brick build-ing with a tower over an opening in the center, through which a train he had once taken had also passed.

The building was empty, the ground littered with crumpled packs of Russian cigarettes. For miles in every direction, there were rows of torn barbed wire.

For once, he was without a biblical or historical analogy. There were abundant atrocities to choose from, from the destruction of the first and second Holy Temples, through the millennia of Exile, from the Crusaders to the Inquisition, but none came to mind when he arrived under the elegantly arched gate that read, ARBEIT MACHT FREI.

For the first time since they had started their mad drive, Fishl stopped the truck, to peer at the unguarded gate.

Perhaps it was the sudden cessation of motion that caused the child to wake, crying.

Rivka said, "I don't want to go in."

He stopped his story.

"I don't understand," Schimmel said.

"I knew I was where I should be."

"So? So? Go on." Almost everyone in the room was hovering about Fishl, waiting for the conclusion of the story.

But Isaac was quiet. He had long since known where Fishl was going, perhaps before Fishl himself knew. He might have seen it on a map, the cinder point from which a fire would devour the world. He looked around the room. Most of the listeners were leaning forward, but Marcus had placed an arm around Miranda's quivering shoulder. Der Schreiber, who also knew the end, because it made a good story, had stopped taking notes, his pen poised midair.

Then Fishl told everyone. "I buried the gold at Auschwitz."

Isaac started laughing and his new teeth sparkled. It was not the bitter laugh of irony or anarchy, but full-throated, gold-glinting genuine humor. It was the funniest thing he had ever heard.

Fishl described the green grass poking up through the blasted, blood-soaked earth at the hole he had found, filled and covered while Rivka waited beyond the gate. "That was what was most strange," he said. "The grass. It was growing. It was alive. And I was alive, too, so I said Kaddish."

Even Miranda knew the word. She said, almost to herself, "the prayer for the dead."

Unable to stop his laughter, wheezing, gagging, and choking on hilarity, Isaac said, "Every prayer is a prayer for the dead."

It took Fishl and Rivka and their baby weeks to travel back the distance they had gone in a night. They took wrong turns, were delayed at borders. The truck broke down and they couldn't fix it, so they abandoned it and hitchhiked. The baby caught a fever, and they waited three days in a field for the child's temperature to subside. But all along, Fishl knew that he had to bring a message to Isaac, just before his new family set off again, for Palestine. A thousand years on one continent is enough.

After it was all over, after the murders, after the rapes, after the old people were stripped and the children were starved, after the Torahs were torn to shreds and the shreds burned, ashes scattered, and the synagogues converted to stables for the cavalry and the graveyards were desecrated, after the living were turned dead and the dead denied dignity, after everything, one could hear a whisper rising out of the forest and the fields and the universities and the churches and out of the bunker in Berlin, the still unfulfilled prayer born of the knowledge that Isaac and Marcus and Fishl and Der Schreiber and Miranda were in Regensburg and others were in Amsterdam and

London and Toronto and Buenos Aires and Capetown and Melbourne and Bombay and Shanghai and New York and Jerusalem and the last Jew, wherever he was, was still breathing, and the whisper was sighing, "No, nein, not After," but that other, age-old, heartfelt, eternal resolution: "Again."

About the Author

Melvin Jules Bukiet's books include *While the Messiah Tarries, Stories of an Imaginary Childhood,* which received the Edward Lewis Wallant Award for the best American-Jewish fiction of 1992, and *Sandman's Dust.* His stories have appeared in *Antaeus, Paris Review,* and elsewhere. He teaches at Sarah Lawrence College and is the fiction editor of *Tikkun.* He lives in New York City with his wife and three children.